T0300789

# THE ENTIRE SKY

ALSO BY JOE WILKINS

**Novel**

*Fall Back Down When I Die*

**Memoir**

*The Mountain and the Fathers: Growing Up on the Big Dry*

**Poetry**

*Thieve*

*When We Were Birds*

*Notes from the Journey Westward*

*Killing the Murnion Dogs*

# THE ENTIRE SKY

*A NOVEL*

## JOE WILKINS

LITTLE, BROWN AND COMPANY

*New York Boston London*

Little, Brown and Company
Hachette Book Group
1290 Avenue of the Americas, New York, NY 10104
littlebrown.com

First Edition: July 2024

Little, Brown and Company is a division of Hachette Book Group, Inc. The Little, Brown name and logo are trademarks of Hachette Book Group, Inc.

The publisher is not responsible for websites (or their content) that are not owned by the publisher.

The Hachette Speakers Bureau provides a wide range of authors for speaking events. To find out more, go to hachettespeakersbureau.com or email hachettespeakers@hbgusa.com.

Little, Brown and Company books may be purchased in bulk for business, educational, or promotional use. For information, please contact your local bookseller or the Hachette Book Group Special Markets Department at special.markets@hbgusa.com.

Book interior design by Marie Mundaca

ISBN 9780316475389
LCCN 2023949231

Printing 2, 2024

LSC-C

Printed in the United States of America

*For my grandfather,*
*who loved the land*
*but loved his grandsons even more*


*And for Justin*

*What else could I write? I don't have the right*
*What else should I be? All apologies*

—Kurt Cobain, "All Apologies"

*Yes,*
*this is the kingdom of lost boys—*

*those longhair, & of hip, rib, & heart*
*delicate as antelope*
*or certain girls.*

*There are so many of us.*

*Our patience that of meltwater,*
*our anger involving pills*
*& wires. Nightwind*

*rattles the barnmouth, stars salt the barnholes,*
*& we are streaks of lean in the alfalfa field*
*when rifleshots*
*pin the night to our backs.*

# APRIL 1994

# 1

AFTER THE PICKUP SPED past, the boy crawled up out of the weeds and cheatgrass and started again down the slope of the mountain road, paperboard guitar case in hand, green canvas backpack jouncing about his ears and shoulders, the cold afternoon light hazed with roaddust. He was moving fast, breathing hard. He could taste it, the dust.

At the one-lane river bridge, he looked both ways up and down the long wing of gravel. No one coming, not as far as he could see. He hugged the battered guitar case to his chest and took off at a near run, the knock of the instrument inside making a kind of music. The rusted struts of the old bridge rose above him and slid over him, and the thick, cross-hatching shadows darkened his vision in time as he breathed, as he ran. When he was halfway across, a fishing boat bobbed around the upriver bend, fly lines curling through the air and lighting on the deep green water. The man at the oars spotted the boy and lifted his chin in acknowledgment.

Fuck. Here he was, a kid — sixteen but so skinny and small people often mistook him for younger — with an army surplus backpack and a guitar running across a nowhere bridge on a nowhere road in the middle of the afternoon. Anyone who saw him would be sure to remember him.

Fuck, fuck, fuck.

He slowed, waved back. Tried to pretend everything was okay, was as it should be. He'd gotten good at pretending. Across the bridge and out of sight, he ran again. His heart sounded hard in his ears. A mile on, the gravel road opened onto a blacktop highway, the tight green-dark corridor of forest opening as well, and now he crouched down and considered.

He was only a few miles east of Nye and figured he couldn't hitchhike just yet. Someone from town might recognize him. He'd ridden the school bus with his little cousins and the few other Nye kids all the way to Absarokee, had picked up the mail at the post office any number of times for his aunt, had been hauled on beer runs to the Trading Post with his uncle Heck. That was before Heck had stopped letting him go to school, go anywhere for that matter. Before it got bad.

Huddled in the grass and pine saplings at the edge of the road, the boy dug his hands into dead needles and gritty, fungal-smelling soil. Don't think about Heck, about Heck's astonished face. The weight of the splitting maul.

His heart a hot, mad animal in him, the boy rocked and leaped up and ran along the blacktop, his footfalls loud, the impossibly large strides of his shadow somehow matching his own — and then he held up, cursed himself for being so dumb, and crashed down through the ditch and into the woods.

He leaned against a pine and caught his breath. He had to be smart about this. These were the hours that mattered most. The road would be faster, but he couldn't risk being spotted. And if he tried to run in the woods, he'd trip over a root or rock and break his ankle. He decided to split the difference and parallel the road just inside the forest. He moved slowly, carefully, watching his every step.

The slope of the land was steep and uneven. The runoff creeks coursed with meltwater. Barbwire fences sliced along property lines. Wherever there'd been logging in the past decades — Heck had at least taught him the woods — the pines grew dog-hair tight, the forest dark and dusty, with sharp dead stobs below the canopy. The boy thrashed through as best he could, though he tore his flannel and scratched his arms where he'd rolled his sleeves up. He was worried the guitar case wouldn't hold or that his shoes, ratty Chucks with slick soles, would blow out. An hour on, maybe more — fuck it — he made for the road.

The hand of the sun at his back, he came up the berm and kicked through the beer cans and deer bones in the verge. The first couple of times he heard a vehicle, he again threw himself into the bar ditch. Eventually, though, he realized he wouldn't be able to tell who was a local and who wasn't, not until he'd seen the gun rack or fly rods in the back window. Not until they were long gone.

The sun dipped behind the blue shoulders of the Beartooths, and the boy shivered. He hoped maybe the fishermen were calling it a day and heading back to their lodges or fancy hotels or wherever they stayed. At his back came the far grind of an engine. He resisted the urge to flatten himself in the weeds and stepped just off the blacktop, stuck out his thumb.

From the vast blackness of the backlit mountains, a vehicle emerged. The wind of its passing pulled at the tails of the boy's flannel and flipped his long, dirty yellow hair across his face. A truck stopped some yards beyond, and the boy finger-combed his hair from his eyes, spied a bristle of fly rods through the Bronco's dusty window. The whole of him unclenched, a hard knot of held breath draining from his lungs.

—Where to?

One of the fishermen, gray waders rolled down around his waist, silver can of beer in hand, was already out and leaning the seat forward so the boy could climb in.

—The interstate, if you're going that far.

The boy lifted his guitar in first, then hauled himself in. He had to clear away plastic boxes of bright, feathery flies and fast-food wrappers and beer cans and crumpled sweatshirts and a couple of grungy ball caps to make room.

—It's a mess back there.

The driver wore dark glasses, despite the fading light, and lifted a can of beer to his lips, sipped.

The boy flinched. The driver, with his short red-brown hair and neatly trimmed goatee, didn't look a thing like his uncle Heck. But the dark glasses, the way he draped his hand over the wheel, wedged the can of beer in his crotch—it was all too familiar.

—No worries, the driver said, his voice deep and steady. We take turns when we go fishing. Driver only gets one beer on the river, one beer on the road.

The other man, lanky, patchy blond stubble stippling his jaw, folded himself into the cab and slammed the door. He grinned at the boy over the back of the bench seat.

— But the passenger, he said, laughing, gets to get shitcanned if he feels like it!

The driver checked his mirrors and eased the Bronco back onto the highway. The passenger, still laughing at his own joke, cracked another Coors Light.

— I'm Zach, he said. That ugly bastard behind the wheel is Cal.

— Kurt, the boy said, though his name was Justin.

— All right, Kurt. The interstate it is. Or, hell, if you want, we can take you all the way into Billings?

Billings was where Uncle Heck had picked him up last fall. Justin remembered the dirty marble floors and the high, intricately patterned ceilings of the old Greyhound station — and when they'd stepped out onto the street, right in front of them was a dancing man with three pink plastic clamshell hairclips in his beard.

Fucking bums, Heck had said. Degenerates. Whole city has gone to shit.

Justin wasn't sure how far east Billings was — he'd thought to hitchhike straight west once he hit the interstate — but his uncle was right, Billings had almost been like a real city. He could likely busk his way into a little money there, maybe enough for a bus ticket. It'd be safer on the bus. And he could sleep more easily.

Pine shadows striated the highway. The evening began to pool and deepen in the road ditches, in the mountain valleys below and beyond. Now that he was sitting, Justin felt a bone-deep tiredness ripple through him. How long ago had he woke, weary and sick, in the predawn forest? He tried to tally the hours between then and now but stopped short of the moment he ran hell-bent from the barn with the maul held hard in his hands — the moment he brought the maul down on the soft place where Heck's thick neck jointed into his chest.

— Billings'd be great, Justin said, swallowing against the bile rising in his throat, the fear and fury and gut-hollowing shame. Thanks.

— No sweat. Zach took a long drink, smacked his lips, and went on.

Good day on the river. Rainbows are running. Cal landed a twenty-incher. At this he punched the driver lightly on the shoulder. Lucky bastard.

Justin's mind flashed to the creek back of the trailer park in Bremerton and the astonishing colors of the spent salmon, their dark, mottled bodies drifting in the shallows.

— Yeah, man, Zach sighed. Good action all around. Always a good day on the river.

Zach drank again and dropped the empty to the floorboards, where it tinged and rolled. Then he hooked his elbow over the bench seat and turned to look right at Justin. Really took him in. Green canvas backpack. Beat-up guitar case. Long blond hair. Silver studs in his ears. Sharp face and small, almost girlish ears and nose. Knob of chin.

Zach studied the boy a moment longer and then, as if deciding, turned to the tape deck.

— You got a guitar there. You like music, Kurt? How about Springsteen? The Boss, right?

Before Justin could answer, the speakers crackled and came alive, and they drove on for a time, no one saying anything but the Boss: who was long gone, who was on fire, who was going down, down, down. The blacktop slid beneath them, the mountains faded into the deepening evening, and Justin leaned into the dusty plastic mesh of the speaker, into the noise, and slept.


When he woke, the details of the evening about him made no fucking sense whatsoever — glowing white fluorescents, a bank of gas pumps, tinny music. Big rigs idling in a wide gravel lot. The smeary reds of running lights. A man in cowboy boots and a blue corduroy ball cap walking stiff-legged toward the glass door of a gas station.

Justin sucked at the air and sat straight up, the story of this last day flooding into him — and now here he was at a truck stop in the back seat of a Bronco, fly rods bent above him.

But where were the fishermen? Where in the world was this truck stop?

He had the sense they'd been parked awhile, as it wasn't the cessation of motion that had woken him. It was something else.

Maybe they knew? Maybe they'd stopped to get the cops?

He should go, go now. He slid his left arm through the strap on his pack and took hold of the handle of the guitar case. He fumbled and found the latch to lean the front seat up. Just as he was about to run, he heard Cal's and Zach's voices drifting through the open driver-side window. They were in front of the gas station, near the ice cooler. Justin eased himself back into the bench seat.

Zach was gesturing with his grocery sack, saying something about his girlfriend, who was a teacher, who knew kids like this. Homeless. Strung out. They'll steal anything not nailed down.

—He's scrawny, but he could be dangerous. I mean, what the hell was he doing hitchhiking out on the Nye Road?

Cal shook his head and spit. He said something that Justin couldn't quite make out. The two men stood there, leaning toward each other, and Cal went on, his voice so low in timbre, it was only a far rumble. Justin closed his eyes and scooted that much closer to the window. Even if he couldn't make sense of it, he liked the sound of Cal's voice, how slow and even it was. The rumble ceased. Justin opened his eyes.

Both men had started toward the Bronco.

Fuck. He should have gone. That was maybe his only chance. Justin kept hold of his guitar case, but loosely, the strap of his pack at his elbow, and hunkered down. He laid his head back up against the speaker and closed his eyes as if he'd been sleeping the whole time.

The doors opened and slammed shut. The engine turned and caught. The Bronco began to move. After a time he could tell Zach was looking at him, reaching over the bench seat.

Oh, fuck. Justin let one eyelid flutter open and watched this tall, long-faced man lift the flap of his green canvas pack and stuff in a big plastic bottle of orange juice, a sack of peanuts, and a fistful of beef jerky sticks.

The Bronco picked up speed as they merged onto the interstate, and Justin couldn't help but imagine the grease of jerky sticks, the sour and salt of orange juice and peanuts. He didn't want to trust it. Not yet. For a long time, he held himself curled and still.

* * *

Both men silent, the music off, no sound now but tires and interstate, Justin finally sat up. Even in the deepening night, he could see they'd come out of the mountains and into a wide valley. Pine-studded ridges, a dark scribble of river sliding bridge to bridge beneath the freeway. Now banks of lights cut the sky, and a phalanx of smokestacks belched blue, orange, and yellow flames, the oily blooms somehow blacker than the night. Pumpjacks nodded in the dark distance.

— The Cenex oil refinery, Zach said, popping another beer. They say that smoke doesn't do anything to you. That the air is fine. I don't know.

The smoke faded, as did the lights.

They came up a high hill, then settled once again into the valley. The moon lifted over the southern horizon and slicked the dark river. As the moon drifted and grew, Justin couldn't help but turn his hands in that sideways spill of brightness. He grinned to see the play of shadows on the back of the seat in front of him — a rabbit, a bird, the devil sign, a double fuck-you. He pulled the sleeves of his flannel up and studied the bruises on his arms, the blues and blacks carrying the shape of a hard grip, the press of fingers, a pattern like wings. He could feel, too, the wings of a bruise at the small of his back. And in the pit of him, a deeper bruising. Justin bit down hard against the choke in his throat, his hot tears. He was glad of the dark, the highway sounds.

The lights of farms and ranches soon competed with the moon, then clumps of lights — trailer parks, maybe, or small towns on the verge of being swallowed — and now regular rows of streetlights along frontage roads and gas stations, warehouses and strip malls.

They were in the city.

Off to the north loomed the dark prow of the Rimrocks, the high sandstone cliffs that cut through Billings. All those months ago, mid-October, Justin stepped off the Greyhound and got into his uncle's truck, and for some reason, Heck had pointed the Rimrocks out to him. The only other thing Justin could remember Heck mentioning was his hair. How long it was, how he looked, his uncle said, halfway like a goddamn girl.

The Rimrocks were dark now, and close.

— You got a place to go?

Zach's voice startled him. Before he could answer, Cal's low baritone cut in.

—We got a room in the basement. Even got its own door. My wife and I don't really do anything with it. There's not any furniture. Except a TV and a VCR. My wife does her aerobics down there. Anyway, we could loan you a sleeping bag and a pillow. It'd be dry, warm.

Justin looked from one man to the other, the dark backs of their heads. They were both clean-cut, fit, maybe late twenties or early thirties, the kind of guys who were used to figuring things out, getting things done. Doing things their way.

—We grilled burgers last night, Cal went on. There's still some in the fridge. Potato salad too. Some Pepsi, Mountain Dew.

Zach leaned over the seat, the drape of his big, long arm.

—Listen, Kurt, you don't have to tell us anything. It's just, you know, you're a kid. We can't put you out in the middle of the city at night. You want more help tomorrow, just let Cal know. Whatever it is, he'll help. We'll help.

Justin could taste the potato salad, the pop and fizz of a cold Pepsi. But he was too close to the mountain yet to trust anyone, too close to the trailer—to what he'd done.

Heck lying there in a puddle of blood.

—Okay, Justin said, his heart squeezed in a vise. Thanks.

# 2

Here at the hill's crest, the world was two parts grass, three parts sky, and a pure measure of unraveling light. The nose of Old Blue, a Ford full-ton, tilted down the steep face of the Seventy-Nine Hill. The engine caught and revved on the grade, and as he drove, the man felt the sadness and heart-scatter of the past weeks whirl away in a gust of prairie wind.

As the hill flattened, he hit the gas and splashed through the south fork of Willow Creek, puddles here and there filigreed with ice and maybe sixteen inches of clear, moving water in the depths of the curving channel. Old Blue bounced up onto the long straightaway, and the man, Rene Bouchard, seventy-one years of age, shifted into third, dust barreling up behind him. The fences were in bad shape. Posts leaned like loose teeth. The barbwire bellied, broken here and there. Winter had been hard, and he hated to admit it, but he hadn't given the place the work it needed these past years. Rene lifted his foot off the gas and coasted as he neared the pastures, the corrals, and the shed.

Out front of the camphouse, a low-slung, tin-roofed cabin, he slowed to a stop. An iron boot scraper squatted at the lip of the plank porch, and two straight-backed wooden chairs flanked the camphouse door. On the north side sat the rain barrels, the drinking-water cistern, and the pump, all up on railroad ties. From behind, the long white snout of the propane tank poked out. Directly south of the house, a wooden fence enclosed the garden Viv had always insisted on, the bed thick now with dry, matted grasses and the yellow-green stars of weeds. A footpath bordered with river rocks led off the porch, around the garden, and into the cottonwoods, willows, and chokecherries. The trees and the contortions of the land sheltered from view the outhouse as well as the far reaches of the trail, which led to a wide gravel bar where the north and south forks of Willow Creek met. You could cross the north fork stone by stone and clamber up the high cutbank. It was there, facing west, that Rene had long ago built a split-log bench, Viv's sunset bench.

Well, he was home. And for the last time.

He cranked up Old Blue's windows, pulled the handle, and shouldered open the pickup's door, the hinges creaking. He worked his arm down one sleeve of his quilted flannel jacket, then the other. The day had been almost warm, but the cool edge of evening was in the breeze.

He studied the dust of the road, the untrammeled grass about the camphouse and corrals. No sign of the sheep, or of Bassett, his winter sheepherder of many years. He thought to haul in the few supplies he'd brought—a couple sacks of groceries, his .243—but Rene had his one chore, and ranch work, as he'd always told his own, came first.

The shed door opened into shit-and-straw-scented darkness, and Rene moved by bone memory. He dippered oats into a metal pail and, beneath the broken-peaked roof, walked the belly of the shed. The high, south-facing windows let in just enough dirty light to lean blacker shadows away from the support posts, pens, and lambing jugs. Soon, the shed would fill for lambing—the bleats of ewes in labor, drift of hay dust, scent of blood and iodine—but for now, it was one long emptiness. At the far end, he slid the bolt open and pushed the gate to the side on its rollers and blinked at the sudden sunset colors that met him.

Rene called out to the dry hills, clicked his tongue, and shook the metal pail, oats rattling, dancing—and over the grassy gusts of wind came the pounding of hooves. Nine Spot crested the hill first, the blue-black of her tossed mane and slim shoulders, then Big Red, looking as ever like a horse made somehow out of bricks save for the long white lick down the center of his nose. Rene called again, shook the pail, and felt even before he put his hands to them the good, rippling hides of horses.

The chill of winter yet pooled in the camphouse's shadowed corners and clung to the bare wood of the walls. For the last, slanting light, Rene pulled back the curtains. In the kitchen, he lit a fire of crumpled newspapers and wood shavings in the stove, then knelt and slowly laid himself all the way down, his left hip and lower back grinding in protest. With his shoulder and cheek mashed against the thin layer of dust and mouse droppings on the pocked linoleum, he punched the sparker until the propane burner below the fridge caught.

He finagled a hand underneath himself and pushed up and managed to get halfway to standing only to collapse onto the long bench in front of the table. He sat a moment and breathed as the pain flared and faded, as his heart galloped and slowed.

When Rene was sixteen, cowboying out on the Comanche Flats, his horse had spooked at a rattlesnake. Rene Bouchard was born to the saddle and had been bucked off plenty, but this time his left foot caught in the stirrup. The horse, young and full of spit, dragged him across the prairie a good long ways before he finally twisted free. Rene lay sprawled in the dirt and knew he was lucky he hadn't been gutted by a cactus or any other damn thing. Still, with his left leg mangled, he had to crawl nearly two miles back to camp, where the other cowboys loaded him into a Model T and drove him to Billings. The old country doctor, a bulldog pipe clenched in his teeth, did what he could, but the healed leg came out an inch shorter than the other. Though he could still ride and work with the best of them, Rene had limped ever since. As he aged, the limp settled into a near constant pain in his hip and lower back.

Just so long as he could stay off the floor, he thought now, the heels of his hands pressing on his knees. Stay on his feet, in the saddle.

Outside, the wind blew in curves and circles. Bits of dust and dead grass ticked against the metal roof and the lead-glass windows. Rene hauled the supplies in from Old Blue and filled the fridge, cupboards, and drawers. With Lianne gone to Billings for the day, he'd taken his one chance and pretty well emptied what was left at the house in town. Stocking up at the ranch was an old habit, but Rene needed only a handful of days out here.

Enough time to saddle up Nine Spot and take a ride, sit in the night beneath the stars with a glass of whiskey. He told himself he wouldn't go check on Bassett, who was out with the sheep in one pasture or another. No, he'd do the few things he came to do, then he'd take a seat on Viv's sunset bench, prop his rifle on the hard prairie earth, and lean himself down onto the point of the blue-black barrel. Shoot himself through the heart.

Rene fed lengths of juniper and pine to the fire. The stove creaked and warmed. He tied back the thick wool hangings that served as doors for each of the bedrooms to get a little warmth in there. The kids used to sleep in the bunkbed room, a set of slim army surplus bunks along each of the three walls. Lianne, the oldest, always took the top bunk by the window, Keith and Dennis fought over the other two top bunks, though there wasn't really any difference, and Franklin, the baby, was left with one of the bottom bunks, usually the one below Lianne. Rene stared a moment longer at the raw board walls, the stain of old rain etching the window glass. So many years held in that still, small space. He let the curtain swing back into place.

In the kitchen, he ran the water to clear out the rust and spiders and set the percolator on the stove for coffee. Then he swept the floor, filled the kerosene lamps, and lit one against the slow-gathering dark.

What else was there to do? He stowed his .243 in the rack in his bedroom, the shells in the top dresser drawer.

He eased himself down into one of the two easy chairs. A bloom of dust rose as he gave his weight to the springs. The coarse fabric beneath his hands, the shape of the chair at his back — it all felt so familiar. And so goddamned different. Ah, Viv. Who would hold him or any of them together now that she was gone?

Hell, they'd already been falling apart for years.

Opposite where Rene sat, above the long bench and table, the bird feeder at the window was empty. With the days already tilting toward spring, the songbirds would be back soon. There was dry corn and a bin of sunflower seed in the barn.

Well, it didn't matter much, not much at all, but at least it was something he could do.

# 3

OFF TO THE WEST, rags and tracers of deep orange and vermilion were snagged in the broken teeth of the Bull Mountains. A little higher, the whole sky was rose laced with lavender. Higher yet, periwinkle and cobalt. And in the east, the sky shone the gray-blue of nighthawks on the wing.

She had forgotten the casual, stunning brilliance of a sunset in eastern Montana. And not a soul out to see it, Lianne Parker thought, taking in the empty gravel streets, the tumbledown houses and slumped double-wides, wind pulling at the weeds. She popped the trunk and loaded two paper grocery sacks into her left arm and got another in her right, then made her way up the curving concrete walkway and onto the low porch, where she maneuvered open the screen door and knocked with her elbow.

—Dad, she called. Would you get the door?

Lianne blew a flyaway strand of hair from her eyes and looked west once more to catch the last colors, though from here the neighbor's cottonwood obscured the view. The tree was a gnarled, half-dead thing. Hunks of bark and finger-thick branches littered what passed for a yard, mostly tufts of crabgrass. They should have that thing taken down, Lianne thought. Cottonwoods were so messy—the fluff in the spring, dead branches and sloughed bark all year long. It was ugly, even dangerous.

And if it was gone, if it had been gone, Mom could've sat on the porch these last weeks and watched the sunset.

Lianne's throat went tight. The tremors that had racked her without announcement since her mother's death began once more in her chest and radiated out. She clung to the grocery bags and the crinkle of their thick brown paper.

—Dad, she called when she could get her mouth around the word again. Dad!

She wasn't even sure who lived next door anymore in that bungalow with the untended yard. When she was growing up, it was the Kantas, Sandy and Ethel. But Sandy had been gone a long time now and was an old man even when she was little. Lianne remembered the exact way he tilted his hip and swung his wooden leg out in front of him. A souvenir from his sightseeing trip to France, he always joked, meaning of course the war. Ethel must be gone as well, though Lianne hadn't heard of her passing, or if she had, she'd long forgotten.

A dust devil whirled to life and spun itself out. What might it be like to blessedly forget?

Lianne had stayed with her mother in those long last moments, twenty-six hours from when the delirium set in. Her brothers Keith and Dennis had been there in the beginning; the whole family had been there, kneeling, hovering, or perching on kitchen chairs pulled into a rough circle around the old Naugahyde couch, where their mother or mother-in-law or wife lay thin and dream-racked and covered in blankets. There was no term for the stage the cancer was in. It was everywhere; it was her.

Last winter, as nothing worked, nothing helped, Viv had finally refused any more treatment. And she wouldn't stay in the hospital either. Of course Rene had backed her. The flint in his eye and the set of his stubbled jaw—every fresh-faced doctor in the place backed off when they saw this rough-hewn cowboy coming down the hall, saying he was damn well going to take his wife wherever she wanted, which was home, thank you much.

Lianne was the first to come help care for Viv, though as the weeks went on, the family slowly gathered. At first, it'd been like a reunion of sorts, just like Viv wanted. Casseroles and stories, grandkids giggling and darting about pell-mell. They hadn't all been together since forever, and that's how they said it — *since forever* — though in truth, it wouldn't have been so hard to tally all those silent, bygone years. They did no such accounting, at least not out loud. One evening, everyone piled into the front room, and Rene pulled his harmonica from his pocket, which he seldom did anymore, and played tunes from his cowboy days — "Moonshiner" and "Will the Circle Be Unbroken?" and "Tie a Knot in the Devil's Tail." The grandkids wheeled about, and Dennis and his second wife, whom Lianne had met only once before, jitterbugged with surprising grace across the creaking wooden floor. Viv, sitting against a bank of pillows, clapped and sang along, tears slicking her dark eyes, a smile on her lips.

But then Viv fell while making her way to the bathroom. Then she was awake less and less. Then, finally, when she was awake, she was barely there, her words slippery, ribboning into nonsense. Some hours into this new, strained reality, Lianne handed the cup of ice chips to Keith and rose to stretch her knees and back, and her mother's hand shot out from beneath the scratch of wool blankets and grabbed her by the wrist, those muscles and bones remembering their old mothering strength.

— Pockets, she said, her voice falling, breaking into sibilance.

They'd called Lianne High Pockets as a girl. For how fast she grew.

— Pockets, Viv said again, her eyes flapping open. Help me here. I can't.

In horror, Lianne watched as her mother tried to raise her shoulders, tried to sit up, and, no, she couldn't. Lianne knew, then, what needed to be done and filled a bucket with warm water, gathered soft rags. The wastebasket and clean sheets and blankets.

The day after the funeral, her brothers had packed up their families and left. Marty, Lianne's husband, agreed to stay until the end of the week but then wanted to get their boys, Trent and Frank, settled back in Spokane before the school week started. Lianne had let Marty think she was caravanning back with him, but once the boys were seat-belted into his Lexus, she shook her head. She needed more time. Her father could barely get himself up and shaved in the morning, let alone answer the condolence cards, cook, clean, or do any of the other dozen daily tasks that needed doing. It wasn't a lie, but it wasn't the truth either. Lianne knew the only reason Marty didn't try to rationalize her into submission right there—one of his specialties—was that her father was watching them from the front porch, the old rancher Rene Bouchard, his thumbs hooked in the front pockets of his blue jeans.

Marty looked at her—studiously not looking behind her—and ran a hand through his thinning hair. Even more than losing an argument, he hated a scene. When would she be home? he asked. Soon, she said, and put a hand to his chest. Soon.

Lianne had left Delphia, Montana, over twenty years ago. It had long been the kind of place everyone said you had to leave if you wanted to make something of yourself—even more so if you happened to be a young woman who wanted to make something of yourself. She'd visited over the years and so had noticed when the Depot Café burned down, when the Sportsman Bar went out of business, when the trains quit running and the tracks were pulled up for salvage, and when, in the late '80s, farms and ranches went under one after the other—but she hadn't lived here, hadn't felt the place shape her days or seen the world through a scrim of dust and distance in all these years. She'd left family and land and all the old, worn-out expectations, all the grievance and grief. But today, as she'd done every ten days or so across the months she'd been back in Delphia, she'd driven ninety miles to Billings just to grocery shop. And then driven right back.

Lianne shifted the weight of the grocery bags and squinted to see through the gauzy white curtain over the rectangle of window in the front door. She could make out one arm of the couch, the dark hallway that led to the kitchen, and she felt it again—the house was wrong. Too small, the sloping roof of the porch too low and close. When she dreamed of Delphia, of this house, which even twenty years gone she did often, there were hallways and rooms on end, high windows lavish with light.

—Dad, she called, pounding with her elbow. What the hell? Open up!

Then she saw it: Old Blue, her father's ranch truck, was missing from the driveway. Her mother was dead. Her brothers had scurried home. And she'd come back today to find that her father, like a boy, had run away. Again, she was the only one.

Rene was at the ranch. Even if he'd taken Viv's Oldsmobile or bounced off on a pogo stick, Lianne knew that's where he'd go. What was he thinking, lighting out for the territory like some geriatric Huck Finn? Lianne and her brothers had a 50 percent share of that ranch now, their mother's half, which meant they could force Rene to sell if they wanted. The day before the funeral Keith pulled Lianne aside and told her he'd had coffee that morning with Orly Pinkerton, one of the big ranchers in the valley. Orly'd made an offer, Keith said, a good one. Then Keith dropped his voice a notch lower, his eyes going wide as he whispered the number. Lianne cursed now and fumbled for her keys. She nearly dropped a bag of groceries but finally got the door open.

Inside, the dining-room light shone dimly, the silhouettes of dead moths littering the bottom of the frosted-glass fixture. She'd scrub the place up before she left. Water the lilacs, clean the house, haul her father back home. Even when she was a girl, she'd always had the longest list of chores. Whenever Lianne complained, Viv, a bristle of sewing pins in her mouth or her hands deep in the dishwater, told her she'd better get used to it.

Maybe she had. Maybe that's why she was still here. Lianne shrugged the grocery bags onto the counter and went back for the rest.

It was nearly dark by the time she'd finished unloading. She put the percolator on for coffee and lifted the phone, which hung near the doorway to the mudroom in the back of the house, the long yellow cord curled below, the old rotary gears still clicking and unwinding just like they had when she used to call JB or Ves or any of her high-school boyfriends, and dialed Marty.

He answered on the second ring with his usual greeting—bright and sure, no matter the time or circumstance.

—Hey, she said, it's me.

—Was wondering when you'd call. The boys too. Trent practiced his roping all day. Wants to show Grandpa Rene, of course. And Frank made another card for Grandma Viv. Marty paused, as he always did when he was coming to the point. Of course, they've been in bed for a while now.

Even on a Saturday, Marty was a stickler for mealtimes and bedtimes and just about every time in between.

— Sorry. Didn't realize how late it was.

— So, when are you coming home?

Lianne stepped into the mudroom and opened the back door. She'd put in for bereavement leave at the community college before she'd come back to help with Viv — Rene had of course called her, not Keith, not Dennis — so she wouldn't have to be back again until the fall. If she ever went back. She hadn't told Marty yet, but a couple of months ago, a friend from grad school had called with an offer — a sabbatical replacement for the coming year at the University of Idaho. The pay was better, and she'd be teaching creative writing rather than composition. But of course, she'd be away again. The university was two hours south of Spokane. As it was, Trent and Frank, eleven and seven, hadn't really seen their mother — save for the week before and after Viv's death — in nearly two months.

Through the screen, the chill of the prairie dark pricked at Lianne's face and neck.

— Dad ran away.

— He what? Marty's voice was suddenly perfectly urgent and concerned. Oh, Lianne. I'm sorry. Do you need me to call someone? I can —

— No. I'll just, well —

Lianne pushed open the screen door, the long curly cord coming taut, and the night closed around her, enormous and dark, the sparks of stars.

— He's at the ranch, she said. Probably lucky he didn't run off before the funeral. I might let him stew for a few days, but I'll have to do something. He's too old to be out there on his own anymore.

Lianne could hear the low classical music Marty liked to play in the evenings, the churn of the dishwasher. They had been married the summer after she graduated from college, and for a long time she'd marveled at how measured and predictable Marty was, how in control. He breathed down the line, slow and even.

— I fly to Chicago a week from Monday for the directors' meeting, and the boys have spring break that week. You'll have to be back by the weekend. Sunday at the very latest.

Shit. She'd forgotten all about spring break. She should have just kept the boys with her. They doted on Grandpa Rene, and he likely wouldn't have run off if they'd been around. And who cared if they missed another week of school, especially the week before break? But of course, Marty would have cared, which was likely the reason Lianne hadn't brought it up in the first place. Across the twenty years they'd been together, he had somehow trained her *not* to consider the possibilities, to imagine anything different.

Before Marty could pin her down, write a date and time in his planner, Lianne said her goodbye and reached the phone back into the house.

She walked out from beneath the canopy of the ash tree and into the night.

The moon rose low over the hills; its light shadowed the ridges and washes and coulees. Delphia wasn't much more than a four-by-five grid of gravel streets, so it didn't matter where in town you were, you were always close to the edge. These past weeks, Lianne's whole heart and self had been given over to her mother, the fact of her lying there on the couch, her sunken veins and fragile bones and spasms.

Now, though, Lianne felt herself lifting, stretching, looking out for the first time in a long time toward the horizon, the dark breadth and presence of the flats and hills, the many prairie miles rolling away to the north, toward the Bouchard Ranch.

# 4

BENEATH THE NEON LIGHTS, two women, bangs piled impossibly high, shared a cigarette. The one in the jean jacket leaned in and said something to the one in the sleeveless blouse. Sleeveless, eyes wide in pretend shock, pushed Jean Jacket in the chest. Jean Jacket pushed back. They stumbled, laughed. Sleeveless flicked the cigarette into the dark, and Jean Jacket pulled two sticks of gum from her purse. Both women chewed hard and fast and as if on cue hocked their respective wads of gum at a trash can. Sleeveless swung open the door of the bar, country music spilling out, and both women sashayed inside. Across the street, Justin lifted himself up from where he'd been crouched down behind a dumpster.

They'd pulled up to Zach's apartment, and while the men were busy peeling off waders and breaking down rods, Justin had stuffed one of the ball caps from the back seat into his pack, slipped out, and run. Zach yelled for a time, said he shouldn't worry, that they could help, but Justin held his guitar tight to his chest, the night air biting at his lungs. He turned one corner, then another. Kept running.

Those guys thought they knew everything; they didn't know anything.

He just hoped they'd be too embarrassed to tell anyone—Cal's wife or Zach's girlfriend, the teacher—that some kid ran on them. They didn't have the right name, and even if anything from Nye made the newspapers in the next days, he'd started at Absarokee too late for school pictures, and he didn't think there were any photos of him in the house either. He worried about the guitar. If that somehow made the paper, it'd be a dead giveaway. Couldn't be helped, though. He wouldn't leave his guitar. No fucking way.

The parking lot finally empty, Justin loped across the street and tried the door of the first vehicle he came to. Locked. So was the next. But the third swung wide.

Carefully, he leaned his guitar and backpack up against the wheel well. He checked once more that he was alone, then hoisted himself up onto the bench seat. He found a nearly full pack of cigarettes — Winstons, even — stuffed between the sunshade and the ceiling. A big sack of sunflower seeds by the gearshift. An unopened can of Mountain Dew in the cupholder. A white box with two sugared doughnuts left wedged into the other drink holder. And, fuck yes, a six-inch knife in a leather sheath in the glove box. This morning, he wouldn't have gone back into the camper for anything, Heck twitching and bleeding out in the doorway, and so left the poncho and flashlight he'd stashed beneath the mattress, the knife beneath his pillow. It didn't rain here like it did in Seattle. A flashlight would have been nice. A knife was even better.

Justin stuffed the cigarettes into the front pocket of his flannel, wolfed down both doughnuts, and chugged the Mountain Dew, fizz and sugar burning his nose. Then he slipped out of the cab and gingerly shut the door. He buckled the knife to his belt and opened his pack and tried to shove the sunflower seeds inside. But then — that music, loud voices.

He flattened himself against the blacktop.

Footsteps, laughter, the shuffle and scuff of bodies. A man's voice rising above the others.

—I told you. I fucking told you!

Justin's heart slammed up and down, felt too big for the bounds of his body, as if in the course of beating, it might crack his ribs and bust his spine.

The footsteps came closer. No, not footsteps. Bootsteps. The leather scratch of them against the blacktop, bits of gravel. Cowboy boots. A bunch of them. A dozen, maybe. Even if the cowboys were too drunk to figure that he'd hooked anything, if they got hold of him, they'd see his long hair and the holes in his ears.

Justin clutched his guitar case by the handle and his pack by one shoulder strap. He breathed once, twice, and scrambled to his feet. The pack, which he hadn't had time to close properly, twisted and spilled. He grabbed at what he could and ran. Flat out ran.

Behind him the cowboys called and laughed.

— What the fuck?

— It's a fucking kid!

— Hey, kid, you dropped your seeds. And your undies!

# 5

THE WIND STILLED; THE darkness trued and deepened. In the distance, the flash and wobble of headlights tipped down the Seventy-Nine Hill. Rene threaded his arms through the quilted sleeves of his jacket, squared his hat. He worried it was Lianne already come to argue him back into town. Well, he'd meet it head-on. Whatever it was.

Sharp, blue-tinged lights scoured the road, the corrals, and the shed. With the flat of his hand, Rene shaded his eyes. The pickup, a red crew-cab Ram, swung around and pulled to a stop in the road right behind where Old Blue was parked, as if hemming him in. Rene didn't recognize the truck — brand-new — but could about guess whose it was.

The engine rumbled, the headlights tunneled into the night, and Orly Pinkerton crawled out of the cab and hitched up his jeans. He nodded at Rene, stuck his hand out.

— Didn't get a chance to say so at the funeral, but I'm sorry about Viv.

Rene shook the man's hand and stepped back. Orly was over six feet tall and big across the shoulders and in the belly. His place was some miles down the river, so Orly was a neighbor of sorts. Rene wished he'd shut that pickup off, kill the lights.

— Thank you, Orly, but I'm betting you didn't drive all the way out here after supper just to shake my hand.

Orly pretended to shy and scuffed his boot in the dirt.

— You seen right through me, Bouchard. My boy was out fixing fence this afternoon and happened to spy you driving the Mosby Road. I figured you were out here, that this might be my chance.

Times like this, Rene wished he still smoked. A cigarette would give him something to do with his itchy hands.

— I'd like to make an offer, Orly went on. I imagine it's getting to be a burden, all this land. Time you hang up your spurs and take a rest, Bouchard.

Rene was thankful now for the noise and the glare. It hid how hot he was, how quickly Orly had gotten to him.

— No, Orly. No, thank you. I won't be hearing any offers.

Orly sniffed, swiped at his nose with a thumb.

— Your boys got plans out here? I seen them at the funeral. Good-looking boys. That Keith was quite the ballplayer in his day. But isn't he down in Colorado now? And the other one's with the highway patrol, right? Looks to me like your boys might not be interested.

Orly paused like he was making some kind of speech, took a step closer, clapped his big hands together.

— Anymore, you gotta have an eye on the future or else it'll up and bite you on the ass. We can't be doing things like we used to do. You see town about falling apart, right? Well, I'm going to keep this town afloat. You sell to me, Bouchard, and I'll make this land matter. I'll make it pay.

Those headlights hung wide shadows from Orly's hat and shoulders. Rene reached back and opened the camphouse door. He bit down hard on all his heart would have him say.

— I'll say good night, Orly. I got work in the morning.

Orly started in on something or other, but Rene turned away. He just didn't have it in him. He hobbled back into the camphouse and shut the door. That big diesel growled on down the road and was gone. Goddamn.

The fire in the stove snapped and burned, the calls of coyotes rang and faded and rose once more, and after a time, Rene touched a match to the Coleman lantern and dialed the flame to a steady yellow-white. He stepped back out onto the porch and couldn't help but pause and crane his head back and reckon the stars, the spill of the Milky Way wide and bright in the heavens.

The moon ghosted up over the hills.

A body gets tired, Rene thought, it's true. But not tired of this. You likely can't ever get enough of this. Rene stepped off the plank porch and moved slowly, feelingly, around the north side of the camphouse. He held the lantern up and out.

There it was, ringing the cistern, poking out from underneath the railroad ties—mint, the leaves tough but greening again with the rain and the recent run of relatively warm days this early April. After the long day of work, when they'd dug the well, installed the pump, and horsed the cistern up onto the heavy, creosote-dark ties, Viv had surprised him. She'd gone to the truck and ferried back a single nodding stalk of mint, which she planted in the broken earth below. That was more than forty years ago now, Rene thought, running his hand through the bristling stalks. The heady smell rose in the night.

Inside, he poured an inch of bourbon into a tin cup, worked a mint leaf between his fingers, and dropped the broken leaf into the liquor. Viv had always liked a sprig in her sun tea, and though he'd given up smoking when they married, then quit the bars when the kids were little, she'd allowed him his whiskey on a weekend.

Today was Saturday. Maybe. He'd lost track. He sat once more in his easy chair and sipped.

Orly and his talk of boys, his talk of land. To hell with Orly. If the son of a bitch ever did get his hands on Willow Creek, well, at least Rene wouldn't be around to see it. Which was poor goddamn consolation. Rene burned his scarred and calloused hands up and down the arms of the easy chair. He tried to quiet the tremors in him of shame and confusion, even fear. Lianne was by a country mile the toughest of his children, but she'd take it hardest, too, what he planned to do. She was the one who put in the time with Viv there at the end, and he'd told her the other day she'd done enough, told her to go on home to Spokane, to her husband and her boys. But she wouldn't, and he knew she wouldn't, and she maybe saw in his eyes a shadow of what he planned. Now, hell, she'd be the one to find him. Rene took another swallow, near half his glass. The whiskey swam his vision a moment. It couldn't be helped. It was just the way it was. The hard, sad way it sometimes shook out.

Mint and smoke on his tongue, the inerrant prairie dark at the window, the chalk light of the moon.

It was about all he had left. He'd enjoy it while he could.

# 6

THE NIGHT WHEELED AND spun.

Justin ran down alleys and up wide, blasted streets. The red eyes of traffic lights streaked his shoulders. He clasped the guitar to his chest, his backpack bouncing all around. Kept running.

Fucking fishermen, fucking cowboys. He was crying. The night bit at the wet of his eyes.

In front of him now the Dopplered ring of sirens sounded; a quick bleed of color flashed between the buildings — and he froze.

Took his bearings. Ran the other way.

After a time, Justin found himself on a street tunneled by great tall trees. The deep fissures and crenellations in the bark held shadows that suggested birds, language, faces. He thrashed through a hedge and emerged in a yard as big as a city park, the back of a grand brick house, at least three stories, bathed in low light. Through a phalanx of windows, the empty dining room was lit and immaculate, flowers at the center of the table, a white tablecloth. It was the kind of thing he'd seen on television and never believed. Even the smell of the place. No mud or trash. Nothing burning. Just the first soapy, sweet suggestion of blossoms, great hanging masses of tiny flowers nearly ready to erupt.

The whole place gave him the willies.

He crashed through the hedge on the opposite side of the yard and was down the gravel alley and up the next street running, running.

Now he was rubbing shoulders with slick bank buildings, glass-walled restaurants and bars. The wind clattered cans in the gutter and disarticulated the smoke still rising from a door-side ashtray.

Justin slowed and doubled back.

He set his guitar down, plucked a smoking butt from the sand, and pulled a Winston from his pocket. He pressed the two together and breathed in. The Winston kindled; the smoke filled him. He dragged deep and quick — but caught himself, slowed. Leaned into the bricks.

It felt so good to still into a cigarette, to feel like you had a reason to be in this one place you were. A rind of moon showed behind the dark skyline. This was likely the kind of place to busk, he thought now, near a bar like this. He noted the outlines of the buildings at his back and across the street. But now he should find someplace to hole up and grab an hour or two of sleep.

The Rimrocks were to the north, there, so he'd been running a ragged line east since that siren spooked him. But he didn't know where the bus station was — somewhere he could at least find a bench to curl up on — didn't know Billings at all.

He tasted the burn of filter and reached for another Winston but stopped. He ought to try to make them last. He flicked the butt to the sidewalk and fished in his bag for one of the beef jerky sticks Zach had stowed in there while he was pretending to sleep. He skinned the plastic and chewed the tough meat. Teriyaki, sweet and salty. He thought again of the fishermen and wondered at the ride, the OJ and peanuts and beef jerky, the offer of a place to crash. Wondered if he should have trusted them.

No, fuck it, he couldn't think like that. Running was the best bet after what had happened, after what he'd done. As if from a long way off, Justin saw himself laid out on the forest floor in the predawn light. In his bones, the stretch of his sinews, he felt the centrifugal force of the swung maul. It was as if he'd swallowed it all, the slosh of it in his belly. He hoped he wouldn't be sick. Shaking some, he lifted his guitar and took off down the sidewalk.

The high, slick buildings slowly gave way to abandoned hotels, old houses with sagging porches and bars on the windows, squat buildings that ran, seemingly without entrance, the whole of a city block.

He'd been keeping the Rimrocks in front of him or over his left shoulder, and he followed now the burnished railroad tracks in that same direction. For a time, he jumped from railroad tie to railroad tie, careful not to touch the ashy gravel, like it was hot lava from one of his little cousins' games.

The sky lightened almost imperceptibly, from dark to near-dark, and in front of him, the tracks multiplied beneath a bank of sodium lights that shone on buildings and platforms. He didn't want to risk that. He angled south, down through the no-man's-land between the tracks and the highway, dry weeds and burrs slashing at his shins.

He came up over the road and cut east toward a wide parking lot, corrals or something behind the false-front building.

Yes, those were corrals. Corrals in the city. And the sign on the wooden building read BILLINGS PUBLIC LIVESTOCK AUCTION.

Justin boosted himself up over a low fence and crossed a small half-moon of grassy pasture, and at the next fence, this one higher, made of cold metal pipe, he slid his guitar through the bottom rungs, climbed over the top, and leaped to the ground.

His feet landed in soft, churned dirt and manure. The smells of sweet-rot and dry grass were just about enough to knock him over. But where there was the smell of shit, there were animals, straw — there was warmth and sleep.

The chute he was in broke into three different chutes, each leading toward one of three barns in parallel. He aimed for the one on the right and wondered what he'd find inside. Cows, most likely. There were cows all over the mountains out of Nye. Sometimes he thought about what he'd tell the guys in Seattle about Montana. That there were more cows than people, that there were honest-to-God cowboys wandering around, that the whole place was like going back in time.

That it was scary as hell.

The high barn door slid to the side on a screeching wheel, and the dark inside was oceanic, impenetrable. He blinked and the shapes of metal pens and wooden stalls gradually resolved. Then the tremendous, slow-breathing shapes of horses, their great long heads hanging over their gates.

The nearest horse side-eyed him, cocked the flutes of its ears.

Except for dogs, of course, and raccoons he'd thrown rocks at, and the time at the trailer park in Bremerton when he'd watched a beautiful, dignified skunk waddle from trash can to trash can, Justin had never been this close to something so warm, wild, and alive. If he took a step and reached out, he could run his fingers along the short, fine hairs of the animal's jaw, the dark flower of its nose.

The horse snorted loudly, and Justin fell back against the barn wall, his guitar knocking and sounding. He gathered himself and saw he'd fallen onto a set of stairs. There was an old barn full of bats and mouse shit behind his uncle's place, and even if he was a city boy, he knew enough to make his way up to the loft and wedge himself between the wall and a bank of straw bales.

With the straw at his back and beneath his heavy head, he breathed and blinked and saw again Heck's astonished, terrified face, the bulk of him framed in the camper's slim doorway.

Fuck him, Justin said to himself. He closed his eyes and said it again, chanted it—*Fuck him, fuck him, fuck him*—until he fell into a black, thrashing sleep.

# BEFORE

# 7

Most folks out in this part of the country didn't want to admit it, preferred to paper over it with prayer or reactionary politics or all the old, worn stories, but everybody could feel the weight of it now, how they had to work against the tilt, the lean, the gravity of this new reality pulling at them as if they were all scrabbling up a steep hill in loose dirt. Rene had come of age in the dirty '30s, when the fields failed, the cattle turned bone-skinny in the unforgiving sun, dust sifted under doors and windows, and there was nothing but squirrel stew for supper. Then, like all the other boys and men, he'd tried like hell to get drafted, though his bum leg branded him 4-F—and even so, this world they had now was somehow meaner, sharper. Big and wide and ragged at the edges.

He thought of the Langs, the family next door, who'd moved in after Ethel Kanta left to live with her daughter in Great Falls. It wasn't so long ago, maybe '87 or '88. The two older girls, likely Crow or Cheyenne, were the woman's from before. Rene only ever saw her, the girls' mother, through a window or leaning out the front door, smoking. A short, husky woman with dark eyes and black hair. He didn't know her first name. Dan Lang was clearly the father of the two little boys, all three of them towheaded, their eyes and noses and mouths tight in the wide, round planes of their faces. Those boys were the ones. The older boy couldn't have been more than ten or eleven the first time Rene caught him hooking a can of gas from his back shed. When Rene marched him next door, Dan, shirtless, tinkering with that rust-red sports car of his, held the boy up by his thin wrists right there in the street and whacked his backside till he was crying. But ever after, Dan wouldn't so much as say hello to Rene, as if Rene were the one who'd done something wrong.

Later, over coffee at the drugstore, Rene mentioned it to the school principal, whom he'd been friendly with, and the principal shook his head and smoothed his chin beard. Those boys were goners, he said. That was the word he used—*goners*—and then he cataloged the older boy's transgressions. Rene felt something hollow in the pit of him. He never told Viv about any of it. She was tougher than he was, that was a fact, but he couldn't imagine himself saying those things to her, the things that boy had scratched on a stall in the elementary-school bathroom. It embarrassed him, set his heart knocking and his rangy hands wishing to grab the handle of something and get to work. So, as if the Langs were the best of neighbors, Viv kept on bringing over iced tea and homemade cookies while Rene started locking their doors at night, something he'd never done in all the years they'd lived in tiny Delphia, Montana.

But we were talking about before.

Before the Langs moved in, before the farm crisis of the '80s shattered family after family, before Rene had begun to feel the world tilt so and slip away.

Long before all that, say thirty years ago, 1964, when his own children were young, when, come lambing season, he and Viv would pack up the original Old Blue, a '56 Ford full-ton, the first pickup with seat belts they'd ever owned, and leave for days or even two weeks at a time to live at the ranch. Ethel Kanta, her own children mostly grown, would come by in the evenings to make dinner for Lianne, Keith, Dennis, and little Franklin and get them to bed and then come over again in the morning to cook eggs and pancakes. She'd send the older three off to school and take Franklin to her place for the day. When Viv or Rene came back to town for groceries and to check in, Ethel would give her report, and it was almost always good: Lianne was getting her homework done, as was

Keith, and both were helping keep Dennis in line. Franklin was cleaning his plate at lunchtime like he was supposed to, to grow big and strong, and *Look here,* Ethel would say, *I set up my easel for him, and he made these paintings for you. Says they're sheep. You see?*

Rene did see. He framed and hung one of Franklin's paintings in the camphouse above the easy chair he favored. It was a big fluffy sheep, the white of its fleece an absence rather than a presence, a being given shape and substance only by the landscape surrounding it — a field of the greenest grass, a true-blue sky, butter-yellow sun smiling in the corner. Yes, in those days the sun shone down, and the rains came, and the wind in its turn, and the cold, and the Bouchards butchered their own lambs and stacked the hand-wrapped packages in the deep freeze. They canned tomatoes and green beans, pickled cucumbers and carrots and a bright, hot horseradish. They stowed sacks of potatoes and squash in the cellar. They handed boots and shoes down from one child to another. They never ate out or traveled — extravagances like that simply didn't occur to them — no, they made do with what they had, pinched every penny, some years just barely scraping by, but after a time they owned the land outright, and day after day Rene Bouchard bent his back to the work he loved, sheep ranching, and his fierce, lovely Irish wife was right there beside him, as good on a horse as he was, and their children were safe and cared for, and even if they had to keep an eye on Dennis, they were good kids, smart and willing and kind.

And the plains of eastern Montana in 1964 felt that way, too, like if you were smart and willing, the world would surely be kind.

# 8

AND WHAT DID JUSTIN remember? What did he flinch at in his straw-strewn sleep?

Once, there'd been a hotel room with beige carpet, two beds with dark-patterned spreads, fake wood on the walls, a wide mirror above a low chest of drawers, and out the window that cranked open only a fist's width ran a sick river of lights on a strip of six-lane highway, the thrum and grind of traffic.

Where were they even going? What trip would have necessitated that they — father, mother, and son — stay in a hotel? Were they visiting someone? Maybe his dad's mom in Wenatchee? Maybe his mom's one good friend, in Spokane, who was also his godmother and sent him a two-dollar bill tucked into a jokey card twice a year, on his birthday and at Christmas? Were they going to the coast? Or that German town in the mountains? He had no memories of such trips, but there were pictures, square Instamatics. Justin found the cloth-covered album years later while dumping drawers, scrounging through the wreck of his mother's place for money, cigarettes, anything. He sat in the ruins and turned the plastic pages. His mother's curly ginger-brown hair blown in the ocean wind. His father, hair yellow and straight, like his, grinning maniacally and hefting an enormous beer stein.

But no matter where they'd been or where they were going, that one evening they were there together, in a hotel. Justin was seven and sat kicking his legs on the foot of the bed, as near to the TV as he could get. It was New Year's Eve, the celebration in New York City getting under way. He couldn't believe that in a few hours, even here, clear across the country, it would no longer be 1985, which was the only year he'd ever really been aware of, as if the ones that had come before were just practice for this one — and 1985 was such a good, safe number for a year, much more solid than 1986, which felt thin and slippery in his mouth. Every time he said it to himself — 1986 — it somehow unraveled, got away from him.

Fireworks bloomed on the curved screen. Justin turned to find his parents leaned into each other, laughing and tipping cans of beer to their mouths — Rainier, the pretty red *R* on the white can — and he didn't know whether it was the unfamiliar hotel shadows on the caves of their eyes or the pure curiousness of being allowed to stay up late and sleep in the same room as his parents, but his father and his mother suddenly looked to him like strangers, like in this new year, 1986, they would not be who they had been in 1985.

Justin was suddenly sure of it.

—Mom? he said.

—J., she said, though she wasn't looking at him. She was leaned back against the headboard, her eyes closed. A slack, dreamy look on her face.

Terrified, Justin launched himself at his mother. He spilled her beer, and the front of his shirt and his pants were wet, and there was a big wet spot on one of the pillows too. There was a lot of yelling then, and his father, furious, took him by his arm, those strong fingers biting to the bone — all the people on the TV singing and crying and hugging one another — and hefted him into the air. Justin must have landed on the other bed, yet the last thing he remembered as he flew was the orange and red smear of lights out the hotel window, everyone going somewhere, going away.

The day's light began to burnish and faintly glow in the barn below, the nickers and stamps of horses awaiting their morning feed, but Justin burrowed into the straw, twisted himself into another memory, another dream.

Bremerton, early afternoon, a low, gray quilt of cloud, the day's mizzling rain giving way, everything damp, dripping, and his mom had friends over — people he didn't know, men with mustaches and big, dark glasses, women wearing jeans and heels — so he had to go play in the street. That was what she said: *Go play in the street.*

Two houses ago that had been something both his mother and his father would say when they came home from work tired and he asked too many questions, when they were grilling on the weekend, letting loose, and he was underfoot. But back then, after they said it, they'd laugh and tousle his hair, and so he was to understand it was a joke, that they would never, ever want him to truly do such a thing.

Yet Justin was nine now, almost ten, and across the last months, his father had faded into abstraction. Like the new Air Jordans he wished for, or eggs for breakfast, or staying in the same school the whole school year, his father existed as an idea, a thing technically possible but wildly unlikely, much the same as an intricate and alluring toy you'd see advertised on Saturday-morning cartoons and dream of but know you could never have, and thus such a thing would be part of your life, in a way, just not as a physical presence, not as something that could be measured, reckoned, loved, manipulated, raged against, forgotten.

The one time Justin asked why his father didn't come home anymore, his mother pulled a pack of Winstons from the freezer and lit one on the stove coil.

— J., honey, she said, letting loose a lungful of smoke. I'm trying here. I'm fucking trying.

He stood there waiting for more. There had to be more.

She wiped at her eyes and parked her cigarette in an ashtray, plunged her hands into the sink water.

— Why don't you go play in the street?

Mostly, Justin pedaled his bike around and around the loop of trailers, pretending he was piloting an X-wing or the *Millennium Falcon*. He knew how to take the corners at speed and which ruts and potholes were good for wheelies and which ones would wreck your spokes. He'd watched the three older boys who haunted the trailer park do just that: bend spokes, shred gears, tangle chains. Somehow, those boys always had new bikes to destroy. They had knives, sacks of candy, and matches, sometimes fireworks or brass knuckles or ball-peen hammers. Justin followed them at a distance and studied the leaning way they walked, the wings of their bony elbows, the hard spatter of their laughs, how they twisted their shoulders to spit. As they moved on, Justin would crouch down by whatever wreckage they'd left. Lift the greasy, busted bicycle gears or pick hacked bits of plastic action figure from the scars in a stump.

This day, told to go play in the street, he followed the older boys to the far end of the loop, behind the last trailer, where the wet, green land went wild again and dropped steeply into a ravine. Justin dragged his bike off into a tangle of ferns and ivy and squatted down, waited. Many times, he'd stood at the mossy lip of the ravine after a weeks-long rain and heard the sucking roar and rush of whatever was down there, but he hadn't yet dared to descend himself.

A sputtering rain came and went. The voices of the older boys drifted up out of the green expanse in snatches. Shouts and laughs. Curses, exclamations. Then a series of small explosions Justin guessed were firecrackers. And up the slick trail the boys came, scrambling and pushing and grabbing at one another, something glinting on their hands, arms, and faces. They sauntered down the street, their shouts and laughter fading.

Justin lifted himself from the damp cover of sword ferns and started down the trail on his backside, grabbing at the bushes and digging his feet into the soft earth. Thin, whiplike branches slapped at him, and the steep slope gave way to a close, overgrown creek bottom. The creek itself was maybe four or five feet wide and clattered with spring rain. Its course bent around boulders and beneath the convoluted roots and straight-rising trunks of cedars and firs, and Justin felt his heart lift and expand. These green, muddy banks would be his one place. His world.

But first he had to clean up the mess. He followed the trail of winking scales and bright meat to a shallows downstream where the older boys had stuck firecrackers in the mouths and anuses of spent salmon and blown them open, tearing gaping holes in their faces and bellies, scattering loose guts and scorched flesh. Before he disappeared, Justin's father used to take him every autumn to Kellogg Island; there he'd lift Justin onto his shoulders, and together they'd watch for the bright backs of salmon as they swam up the Duwamish. If the pinks were running, the river mouth fairly boiled with fish, and Justin and his father pointed and called out — *There, there, right there!*

Now here were the insides of these astonishing creatures, red and dull, and Justin was sad and sick, even angry that boys or anyone would ever think to do such a thing to something so beautiful and blameless. He gathered the slippery bits and pieces and set them loose in the swiftest current. As they corked and turned out of sight, Justin wondered where this little creek ran, which river it entered, and where that river entered the sound. He squatted down to scrub the blood and silver scales from his hands. The creek water was so cold it ached his bones.

# 9

ON THE LAST DAY of school, Lianne's parents would meet the children at the house in Delphia. They would even leave the ranch untended for a day to mark the occasion.

They'd all sit at the table in the front room, and each of the kids, as well as Rene, who had an awful sweet tooth, would get a fresh-baked oatmeal cookie and a tall glass of milk. In turn, the children were to hand over their report cards, final papers, art projects, and things of that sort. Viv and Rene would adjust their eyeglasses and study each of the documents. Rene leaned back in his chair and every so often smoothed his hand over his unruly thatch of short, dust-colored hair. Viv sat up straight and pursed her lips. It was all Keith and Dennis could do to keep still, to resist giggling or kicking each other under the table. Lianne scowled at her brothers, and under her gaze, they straightened up. She could give a mean snakebite. Lianne liked that she was at the top of her class, liked especially how her father, who had only an eighth-grade education himself, was so proud of her. Viv, who hadn't said yes to Rene's proposal until she finished an associate's degree and worked six months as a financial secretary at a bank in Billings, expected Lianne to get top marks, but to Rene, Lianne's smarts—as he always called them—were a true delight.

Now he clicked his tongue and grinned.

—Well, Pockets, I don't know where you got your smarts, but I believe you got your good looks from me!

Lianne smiled and blushed, and Viv peered over the top of her glasses and nodded. It was 1968, and Lianne had just finished eighth grade. Straight As again. Next it was Keith's turn, then Dennis's, who struggled with reading but was trying. Last was little Franklin, who was always picking bouquets of clover and dandelions or drawing special pictures for people and was a favorite of all his teachers, though they fretted over the fact that he was so shy around the other boys.

When the end-of-school ceremony was over, the whole house shifted into motion.

Viv and Rene cleaned out the fridge and freezer and gathered boxes of books, newspapers, garden seeds, and other necessaries. The kids packed their own suitcases and a pillowcase each of books and toys. They all made sure they had their jackknives, and the boys each had a sling-shot. Lianne's .22 lived in the gun rack in the rear window of Old Blue, below her father's .243, but she had to use her own chore money to buy ammunition. A rifle was a tool, Rene had said, and if you wanted to toy about with it, you were on your own, so Lianne packed the paper boxes of bullets, which she'd bought the day before at the Lazy JC drugstore, in the corner of her suitcase between pairs of socks and white underclothes. And she was ready for the ride to the ranch, ready for the story.

The story of the ranch was the story of her father and of her mother, and so it was her story as well. It had the force of a river at melt, of a storm at its blackest, and though she'd heard it near on a hundred times, Lianne felt every telling ripple in her blood and bones.

Rene's people had tried for land everywhere they'd washed up. The slash pine country of Louisiana. Oklahoma, where they rode in the land run of 1895 and came up with 160 acres of scrub and salt flats. And finally Montana, where in 1908 Rene's grandparents settled on a homestead north of the Yellowstone, on Canyon Creek, the first good land the Bouchard family had ever called their own, a whole section of it, 640 acres, as part of the Enlarged Homestead Act. But his grandparents had their own passel of nearly grown children, and as often happens, the land was over the years whittled down and down.

By the time Rene came along, in the winter of 1923, his crib a boot box set on a woodstove, his grandparents had just enough acres left for a few head of sheep and a garden plot. Still, that stretch of sagebrush and bunchgrass up Canyon Creek was the only home Rene truly knew, shipped off as he was to his grandparents' house whenever his parents fell on hard times, which they did more and more as the years went on. Rene's father, Floyd, the youngest of the Bouchard boys, was lean and sandy-haired, a fast-talker, a man perpetually on the edge of a wild idea or a fistfight. Floyd was tough on his wife, a slip of a woman who nevertheless seemed to be the only person in the world who could keep Floyd close, and tougher on his kids. He hated any kind of work, gambled away every bit of land he'd inherited, and ended up running Canadian rum down through the Missouri Breaks. As revenue agents ransacked his father's Model T, Rene sat on the hollow seat filled with liquor bottles packed in straw. He had an old harmonica in his shirt pocket and he took it out and blew into it gently as his father, flat cap scrunched in his hands, protested on the side of the road.

Not so many years later, at the height of the drought and the dust, when thousands upon thousands of homesteaders turned refugees streamed west once again, eastern Montana one more in a long line of busts, Rene figured eighth grade was good enough for him and took off to go cowboy up on the Comanche Flats for a big cattleman named Pete Schuster. He was three years into the job when one Sunday, his father showed up, working that same flat cap in his hands and claiming they were hard up and Rene's littlest brother, Junior, needed this and that and the other thing.

Rene always shook his head at this point in the story. He'd caution Lianne, Keith, and Dennis, even Franklin, he'd say, *You watch what you do when you're young and strong and dumb. Just because you can doesn't mean you should.*

The hard, young cowboy Rene stood there with his arms crossed, his head tilted against the prairie sun. He knew his father's story was all some slapdash mix of half-truths and outright bullshit, and he knew, too, that it was Floyd's fault. Whatever it was, it was Floyd's fault. Rene spit at his father's feet. When Floyd swung, Rene ducked and stepped smartly to the side, brought his fist up into his father's gut once, twice, and then hit him across the jaw. Floyd fell to the ground, and Rene put a boot to his chest, told him, as the other cowboys spilled out of the bunkhouse, that they were good and done, that he better not ever come around here again begging like the dog he was.

Lianne studied the shift of her father's stubbled jaw, noted the cadence of the telling as he came to this pivotal moment in the story—those one, two, three punches—and marked the lift in his voice as he went on, as he told about his years cowboying for Schuster, about trying to sign up but being turned down for World War II, about meeting Vivian Ahern at a dance one Saturday night in Acton, about their years of courtship and Viv encouraging him to study for the grain-elevator operator's license and him passing the test, about the string of elevators he ran for the next years, from Moccasin to Dutton to Conrad, each elevator a little bit bigger, the pay better—and the whole time, he was saving for a ranch of his own. Even when he was a scrawny cowboy sitting on another man's horse in a borrowed saddle.

Rene looked right at Lianne and said that all those years ago he'd promised himself he was going to do things right, said he knew just about exactly how—he'd do the opposite of what his own father had done. And in 1952, Rene and Viv put a down payment on three sections along Willow Creek, a spread thirty miles north of the little railroad town of Delphia. They'd added to it over the years, some land bought outright, some leased from the BLM, until eventually the ranch spanned ten sections, ten square miles, better than six thousand acres. And that's where they were headed for the summer—to their ranch, the Bouchard Ranch.

Lianne sat in the middle of the bench seat, right beside her father, and listened to his every word. Keith and Dennis rode in the truck bed, their backs up against the cab, bits of dust and straw wheeling in the roadwind. Viv leaned into the passenger-side door with Franklin on her lap. She was silent most of the time, though now and again interrupted Rene to add a detail or reel him back when the story got away from him, which, when she was a girl, Lianne always resented—her mother not letting the story of the Bouchard Ranch billow, grow, and fill the whole known world.

# APRIL 1994

# 10

LIANNE ROSE IN THE early dark and pulled on sweatpants and a T-shirt. Downstairs, she plugged in the percolator. While it gurgled and chugged, she curled up in the front room and opened one of the books of poetry she'd brought with her, Philip Levine's *What Work Is*. As always, Lianne had brought too many books and hadn't yet had a chance to read any of them.

Under the yellow shawl of lamplight and against the worn nap of the easy chair, she got caught not quite halfway down the page:

> *You love your brother,*
> *now suddenly you can hardly stand*
> *the love flooding you for your brother,*
> *who's not beside you*

The percolator coughed. Dawn shone weakly at the windows. Her parents had never bothered with the extravagance of a camera, but in high school, graduating from Ethel Kanta's easel and watercolors, Franklin had saved up and bought a Kodak, which he carried night and day, and every one of the framed pictures Lianne could see now — on the end tables, atop the bureau, hung here and there on the walls — was Franklin's:

Lianne, back from college, a flower in her hair, curling up on this very chair, her bare feet tucked under her just so.

Keith — so young! — holding a leather basketball at his chest with both hands, as if without warning he might send a hard pass your way.

Rene leaning against the porch rail in his brown suit, red handkerchief knotted at his throat, the sky behind a breakaway blue.

And her mother, Viv, in chiaroscuro black and white, bending over her sewing machine, tailor's tape draped around her neck.

Viv had never been a big woman, but she was anyway formidable, her words sure and sharp, her thick waves of Irish hair always done up with silver combs. In those last hours, though, she could barely speak. Wisps of gray haloed the bony angles of her face. As if reading instructions from beyond, Lianne watched Rene with her. It hadn't always been easy between them, forty-odd years never could be, but they had been in love, and Rene stayed at his dying wife's side despite everything that told him this wasn't work for a man, that he shouldn't see her this way, that for his own dignity and hers, he should leave.

Love, thank God, was stronger than all that.

With his thick, gnarled hands, hands that had birthed lambs and nestled the rifle barrel in the lame horse's ear, Rene gently tilted his wife by shoulder and hip so she could be cleaned. He knelt on his cracking knees as if in supplication and slipped ice chips between her cracked lips. He sat as near to her as he could.

But love, too, has its limits.

Lianne and Rene were tired, the both of them dog-tired, and the only two left. They had begun to imagine this hard vigil might go on forever — when suddenly Viv's breathing deepened and her eyes focused, cleared, and she looked right at her husband, who knelt beside her with his hands on her forehead, and asked, as if she were asking about the weather or if he wouldn't mind putting on some coffee, if he'd go get Franklin for her, that she'd like to talk to him. Did he know where Franklin had gone off to?

Would Rene go get her baby for her? Please?

Lianne pursed her lips and lifted a finger as if to shush her own dying, delirious mother, but no sound came. The only sound was Rene rising, his weathered joints grinding as he pulled himself up. He squared his shoulders, took one last look, and walked away.

Lianne stayed by her mother's side. She talked and talked, though now she couldn't remember a single word she'd said. That last hour, Viv said nothing. She sank ever into herself. Her breath went ragged, it rattled in the back of her throat, and she died.

Now, with the hem of her T-shirt, Lianne dusted Franklin's photographs. With the rest of the morning, she set herself to finishing the job.

Upstairs, she stripped the beds and swept cobwebs from the corners of the ceilings. She wiped down walls and dusted sills and shelves, vacuumed everything she could vacuum. She got a load of laundry going, then scrubbed the floors and stairs with what was left of a bottle of orange oil. Finally, she scoured the bathtub and toilet with Comet, the smell watering her eyes.

Lianne stood in the front room, sweat sticking flyaway hairs to her temples, and took stock. Everything was as clean as it could be—and it was all so old and worn, it didn't look that much different. Viv and Rene had kept the house up—there was no damage or rot—but they simply didn't believe in new things. The carpet in the front room, a hard gray-brown, was older than Lianne was, and most of the furniture was close. Rinsing the fluted schoolhouse-style fixture that hung just inside the front door, she noticed *1944* stamped on the inside of the glass, likely the very year electricity first came to this far part of Montana. The blue-white light of morning streamed through the south-facing windows, and even over the orange oil and bleach, Lianne could smell the dry waft of prairie dust.

She took the broom out and swept the porch and curving walk. Next door, the screen to the old Kanta house was propped open with a man's work boot. A woman leaned into the open doorway and smoked. Lianne waved. The woman nodded—long black hair, a round face—and reached down for the boot.

The day came on blue and wide, the warmth of it tingling her skin. Lianne turned and turned again, taking in the horizon at its every distance.

You'd never be able to take a picture of this. You'd never be able to get it all.

Just as Lianne stepped inside, a big red pickup pulled up next door. The driver left the engine idling and sauntered down the neighbor's cracked walk. He was even bigger than she remembered. Heavier, surely, but the pure dimensions of his steak-thick hands and face — the physical facts of Orly Pinkerton—didn't quite seem reasonable to Lianne anymore. Orly rapped on the screen, waited.

To get a better look, Lianne crossed to the west-facing window in the front room. The woman she'd just seen smoking had stepped out of the house and folded her arms over her chest, that curtain of black hair falling across her face. Orly moved his hands lazily as he talked. Now took leaned forward. The woman stood in the doorway on the raised porch, but Orly still towered over her. This was about money, Lianne thought. Rent, maybe? It made sense. But it still felt — what was the word? —*discomfiting*: Orly offering to buy her father's ranch, Orly owning the place next door here in town as well. When Lianne was a girl, Orly Pinkerton had been just another big talker, his belt buckle wide and shining, even if his cattle ran to bone-skinny, even if his first wife ran off with the shaggy-haired, bell-bottom-wearing music teacher at the high school. But in the late '70s, as the oil crisis ramped up, wildcatters fanned out across the country. A few ranchers got lucky, but in '78 Orly got the luckiest of all. Lianne remembered because she'd just finished her master's thesis and was back that spring for the last funeral.

Orly put a boot up onto the lip of the porch, and the woman's boyfriend or husband was suddenly there in the doorway, shirtless, his hair slicked back from a shower. The man was the one talking now, as if whatever the woman had said before wasn't good enough. Orly poked a thick finger into a thicker palm. The man started to say something but swallowed. Nodded. Orly grinned and touched the brim of his cowboy hat, started back toward his pickup.

Not really deciding, just doing, Lianne hurried to the kitchen. She poured two mugs of coffee, pushed her way out the back door, and came around between the houses. The pickup door groaned closed; the frame took Orly's weight. For some reason Lianne wanted him to see her, to know she was here. Still, she kept her eyes on the neighbor woman. The man must have gone back in.

—Coffee? Lianne asked, raising her voice above the rumble of the diesel engine.

The woman looked at Lianne, then over her shoulder at Orly. She took one of the mugs.

Orly's truck caught a gear and rolled down the gravel road.

—I hope it's okay black, Lianne said, her voice dropping as the sound of the engine faded. I'm Lianne. Rene and Viv's daughter.

The woman sipped and tucked a length of hair behind her ear. She was maybe Crow or Cheyenne. If you followed the old roads, the Crow Reservation was just over the Bulls and up the Big Horn, maybe two hours at most. The Cheyenne Reservation wasn't that much farther. Still, Delphia was a world away.

The woman introduced herself as Mariah White Bear.

—Sorry about your mom, she said. She was a good lady. Kind to us. Mariah gestured at the yard, the overgrowth of Viv's gardens. I imagine you'll be getting your beds ready soon.

—My mother always liked flowers, Lianne said.

—I used to garden with my grandmother. I'd like to put in some beds myself, but Pinkerton said we had to keep it all in a lawn.

—So Orly owns this place?

—Owns half the town. Used to not be so bad, but then one of my boys got into some trouble and now it's every little thing. Made Dan sell his old car the other month. An eyesore, he said. Now he says we're not keeping the place up. Wants Dan to take this tree down and do about a dozen other things. Dan barely gets enough time off to sleep.

Lianne couldn't help it; her first thought was, What kind of trouble? — as if a boy's trouble excused a man's bullying—and her second was that Orly was right about the tree.

Mariah must have read her hesitancy. Before Lianne could respond, Mariah thanked her for the coffee, said she'd wash and return the mug. Then she disappeared inside.

Lianne knew every room and shadowed corner of Mariah's house— Orly's house—had spent hundreds of afternoons there as a girl helping her brothers with their homework, slicing Ethel's fresh-baked bread for a snack and slathering it with butter.

She wandered back to her own porch—or, rather, her parents'—the garden beds weed-choked, the walk swept clean. Lianne sipped at her coffee and thought again about Mariah's boy and trouble, about her own boys and distance, about the distant, troubled boy her brother Franklin had been in the rooms of both these houses.

# 11

In the half-dark, Rene gasped awake from flood dreams—water spilling over creek beds, topping cutbanks, running fast and impossibly black.

He'd had these dreams of water all his life, though the details had shifted with the years. When he was a boy, slick, finned monsters had cut the dark, churning waters, but soon enough it wasn't what plied the flood but the flood itself. As a young father, he'd dreamed of lead-colored clouds massing on the western horizon, great stacks of them—and as the first fat drops stung the cracked earth, the stink of petrichor, he'd scramble about, trying to gather his children, one, two, three, and four, in his arms, though invariably he'd slip in the gravel, catch a boot in a tangle of cattails and stumble, lose a child, turn back for the lost one and so lose his grip on the others. In the last year, across Viv's diagnosis and decline, the dream waters had receded, and Rene found himself the tallest thing in a hundred prairie miles, scanning the broken circle of the horizon, sure at any moment clouds would billow into view, though they never did. He stood heartsick at what he knew was coming but couldn't for the life of him see.

Last night, a little whiskey behind his eyes, he'd fallen asleep in the old feather bed, and the waters had risen and churned as they hadn't in years. Rene had kicked and dived, he'd clung to the great, jostling limb of a cottonwood, he'd swum desperately for the shore—and woke before he ever touched it.

Now, the world blue-dark and still, Rene put the percolator on for coffee and browned a heel of bread in the cast-iron. He slicked it with margarine and ate standing at the window.

Orly's late-night visit had loosed something in him. He hadn't planned to, but he thought now he'd ride out and check to see that Bassett was doing right by the sheep, or right enough. Rene was one of the last ranchers doing things the old ways. Save for when the sheep were penned up in the shed and the corrals for lambing, he grew them on grass. He kept a herder with them and a dog, against overgrazing as much as coyote kills. It was the land that mattered, what fed and held and allowed them all. Even if Orly Pinkerton could afford to buy new pickups and shiny center-pivot sprinklers and closed-cab air-conditioned combines and the whole rest of the goddamn valley, Rene didn't want any part of it. He didn't imagine for a moment it would last. Corn and soybeans out here? These big machines throwing up dust in this dry country?

Rene Bouchard had all his life tried to do right by the land. And even if his children could sell the place out from under him now—signing on a dotted line, they could undo everything he'd ever worked for—he'd make sure things were right with the ranch once more. Then he'd do what he'd come here to do.

He sipped coffee and chewed his toast. From down near the creek, a red-winged blackbird let loose two metallic notes. The watery night ached away. The day, as it does, trembling, rising.

Meadowlarks called in the crystalline air, and Rene set out, the sky clear but for a few clouds feathering the horizon. He reined Nine Spot through the creek shallows and up the hill. The gate was hanging open. How many times had he told hired men, and before that his own children, to close the goddamn gate? Lianne had always done it, the only one who had. Rene stepped the horse around the wire tangle and rode on. He could tell by the graze and sign, the grass cropped but greening, the hard, dry pellets of sheep shit, that Bassett had had the herd in this pasture ten or so days ago. He went ahead and checked each of the three wells, which were positioned along the fence lines in four parallel pastures, each a quarter of a section. He found the pumps greased and the metal gas cans full. The stock tanks, too, had been cleaned, save for the intricate patterns of salt-white alkali where the last of the hard water had evaporated.

Well, at least Bassett had taken care of that.

The first warm winds of the day leaned against the bunchgrass and sage, blew in gusts down the hills, and whistled through the coulees. The long shadows slid back into themselves. Rene lifted his straw cowboy hat to feel the breeze. He clicked his tongue, and at a clip he and Nine Spot set off back the way they'd come, stopping to close every gate behind them.

The sun quartered the sky as Rene rode into the artesian well pasture, into Bassett's camp. The sheep wagon was parked in a shelter of cottonwoods, Bassett's yellow GMC nosed in nearby. A length of nylon rope ran from the wagon to the silver side mirror of the pickup, and a few of Bassett's shirts and socks and handkerchiefs fluttered in the breeze. The sheep had grazed north this morning, and on a rise fifty yards off, watching the sheep, sat Finn O'Malley—tense, aware, always ready—Rene's border collie and heeler mix.

Rene swung off Nine Spot and winced as his bad leg took his weight.

—Bassett, he called out. You dead or alive?

A general rustling shook the round-roofed wagon, which sat on four wood-spoked wheels, the iron tongue dropped down to the ground for stability. Both the top and bottom half of the Dutch door creaked open, and Bassett crawled out and down the short ladder wearing only boots and a pair of long johns, pale, coffee-colored stains swirling the ribbed cloth, which hung loose at the man's thighs and seat and belly.

—Well, you look alive. Mostly.

Bassett blinked and sniffed, lifted the flat of his hand to his rheumy eyes for the morning light. The man had somehow grown even smaller, his chicken legs and thin chest, shoulders sloping down. The sun-dark skin of his face hung slack, his lips collapsing for the vast gaps where he'd lost teeth. Rene had known Thad Bassett going on fifty years now. He'd been a new hand, a scrawny runaway, in the last years Rene had cowboyed out on the Comanche Flats. Rene looked Bassett up and down and wondered again at what in the intervening years had turned them down these paths, that Bassett was yet a hand, that he was a rancher. There were little things—gates left open, days lost to hangovers—and Rene had indeed gotten hot and fired him a time or two, but on the whole, Bassett had been a good herder and had worked seasonally for Rene for many years now. Maybe it was luck, or maybe—and Rene hadn't considered this before—maybe it was a choice. Maybe Bassett never wanted what Rene had, what had come now to grief for him.

—Renny, Bassett croaked. Didn't believe I'd be seeing you yet. How's Viv?

—She passed a week ago.

—Hell, Bassett said. Renny, I'm sorry. She was a good woman. Treated everyone kind. You don't always find that. Leastways, I don't.

It was as long a string of speech as he'd heard from Bassett in some time, and he knew the man meant it. Rene dipped his chin and shifted his hat on his head.

—How're the sheep?

Bassett swiveled to the north and smacked his lips.

—That dog of yours does most of the sunrise work. I been sleeping a good part of the day so as I can sit up nights for coyotes. Only one kill so far, an older ewe. She was dry this spring.

Rene nodded. That was better than he'd hoped, to have lost only one and without a lamb at that.

—How about lambing? Any showing yet?

—There's some getting close.

—How close?

—Next couple of days, I'd guess.

Rene swung his hat from his head and slapped it hard against his thigh.

Like that, the heat rose up in him, Bassett's failure all he could see. You had to jug lambs up when they were born to keep the mothers nearby and the lambs fed and safe. Otherwise, you'd have them dying of this and that and everything else. Too often, in Rene's decades of experience, sheep seemed flat-out determined to find a way to die. With lambs coming in a matter of days, the sheep ought to be back in the corrals, and Bassett should have readied the shed.

— They start dropping lambs out here, we'll have a hell of a mess on our hands.

— I'd been thinking, Bassett said and rubbed at his watery eye, I'd trail them back tomorrow. Like I said, that dog pretty much does it on his own.

— Not unless you tell him. Rene bit the words off, then raised his voice and made a counterclockwise circling motion with his right arm.

— Away to me, O'Malley! Away to me!

The dog cocked his ears and circled to the right of the herd. The sheep lifted their heads and tensed, began to bunch.

— Wide around! Rene called. Wide around!

O'Malley came around the other way, and the herd became a trembling mass of bleats, wool, and kicked dust.

— Take 'em home, O'Malley! Home!

The dog had his own head now, running back and forth behind the herd, occasionally nipping at a hind leg, though easy, careful not to push the pregnant ewes — some nearly as wide as they were long — too hard.

Rene turned his attention again to Bassett, who was still working at his eye with the heel of his hand. This was going to gum up his plans. It'd take better than two weeks to lamb the whole herd out, and at the very least, Lianne would be out to see him before she drove back to Spokane. But Rene Bouchard simply couldn't do it. No, not even here at the end could he let Bassett stay on after not doing the work he ought to have done. Rene kicked at the scalloped dirt. Well, hell. He'd lamb the herd out one last time, then take care of his own business.

Rain, sun, wind, bad ranch hands — he'd make it work. As he had all his life.

— I'll ask you to pull the sheep wagon back to the camphouse with your rig. I can write you a check for the second half of your pay there, before you go on your way.

Rene put a hand to Nine Spot's neck and tightened his grip on the reins.

— It'll be a job to lamb out two hundred head, Bassett said, finally pulling his hand away.

A quick star of pain winked in Rene's hip as he swung into the saddle.

— It will indeed be a job, Rene said, reining the horse around, the pain yet bright in the bone. And I believe I'll do it just the way I like it done.

They'd thought to name him something easy early on — Bill or Sam — but one bright day Viv, pregnant as could be with Lianne, had leaned down and lifted the first little pup sheepdog they'd ever owned and pronounced him a Frenchman. He was such a handsome fellow, she explained, what with that little white bib and those white socks, and romantic, lots of licks and cuddles, but look here, he was curled up and brooding in the corner on a sunny day.

— He's given to lonesomeness and ennui, Rene, just like you. How about Charles Laurent?

Viv had named all their dogs after that, and each had been either French or Irish. For Rene, dogs were mostly a necessity of the work of sheep ranching. But he'd gamely pick up the new pup and hold him to his face, the short-furred muzzle, those sharp, tiny milk teeth.

— Yes, he'd say. You're right, Viv. He's Irish to the bone.

Now Finn O'Malley bellied himself down in the dirt and grass just outside the corral gate, ears cocked and head up, as if he'd never witnessed anything more exciting than a pen full of bleating sheep. Rene hobbled over and latched the gate and turned and stood a moment in the hoof-churned dust and shit. Goddamn that Bassett. Rene spit. He would never, not ever in his life, understand a man not doing what he ought to do. He walked stiff-legged over to the stock tank, the sheep already massing around the bright empty tin, and lifted the red handle of the spigot. The pipe coughed. Water unthreaded and fell. Rene watched the sheep give their muzzles to the pooling waters and realized he was thirsty himself, terrible thirsty. He cupped his hands beneath the cold flow and rinsed his face. Cupped his hands and drank.

With wooden panels he penned up the hay and straw and built paneled fences around the oat and corn and bean barrels as well. He spread straw around the wider space of the shed and pitchforked clean the lambing jugs along the southwest wall, then strawed the bottoms and made sure there was a metal water bucket in each. He penned off the area near the jugs, around the utility sink, where he kept his lambing records on a high wooden table and his sheep-birthing supplies in a metal tub beneath. The shed ready, he shut off the stock tank and hooked up a float. Then the real work began. He backed Old Blue up to the haystack on the far side of the corrals, loaded three dozen heavy alfalfa bales, drove into the main corral, the sheep milling about but O'Malley keeping them from bolting into the pasture, and restacked the hay in the feeder at the center. He had enough in him for another load but figured he shouldn't risk any more, his legs and arms light, trembly, his breath coming hard. There were some things he could yet do without much trouble, but loading hay was young man's work. He knew it, and hated it, and though he didn't want to think on it just now, he'd likely have to refill the feeder every few days or so. He shifted his weight, and the pain jostling his leg and hip swirled and rearranged but didn't dissipate.

Lord, the work itself might finish him off.

Rene Bouchard swallowed at the grit in his throat and limped toward the dust-streaked light at the shed mouth. He'd nap an hour, then have O'Malley help him turn the sheep into the shed for the night.

# 12

LIANNE STEPPED UP ONTO the sidewalk and into the small foyer of the aluminum-sided Quonset hut, which had been thrown together after the two-story French-style building that housed the old Depot Café burned to the ground. A coatrack ran along the back wall, a low bench to the right, six or seven pairs of overshoes and especially muddy boots tucked up under it. The door on the left side led to the Snakepit Bar, even now serving red beers and shots of Beam. Lianne pushed open the other door, the one to the right of the coatrack.

Fluorescent light polished the crosshatched linoleum. A drink cooler hummed along the wall. Six white plastic tables and a smattering of folding chairs occupied most of the dining space — a circle of farmers coffeeing up at one of the tables, a man and a woman bending to burgers at another — and the till sat up front on a low counter scattered with old newspapers and magazines, racks of candy and cigarettes behind it. The kitchen, which led into the bar, opened to the left of the till. Lianne could just see eggs, bacon, and hashbrowns popping on the grill, and despite the aesthetic deficiency of the place, eggs and hashbrowns sounded just about right. Comfort food. Good for grief.

She took a seat near the window, for the light, and lifted the laminated menu from where it was tucked between a napkin holder and a jar of powdered coffee creamer.

—It's all about the same as you'd remember it, I'd guess. Nothing new.

One of the farmers scooted out of the circle and leaned toward her in his chair. Lianne was about to nod a thanks, then strategically position her own chair so that she didn't have to continue the conversation—when she recognized that unruly dark hair, those deep-set eyes.

—Ves?

—Lianne.

She'd seen him, of course, at the funeral. But he'd been dressed in dark jeans and a jacket then. And there'd been no reception—Rene had said he couldn't stomach it—so besides her own family and a couple of friends from Spokane who'd called, she hadn't really talked with anybody all these months she'd been home.

Ves Munroe pulled his ball cap from his head.

—I'm awful sorry about Viv. She meant a lot to folks around here. We'll sure miss her.

Lianne knew this was coming and both hated and wanted to hear it. She stilled her tremors and tried to turn the conversation. Ves beat her to it.

—I hear you're a college professor. I always figured you'd be the one for something like that. I believe you'd read about every book in the library by the time you graduated.

Though she knew the distinctions likely didn't matter, Lianne always felt dishonest when Rene or Viv or anyone here called her that. She only had an MA and was just a lecturer at a community college. Years ago, she'd planned on a PhD, had finished her master's thesis and was applying to doctoral programs—but then, in the spring of '78, she'd had to leave all that behind.

—I don't know about every book in the library, but I enjoy teaching. And it looks like I might be moving to a new university in the fall, she added, feeling herself shine to the praise. A bit of a promotion.

Ves widened his eyes and nodded. Lianne studied the menu.

—How're the hashbrowns?

—About like you'd expect.

—That bad?

Ves laughed and smoothed his ball cap back onto his head, that shaggy hair of his poking out in thick tufts.

—My girls swear by the curly fries.

—Girls?

—Daughters. Three of them, if you can believe it. Don't know what I did to deserve it, but that's the way it is.

Lianne assured him it was just what he deserved, and they both laughed. Ves's wife, Connie, one of the Turley girls—Lianne remembered her in her cheerleading uniform, alabaster legs and arms, fiery red hair framing her face—had taken a job at an insurance agency in Billings and so was gone most of the week, which meant Ves was Mr. Mom.

—It's an education, Ves went on. Right now my youngest, Amy, is all broken up over that singer she likes. Could barely get her out of bed this morning.

The waitress came by—unsmiling, smelling of menthols—and Lianne ordered eggs and toast with a side of curly fries. She took a sip of water.

—Which singer? What happened?

—Oh, you know, that one who screams all the time and doesn't make much sense. Cobain. I guess they found him—and here Ves paused and studied the knot of his hands in his lap—well, they found him dead the other day. Suicide.

Lianne swallowed. She'd heard the songs on the radio, could picture the face, the mess of blond hair.

—He was young, wasn't he?

—He was.

—That's sad.

—It is. And I told my Amy that too. Even if his music isn't quite my cup of tea. Ves paused, continued. Well, Lianne, it is awful good to talk to you. But I should get back to the lies these fellows are telling. I'll let you alone.

He turned to scoot his chair away, but Lianne reached out and touched his shoulder.

—Ves, I wondered if I might ask for a little help. With Rene. He's run off to Willow Creek.

—The fellows were just talking about that. Ves chuckled. Rene had Thad Bassett out there herding for him, but as we speak Bassett is bellied up at the bar in the next room.

Lianne's vision swam a moment, and something like fear rained down through her. Her father was truly alone out there. He had, in fact, engineered an even deeper loneliness. She planted a palm on the roughened plastic of the tabletop.

—You all right?

It took her a moment to realize Ves had leaned that much closer, placed his hand on her knee. It was the kind of thing he'd have done when they were dating, when they used to come down to the Depot Café for malts and Lianne would complain about her dad and Keith fighting again or her mother expecting too much of her.

Ves sat back and made a show of lifting his ball cap, running a hand through his hair.

—Sorry, Lianne. I wasn't…well, anyway.

She could tell he was embarrassed. So many men got angry when they got embarrassed. What kind of a man was he?

Ves swallowed and went on.

—I don't know if I'll be much help with Rene, but I'm happy to try. I'm hauling a load of culled heifers to Billings this afternoon, but about any other time works. I got the same number I had in high school. I imagine you remember.

Lianne studied his windburned face, those deeply lined eyes. Ves was better-looking as a man than he had been as a boy. But he'd been such fun back then, always some scheme sure to land him in heaps of trouble—one night he managed, using a come-along, tow chains, and the ramp from a big stock trailer, to haul the principal's car up on top of the school building. He was a senior when they dated, and she'd been a sophomore. So he was, what, forty-two, forty-three? Still, even for daughters and sons and years and whole worlds between them, it was true, she knew his number, could likely close her eyes and dial the old rotary phone by muscle memory.

—Say, Ves broke in, if you're around, you ought to come over next Sunday. We're branding. Maybe we could haul Rene back in time to give us a roping lesson?

The waitress slid a white plate of eggs and toast and a red-checked paper basket of curly fries in front of Lianne, the napkin-wrapped silverware clattering to the tabletop.

Lianne, lost in the years, found herself flustered. Ves grinned.

—I don't imagine those fries will hold up too long. You best eat. Give me a call if you like.

# 13

It was the same here as anywhere. You looked for a patch of sidewalk, courtyard, or park that had plenty of foot traffic but room enough, too, for passersby to stand and listen a moment and not obstruct the flow. You didn't want to put anyone out.

In a plaza beside a bank, the red stones of the building flecked with quartz, Justin took out his earrings and stowed them in his pack. He finger-combed his hair and buttoned his flannel, made sure his jeans weren't sagging too much. Traffic, and a few birds crying overhead, the drift of disembodied voices—city sounds, their sheer, harsh, unsyncopated noise new to him again.

He clicked open his guitar case and lifted out his Alvarez. There were a few scratches here and there, and he could use new strings, but it was still about the prettiest thing he'd ever seen, the warm red honey of the wood, the bright, winking curves and lengths. He turned the open case around and pushed it out in front of him with his foot, wishing he had a few bills to seed it with. Justin sat with his back against the sun-warm stones and tuned the guitar for a time. Then readied himself. Then began.

Sometimes when he sang, he forgot where he was.

Maybe back in Seward Park, at the amphitheater. Maybe in honors band, his teacher's bald head gleaming at the front of the room. Maybe in the living room of the duplex in Rainier Beach, his mother smiling her closed-mouth smile at him from the kitchen. He was everywhere and nowhere, he was with the songs, the textures and mysteries of them, the worlds they built in the air, in the wide rooms of his heart.

Justin played hard and fast, then palmed the strings to silence and opened his eyes. Already, a few bills were in the case, some change. Maybe half a dozen listeners lingered, a few of them moving on before he could start the next song. A young guy in a convenience-store uniform stepped forward, riffled through his billfold, and dropped in a five.

—That was great, man. Really great. You sound a lot like him. Even sort of look like him. Hell of a tribute.

He didn't know any other way to sing. Not anymore. Not after years of trying to sound like Kurt Cobain. The fact that Justin looked a little like Cobain—lank blond hair and thin, elfin face—was pure coincidence, but it meant something to him. Back at Seward Park, among all the other sad, lost boys, it had made him think that maybe he, too, was destined for something more, something better. Anyway, he used to think that. Now even just busking in Seattle—far from Montana and every memory of his uncle—sounded like about the best a boy could hope for.

Justin wasn't sure what the guy had meant when he said *tribute*, but you didn't argue with a fiver. He nodded, murmured a thanks, and launched into "Lithium." He played and sang and gathered most of the money after every other song, leaving only a few quarters, a bill or two.

The music filled him and buoyed him and finally wrung him out.

His guts thinned with hunger. His fingers suddenly weakened against the strings.

Sunlight leaned and shattered on the square outlines of office buildings. A stale wind skirled soda cups and bits of paper. Justin gathered the last round of bills in the case, counted out the money in his front pocket, and, holy fuck, he'd made over fifty dollars. Twice as much as he'd figured and better than he'd ever done by a few bucks, even on the days he'd nabbed one of the good spots along the outer trail in Seward Park. He didn't know what to make of it. He didn't care. All he'd had to eat in the past day and a half were jerky sticks and peanuts. Justin hefted the guitar and his pack and made for the Subway down the block.

He liked the Italian herb-and-cheese bread best and always got the cold-cut combo, since it was the cheapest and you could still load it up with everything. Cheese. All the vegetables. Extra mayo, mustard, vinegar and oil. Parmesan. Salt and pepper. With the wadded bills hot in his pocket, Justin ordered two sandwiches and grabbed a cup for water. When the teenagers behind the sandwich line weren't looking, he filled it with orange soda, then took a back booth, near the restrooms.

The first sandwich more or less disappeared. Justin pinched up the last bits of lettuce and cheese, then smushed up the crumbs on the wrapper and ate those too. He unwrapped the second but forced himself to wait. He went into the bathroom, hauling his guitar with him just in case. He pissed, then stripped off his flannel and T-shirt and scrubbed his armpits and neck and arms and face, let the warm water run and run, then washed his hair as best he could. The white sink was soon streaked with grime. A ribbon of smooth brown paper towel poured out of the dispenser as he cranked its silver handle. Justin cranked and dripped and cranked and couldn't believe how ridiculous it was. Didn't they know someone like him would come along? He tore the long towel from the dispenser, dried himself, and stuffed the great wadded brown flower of towel into the tiny garbage.

Back in the booth, he put his earrings in again and drained his pop.

The teenagers were totally outgunned by a mom with three kids in tow. One of the kids, a boy maybe four or five, sobbed in that slow, deliberate way children do when it's clear they've lost the heart for it but haven't yet gotten what they want. Justin slipped over to the pop machine and refilled his cup without ice, orange soda slopping over the brim, and took a swig, another, and drained the cup, sugar sparking up and down his bloodstream. God, it tasted good. He refilled once more, Mello Yello this time, for the caffeine, and grabbed a newspaper from the scattered pile atop the trash bin. He figured he could soak up a good hour here, then, by the time he made his way back to the barn, the cowboys would be done with whatever it was they did all day, and he could sleep again in the warm straw above the horses.

Justin slid back into his booth, laid the newspaper out in front of him, and hefted half of the second sandwich. He liked to read whatever he could get his hands on — newspapers and magazines, books, the back of a cereal box — and was thinking, too, that he'd flip through for any news out of Nye, but there on the front page was a picture of Kurt Cobain. He couldn't make any sense of it. Why in the world would there be a picture of Kurt Cobain on the front page of a newspaper out of Bumfuck, Montana?

Then the headline slid into focus: KURT COBAIN FOUND DEAD.

Justin dropped his sandwich, shreds of lettuce and a half circle of tomato spilling. He read the headline again and again. He tried the tiny black ants of newsprint, but beneath his gaze they shifted and blurred, ran off in all directions. It didn't make any sense. No fucking sense at all.

The sobbing boy stood on the bench two booths up and stared at him, but the boy wasn't sobbing anymore. The sound was his own, Justin realized, a breathy, drawn howl bordering on a scream. Everyone was looking at him, looking right at him.

Justin grabbed his shit and was out the door, still cursing, crying; was better than two blocks away, the cold biting at his eyes, the evening coming on, when he realized he'd left his pop and stupid fucking cold-cut sandwich just sitting there.

Fuck, fuck, fuck!

# 14

THE MOON HUNG OVER the hills, gold and swollen, and the sheep were surely bedded down where they shouldn't be, out in the corral with no real protection at all from coyotes. Rene slapped his cowboy hat onto his head and was out the door, shuffling toward the barn. He'd napped too long, right into the evening. O'Malley's whining was what finally woke him.

As he crossed the dirt road, his whole body felt stove-up. Like he needed to undo each and every bone, grease the knobs, and then fasten them back together. Shadows fell darkly from the shed corners and corral boards. O'Malley at his heel, Rene came around the side of the corral, talking softly the whole time.

—Up, sheep, up, sheep. Let's go, there we go. Sheep, sheep, sheep.

He slapped his thigh and whistled softly and made the nonsense noises all sheepherders make to speak with their flocks, and in response the sheep rose and bunched and baaed lazily at one another, currents and whirls of dust rising in the moonlight. Rene clapped, the sound sharp in the dark, and raised his voice and sent O'Malley around, and the sheep spilled into the new, dry straw he'd laid down in the shed. An easy chore. But one you goddamn well ought to do before nightfall.

He put his shoulder to the shed door and heaved. The roller squealed on its rusted track and the heavy pine panel slowly closed. He dropped the metal hook into the eye. No coyotes could get in now. He could yet hear the sheep baaing and settling. As if soothing or blessing or asking forgiveness, he pressed the flat of his hand to the rough wood of the shed.

Back in the camphouse, Rene lit the kerosene lamps and tossed a match on the crumple of newspaper and lengths of kindling he'd laid in the cold stove, set the percolator on the burner above the fire. He rooted around in the fridge and came up with a carton of eggs and a bony hunk of roast beef, its grease hardened along the bottom of the Tupperware. He had flour and milk and baking powder enough. Rene lit one of the propane burners and dialed it low, after a moment slicked the cast-iron with beef grease and set to it. O'Malley had wolfed his kibble and laid himself out on the braided rug by the front door. As soon as he smelled grease, though, he whined low in his throat.

—Bassett ruined you, didn't he? Fed you pancakes every damn day? I told the man to make it a treat.

The batter popped on the skillet. Rene flipped the cakes and dropped the first two on a tin plate, let them cool before he set the plate on the floor for O'Malley.

—Don't ask for syrup. There ain't any.

Rene lifted the last of the cakes from the cast-iron, spooned more beef grease into the pan, swirled the melt of it. He cracked two eggs. Dashed salt and pepper onto them and thought maybe he'd been too hard on Bassett. Thad wasn't a man too proud to take correction, and he was right as rain that lambing out two hundred head of sheep was going to be a hell of a job, especially for a stove-up old man like him. He over-easied the eggs, the whites laced with fry, the grease popping, and thought that if he absolutely had to, he could get a neighbor to help. There wasn't anyone left on the Dejagher place, that boy of theirs had moved into town and spent most of his time on a barstool now. The Pinkertons were the next closest, a few miles farther south, but Rene didn't want Orly Pinkerton anywhere near the ranch. And if he'd gone that far, it wasn't much farther to Ves Munroe's place, or even the Kincheloe spread, there at the bend of the river, where one of old Elner Kincheloe's sons-in-law would surely help him out.

The percolator chugged. Rene poured himself a cup, then plated a couple of cakes and his runny eggs right on top of the cakes. He sat at the long table, where the kerosene lamp threw a wavering light. O'Malley came over slowly, as if Rene might not notice, but eventually nuzzled his black-and-white head right up against Rene's thigh.

— Turned you into a beggar, too, I see.

Rene sawed off a bite of cake sopped in yolk and tossed it over his shoulder. He doubted it even hit the ground.

Later, the cast-iron wiped out and the rest of the dishes scrubbed, the camphouse almost too warm for the fire burning down in the stove, he lowered himself into his easy chair. After his nap earlier in the day, Rene knew he wouldn't sleep for some time and so drifted into the loose hours like a johnboat unmoored in a flood, unfastened to anything on the earth.

On the AM radio they called it a crisis, a tragedy. But more and more Rene thought it a farce — the way this whole high, dry plains country, once dotted with small farms and ranches from end to end, was emptying out, the next generation leaving as fast as they could or, if they stayed, buying big machinery and running too many cows and still losing the family land. Ranch after ranch taken back by the banks and leased to oil or coal companies — scoria roads and chemical spills, salt lagoons and strip mines. Other spreads were bought up by rich men and subjected to their whims, whether constructing tracts of elaborate log houses in the Missouri Breaks or raising emus or what have you.

Better it went wild. That it was left alone. Once, years ago, walking fence on the high flats east of the camphouse, he'd spied a slick of white and knelt and pulled from the prairie earth a buffalo skull. He held it a moment and marveled at the immense, intricate architecture, though even as he did, the skull crumbled to dust in his hands.

Moonlight polished the windows. O'Malley twitched through a dream. Rene blinked and rubbed at his stubbled jaw. He thought to pour a whiskey but didn't want to make a habit of it. He'd be out here longer than he planned now and didn't relish having to resupply at the one sorry excuse for a saloon they had there in Delphia.

From the wire rack alongside the easy chair, he pulled an old *National Geographic* and studied the cover, an underwater shot, the ocean a deep blue-green, the camera angled toward the diffuse, refracted light far above. Just as he was about to fan the pages open, he noted the date, April 1978, and dropped the magazine back in the rack with a thunk.

Hell and goddamn.

Nearly sixteen years now. And the great black hole inside him yawned as wide as ever, as deep. An ocean of blackness. No light for miles.

Rene Bouchard forced himself now to take these loose hours and do something he hadn't done in years: to think of his boy, of Franklin.

Tall, though not as tall as Keith, and so much thinner than both Keith and Dennis had ever been. His black hair was thick and wavy, like Viv's, though both Lianne and Franklin had Rene's face, a long tapering rectangle split by a Roman nose. But some things were Franklin's and Franklin's alone — the way his eyes lit up when he was taking his pictures, how thoughtful and serious he was, how he was always willing, no matter what was asked.

Christ Jesus. He wouldn't sleep without the whiskey. Not now. Rene heaved himself up and crossed to the sink. Pulled the bottle from beneath.

# 15

SHADOW-BLIND, FURIOUS, JUSTIN RAN sidewalks, streets, alleys. He knocked over garbage cans and angled across busy roads, horns honking in his wake, the squeal of brakes.

He spied near a dark storefront a tumble of bricks. His muscles worked at his bones of their own accord — the arm reaching down, the hand closing round. He launched a brick through the glass. The shatter was terrific, the sound loud and sustained, the final shards tinkling, bell-like, as they fell to the ground. A gleaming heap of glass.

Why did this shitty world have it in for boys like him? Why did he always have to do such stupid shit? He sprinted he didn't know which way away.

In an alley, he squatted behind a dumpster and breathed and made sure his pack was buckled shut, the latches on his guitar case snapped. He worked a shirtsleeve over his leaky eyes, blew his nose in his hand and wiped it on his jeans.

He had to get out of Billings. Go now.

He didn't want to risk hitchhiking again. He thought of a train, like some old-time hobo, but ever since the apartment near Boeing Field, he'd hated the sounds of trains, so much clang and rattle. He leaned the bones of his back up against the dumpster and tightened the laces of his dirty Chucks. Unbidden, the calm of the morning came to him, that pickup easing into the lot out front of the auction yards, the low trailer it pulled. He'd seen straw sticking out the bottom slats. Maybe he could ride away from here as warm as he'd been last night, in a bed of straw.

Like that, he was up and running again.

The auction yard was still busy—the squawk of the PA, shouts and snatches of laughter, the grunts and slobber-screams of stock—and so on the other side of the highway, on his belly in the weeds and cheatgrass, Justin stilled his wild heart. He lay down and waited. After a time rolled onto his back. The rising moon stretching toward full, its light painting the underbellies of the clouds with sure, bright strokes.

The spark and growl of engines, and pickups began to stream from the lot. Justin eased up, crossed below the auction yards, and, as if he belonged, walked right into the unraveling crowd of ranchers and farmers and wives and children. He'd tucked in his shirt and twisted his hair up beneath the ball cap he'd taken from the fly fisherman. Here in the night, he didn't look all that different, and when you lived like he had these past years, you got good at pretending. Good at being who you needed, in the moment, to be.

He made his way down a column of parked trucks, touching the slick nose of each. Near the end, a big two-tone pickup, cream and a shade of brown, idled and chugged, but no one was in the cab. From the hitch hung a metal trailer, dark and empty.

Justin studied the crowd. No one was eyeing him, no one coming his way.

The latch took some figuring—he had to lift up against a spring, then pull the bar out, but then he was inside.

The sour reek of cowshit and piss flooded his mouth and nose. He could taste it with his teeth. He pinched his T-shirt up just below his eyes and tried not to step in any loose pats. At the very front, where the metal walls came together in a V, he squatted down and touched the straw, the walls, the floor. His hand came away dry. He nested himself in—his guitar behind him in the metal fold, his pack a pillow against the trailer wall—and waited, the yard lights and moonlight slatted by the trailer siding.

A man's voice rose above the others, a note of laughter, a call of good-bye, and the truck jostled. The yard lights, the lights of pickups, and even the moon swung crazily as they turned in a wide arc and rattled over the gravel lot. The trailer hinge squealed, and the bump at the highway's lip bounced Justin into the air—but then they were on the blacktop, the wind picking up, whistling, wheeling dust and straw.

It was only then that Justin realized he had no idea where they were going, only then that the land seemed to stretch and reach and spread in every direction—so much Montana.

He lurched up, fingers gripping the cold metal, and tried to see what he could through the narrow openings meant for animals. The interstate was right there, just south of the auction yards. He'd somehow thought they'd merge onto I-90 and travel west and ever west. Had never considered any other possibility.

Oh, shit. Oh, fuck. Oh, where were they going?

The truck slowed at a traffic light, and the dark hulk of the Rimrocks showed to the left, which meant they were traveling north. A splash of green, and the truck moved around the prow of those sheer sandstone cliffs and rose up out of the river valley, and soon they were rolling through the fringing of the city—grocery stores and used-car lots and fast-food joints, a wide Kmart—and the streetlights slid away, a two-lane highway rising into the hills, into the night, the burn of moon and stars.

Justin fell back in the straw. He'd felt this way before—gutted, blown open, like those firecrackered salmon down on the creek—and there was nothing to do about it. You just had to take it. You just had to ride into the dark distances, ride as far as they took you. Huddled against the roadwind, the juddering frame of the trailer, he curled up as best he could. After a time, he slept.

His dreams were shot through with shadow and intimation, with bands of light, the thin tall pines up Nye Creek, a wind shaking the night's rain from the cedars on the creek back of the trailer, Cobain's beautiful, shotgunned face, his uncle finally understanding what was about to happen, finally screaming.

Justin woke to his own screaming.

# 16

A KNOT OF MILLER moths fluttered and spun around the kitchen light, and Lianne shifted the phone to her other ear.

—How about a flying story? What do you say to that?

Frank's little mouth was so close to the receiver she could hear his quick, wet breaths, the movement of his lips.

—Okay, yes. But we have to fly together. Okay? Okay, Mom?

—Fly together. Gotcha. Once upon a time—

—No, wait! I need my blanket!

The clunk of the receiver sounded down the line, and she could hear Frank—always some combination of exuberance and terror—running here and there, yelling for his blanket, the one Grandma Viv made him, and Marty's faraway, measured voice asking him to quiet down, telling him just where the blanket was.

—Okay, Mom, Frank said, his breaths even lighter, quicker. I've got it. I'm ready.

So Lianne told her younger son the story of a little miller moth named Franklin who lived in a crack in the bark of a cottonwood tree, and he slept all day because miller moths are nocturnal. In the evening his mother would wake him and say, Franklin, my little moth, let's fly together beneath the stars. But Franklin was worried. His wings were new, and he didn't know if they'd hold him up high in the night sky. Franklin's mother came to him and told him that his wings were strong and getting stronger, that all he had to do was flap and follow her, that even from the very beginning, he was made to fly. So Franklin crawled to the tippy-top of a cottonwood branch and leaped into the sky and —

Marty's voice cut across the story.

—Bedtime! Bedtime for all little boys.

—But I'm not a little boy, Frank whined. I'm a miller moth!

—Bedtime for miller moths too. Let's go. Here, hand me the phone.

—Miller moths like the nighttime, Dad! That's when they fly! With their mamas beneath the stars. They're noc...noc...nocturnal!

Lianne could hear Frank's voice begin to bend and waver, break. Why did some hand fashion sons so different from their fathers?

—Marty, how about I just—

—Bedtime, kiddo. We'll get Mom on the line earlier next time so you actually have a chance to talk. She'll have another story. She always does. Go on.

Frank's whimpers and sobs grew louder for a moment, then faded. When Lianne had first readied to come back to nurse Viv, she'd spun tales of leftover pizza piling up in the fridge and hours of cartoons after school, and Trent and Frank had thrilled to the idea of living the bachelor life with their dad. What visions were behind their eyes now? Lianne thought of Ves taking care of his girls all week, of all the weeks she and her brothers had spent in Delphia with Ethel Kanta, of those last summer days she and Franklin spent out at the ranch with her father. Of the ways families are variously knit and unknit.

Frank in full meltdown mode now, Lianne managed a goodbye and hung up. Frank had always been a tough kid, colicky and mercurial, and she'd handled the better part of his intensity over the years. She was both relieved and ashamed to be away, to let Marty take his turn. Lianne was suddenly exhausted.

Upstairs, she clicked on the bedside lamp and slid out of her jeans, unbuttoned her blouse, unhooked her bra. She pulled on a T-shirt and crawled into bed, the same bed she'd used all through childhood, a sunken twin with busted springs, pushed up against the wall below the window.

Lianne drifted in near sleep. Or, more precisely, on thin and dusted wings, she flew.

She flapped and spun above the house, wove her way through the intricate branches of the neighbors' cottonwood, and flapped higher yet, above the gravel streets, the slumped farmhouses, the double-wides and empty lots. The highway a thin, gray line below, she followed it east, as if flying toward the ranch, though before the Mosby Road, she turned with the dirt track that led up Cemetery Hill, and fell then, tumbled through the air on useless wings. The granite stones—her mother's, her brother's—rising to meet her.

Moonlight at the window, bright and sinless, and Lianne sat up gasping, her heart shivering. With the hem of her T-shirt, she wiped a sheen of sweat from her forehead and neck.

It was likely past midnight, she thought, but by the light of the moon you could find your way wherever you were going. She pulled on a sweatshirt, lifted the jeans she'd laid across the foot of the bed. She slid her journal into her back pocket and grabbed a pen. She didn't bother with socks but laced up her tennis shoes—and moments later craned her head back beneath that high, white gibbous moon. It struck her as ridiculous, the brightness of it, the outsize generosity of such light—and what had any of them ever done to deserve it?

When they'd first moved to Spokane, Lianne was still writing. She'd published a handful of poems those first years, and for a while, it felt like it all might be building toward something. But then Marty made partner, then the boys showed up—and suddenly it seemed impossible to find time for much of anything. And writing had never made sense to Marty. All that tinkering and fretting, only to publish a poem in some obscure journal? The job in Idaho, she knew, wouldn't pencil out in Marty's book either. It wouldn't matter that she'd get a raise, that she'd get to teach poetry. For Marty, it'd be about the distance, and he'd be right—it was too far to commute each day. How far was she willing to go?

The night was wide and still, stars ringing the horizon, the moon high above. Lianne crunched through the gravel. She hauled in great breaths of chill air. At the foot of Main Street, she swung open the chain-link gate that led to a small park, a bank of four swings, two teeter-totters in parallel, a cockeyed merry-go-round. She sat in a swing and kicked it into flight.

Through the moonlit dark she flew back and forth and slowly stilled.

A pair of headlights shone over Korenko Hill west of town. She watched them come on, the sound of the engine catching up to the lights, the vehicle—a pickup, she thought now—coasting as it came through Delphia. Yes, a Ford F-350 hauling a metal stock trailer. Years ago, she would have known whose rig it was, might even have had an idea of where they were going, where they were coming from. The pickup sped up as it headed east.

Lianne pulled out her journal and let it fall open. The night was wider yet, and colder, as she put a pen to the page.

# 17

JUSTIN GRIPPED THE METAL and shivered in the rushing, straw-bitten wind. His whole body ached, one big raw bruise. He had no idea how far they'd traveled or where he was. He thought now to stay awake for the remainder of the journey, to figure the lay of the moonlit land.

The two-lane highway was shoulderless, the bar ditches shallow and matted with grass. On both sides, fenceposts whipped by, lines of barbwire sagging and rising. To the right, fields sloped down to a dark ribbon of river flanked by leaning, messy trees, then, beyond, the land lifted into sudden ridges and broken rocks; mountains like he'd never seen scattered and tumbled. To his left, a wide grassy plain rose slowly into low hills.

Through the trailer slats spilled the hard bone-light of the moon.

No traffic at all, and only the occasional light of a faraway farm or ranch — here, then gone. Against the cold, Justin piled straw over his legs, flipped up the collar of his flannel. The rig growled and geared up a low hill. It picked up speed down the other side, the lights of a small town winking in the distance. The wind whistled.

The truck slowed at the edge of the town, such as it was, gravel streets and trailers and dark-windowed houses and one line of big, blank-faced brick buildings. In a small teardrop of park along the highway, Justin thought for a moment he saw someone on the swings. But then they were through town—blink and you'd miss it, just like Nye—and it was likely only a trick of wind and moonlight.

They sped up and over another hill and down a straightaway and crossed the river as it bent sharp to the left. Not far beyond, the pickup slowed and swung left as well, onto a gravel road that once more followed the river as it ran this new direction.

The trailer banged and clattered in washboard ruts. Justin tried to steady himself but ended up bounced onto his ass, had to crane around to see where they were going. The river and the trees and the big open country. Hills and plains darkened into the night.

They turned left again, perpendicular to the river now, and bumped over a cattle guard. The nearly empty trailer jounced and slammed back down, and his head banged against the metal wall. They drove a road more dirt than gravel. Justin gripped the trailer slats all the tighter, got up onto his feet. The rig was aimed at a scatter of lights this side of the trees fringing the river. As they came nearer, he could make out a house and what looked to be a garage or machine shed. Beyond that lay a dark barn, corrals, and trees.

The pickup pulled to a stop out front of the shed. Justin cursed himself for not leaping out of the trailer earlier. He threw himself down in the straw. He didn't know if the driver would unhook the trailer or wait for tomorrow, late as it was, but he didn't want to take any chances. He could hear the pickup door unstick and creak open. Through the lowest slat he watched a man climb out and stretch, pull his cowboy hat from his head, then stand there a moment beneath the light of the moon. The man turned and studied the trailer—Justin's heart sounded the hollows of him—but after a time ran a hand through his hair and spun on his booted heel toward the house.

Gravel crunched under the man's boots. A dog rose from the top concrete step and trotted out, lifted its nose to the night, sniffed. Justin willed his heart to still, his breath and every muscle to unshiver. Please, please, don't let that fucking dog start barking.

The man opened the door and gave a low call. When the dog didn't react right away, the man slapped his thigh. The dog tucked tail and hustled inside. Justin breathed, settled back.

A light clicked on, then off, downstairs. Another light clicked on upstairs. Ten minutes later, that light, too, went dark. Now only the porch light shone. The man must be asleep. The dog was in the house.

He gathered his things. At the trailer gate, he reached his hands through and worked at the latch, trying not to let metal bang against metal. Finally, the door swung open. He didn't bother closing it. Who would ever think a boy rode back here? Who would ever imagine a stow-away like him?

In shadow, Justin reckoned the moon, the stars, the river. He didn't know yet which way was north or south, east or west—that would have to wait until the sun snuck over the horizon in the morning—but he didn't want to risk going back toward that little town. He hadn't liked the look of it. Too much like Nye.

No, he'd keep to the river was what he'd do, move the same direction they'd been driving. It'd lead somewhere, a highway at the very least. Then he could hitchhike his way west.

Justin circled around back of the shed and was off through the grass into the dark trees.

He moved quickly for a time, following faded cow paths, but as the moon angled off toward the horizon, the light stretching, shadowing individual blades of grass, he slowed. He didn't want to hurt himself out here. Wherever here was.

After an hour or so, he rested on a downed tree, the bark sloughed off and the wood beneath white and gray and going soft. He ate a jerky stick and a handful of peanuts and slugged down the orange juice. He licked the last of the sticky, gelatinous juice from the plastic lid and capped the bottle and stowed it in his pack.

Below, the river cut through its bank, this river—shallow, slow, and beneath the light of the moon a muddy brown—so different from the white mountain creek crashing through the woods at his uncle's place.

And he suddenly couldn't help it. He felt himself hover above that little clearing of pines, the buckling farmhouse, the camper, the barn, the still-smoldering burn pile, the one road snaking through the trees. In this waking dream, Justin watched the brown snout of his aunt's Astro van nose up the road on the way back to Heck. The engine worked against the grade. His cousins squabbled in the back, smelling of milk and sunlight.

Weeks ago, Gracie, the littlest one, spilled a beer that Heck had forgotten on top of the television, and in a rage, Heck broke her arm. Justin's aunt gathered Gracie and took her outside and loaded her into the van, said, her voice so quiet you could barely hear, that she and the kids were going to stay with her sister in Wyoming for a while.

Somehow, her near silence silenced Heck, who a moment before had been screaming, lunging, swinging at the walls. Now he hung his big fat head. Now he helped buckle the littler children into their seats.

Justin knew better. He knew that as soon as his aunt and cousins left, things would get even worse for him. As he helped his aunt pack a suitcase for the kids, Justin pleaded with her to take him. She zipped the suitcase closed, hugged him quick, and let go. He was Heck's blood nephew, not hers. Her sister wouldn't have him in the house.

Justin cursed her as she loaded up to go. Chucked rocks as the van pulled away.

And now, as Justin drifted above the dream pines, that anger boiled up in him again, alongside a deep, ungovernable sadness. If he could, he'd dive down and run the van off the road. He didn't want her to ever go back. Didn't want her to park by the house and help the kids inside, a pink cast on Gracie's arm, didn't want his aunt to call his name, to check the barn, the burn pile, the camper—where she'd find, like a fallen tree, Heck's body in the doorway.

The moon threw long, stretched shadows, the stars wheeled, and Justin was up again trying to outrun his dreams.

# BEFORE

# 18

HE FIRST HEARD THE music when he was eleven.

They'd left the trailer park in Bremerton — Justin yet dreaming of the brush of sword fern at his knees, blackberries purpling his palms, the shadowed roothouse he'd cleared beneath an enormous western red cedar, how that wall of cool dirt just fit the curve of his thin back — and he and his mother were living in a one-bedroom apartment north of Boeing Field. The complex was a square U, clanging metal stairs zigzagging up to the third story, where their unit sat halfway down the east side. The windows opened on the steel and cinders of the railroad tracks and an elevated stretch of I-5, traffic a constant clangor, trains rattling through at all hours, and, without warning, jets roaring over, obliterating for a moment the sounds of the neighbors, who turned their TVs up and let their babies wail and slammed doors and yelled at one another in half a dozen languages. And three, four, five nights a week there were his mother's sharp, drunken barks of laughter, the low, quick, cajoling voices of the various men she brought home from the bars.

Justin would lie on his bed in the dark — the bedroom his, the rest of the apartment hers — and in an attempt to block out the noise, he'd tune through the radio, turning the knob slowly, so as not to miss a thing. He'd twist the antenna, flagged with tinfoil, one way, then another, angling it toward the window this time or even just holding on to it, his body the conduit, his own bones carrying the signal. Up and down the FM band, he could usually tune in better than thirty stations. He'd listen to the Super-Sonics game for a while, then turn the knob down to find preachers bellowing and breaking into song and sometimes whispering, even weeping. There were late-night shows about UFOs, angry call-in shows about the news, and music, so much music, when, for as long as he could remember, his had been a house without.

His mother and father had never bothered with music, though sometimes, when they lived at the trailer park, someone over for a barbecue would roll the car windows down and play something loud and sure of itself on the stereo. A Mexican family lived in the trailer park as well, and on Sunday afternoons the man of the house would sit in a lawn chair and drink yellow beer in clear glass bottles and play his guitar. Justin would coast as he biked by, marveling at the sad, intricate sounds lifting from the wooden body of the instrument and the man's own throat.

He marveled at all the music: The swaggering rock he remembered belting from car stereos. The silences and crescendos of the classical station. Lonesome, warbling country tunes that reminded him of the songs the Mexican man sang. The Top 40 Casey Kasem counted down each week, and on lined notebook paper with blue pen Justin listed the songs, noted which ones moved up and which ones moved down and what, then, he should record on his one cassette tape. Bon Jovi this week. New Kids on the Block the next. Madonna. Richard Marx. Mötley Crüe. He taped the hits all summer, and eventually Skid Row bled through Billy Joel, Garth Brooks blended with Debbie Gibson—and he liked it when this happened, the strange juxtapositions and sonic disruptions even better than the songs themselves.

There in the dark of his room, the sharp, discordant noise of the neighbors piercing the walls, the lights of late-night traffic stretching and disappearing behind broken blinds, Justin let the bleeding notes and twisted sounds fill him, and so was ready, then, for when he first heard it, the music that would be his.

Low on the dial one weekend afternoon—with his mom not home, what else was there for a boy to do all Saturday except eat sugar cereal in his underwear and listen to music? — he found it, the lone, bending bass riff joined by drums, then suddenly split by distorted, driving guitar, and, most of all, that voice: in the man's throat and nose, deep but breaking at the edges into a kind of glassy, animal scream, as if he didn't care and at the same time this song right now mattered more than anything else in all the blasted world.

Justin stopped dead.

He fumbled his bowl onto the chipped vinyl counter and wheeled into the bedroom. Behind him, the bowl wobbled and fell, milk and soggy Os splattering the cabinets, puddling on the linoleum.

He didn't care.

He turned the radio up, up, up.

As the song faded, Justin grabbed his notebook and pencil. When the radio man said the band's name, said *Nirvana*, he wrote it down, wrote *Nirvana* and underlined the word and circled it and in the deepest, safest roothouse in his mind put that astonishing sound in the same place he kept the clatter of the creek, the drip of ferns and cedars.

Put it there and closed his eyes and let it play again and again.

# 19

It was different with the boys. Or it became that way.

When he thought about it now, he was never sure. Had it really only been Lianne who put her shoulder to the work? A girl, he'd thought, wanted to go off on her own, but a boy who stood to inherit a ranch — why, that had been his one dream. Had Rene Bouchard somehow seen his own boys and not seen them? Or was the world even then beginning its wobble and tilt?

The summer of '71 had been hot and dry. Fast black storms rolled through most every afternoon, hauling wind and heat lightning and blue-dark ropes of virga burning off before they hit the cracked flats. By late July, Willow Creek was nearly dry, the only water left warm and slow and stinking. Rene had split the herd — the largest he'd ever run, a thousand head of sheep — which meant more exposure and likely more coyote kills, but he didn't want to put too much pressure on any one of the wells. He and Lianne had been seeing to the bulk of the herd, which was on two sections to the immediate south and east of the camphouse. Every morning, while Lianne slept, Rene rode out early with the sheep and ran each of the pumps until the stock tanks were full, the sheep sucking at the water even as the pump motors coughed and knocked and churned. Every evening, Rene and Lianne gathered the sheep back into corrals, where they'd secure as many as they could in the shed, and then Lianne would sit up the better part of the night with the others in the corral, a rifle across her knees.

Keith and Dennis were camped miles to the north, in the section with the artesian spring, which ran year-round clear and cold, though slow. With the north fork of Willow Creek dried down to the dusty wink of agates and alkali, the artesian spring was the lone source of water to the north and could keep up with only two hundred head or so of sheep. The boys had a tent, a rifle, and a horse between them. They were to keep the stock tank clean and move with the herd as needed, taking turns during the night with the rifle. Without any kind of enclosure for the sheep, Rene knew, there'd be more coyote depredation than he'd like, but it was too far and would take too much water, grass, and time to trail this part of the herd back each evening. He just hoped the boys were staying up as late as they could and putting the fear into those old dogs.

Once a week or so, Viv and Franklin took Old Blue out to deliver food to Keith and Dennis, but this particular noon, Rene rode out himself, his saddlebags full of apples, roast beef, saltines, cheese, hard candy, and .22 shells. Great stacks of white cloud scudded overhead, burying the grass and cactus in rippling underwater shadows. Then the high, hot sun shone again, the prairie made bright as windblown bone.

After a mile or so, Rene reined Eight Spot off the dirt road and took to the hills. He thought he'd circle the boys' camp, maybe get his own rough count of the coyote kills to square with theirs. He came on bones and wool and desiccated flesh a good ways from the artesian spring. Not a fresh kill—the carcass had been bird-pecked and scattered—but from this summer for sure, maybe three weeks old, which was when the boys first took this part of the herd north. Eight Spot shied and crow-hopped a time or two. Rene turned her, put the flat of his hand to her neck, could feel beneath the taut hide quick charges of blood.

He rode the hills. He found kills everywhere. Bits of wool and entrails strung through the sagebrush. Bellies opened and gnawed. The faces, too, the haunches and assholes. The stink of rot scoured his nostrils, his throat. A kettle of turkey vultures drifted darkly on the horizon. Rene's count, if you could call it that, for the mess of it ran into the forties. He was nearly sick.

He turned Eight toward the spring and rode hard, puffs of dust lifting from the dry hardpan. He came on the boys horsing around in the stock tank, both naked as jaybirds. They didn't see him for a time, and then they did, and they stood there, wet and sunburned, the water in the stock tank dirtied with the mud of their feet, with rust and yellow-green blooms of algae. They were fifteen and fourteen that summer. Keith had been playing on the varsity basketball team since the eighth grade and was a couple inches taller than his father. Dennis was thick in the shoulders and through the legs and likely heavier than Rene, who'd been rangy all his life.

Rene was as furious as he'd ever been. He thought of that moment at the bunkhouse when Floyd showed up with his hat in his hands asking for money, and, no, he'd been calm then, ready. He'd known what he planned to do. And he'd done it. He had no idea now.

The boys covered themselves with their hands. Keith made to get out of the tank. Rene shook his head. Told him to stay right where he was. Then asked after the count. The boys looked at each other, shrugged. Keith said he thought maybe twenty.

— There's better than forty head of sheep dead out there in the hills. You boys have been goddamn worthless.

Rene spit. Eight Spot stamped and snorted.

— I've told you before that what's easy is seldom what's right. And you've done what's easy. You've done wrong. This is a sad, wrong thing you've done.

Dennis hung his head and started to say something, but Keith interrupted, his chin lifted.

— Then send us home.

It took Rene a moment to understand that Keith meant town, meant the house in Delphia. That's what his boy meant when he said the word *home*.

# 20

JUSTIN TURNED TWELVE, THEN thirteen, and they were living in Rainier Beach, in a duplex on a relatively quiet stretch of Sixty-Fourth Avenue. With two bedrooms, a bath and a half, and a concrete patio in the backyard, the place felt enormous, astonishing, revelatory. His mother had found steady work entering data in a computer all day. She'd done receptionist work when she was younger—and prettier, she always added—but with Boeing booming, the company was taking anyone who could type, whether they were pretty or not. His mother laughed at her luck. She said the work was boring as hell but came with benefits. She said it again—*benefits*—and he knew those were good things, though he didn't know what, exactly, they were.

The benefits Justin understood were the bedrooms and the bathrooms and really everything about the duplex: the three straight, tall, cinnamon-barked fir trees shading the backyard, the old woman who lived on the other side of the duplex, Mrs. Gribskov, her two yappy dogs circling and sniffing at his ankles, the plates of sugar cookies she was always leaving on their doorstep. Another benefit was that his mother had to be up early to blow-dry her hair and catch the 7:05 bus, which meant she was in bed after the late show, which meant, save for Friday and Saturday nights, she'd pretty much given up going out to bars. After a couple of months, she'd even saved enough to put a down payment on a used Honda Civic. Every Sunday after that, they drove to the Safeway at the corner of Rainier and Seward, where from the far side of the parking lot you could make out a blue-green slice of Lake Washington, maybe a motorboat or two ribboning the water.

—What do you say, J.? his mother would ask, rolling a cart down the chilled dairy aisle.

—I say, Justin would muse, tapping his chin, studying all the bright offerings, it's a good week for cheese sticks.

—Cheese sticks it is!

With a flourish, his mother would toss two plastic strips of them into the cart alongside Lunchables and pudding cups and electric-blue Gatorade and whatever his mother wanted to try, maybe Parmesan-stuffed tortellini, and they'd smile at each other, mother and son, and it was like they were getting away with something, like no one else in the world knew—and this, then, was the benefit that mattered most, that day after day, week after week, they could pay for things, could begin to rely on things to be there, to hold a known space in their lives and offer utility or comfort. To a boy used to the furious disarray of a given span of hours—let alone of a day, a week, a month, a school year—such order indeed felt holy, like evidence of the unseen, a system of belief, faith itself.

Justin was so small and relatively well behaved that his teachers assumed he was brighter than the other kids, that he'd skipped a grade or two somewhere along the line. His seventh-grade year, his first at South Shore Middle, Justin was slated into advanced English and math. He did well enough that he was allowed, that spring, to apply for competitive electives for his eighth-grade year. He chose drama and honors band—he'd taught himself to play guitar and drums—and got into both. What's more, that next year, he was still there, in the same school, still living in the duplex on Sixty-Fourth. Justin had small parts in both of the stage shows that winter, but what he truly shone in was honors band. Just a few weeks into the school year, his band teacher, bald, kind-eyed Mr. Hollowell, told him he had a gift, that he should keep practicing, and soon Justin was sharing lead on the drum set for the pep band and chosen as one of the rhythm guitarists for the jazz ensemble. It wasn't his music. But it was music.

That spring, as the last of the winter rains gathered and grayed the sky, for his fourteenth birthday, his mom bought him a shining blond-and-rosewood Alvarez Artist Series acoustic guitar. His mother's new boyfriend, Rick, had come over for the party, but today not even Rick could ruin things, because look at this guitar. The curves and strings and shadowed hollows, all the music held silently within. The Alvarez glowed on the cream-and-steel Formica table, right by the Safeway cake, thickly frosted with a border of blue notes and his name spelled out in yellow letters.

Justin almost didn't want to touch it.

—Go on, J., his mother said. She was standing behind him. She wrapped her arms around his neck and gave a quick squeeze, then gently pushed him toward the Alvarez.

Justin picked it up, touched the shining curves, the taut strings.

—Play something, she said. Whatever you want.

He plopped down in the nearest kitchen chair and gently strummed the first chords of "Come as You Are" and glanced up. His mother was smiling at him, a big, wide smile. She had a dental bridge that didn't fit well and so seldom let herself smile like that, with her teeth showing. Justin sang the first verse softly, slowly. Just as he got to the chorus, Rick's chair screeched out from under him.

Justin palmed the strings to silence.

Rick was a mechanic—had met Justin's mom when she took the Honda in for an oil change. Or he was a mechanic when he had work, when he hadn't managed to piss off his latest boss and get fired, and he favored T-shirts with the sleeves cut off and tight blue jeans, his chest and belly massive, his hips and legs so cartoonishly skinny Justin always had to fight the urge to laugh. You didn't laugh at Rick.

Still standing, Rick forked up his last bite of cake.

—That one of those faggy outfits you're always listening to? he asked, white frosting on his lips and teeth.

His mother put a hand on Rick's arm—her smile tight now, thinned nearly down to nothing—and made a show of picking up plates and forks.

—J., why don't you go practice in your room. Rick, there's beer in the fridge. I'll get you one. You want to see what's on TV?

Justin didn't even care that his mother had covered for Rick again; he simply disappeared into his room and locked the door, stuffed a towel in the crack beneath so the music would be his and his alone. He sat on his bed and touched the Alvarez up and down, the strings and curves and frets, the neck and headstock. And now that he knew this guitar, his guitar, with his fingers and hands and whole body, he began to play, softly, carefully, the sounds becoming part of him, becoming him.

Across that spring and summer, he practiced nearly every day, and it didn't take long for him to figure out how to bend and break the chords, how to make the lovely, ragged sounds that spilled from the round mouth of the radio.

The sounds spilling now from his hands, his mouth.

# APRIL 1994

# 21

Lianne woke to the ringing of the phone, her heart askew. She sat straight up in bed and from all the way downstairs, the phone sounded again — that hard, loud, mechanical *briinnggg*.

She hadn't gotten back into bed until after two a.m. and glanced now at her watch. Just before six in the morning. If it was Marty, it was an emergency, that was sure. But she doubted it was him. Marty wasn't the kind for emergencies. He was always so well prepared, nothing could possibly be an emergency. There was no phone out at the camphouse, so it couldn't be Rene. Keith? Dennis?

Lianne pulled on a pair of sweatpants and felt her way down the hall, the phone ringing, ringing. Keith, his gifts always more extravagant or expensive than they needed to be, had given Rene and Viv an answering machine for Christmas a few years back, but they'd never connected it. Televisions, microwaves, answering machines — her parents didn't believe in such frivolities. Lianne gripped the banister and pounded down the dark stairs and across the living room, the pale rose glow of morning filling the front window. In the kitchen, she clicked on the light above the sink and closed her hand around the phone mid-ring. She lifted the receiver to her ear.

—Hello?

—Is this Lianne Bouchard?

It didn't matter if her last name was Parker; she was always a Bouchard here in Delphia. Lianne breathed and swallowed, collected herself.

—Yes. Can I ask who this is?

—This is Bill Harney, up at the school—I'm the principal—and we've got ourselves a situation.

Harney went on to explain that the new librarian and English teacher—a young guy just out of the teachers college in Billings and a bit wet behind the ears—had been having a rough go of it in the classroom and, according to the note Harney had found slipped beneath his office door this Monday morning, had quit and left town.

Lianne was confused.

—But what does any of this have to do with me?

There was a pause on the line, as if Harney didn't quite believe she didn't understand, as if his intentions should have been crystal clear.

—Miss Bouchard, I hear you are an English professor and that you find yourself in town for the next few days. I'm asking if you might substitute for us. We're in a bind.

Lianne laughed out loud, a short, quick laugh that she tried to hold back. She didn't even have a teaching certificate, she said, let alone one valid in the state of Montana.

Now it was Harney's turn to chuckle.

—Well, now, that does indeed matter in certain locales. But not here. In fact, though I don't especially like to admit it, I have been forced a time or two to hire substitutes who haven't even graduated from high school. Miss Bouchard, I assure you, you are more than qualified.

She could hear Marty's voice in her head: It's not your problem. It doesn't have a thing to do with you or your family. Tell him no. But Lianne had always had a hard time with no—Marty was a case in point—and even more, she was her father's daughter. If there was a job that needed doing, well, you did it.

—What time do you need me?

Harney explained the schedule: Three English classes in a row—seventh-, eighth-, and ninth-graders—then a library period, then her prep, which was also lunch, and she was always welcome to a tray. Lianne asked about a curriculum or any lesson plans. Harney thought there might be some things in the library but assured her that whatever she wanted to do was just fine.

—This is the first time we've had a college professor in a classroom here in Delphia. Hell, have them do jumping jacks if you like!

Lianne got the name of the school secretary, who'd have paperwork for her, and hung up.

The light shifted toward pale straw and began to fill the quiet kitchen. Lianne poured a bowl of breakfast flakes and sliced a banana on top. She showered and pulled on her best jeans, a blouse, and a light sweater—and all the while she was planning activities and assignments, making a mental list of poems she thought might truly speak to the sons and daughters of Delphia.

# 22

THE RED-GOLD GLOW OF dawn built behind the far hills, the near trees, and for what seemed a long time now—hours beyond counting or consciousness—Justin had been hearing music, as if melody lifted from grass and cold dust, rhythm clattered down from the few high clouds massing and jostling on the dim horizon, the music both his and not his, as if the chords and rhythms had been stretched to accommodate the river and the wind, as if the screaming songs shuddered at the same frequency as the dying stars.

He'd been walking through his own dreams.

The cottonwoods thinned and fell away. He climbed, awkwardly, over a barbwire fence and started across a shorn and diked flat, a field. Upriver sat a big house with a wraparound porch, black smoke curling from a stone chimney, lights in the windows, and someone—wide hat and dark boots—getting into an enormous red pickup parked out front. Justin took another step and heard a raised voice. The man in the pickup had gotten back out, was gesturing at him.

Justin shook himself fully awake. He was only fifty yards away. He could see the man's belt buckle, the shine of it as first light broke through the trees.

Oh, fuck.

He ran straight at the river, leaped down the bank, and splashed through the muddy shallows. He was up the far side and into the trees running north—he knew it was north now because of the rising light—and his breath roared, his steps fell hard against the snap of branches, the pull of the river.

The predawn air stung his eyes, the back of his throat.

He broke from the trees into a stretch of tall grass—and slammed straight into an overgrown barbwire fence.

Justin pitched over the wires and landed on his back, guitar clanging down beside him. He couldn't breathe, couldn't breathe, couldn't fucking breathe—and his lungs finally ballooned.

He sucked at the riverine air and curled himself into a ball and shook. Touched after a time his belly. His hand came away slicked with blood.

An engine growled, and Justin flattened himself down in the grass, the wounds on his belly flaring. Through the grass and trees, he spied that same red pickup rolling slowly down what must have been another dirt road, and two men—that huge one and a slightly smaller one—in the cab craning their heads out the windows. If he hadn't hit that fence, he'd likely have run right into them. Jesus, fuck. He had to be more careful.

The pickup disappeared around a bend in the road. Justin waited and shivered and chanced rolling again onto his back. He let his head fall to the earth and watched the high-running clouds, the curves and ribs of them stained with sunrise. He concentrated on breathing. He counted to one hundred, then scrambled to his feet and dodged from tree to tree, sprinted across the dirt road, and kept to the thickest woods until he came to the mouth of a small creek, the slow, greenish waters drifting into the heavier, darker flow of the river.

He sat in the grass and ate a jerky stick, a palmful of peanuts. His heart stilled; his head cleared.

Justin could feel the sticky wetness of blood gathering at the belted waist of his jeans. He slid off his flannel, then pulled off his T-shirt. With the T-shirt, he wiped at the blood, felt the stark ridges of his ribs, then tied the torn flannel like a bandage around his middle. His uncle used to spit at how scrawny he was, used to tell him if he didn't beef up, he'd toss him in a gunnysack and drown him in the creek like you would a batch of cats. Justin had had a friend in the pep band—she played percussion, like him — and she used to put her fingers all the way around his wrist. It was ridiculous. He was so fucking skinny. Now Justin laughed, shook his head, and blinked back tears. He held his ruined shirt against his stupid crying eyes and shook and finally wiped his nose and tossed the torn, blood-smeared T-shirt to the ground. He rooted around in his backpack for another flannel and settled that good soft scratch across his shoulders.

Upriver and to the east, he could just make out the dark outlines of three oil pumpjacks, black hammers falling toward the earth before lifting back up into the sky, the metal hum of them even now in his ears — he didn't want any part of that. Justin thought of how good and safe the creek behind the trailer park in Bremerton had been and now followed this other nameless creek west.

He passed through a stretch of burned country, sharp bits of red gravel, layers of ashy black dirt, rocks sinuous and wind-warped, coulees serpentine and shadowed. He maneuvered up and out of a tight crevasse and came on a massive earthen cone jutting up well over a hundred feet, the surprise of it like turning to spy Mount Rainier as the clouds cleared.

He kept on.

He trudged up hills, took his bearings on the flats. To keep himself awake, he knelt now and again in the muddy shallows and plunged his head into the slow, pooling waters.

Some time ago, he'd come to a well-traveled gravel road and bent himself through the culvert, the creek lapping at his shins. Since then, he'd seen nothing that betrayed any kind of human habitation but fences, the black dots of cows.

The land unraveled in all directions.

He was alone.

He'd thought he'd run into a highway. He was beyond highways. On his way from nowhere to nowhere. Moving through the music of wind and grass and his own humming blood.

It was some hours yet before noon. He stood on a grassy bank. Before him, the creek split again, one branch running down from the north, the other gliding in from the south and west. Each was roughly the same size, two or three feet across, a foot or so deep, maybe half the width of the main branch he'd been following. The land to the north flattened and finally broke along the horizon line. To the west rose hills beyond hills and in the blue distances the far suggestion of mountains.

Justin waded across where the two branches of the creek met and sat on the gravel bar on the far bank. The rocks were smooth and white-rimmed, bright here and there with a freshwater mussel shell. He pulled off his Chucks and set them out to dry, wrung out his socks. He palmed a flat rock and side-armed it, hoping for a skip. He missed altogether, the rock huffing into the dry grass across the creek, a puff of dust.

He had the sudden vision of each of these creeks splitting, and splitting again, and again, and finally, no matter which way he went, he'd be following a track of dust.

He'd die out here.

What a stupid place to die. No one would ever find him. It was so stupid it was almost funny, the kind of thing he and the boys at Seward Park might laugh about as they passed a pack of smokes, as they strummed and sang.

God, but he wished he had a lighter. Stupid that he didn't. Stupid like his mother putting him on a bus to Montana. Stupid like believing it might work at his uncle's place. Stupid like stowing away in a trailer full of cowshit and straw. Like following this stupid creek all day and ending up way out here.

Stupid like Kurt Cobain being dead. Stupid, stupid, stupid.

It had all gone to shit. Well, he'd just lie down and die. It was the next stupid thing to do.

Justin slid his pack from his shoulders and let his guitar clatter down. He lay back on the gravel. The rocks were warm beneath him. He rolled onto his side, the cuts on his belly pulling and burning with the motion, and slung an arm under his head. He was exhausted, a second or two away from sleep, but as he studied the trees, the branches scratching at the sky, the dry, yellow grass shifting in the wind, he saw, parting the grass, a clear trail leading up the bank and through the willows.

# 23

MOST OF THE SHEEP stood chewing their cuds. A few were yet asleep and so staggered up—pregnant as they were, it took some doing—and bleated softly as Rene walked the perimeter of the shed. Then, so as not to miss anything, he crossed back through the middle of the herd, the exhalations and grunts of sheep, the waxy musk of lanolin. He'd thought a few might be showing—a burst water sack, a line of blood, even the first tiny hoof poking out—but nothing. Maybe Bassett had been right. Maybe he still had time.

—Good sheep, he said. Good mama sheep.

He patted the withers of the ewe following him, the tight, greasy curls of wool, and she tensed a moment but relaxed beneath his hand and was the first one to slip out the shed door after Rene rolled it open, the first one to get to the hay he'd laid down in the feeders.

Another late night, another couple of whiskeys, and Rene had slept in. Or what passed for sleeping in for him. Then he took his time over coffee and biscuits and, after a visit to the outhouse, had readied the feeders. Now the full light of day spilled through the open shed doorway, and the sheep baaed and went swaying and waddling out into the corral. The grinding sounds of their chewing and the dry green smell of hay wafted in the still air. Rene walked the shed again to make sure he hadn't missed any spots of blood in the straw, then crossed to his lambing station and in the blue spiral-bound notebook made his first entry of the season:

*April 11, 1994 — The shed ready for lambing, the sheep gathered. None showing yet. All is fine with the camphouse.*

He paused a moment, pen yet in hand, and added another few lines:

*Saw a boy this morning down near the creek, had himself a guitar. I believe he saw me as well.*

Rene stowed the pen in the spiral binding of the notebook. Stood there for a time.

Above, along the row of windows that lined the broken-peaked roof, light streamed in and gathered, the whole of the shed glowing, motes of dust riding the light. He knew he ought to drive to town and call his boy Dennis, who was with the highway patrol out of Roundup, which would mean all the right gears would get to turning. There wasn't a deputy or any other kind of law enforcement in Delphia, but they'd send someone down to fetch the boy, eventually. At the grain bin, Rene filled a metal pail with oats and crossed to the west entrance and slipped out and called for the horses, who came down the hill slow and side-eyeing the shed, which was closed to them now. They tossed their manes, not liking the mess of sheep. Finally, they sidled up, and Rene fed them each their share and stroked their foreheads and muscled necks. He wouldn't need them for a while, wouldn't have time for them, and Big Red wouldn't care, and Nine Spot would pout and hold it against him. The summers his children had worked alongside him, the horses had gotten plenty of attention. But he was on his own. Had been for a good long time. The metal bucket, empty now, was light in his hands.

You heard awful things about kids these days, but what if he did what he would have done thirty, forty years ago? What others had done for him when he himself had been a grubby kid on the cowboy line looking for work, for three squares and a place to lay his head? Hell, Rene thought, there wasn't any harm in it. Save maybe to his own self, which didn't matter so much. Not now, not considering.

Rene stowed the oat pail in the shed. O'Malley, who wasn't allowed inside either so as not to disturb the sheep, came slinking up to him, kept right at his heel, and together they checked that all the corral gates were latched, that the float on the stock tank was working properly. Then they loaded up into the cab of Old Blue and drove around the far side of the corrals and with the tailgate down backed up until the truck bumped right into the haystack.

Rene's arms and chest were still sore from loading hay yesterday, and his hip flared with pain as he hauled himself up into the pickup bed. But he didn't have to hurry, not today. With both hands he pinched the strands of twine, then got his good knee up under the bale and hefted it and turned and crossed the bed as quickly as he could and dropped it just so. It was an art, stacking bales in a pickup bed, and if you did it right, you could load three dozen into a full-size truck. It got harder as you went, though, having to toss the hay bales up above your shoulders, the scratch of it at your wrists, down your collar.

At each breather, and he took plenty of them, O'Malley hopped up into the pickup bed and leaned into Rene's leg.

— You act like getting a pat on the head is downright necessary business, O'Malley. I believe you've gone soft.

Once the bed of Old Blue was finally loaded four layers deep, Rene and O'Malley drove back around the corrals and parked by the shed. He wouldn't unload just now. Maybe he'd wait for the cool of the evening. Maybe even after he'd shut the sheep up for the night, beneath the stars. That'd tire him out just as well as the whiskey. Likely better. He pulled his hat from his head and slapped the hay dust from his jeans. Then he turned toward the camphouse and what he thought he might find inside.

The one window in the bedroom faced north, and this early in the spring, the light filtered through weakly, light the color and heft of dead grass. A paperboard guitar case leaned against the wall at the head of the bunk below the window. A green pack rested next to it, a pair of dirty sneakers piled by the pack. The boy slept in the bottom bunk. He was in his clothes, the collar of his flannel showing and the cuff of his jeans where he'd kicked a foot out from beneath the blankets. He had a thin face, dirt and sunburn on his neck and cheeks and forehead. Long yellow hair tangled on the white pillow slip, pink roses and faded green thorns crocheted along the edges. In his sleep the boy had gripped in his two fists the hem of the blanket, gripped it hard. Rene thought he wouldn't be able to get it away from him. Not even if he tried.

He backed out of the room and untied the dark wool curtain and let it fall into place. O'Malley hadn't gone in but bellied himself down on the camphouse floor facing the bedroom. His ears up, eyes wide. He glanced at Rene, then back to the doorway.

—I don't know about this either, Rene whispered. But you could fill a goddamn pickup truck with what I don't know.

At the counter, Rene mixed another bowl of pancake batter and fried cakes on the cast-iron. He ate the first two himself, rolled up with a pat of margarine and a dusting of sugar, and fed the next two to O'Malley. Then he fried eggs, put them alongside the rest of the cakes, and set the plate on the table next to a fork and a paper napkin. He heated the morning's coffee, still in the percolator, and poured a mug. Then thought the boy might be too young for coffee and switched the mug out for a tin cup of water. Wished he had milk or juice or something.

Rene sipped at the lukewarm coffee himself. He hadn't known what he was walking into—whether the boy would be awake, if he'd have trashed the place—but a boy out here on foot would be above all hungry and tired. Before he'd set off for the shed, Rene had hid his .243 and box of shells beneath the one loose floorboard in his bedroom. He'd left out three camp biscuits and a hunk of cheese, had tied back the curtain to the kids' room. Made sure there was a blanket on the bed.

He lifted his hat from the peg on the wall and opened the front door; the afternoon clear and edging toward warm, the smell of sage and creek rocks riding a wind that drifted and turned from the south. They'd get blossoms soon, and the grass would green and lengthen. Rene clicked his tongue at O'Malley. The dog shivered but still stared at the doorway to the bunk-bed room. Rene clicked his tongue again and said the dog's name, low and quick, and O'Malley scooted out into the light, tail between his legs.

Rene stood on the plank porch for a time. He drained the coffee and set the mug on the chair and slapped his hat onto his head. Then started across the road to the shed. He could feel the give of the earth beneath his boot soles, the light in his eyes, the dust of years in his lungs.

Franklin had just turned seventeen the first time he'd tried to run. Rene couldn't tell how old this boy was. This boy with the long yellow hair, silver earrings in his ears.

# 24

WHAT LIANNE COULDN'T QUITE make sense of was the fact that the school smelled exactly the same. Not that she'd carried the smell with her these twenty years, no, but that as soon as she pulled open the double glass doors, she breathed—lemon floor wax, rust-bitten lockers, gym shoes—and remembered everything.

Lianne shook hands with Principal Harney, a short, fleshy man sporting a thick mustache, gathered the paperwork, as well as a ring of keys, from the school secretary, then made her way down the hall. She'd spent a good amount of her school years in the library—which had been new her sixth-grade year, part of an addition to the old two-story schoolhouse built in the 1920s, K through 12 all still in the same building—and even now, the memories of those afternoon hours, unfolding an algebra problem at the end of a chapter or diving into the possibilities contained in those rows of tall metal stacks, five of them, to be precise, thrilled her.

She'd forgotten, though, how small the elementary-school side was, squat shelves along two walls, a bright rug with sitting spots, and a book display on one side of a big wooden desk. On the other side of the librarian's desk was an instructional space for older kids, a dozen desks in mismatched rows, and a chalkboard on wheels. Beyond that were the stacks, though only three remained and they didn't seem nearly so tall or full as she remembered. Rather than containing sunlight and possibility, the library struck her now as small, dark, close. The blinds were pulled; the overhead fluorescents snapped and hissed.

She rummaged in the desk for lesson plans, a curriculum, anything. Found a gradebook, the last entry dated late February, as well as a crinkled pile of what looked to be student papers waiting to be marked. Lianne slammed the drawers shut and breathed. She could do this. She was used to composition classrooms of thirty and forty kids. What's more, she knew these ranch kids. She'd been one herself.

She zipped open the blinds and turned off half the overhead lights. On the chalkboard she wrote her name—*Ms. Bouchard*; it'd only add to the confusion if she insisted on Mrs. Parker—and underlined it. Then she wrote the beginnings of three sentences:

*If you really knew me, then you'd know...*
*My best days are when...*
*Sometimes I dream...*

The first bell sounded, and the seventh-graders straggled in, a few pairs, then a scrum of five, followed by three scurrying in on their own, one after the other, an ellipsis of dishwater-blond heads. They looked so impossibly young, their faces smooth and round, and not at all like her college students. No, they reminded her instead of her own boys, just bigger. Big little kids. She felt a pang of lonesomeness for Trent and Frank, but tamped it down.

Lianne took the roll and set them to work writing a paragraph for each sentence starter. Then she partnered them up to peer-review each other's drafts. She could tell they were scandalized by not being able to pick their own partners, but she insisted, and each pair had to bring up their drafts to get their peer-review comments approved before the end of class. Tomorrow, they'd work on responding to the peer review and get started on a final draft, which would be due the day after.

The blocks were only fifty minutes, and though in her second class she could tell two of the eighth-grade boys wanted to get themselves into trouble in the worst way—and would have if she'd left them any room for it—the first two periods went quickly, uneventfully.

The ninth-graders milled about outside the library until the very last moment, and right away, Lianne detected a cultural split developing here in the first year of high school. Most of the seventh- and eighth-graders had worn the ranch-kid uniform—Wranglers and boots, a T-shirt or Western-style snap shirt—but a smattering of the ninth-graders sported baggy Levi's or cargo pants and Nikes, Doc Martens, or Chuck Taylors instead of cowboy boots. They were trying, as best they could, to look like the hollow-eyed kids Lianne saw haunting the parking garages and side streets of downtown Spokane, skateboards and guitars and ballpoint tattoos inked up and down their arms. Lianne thought of Ves's daughter and her grief over that screaming singer—and, yes, there she was, halfway down the roster: Amy Munroe.

Lianne called the roll and noted Amy, a tall kid with curly hair that fell everywhere. Despite her faded jeans and unbuttoned flannel and that reddish-brown hair, Amy bore a striking resemblance to her father. Even if Lianne hadn't talked to Ves the other day, she would have seen it—those high cheekbones, those pale green eyes. Yet Amy shared none of her father's goof and grin, at least not this morning. The girl slid herself down in her chair and stared at the knot of her hands on the desktop, the look on her face weary, sad, and so, so over it.

Lianne set the students to work on the same project she'd given the earlier classes, then partnered them up and strolled through the rows, the light at the windows hazed with dust, the shadows of junipers and cottonwoods at play across the glass. The ninth-graders scribbled earnestly, Wranglers and baggy, faded Levi's alike, and Lianne thought maybe she could write a grant proposal for some new books, though almost as soon as she began penning the argument in her mind, she forced herself to stop. She'd been here only a few hours. She'd be gone at the end of the week.

The bell rang, catching her off guard—she hadn't checked their peer-review comments yet, so she lined them up by the door for a cursory approval. A few moaned that they'd be late to their next classes, but Lianne knew that if you asked something of students, you had better be prepared to follow through. Especially on the first day.

She stood just outside the doorway, checking papers in turn. The last group was Amy's. She'd been paired with a boy, another one not wearing the standard outfit — baggy jeans and white, unlaced Nikes for him — and they'd both written far more than their classmates, their peer-review comments lengthy and full of exclamation points. Lianne mentioned this as praise, and both smiled at her words, nearly lifted onto their toes. She handed their drafts back, and they skipped to their lockers.

The bell caught the two of them still extricating books and notebooks, and Lianne stepped into the hall, about to offer to write a pass, but they sprinted away, laughing and grabbing at each other as they turned the corner.

Lianne stood there, the smells of floor wax, rust, and teenage bodies drifting in the suddenly still hallway, and she knew that feeling — how delightful a little bit of trouble can be.


Thinking on it, Lianne had taken a glass of wine to the porch, had almost convinced herself to start a pros-and-cons list, like Marty was always telling her to do, but she finally just called the man. Ves chuckled, said sure. He'd get something on the table for the girls, then meet her in town for dinner.

Lianne was the only one at the café, though the Snakepit, the bar on the other side, was doing a brisk business, at least as far as she could tell from the jangly country music, the pop of pool balls, and scattered eruptions of laughter. She sat at the same plastic table she had yesterday, the one nearest the window, and the same unsmiling waitress waddled silently away when Lianne asked if it was possible to get a beer here, on the café side. A moment later the waitress ferried back a can of Bud Light, the top already punched.

Lianne sipped at the beer and watched the evening gather. The café sat across the street from the Lazy JC drugstore and the little teardrop park, the swings twisting and shivering in the wind, the tall grass along the highway waving and falling, the dry seedheads nodding nearly down to the earth. The school day had shifted something for her. She found herself looking now not for the absences but for what was yet here — the wind, the evening blues and lavenders, a cold can of beer at hand.

The café door swung open, and Ves Munroe stomped in.

— Well, hello to the new schoolteacher!

He lifted his cowboy hat from his head and pulled out a chair. Lianne noticed he was wearing dark blue Wranglers that likely hadn't seen the inside of a barn. His felt hat was a rich black.

— I could barely get Amy down for dinner this evening, Ves went on. Wouldn't stop scribbling on that assignment of yours.

Lianne smiled, sipped at her beer.

— You might have yourself a writer there, Ves. She strikes me as a sharp cookie.

— Sharper than her old man, that's for sure.

The waitress appeared again. Ves ordered a beer, and they both decided on the special, sirloin steak and a baked potato. In the silence that trailed the waitress, Lianne couldn't help but feel like the girl she'd been all those years ago — nervous and delighted, wanting to be right here, wanting to be far away from here. Ves grinned and shook his head.

— Yes, I believe my Amy might do just like you. Head off to college and never look back.

Someone must have hit a jackpot, as one of the video poker machines on the bar side beeped and whirred and kachinged. Lianne shifted in her plastic chair. He hadn't come to dinner just to critique her life decisions, had he? Ves must have read the look on her face.

— I didn't mean it like that. I mean, you know, she's going places. Just like you were. Like you have.

— Well, thanks, but it seems I've gone just about as far as you. Here we are.

Ves laughed again — he was easy with a laugh — and lifted the beer the waitress had just set down in front of him.

— Here's to right where we are!

They drank and lapsed again into a silence. The bar sounds crested, fell.

— Tell me about yourself, Ves Munroe. How's ranching? Your girls?

Just as Lianne remembered, Ves was a talker. In fact, he got downright animated. First, his girls — Tiff, Lori, and Amy. The older two, twins, would graduate this spring and were thinking business college in Billings, the same one their mother went to and that had landed her that insurance job, though if Tiff wasn't careful she might end up stuck with the oldest Pinkerton boy. Amy, of course, was turning out not a thing like the other two. This newfangled music of hers, and she won't even think of buying jeans at the same stores as her sisters. No Shipton's Big R or Tractor Supply for her!

— How does Connie handle it? Amy's rebellion, if it's okay to call it that.

Ves halted mid-sentence. The linoleum underfoot was streaked with dust and here and there heels of mud from the day's passing of boots.

— Oh, you know how it is. Fathers and sons, mothers and daughters. They get awful crossways of one another.

Lianne bit her lip. This was the kind of thing Marty, if he were here, would have tried to paper over in the moment, then scolded her for when they got home. And the trouble was, he'd have been right — it wasn't any of her business. Christ, she hardly knew Ves anymore.

She tried to turn the talk to ranching. Ves obliged. He was running what they called a grass-fed herd now — no shipping to the feedlots for finishing — and selling directly to a couple of high-end restaurants in Bozeman and Missoula as well as a chain of fancy supermarkets on the West Coast.

— We're doing more of our work on horseback so as not to tear up the fields with four-wheelers and whatnot, and instead of watching the futures prices out of Chicago and maximizing sale weight, we're just try-ing to grow a healthy cow and keep the grass happy, which means we get to keep on doing what we like to do. And those supermarkets in Califor-nia, they love it! Sell a pound of our grass-fed beef for three times what they charge at the IGA in Billings.

Ves sat back in his chair and took a slug of beer.

— Reminds me of the old days, of the way the old-timers — Rene being a case in point — ran their spreads. Speaking of, when did you want to drive out to Willow Creek?

Lianne had wanted to ask Ves if he'd ever read Wendell Berry, wanted to tell him about the new co-op in Spokane where she'd started buying grass-fed meat herself, the first beef that tasted even half as good as the beef they'd traded lamb for growing up, but at the mention of Rene she dropped her elbows to the table. She'd almost forgotten. Or she'd let herself forget.

—I don't know. Probably need to find someone to work the lambing, which I hadn't even thought of until you told me Dad fired Bassett.

The waitress set two enormous white plates down in front of them—slab of steak, foil-wrapped potato on each—and wooden bowls of lettuce salad. Ves picked up his knife and fork.

—I can ask around about lambing help. Best thing would be to get some high-school kid out there, someone who'll listen. Trouble is, they got all these big writing assignments from their teachers!

Ves grinned at Lianne, sawed at his steak as he talked.

—Speaking of some kid, Orly Pinkerton's been telling a story about seeing a kid walking the riverbank early this morning, before sunrise. Said he couldn't quite figure it at first, but it looked to him like a girl, maybe thirteen or fourteen. Skinny, long-haired, and carrying a guitar. Or at least a guitar case. Orly's older boy saw the kid too. Which, you know, helps with the veracity of the whole situation, Orly being Orly. They set out after her, but guitar and all, she took off like a streak. Ran for the river and disappeared.

Ves speared a hunk of steak, and Lianne, a forkful of buttered potato halfway to her mouth, saw for the second time that day the afterimage of those downtown kids, hollow eyes and lank hair and ragged jeans. You couldn't even tell how old they were. Fourteen? Twenty-four? Or even if this one was a boy, that one a girl. She set her fork down.

—When I was a girl, I remember drifters coming through on the railroad. Men on their own, mostly. But a few women with children too. Some older boys.

—There's homeless folks up in Billings, of course, but I haven't seen any in Delphia since they tore up the tracks. I sort of forgot that kind of thing used to happen around here.

Ves paused and screwed up his face. Went on.

—There was that one fellow, tall and quiet as a mouse. Hard to tell, but we were in high school by then, and I remember thinking he wasn't that much older than us. He built himself a little shanty out of pallets and tarps out back of the Graves Hotel. Even had a mattress in there. What the devil was his name?

—Ernie! Lianne shouted, then looked around the empty café, embarrassed. Sorry, just as soon as you said it, I remembered. Railroad Ernie. He used to carve little animals—

—Out of driftwood.

—Right, he'd sit out front of the drugstore and sold those animals for a nickel. I think I might even still have a couple. I brought them with me to Missoula, put them on my windowsill in my first dorm room. An antelope and a coyote.

Lianne found herself flushed with the memory. As if, along with all that had flooded back to her at the school, along with having dinner with Ves Munroe at the café, she was truly back where she'd grown up, back home.

—Whatever happened to Ernie? she asked.

Ves wiped his mouth with a napkin and set his knife and fork down, took a sip of beer.

—I was just thinking on that. Likely you were off at college, but one afternoon Bob Mix drove his big front loader over and scooped Ernie's lean-to right up. Maybe Mix thought it ugly, but hell, what's ugly is all this old drilling equipment littered about town, and, you know, better than half of it is Mix's. Anyway, Ernie must have left town after that.

Ves took up his fork again, then paused, an almost hurt look on his face.

—I guess I'm glad that kid skedaddled out of there this morning. Orly Pinkerton is a sight meaner than Bob Mix ever was.

Lianne wondered where the kid had gone. Where, come evening, all those downtown kids in Spokane laid their heads. If Rene hadn't gathered his own sad, hollow-eyed child and brought him home, where would Franklin have ended up?

Ves was saying something about work, about readying for branding. Lianne hauled herself back into the moment. Their beer cans were empty, their plates streaked with steak juice and potato skins.

Yes, of course, time to go.

She thanked Ves for the evening and stuck out her hand, which he held. He offered her a ride, but Lianne shook her head. It was only a few blocks. She liked an evening walk. The breeze, the waft of river and sage.

—Well, Ves said, I enjoyed myself.

—I did too.

—Good night.

—Good night.

Ves touched his hat and ducked his head. Only then did he let go of her hand.

# 25

For the stillness, the low and pale light, the thick blanket atop him — that closeness, that warmth and weight — Justin came awake slowly. He drifted and sank. Surfaced once more and shifted, stretched. Finally sat up and took in the details he'd been too frantic and tired to take in however many hours before.

The room was a tight, low-ceilinged rectangle, slim bunkbeds along all three walls and two short dressers flanking the doorway. A small cracked mirror hung from a wire above the dresser on the right, two pairs of dusty cowboy boots tucked beneath the left, the tall shafts fallen over with disuse. The walls and ceiling were bare, dark wood. A heavy cloth hung from a rod for a door.

A high, blue-white sky filled the window above the bed, the blue cut with thin curls of cloud. Sweeping fields of grass. Sage-studded hills. The nonsense wanderings of the creek.

The north branch of the creek, Justin remembered, taking his bearings.

He had thought lying down to die was the one dumb thing left to do. But then he'd seen the foot trail, and he'd gathered his things and followed the trail through the willows and trees until he saw a wooden outhouse — there'd been a few outhouses around Nye — and fell straight down on his belly, his wounds sawing with pain. He was thirsty and starving and cold—and wanting, he realized, for his thirst to be slaked, his belly to be filled.

Wanting, like he wanted music, to live.

The outhouse door clattered open, and a man stepped out. An old man. He situated a cowboy hat on his head and stretched a moment and seemed to consider the creek and the trees, his gaze passing right over Justin as if he didn't see him at all—maybe he was older than he looked. And then the man turned and walked—no, limped—up the trail.

Justin followed at a distance, duck walking. From a tangle of sagebrush, he watched the shadow that was the man enter a small, squat house, the windows lit with morning light, white-gray smoke drifting from a metal chimney.

He sat back in the dust and grass.

He had another choice now, one not quite so dumb. He'd wait for the old man to leave, then break in, find something to eat, rest a moment, run again. Even if he got caught, what was the worst a limping old man could do?

Maybe fifteen minutes later, the man stepped out, crossed the wide dirt road, and disappeared into the shed. Justin bolted for that little house.

Now he sat on this slim, soft bed, having slept he had no idea how long, the light at the window clear and pale and somehow beyond time. Before he'd fallen asleep, he'd drunk straight from the faucet and eaten a fist-size lump of yellow cheese and some kind of hard biscuits he found out on the counter—and still, his stomach growled, and the cuts on his belly pulled and itched. He lifted himself up and crossed the room. Standing off to the side just in case, he pulled back the curtain.

The front room was empty, lit by the stretched light of late afternoon, the blue and slowly incarnadining light of the approaching evening. To his right sat two small easy chairs; between them a table with some kind of fluted lamp atop it, oil trembling in the thick glass bulb. Above the closer chair, a child's painting of a yellowing sheep and a dusty green field hung on the wall. Past the chairs, a small oval of braided rug covered the floor below the front door, a thin window on either side. A long table ran the better part of the far wall, a wooden bench below, a picture window above. Immediately to his left hung another thick, dark cloth—behind it the old man's bedroom, likely—and then the kitchen, such as it was. Some kind of old-fashioned stove, a shallow sink, a small window above the sink cranked halfway open, a round-shouldered fridge with a long chrome handle.

Justin took a step forward. The floor creaked; motes of dust lifted and spun. On the table sat a plate of pancakes and eggs, a tin cup and fork. He picked up the cup and took a swallow. Water. He drained the cup, then took up the plate. Didn't bother with the fork but ate with his hands, ate standing up. The grease on the eggs had congealed; the pancakes were cold and dry. He kept looking out the big window, kept thinking the front door was about to swing open. He wiped up cold yolk with pancake and chewed and gulped—and the place was still. So quiet and ordered and of itself. Him the only dumb, stumbling thing.

At the shallow sink, he untied the flannel he'd used as a bandage and studied the cuts on his belly. Messy crusts of blood, the wounds themselves ridged and tender, the surrounding skin pink and tight. He let the water run, but if anything, it only got colder. With a wet rag, he dabbed at the wounds. He shivered. They'd scar, these three down-sloping lines running nearly parallel to his ribs. Justin dried himself off, dressed, and rummaged in his pack for the empty orange juice bottle. He rinsed it in the sink, filled it, drank it dry. Filled it again. He gathered his things and was out the door and down the dirt road headed north, the direction he'd been traveling the day before, when at the limits of his vision he saw something streak by.

A little black-and-white dog circled hard around from the left and crouched down in the road maybe ten yards in front of him.

Justin angled to the dog's right, and like that the dog was up and directly in front of him again, a little closer this time. Even gave a woof.

Okay, whatever. Justin turned on his heel and headed south at a near run. The dog circled and headed him off. Gave three short, hard barks, those small white teeth showing. Justin stood in the road, the dust he'd scuffed catching the light.

—He doesn't mean anything by it.

Justin wheeled around. The old man stood a few steps this side of the shed, maybe thirty yards off. He'd had a cowboy hat on earlier. Justin had noted that. Now his old man's hair — thin, bristly, just the color of that tin cup — stood on end. And for some fucking reason, his sleeves were rolled up, showing white splashes of skin above his wrists.

Justin's heart galloped. He looked from the man to the dog, then back. Little charges of fear or anger zipped up and down his bones.

He'd been so tired and hungry he wasn't thinking straight. Of course this old man would catch him. It was amazing the old bastard hadn't pulled a shotgun on him already. And now he'd have to make his way through the old man and his fucking dog.

The man hobbled toward him, that trailing limp he'd seen this morning, and Justin braced his feet against the earth. Readied himself.

— He isn't allowed in the shed. Nothing out here to herd but you.

Maybe ten or twelve feet away, the old man stopped, hooked a thumb in the front pocket of his jeans. With his free hand he gestured at the house, the corrals. Down the road. Out to the hills.

— I'm Rene Bouchard. This here is my ranch.

Now the man gestured at the dog.

— And this is Finn O'Malley. That'll do, O'Malley.

Like that, the dog's ears fell, and he padded over and sat down nearly on the man's boots, leaned into him. The old man patted his upturned head. Justin could almost feel the push of the dog's back against his own legs, the warmth, the soft, coarse fur.

— Did you train him to do that?

— The fellow I bought him off, he did the training. I'm just a rancher. But I try to treat him good. Be clear with him.

— Oh, Justin said, and wasn't sure what else to say. Wasn't sure at all in this situation what to do.

— You find the cakes and eggs?

Justin looked to the little house. The plate had been set out for him. He'd just assumed it was for someone else, that he was stealing. He always sort of felt like he was stealing.

— Yeah. Yes.

— All right. Good. Something in your belly. A bit of sleep. I see you got your things. I might recommend against leaving out of here on foot.

Especially this time of day. You're better than thirty miles from Delphia. Darn near a hundred from most anywhere else.

The old man looked him up and down. And Justin waited for what was next—some comment about his hair, his earrings, the sag of his jeans.

—That room you were in. With the bunkbeds. My own kids used to stay there. There's even still some clothes in the dressers. A pair of boots too. Anyway, you're welcome to call that room yours the next couple of nights.

The old man, Mr. Bouchard, shifted his weight.

—Three or four days, I was thinking I'd head into town for groceries. Give you a ride then, if you like.

Mr. Bouchard looked down to the dust of the road as if to give him a moment, and Justin thought of the warmth of that bed, could even now taste the salt and grease of eggs and pancakes, how cold and good that water was, sucked right out of the faucet. He took in the old man, the little black-and-white dog, the solid gray wood of the shed and corrals, a blue pickup parked nearby and loaded with hay bales. Justin reached deep down inside himself, down through the blood and fear and bile, the vigilance and torquing anger, down through all that would have him run, that would have him knock this old man to the ground, kick him until he stayed down, then take the keys to that pickup. He thought back to Rainier Beach, remembered their neighbor in the duplex, the old woman, Mrs. Gribskov, always a plate of sugar cookies and a cup of tea when he visited, her two little dogs sniffing about the floor, hoping for crumbs. He breathed into that long-ago moment, trying to remember how it was done. Rain at the windows. The smell of cut flowers. Mrs. Gribskov puttering about.

Justin swallowed. Looked to the little house, then down the dirt road as far as he could into the hills.

—Okay.

Mr. Bouchard nodded. Shifted his weight again. That limp hurt him. Justin could tell.

—If you're going to stick around, it'd be nice to have a name.

The boy considered how far he was from Nye, from Billings. Everywhere.

—Justin.

—Nice to make your acquaintance, Justin.

Mr. Bouchard reached up as if to tip his hat, only then realizing he was hatless. He gestured toward the shed instead.

—How about you set your things down and give me a hand?

# 26

THE BOY'S SHIRT FLAPPED out behind him as he loped across the road, his yellow hair hanging in his eyes. Rene worked a hand across his jaw and wished he had a hat to loan the kid. Viv and Lianne used to tie their hair back with a handkerchief, but Rene didn't know if he could suggest a thing like that to a boy. Didn't know the rules anymore, if he ever had. Rene put his shoulder to the shed door and rolled it open another couple of feet for what light there was and instructed O'Malley to keep watch. He pulled his penlight from his shirt pocket and stepped into the straw and dust and shadow of the shed. Justin, framed and backlit at the threshold, hesitated a moment, then followed.

Even for the evening light, the shed was dark and still. The Coleman lantern burned across the way, atop the table at the lambing station, and Rene swung his penlight in a slow arc. Most of the sheep were up, chewing their cuds and nosing one another. Some were settled down on their bellies or on their sides. Rene moved through the herd, talking to the sheep. Behind him, the boy breathed.

— Are these sheep?

— These are sheep.

— You don't have cows?

— No.

—Oh.

Before Rene had gone out to find O'Malley herding this long-haired kid up and down the road, he'd had his eye on a ewe in the northwest corner of the shed. She hadn't been showing but was hoofing at the straw. Circling, baaing, huffing. He'd hung his hat up and washed. Lit the lantern.

—Are we gonna feed the sheep?

—They've been fed.

Rene took another couple of slow steps. He could almost hear the gears turning behind him.

—What are we doing, then?

—We're looking for ewes in labor.

The soft crunching sounds of straw. The gruntings and bleats of the sheep.

—You mean labor like they're going to have a baby? A baby sheep?

—Yep.

—Whoa. Really?

—You're just in time for lambing season, Justin. If I didn't know better, I'd have thought you planned it.

Rene grinned at his joke and swung the penlight.

—I believe there's one over this way. Let's take a look.

They found the ewe down, eyes closed and neck stretched, her cheek scraping the straw down to hard dirt. The boy leaned into the cone of light, then straightened up and backed away. The ewe's water had broken. A red membrane pooled at her backside, blood on her wooled legs.

—Is it supposed to look like that? Is that okay?

—Nothing wrong yet. We'll just have to wait and see.

So they did. There in the low, sloped corner of the shed, they waited. Rene clicked off the penlight, to save batteries, and the darkness eddied about them, the hum of the far lantern, the night sounds of the sheep clear and soft, and the warm, ripe smells of dung and lanolin, the rich copper tang of blood on the air. Not long until they'd catch the moonrise, the waxing moon.

Rene clicked the penlight back on. The ewe huffed and turned her face away, straining. Nothing more was showing. Rene touched Justin's shoulder. The boy flinched.

—Here, take this. Rene waggled the penlight. I ought to wash up again.

Rene crossed to the sink and wet his arms up to the elbow. He scrubbed with pumice soap, rinsed, and dried his hands and arms on a small towel hung from a nail. He talked slow and soft as he moved through the herd.

Justin, hearing him, flicked the cone of light from the ewe to Rene, then held the metal cylinder out to him, eager to be rid of it.

—You hold on to that. Keep the light on me. And I need you over here, by the ewe. Kneel down and put a hand on her neck. Talk to her. If she starts to buck or get up, you just hold her down, gentle-like. Can you do that?

Justin looked at him like this was surely a joke, and when he saw it wasn't, he shook his head. His long hair fell again into his eyes.

—Look, I don't know anything about this.

—You don't have to. You'll learn. Just listen.

Rene thought this might be the moment, that this might be too much—the boy would refuse, then turn and run. Do something worse. He was three or four inches shorter than Rene, and angular, skinny. Face a blade, eyes a startling blue. The boy moved either hurriedly or not at all and with a jerk of the shoulders. Rene would have said he looked fragile, already broken—and maybe he was, but there was yet more to him. He'd somehow made his way out here, was still on his own two feet.

Justin looked a moment longer at Rene, to make sure, then swore under his breath and stepped around the ewe and knelt down. Shone the penlight in Rene's face.

—Not in my eyes. Here. My hands.

Rene leaned against a support beam and attempted to kneel. Halfway down, his hip and knee gave way. He hit the dirt hard. The kid bobbled the penlight.

—You okay?

—Just keep that light where I need it.

Rene righted himself and gritted through the pain. Christ Jesus. This was going to be tougher than he'd thought. He put his left hand on the ewe's side and with the other reached in. The ewe tensed and grunted against the pain.

—Oh, shit. Oh, fuck. The light wavered as Justin fell forward, his hand and forearm coming down on the bucking ewe's neck.

—That's right. Hold her.

Rene was nearly up to his elbow now, his nose full of shit and blood and the inside meat of things, the contractions squeezing down on him, and with his fingertips he felt the shoulder—no, the haunch—of a lamb. It was coming breech. That was the trouble.

—I've got to turn it.

Justin made a sound that might have been a curse or a breath, but he kept the light steady, and turn by turn Rene repositioned the lamb—the ewe wheezing, grunting—until he had one foreleg. Had both.

In a clean motion Rene pulled, and the lamb slid into the straw. He ran a finger through its mouth and set it on its mother's belly, where the wet thing gave a thin blat, a pitiful little sound, but it jerked the ewe's head up. She licked at the lamb.

The light had gone jittery.

—Oh, wow! Fuck, wow! You just, you just—you just reached in and got that thing!

—Keep the light steady.

The next lamb was coming now, had been waiting on the first, and it slid free with an easy tug. Rene cleared its mouth as well and plopped it down by the first. Two good-size little ewe lambs.

The mother, still on her side with just her head lifted, fussed over both, licking at them in turn—but then stiffened, gave another baa, and heaved. A third lamb emerged, this one half the size of the other two, a little buck, glassy-eyed and hunched. Rene swiped his pinkie through its mouth, but the lamb wasn't breathing. He bent down and cupped the tiny nose and blew right at its nostrils—one, two, three short, hard breaths—and the lamb coughed and sneezed. Kicked his way to life.

Rene laid this one by the other two and sat back in the straw.

The ewe licked at the lambs and passed the afterbirth, and the whole time the kid kept up a steady stream of exclamations, the light flicking from Rene to the lambs, the lambs to Rene.

—I didn't know there'd be three! Wow, holy shit, look at them! Three of those little things!

Rene hauled himself up, hoping the boy didn't notice how slow. He took the penlight from Justin, then instructed him to pick up the bigger two lambs, each by a back leg. The boy quieted almost instantly and again looked at him like he was joking. Rene would have done it himself, but he didn't know that he could bend over that far or if he could bend himself back up.

— Go on, Rene said, and motioned with the penlight.

Justin reached down and grabbed one lamb, then the other, and lifted them up. The lambs bleated feebly and attempted to kick.

— Oh, shit! They're all wet and bloody. Jesus!

— That's right. Gentle, slow. This way.

The mother scrambled to her feet and licked at the dangling lambs. Rene led them to the line of jugs — five-by-five waist-high wooden enclosures — along the wall near the lambing station and the sink. He swung the door of the first jug open.

— Set those lambs down in here. She'll follow.

Justin did as he was told, and the ewe started in, then stopped, looked around, and finally barreled all the way in. Rene latched the low wooden door behind her.

— Go ahead and get that runt in here too. We jug them up like this to keep the mother close. Make sure she's feeding them right. Most do. Just some need a little help.

Justin ferried the runt over to the jug with both hands underneath him, as if carrying a platter, and set the lamb gently down in the straw by his siblings, both already attempting to get up and totter around.

— Look at those things. Those are baby fucking sheep!

Rene filled the metal pail in the jug with water, and the ewe plunged her nose in and drank deeply.

— She might not have milk enough for that runt. We'll see. Might have to do something about that.

They stood looking down into the jug at the first lambs of the season — and there was more yet to do. They needed to iodine the lambs' umbilical knots and pitchfork up the afterbirth and bury it out back of the shed against coyotes. They needed to enter the births in the lambing log and walk back through the herd again in case any more decided now was the time, which often happened, the flood coming after the first. They needed to heat some water on the stove and wash and get some dinner going. Rene needed an aspirin, needed to sit in his easy chair and think on what he'd gone and done by inviting this boy to stay.

But for now they stood there, these two runaways, shoulder to shoulder, blood drying on their hands, lantern light spilling over them, and watched as the ewe nosed the two bigger lambs to her teats, the little runt finally trying out his thin, shaking legs.

# BEFORE

# 27

For a long time, Lianne wondered if what she'd seen those dusty months on the ranch was evidence enough. And, if so, if she could have bent the course of what was to come, if she could have saved them all. Or, if not saved, at least held them in her arms.

Lianne's first year at the University of Montana had been a revelation. By her senior year in high school at Delphia, most of her classes had been independent studies or study halls, since she'd already taken all the academic courses the school offered, but in Missoula she was surrounded by young people like herself, strivers and thinkers who loved to read and write and talk civil rights or existentialism late into the night. She'd met a boy, a junior engineering major from Spokane, who was already studying for the patent bar. He was organized and kind, as unoffending and predictable as the beeping computers he was so taken with — and so completely different from the brusque, by-the-seat-of-their-pants country boys she'd dated in high school. Though Lianne liked — no, loved — all her classes, she planned to major in English. She'd had a couple of poems published in the campus literary journal and had been selected to be part of an honors seminar over the summer term. But then she got the call — her mother, asking her to come home.

Viv wouldn't be able to be out at the ranch much. She'd miss it but she had to stay with the boys. They were too old for Ethel Kanta to be looking after them. And it just wasn't going to work between Rene and Keith. As it never did, Viv's voice sounded thin, tattered at the edges.

—So it'll just be me and Dad? Lianne asked. That's going to be a lot for the two of us.

—No, Franklin'll be out there.

There was only the one phone in the dorm. A line of girls had already begun to build down the hallway. Lianne turned to the bank of windows that lined the foyer, the mountain light softer than the hard glare of the prairie.

—But he's so young.

—He's thirteen. Your dad had you walking fence at that age.

Thirteen? Franklin was just a little boy. Even last summer, he'd spent most of his time collecting agates along the creek, sometimes helping Viv with the cooking, the dishes. Lianne had to count back through the years before she believed it—but it was true. And it was true, too, that no matter her summer plans, she'd break them. She'd finish this term's exams, then come home to the ranch.

Lianne caught an afternoon train headed east, the tumbling Clark Fork dancing with the tracks, the rocky slopes and forested ridges. Despite the delight of classes and new classmates, she hadn't been prepared for this landscape, had felt claustrophobic on the west side of the state, where mountains blotted every horizon, the greens and blues of the forests refusing to fade. Now the evening shadows swallowed riffle, willow, and fir-dark mountain flanks. Stars sounded the stone-blue wash of sky above the Pintlers.

They left for the ranch the day after she got back, near noon, Lianne sitting in her mother's place in Old Blue, Franklin between her and her father. No stories, at least not until they turned off the Mosby Road. Rene shifted in his seat, eyed Franklin a moment, then started in on the time he'd applied for a job as a grain buyer in San Francisco. He'd taken the train west to Portland, Oregon, then south down the coast. He arrived early in the morning, not enough night left to make getting a room worth it, so through the foggy predawn hours, he wandered the city. By the time his interview rolled around, he'd already decided—and caught the next train back to Montana.

They bumped over the prairie, the heady scent of sage and wild onion thick in the early summer air, and Lianne couldn't see it, the ill-at-ease-in-any-kind-of-crowd cowboy Rene Bouchard wandering the streets of San Francisco in his brown suit and bolo tie, leaning toward the steamed windows of chowder houses, poking at bolts of Chinese silk.

—Is that true, Dad? Did you really take the train all the way to San Francisco and back?

Rene hadn't shaved in a few days, and his whiskers, once a tawny brown, had come in steel gray. He looked out the window a moment. Back at his daughter, his son. He grinned, put his thick hand to Franklin's knee, squeezed.

—Well, Frank, at least I got you left. A sad state of affairs, but at least I got one child who believes his father.

—Dad! That's not what I meant! Why—

Lianne stopped short. Franklin was looking now at Rene with something on his face akin to rapture, to a great and terrible and hoped-for fear. And the thing was, the look on the man's face mirrored that on the boy's.

They were both hurt, both hoping. As if this were their last chance.

Rene squeezed Franklin's knee all the harder, and the boy winced but said nothing.

# 28

WE CLOSE OUR EYES to sleep. Can we ever trust what awaits us when we wake? Or maybe that's the difference, what constitutes the variance, the imbalance between us — the faith any one of us can place in whatever sudden world we might wake to.

Justin went to sleep, and woke, and he was fifteen.

Through that spring and summer, as he had the summer before, Justin walked Mrs. Gribskov's two tiny dogs — Scraps and Eustace, who sometimes peed a little bit on the floor, they were so excited to see him — and between rains, he mowed her small yard. Mrs. Gribskov was ancient, even smaller than him, and though he wouldn't exactly admit it, each week he delighted in the ceremony of knocking and waiting as she shuffled to the door and invited him inside to sit at the small kitchen table with a plate of sugar cookies and a tinkling china cup of weak tea, two swallows full at most. Her half of the duplex smelled of dogs, liniments, and cut flowers, which she had delivered twice a week. She'd worked all her life — was born into cleaning and inventory at her father's corner store, which in time became her husband's corner store — and deserved all the flowers she could afford, she said, laughing at her one late, bright extravagance.

Once they'd finished their cookies and tea, Mrs. Gribskov would reach for her checkbook and, with a slow, quavering hand, pen an almost unreadable check, the slants and loops and curves of her script graceful and oddly alluring, like the black-and-white movies Justin sometimes stumbled across on the television. After she slid the check across the table-top and stood up, Mrs. Gribskov always made a point of shaking Justin's hand and thanking him, telling him what a fine boy he was, which embarrassed him—the thinness of her bones, her cool, papery, somehow perfect skin—because she didn't really know him, did she? Didn't know if he was a fine boy or not.

Justin would cash his check at the Circle K and, in a mizzling rain, catch the bus to Seward Park. At the covered amphitheater, near the water, they'd gather—boys in flannels and ripped jeans, boys with ratty, shoulder-length hair, with hollow cheeks and home-pierced ears, boys who scribbled song lyrics in their math notebooks, boys who nestled the wooden curves of guitars on bony knees, boys who'd break your heart when they strummed and hummed and screamed and sang, who'd break your heart when they hitched up their shirts to show you the cigarette burns dimpling their ribs, boys who'd already quit school, boys who felt safe only at school, boys who after school wandered the streets for hours, hungry boys, skinny boys, boys with smoke and sugar on their tongues, who slid tall cans of malt liquor into the waists of their jeans, who quick-fingered packs of Winstons, who tongued pills from one another's palms, boys who wished to touch other boys, who dreamed of being touched by anyone or no one or, please, God, not that one, not again, boys who hoped above all things that when they opened the door their fathers might turn toward them, boys whose mothers always had two jobs or no job or needed to move, again, for a job, boys who lived with half a dozen cousins in falling-down houses, in apartments, trailers, motels, boys who slept last night beneath a tangle of blackberries at the edge of the park, boys who for one reason or another had gone ahead and descended into the jungle camps beneath I-5, boys who were hurting, who hurt, who hurt themselves most of all—but our boy, Justin, who walked the neighbor lady's dogs, who liked sugar cookies and the bitter, grassy taste of tea, what kind of boy was he?

Like the rain, it depended on the season.

At first he merely sat on the nearby merry-go-round, toed this way, then that, sometimes all the way around, but he was watching and listening, noting the lyrics, the chords and riffs and rhythms, the improvisations and particularities. By the time the tree flowers had fallen, dunes and drifts of bruised petals, cream and peach and so many varieties of rose, Justin was one of them, was curled over his Alvarez, strumming, singing along.

Often, they left a guitar case yawed open in front of the amphitheater, though that wasn't exactly the point. Still, people happened by and dropped a dollar in now and again, which meant a pack of cigarettes to share. It was a kind of musical collective, Justin decided, thieving the word from his ponytailed, bespectacled civics teacher. Each boy took a turn, if he wanted, on vocals, on lead guitar. Each was teacher, each student. What mattered was the music, the wild, breaking, broken sounds spilling across the green and down into the blue, blue water.

Even as the days got longer and stretched into the drowse of summer, Justin most often left before the dark came down, before the joints and pills got passed around. Sometimes one of the boys living in the blackberries would ask him for a couple of bucks. Sometimes one of the boys was hurting for something or from something and so took whatever was in the open guitar case all for himself. One Saturday, sunshowers off and on all afternoon, an older guy, maybe twenty-three, showed up blasted, and without any kind of discussion, the boys rolled him for his jean jacket, knife, and wallet, and Justin began to understand more keenly that there were here—like there had been above his long-ago boyhood creek—edges sheer and dangerous. And far below that sucking sound, something roaring.

On the first of August, a rare heat wave descended. With no AC in the duplex, Justin would go outside and soak himself with hose water to stay cool. On day three of the heat, he knocked on Mrs. Gribskov's door to take the dogs on their morning walk. Scraps and Eustace whined and scratched, but Mrs. Gribskov never came. He called her name. The dogs barked. He didn't know what to do. He knocked again at noon, then every hour on the hour until his mom got home from work. She was hot and tired, her makeup running—no AC on the city buses either—but when he finally made her understand, she said, *Oh, shit. Call the cops. Call right now.*

A six-pack deep that Friday, Rick said something. They were watching TV, Rick shifting and muttering. Finally he got up, pounded on the wall with the flat of his hand, and yelled that he could hardly stand it. That the whole goddamn place smelled like dog shit and dead old lady. Justin had been about to open a Pepsi.

He slung the can at Rick's head instead.

With a meaty whack, the Pepsi split in sprays of fizz. Blood tumbled from Rick's nose, a red waterfall across his lips and chin.

His mother made a sudden, shocked sound — Oh! — and Justin was scrambling backward, Rick up and blindly swinging.

— You little faggot! I'll fucking kill you. You ratfuck, you faggot!

Rick's hand closed around the tail of Justin's flannel. Justin slid one arm out and had just about shucked the other when Rick wheeled around with a kick and that caught him in the thigh. Justin felt his muscles pulverize, the toe of the boot strike bone. The pain was boundless, a black mountain rising in him and out of him and falling back down on him.

He collapsed, gagged.

Rick grabbed him by his shirt front and slammed him up against the wall — and Justin threw up all over Rick's too-close face.

Rick dropped him, staggered back.

Justin scrambled into his room and locked the door. He could hear Rick swearing and stomping, his mother trying to calm him down, saying she'd deal with Justin later, she would, don't worry.

— Ricky, honey, why don't we get you cleaned up?

Then his mother made that surprised sound again — Oh! — and Justin heard her hit the wall, the floor.

Silence for a moment, and Justin stood covered in his own filth, waves of pain pulsing through him. He imagined his mother crumpled on the floor, the veil of her hair, her worried, chirrupy breaths — and he almost went to her. He for a moment imagined the two of them leaning on each other, helping each other up, and facing Rick together.

Rick's heavy bootsteps sounded through the duplex.

Justin wiped his mouth with a dirty shirt and quickly changed clothes. He threw his notebook, an extra flannel, the half-empty pack of Winstons he'd swiped from his mother's stash, and all his dog-walking money into his backpack.

He wished he had a knife.

Rick kicked at the bedroom door, the hinges squealing, plasterboard crunching. Justin jimmied the screen from his window, crawled halfway out, reached back in for his guitar—and as the door gave way beneath Rick's boot, Justin was gone.

Those were the first nights he spent at the park, off in the salal and wild grape beneath another boy's blue tarp. They smoked and talked, the slapping sounds of lake water punctuating the city dark. The other boy had a plastic handle of vodka that was a quarter full. They resolved to drink it all. Beneath the sagging tarp, sitting cross-legged, they passed the bottle back and forth. In due time they confessed their various shames and angers and regrets. They held each other and cried and tumbled into blackness.

Justin woke hot and ill, woke alone, the drone of insects in the grass.

He didn't go back home that next day, didn't go back until Monday afternoon, when he thought Rick might be at work. He found his door beaten to pieces, his mother wearing a blue wing of bruise beneath her right eye.

It happened fast after that. Everything simply came apart.

That year his mother spent more and more time at Rick's place. When Justin asked why, when he touched the bruises on her arms, she hugged herself and told him it was complicated, that when he was older he'd understand.

Justin understood things now that he never had before.

He understood all the weight she'd lost, the way she came back to the duplex and slept eighteen hours straight. By late winter, she wasn't working at Boeing anymore; the fridge was empty, the Civic gone. Justin turned sixteen, spent another summer in the park, and started tenth grade, his first year at Rainier Senior High, the building enormous, confusing, full of the smells of bleach and bodies, metallic rings and echoes. Most of his classes had forty students or better. He liked his English teacher, Mrs. Turnbull, a small, stern woman whose voice boomed and rang when she read the Romantic poets. Six weeks in, Justin and a kid he knew from the park were scribbling song lyrics together at the second lunch when they got cornered by some football players. Those guys were so unbelievably big, like cars, houses — they held the two smaller boys to the ground and hacked at the friend's hair with a pocketknife, were about to rip the earrings from Justin's ears when Mrs. Turnbull came around the corner. She was half their size but twice as tough. The football players turned tail and ran. Justin scrambled to his feet and started crying. He was hurt, embarrassed. Mrs. Turnbull put an arm around his shoulders. Instinctively, he shrugged it off, followed his friend down the hallway.

He started skipping school. First just afternoons. Then whole days. No one but Mrs. Turnbull ever said anything.

One evening Justin walked the whole way home from Seward Park — no bus money anymore — and found an eviction notice on the duplex door. His key still worked. There was nothing in the fridge but sour milk, black bananas, some mustard. He found an unopened box of saltines in the corner of a cupboard. He sat at the kitchen table alone, the Formica cold beneath the heels of his hands, and ate a plate of mustard crackers.

Ate another after that.

# 29

For a long time after, Rene thought of that summer as the Bouchard family's last at the ranch, even if it was just the three of them — Rene, Lianne, and Franklin.

Viv and the other boys had stayed in town. Keith was the starting center for the Delphia Broncs, a blue and gold letter jacket always draped across the hanger of his shoulders, and had daily workouts and Friday scrimmages. Dennis was hoping to make varsity as well but spent most of his summer in tutoring sessions so that, come winter, his grades might be good enough for him to be eligible. Viv broke ground for flower beds at the house in Delphia, which she'd never had time for before. She looked over Dennis's studies in the evenings and ferried Keith to his scrimmages. In the afternoons, she had neighbor women over for iced tea on the porch. Rene could see she was enjoying her summer, which hurt a little. They'd had to buy a car for her, an Oldsmobile wagon. If the creek wasn't high, she could get it out to the ranch — but barely. Rene didn't like carrying a note and paid cash with what he got for selling the herd down, but he knew, too, that he had to bank some of that money against Lianne's tuition and the lean winter months. With a smaller herd, they'd make quite a bit less when they sold the lamb crop come fall.

Still, the summer so far had been a good one. With fewer sheep, he and Lianne had more than kept on top of things. They'd even gotten to some work he'd put off. They built a new set of chutes and gates in the corrals and installed a cistern near the artesian well to hold more water through the summer and fall, and with ten square miles of land, there was always fencing to be done.

That morning, Rene and Franklin had driven to the far southwestern edge of the ranch, over the spine of the Gumbo Ridge, the fossil-studded hills that divided the many coulees and draws of Willow Creek from those of Mud Creek. They weren't more than three or four miles from the camp-house, but already the country felt different, the land itself rising toward the Rockies, which you could see in the distance — blue-gray humps like whales breaking the shimmer of the oceanic horizon.

They parked in the sage, and with a bucket of staples, a pair of fencing pliers, a small roll of wire, and a come-along apiece, they walked north. From post to post, they leapfrogged each other, father and son, checking that each of the four strands of barbwire was still stapled down, mending breaks, and sometimes, if an old cedar post was rotting and loose, knocking it the rest of the way out of the ground and leaning it up against the wires as a flag. Later, they'd come through with Old Blue and fill in the gaps with steel posts. Even when you were done for the day, you weren't really done.

The sun arced up and over, beating down. Sagebrush and dry grass scratched at their knees and shins. As best they could, they maneuvered around the sword-leaved yucca and knots of prickly pear cactus. By noon, they were sweat-soaked, grimed with dust. They sat beneath the sharp overhang of a cutbank and spread out lunch — ham sandwiches, sliced radishes, plums. They ate the sandwiches and radishes first, hunched over their meals, then each took a share of plums and lay back against the dirt bank. Rene had wrapped the dark fruit in wet cloth, and the plums still held a hint of coolness. He sucked a stone clean of flesh and spit it into his palm, then wound up and pitched the pit down the length of the coulee. Franklin, sitting below his father, did the same.

They walked on. Rene kept his eye on his youngest son. The boy had given it his all this summer. He didn't have the kind of vision Lianne did — she could see a situation and see all the ways through it or around it.

And though it might yet come, Franklin didn't have the strength and skill with his hands that Rene did. Even despite his limp, it was Rene's genius. It wasn't gracefulness, necessarily, but a wise and expressive strength in the muscles and bones. If it took hands and a strong back, Rene Bouchard could get the job done, was always tough enough. There was some inner reserve in him. Rene hefted his bucket and walked up to Franklin, put his hand to the boy's back as he passed. Franklin, wrestling with the come-along, attempting to mend a break in the second wire, looked up at his father and smiled, the dust on his face cut with rivulets of sweat.

Rene could see the workday was about done for the boy, but unlike Keith, who was prickly even at the best of times, Franklin seldom complained or turned sour. In fact, it was Franklin who'd helped them settle in and kept the days turning gently forward. At dinner, Franklin might get Lianne talking about her studies, which she loved to do, though she left the two of them behind with her confessional poets and Pierre Teilhard de Chardin. Later, at Viv's sunset bench, where they retired most evenings to take in the sky, Franklin would ask Rene for this story or that story or maybe the one about the barn dance in Dutton and old Asa Zaharko's bottle of corn. And as the colors deepened and shifted and finally from east to west darkened down, as mosquitoes lifted from the willows, as nighthawks and bats wheeled above the creek, sipping mosquitoes, they retreated to the camphouse, where by the light of an oil lamp, they played cribbage or read or listened to Rene blow a few tunes on his harmonica. Then they'd dip their toothbrushes in a box of powder and clean up and go to bed.

Behind him now, Franklin cried out.

Rene had gotten in front of the boy by five or six posts. He dropped his bucket and pliers and hustled back the way he'd come — and there was Franklin, in a heap at the bottom of a coulee, his bucket upended and staples strewn everywhere.

The coulee was steep, tight, the bottom a grassless crackle of hard, dry mud. Because of the contortions of the land, Rene had long ago sunk three-quarters of an old pickup bumper in the gumbo mud of spring runoff and strung two fences here. Above, the main fence ran taut straight across the ravine, as if fencing the sky. Below, a makeshift fence curved down and along the coulee bottom, anchored by the rusting corner of the bumper. Rene had already come through here. Franklin should have known, should have crossed up the coulee, where it was easier. It didn't make a goddamn lick of sense to try to scramble down here, especially if you didn't have to. Well, hell, this whole ordeal would slow them down, that was sure.

Rene slid down the incline and knelt by the boy, touched his shoulder, his knee.

—Took a spill, huh? It's tight here. You ought to cross up above next time.

Franklin sucked in a breath, scrunched his eyes against the tears.

—You skinned your arm up pretty good. Anything broken? An arm, a leg? Your backside?

Rene had meant to joke, but Franklin shuddered, rolled nearly onto his belly, lifted his shirt. Christ Jesus. The boy's lower back and hind end were scraped all to hell, blood and dirt and bits of abraded skin. Rene lifted his canteen and tried to wash the dirt and grass from the wound, hoped he didn't see any bone. Franklin cried out at the water's touch. Rene shushed him, rinsed the wound once more, and hitched the boy's jeans down to pick at the spines of prickly pear, Franklin whimpering. He must have skidded through a good bit of cactus and yucca, Rene thought. The wounds were ragged, deep.

—Sorry, kid. That don't feel good. Let's get you up.

He got an arm beneath his son's shoulders and lifted him to his feet. Franklin swallowed a sob but started walking. They made their way up and out of the coulee. Rene told Franklin to wait right there, then went for Old Blue. They drove slowly back the way they'd come.

Near the camphouse, Franklin started crying again, sobbing, and Rene thought it was the ruts in the road, but the boy shook his head. He had just remembered they'd left their fencing buckets in the bottom of the coulee.

—I'm sorry, Dad. I'm so sorry.

Rene shushed him. He helped Franklin out of the pickup and handed him off to Lianne.

He stood there in the dust and sun. He didn't know what to do about this boy. About his boys.

APRIL 1994

# 30

Since he was very young — maybe since that long-ago, unfathomable family trip when the can of Rainier tipped onto the hotel bed and his own small body tipped through the air — Justin had understood that the world was at best unsteady, that the days were no better than rain or wind or whatever fell from the always unforgiving above, and so to make it, to wake and breathe and hope this day for a little music, you had to train yourself to notice the particular colors of the sky, this slant of wind, that pull of tide. The variations, the rules and exigencies. This, for instance, was what you could do when your father was newly absent; this on a Sunday afternoon your mother was hungover. This at the creek, at the park, in the band classroom after school. This with a girl. This with a boy. This in the night. This in the light.

This was Justin's second morning waking at the camphouse.

He stood on the plank porch and blinked against the scraped light. He winged off his flannel, pulled his T-shirt up over his head, held himself, and shivered. Before him, on the ladder-back chair, a tin bucket of hot water steamed. A dull rag hung from the metal lip, a thinning wafer of white soap on the gray wood of the chair. Smoke chuffed from the slender chimney atop the camphouse. The watery calls of birds sounded off in the sage.

The old man had woken him some time ago, in the blue dark, called to him and tied back the curtain that hung over the bedroom doorway. Despite himself, Justin had fallen back asleep. The next time, Mr. Bouchard banged the bottom of a pot with a wooden spoon, said the dog would happily eat his breakfast if he didn't quit wasting daylight. Justin was up and dressed in seconds. Mr. Bouchard handed him a cup of coffee, said he could wash up, then they'd eat. Justin stood there for a time in the front room with his coffee before he realized it wasn't an invitation. Yesterday, Tuesday, the old man had let him sleep past noon, tend to the wounds on his belly, wash all his clothes in the sink — and only then asked him for help in the shed. After dinner, they'd gone straight to bed, Justin already exhausted again. Today, though, there was a different edge to the old man's voice. With a burned-black spatula, Mr. Bouchard had pointed toward the front door.

Justin dipped his two hands into the water and wet his face, his arms up to the elbow, his pits and neck. The heat felt good. It prickled, then loosened his skin. Yesterday had been the first decent wash he'd had in days. And his sleep these past two nights cavernous, unmoving. He could get used to this.

The cool of the morning licked at him as he scrubbed, the lather slick and smelling faintly of milk. He rinsed, the water one notch cooler now, and took in the fading bruises on his arms, the hard, loud scabs that ran along his belly. Gently, he washed the ragged barbwire wounds and patted himself dry with the cloth and hung it across the back of the chair. Mr. Bouchard had told him to pitch the wash water into the small fenced yard along the side of the camphouse, so he did, a bevy of small, yellow-breasted birds scattering at the disturbance. Threads of steam unwound from his face, his hands, and the empty mouth of the bucket. The dry ground gurgled and drank the splash of water.

Back in the camphouse, Justin turned the pail upside down on the counter above the sink, as instructed, and took a seat at the table. O'Malley, the dog, sat on the braided rug by the door, watching his every move.

— We're not exactly what you'd call well provisioned, the old man said, and dropped two tin plates onto the table, a hard-looking biscuit and a slice of some kind of fried meat on each.

Justin knew better than to start in immediately — last night at dinner, the old man hadn't said anything but had given him quite the look — so this morning he waited as Mr. Bouchard lifted the one leg up and over the bench and slowly lowered himself down.

— Just camp biscuits and canned ham, I'm afraid.

The old man reached for his biscuit, and Justin didn't wait for further explanation — he was eating. The meat was hot and salty, the biscuit rich and crumbly. He laid the ham across the biscuit and finished the makeshift sandwich in two bites. Took a bitter slurp of cooling coffee.

The old man was looking at him, his own biscuit halfway to his mouth.

— There's more on the stove.

Justin thanked him and was up filling his plate. He turned to find O'Malley underfoot. The dog cocked his black-and-white head.

— Drop him a little something, if you can spare it, the old man said, and he'll about be your friend forever.

Justin broke off a corner of biscuit and held it out in his palm. O'Malley's nose twitched, the muscles across his ribs shivered. But he held back.

— Go on, O'Malley. It's all right.

At the very instant of the old man's voice, the dog lipped the biscuit from Justin's palm and gave his fingers a thorough licking for good measure. Justin grinned and patted O'Malley's head. He sat down and took another drink of coffee, which didn't taste good, exactly, but seemed like what he ought to do. Mr. Bouchard clearly put store in coffee.

After breakfast, Justin scrubbed his plate and fork and set them in the rack near the sink, then rinsed his coffee cup and set it by the percolator on the stove. He had watched the old man do just the same a moment before.

Now Mr. Bouchard handed him a pair of leather gloves, told him he thought these would fit. He was sorry, he said, but he didn't have a hat for him. Justin could tell this, too, mattered to the old man, like the coffee, and so he tried to assure him it was okay, that he had a ball cap in his backpack but didn't like wearing it, which was the wrong thing to say, as the old man sucked his teeth and looked at him like he was talking nonsense.

They stood a moment on the porch and took in the view. Clouds drifted by, their shadows on the prairie below like great, dark ships moving of their own accord and dignity. And the clatter of the creek, the intricate whistle-songs of birds. He'd have to ask the old man about the birds; he'd like to know the names of those little yellow birds.

—We going to check for baby sheep?

—Already did, Mr. Bouchard said and side-eyed the boy. While you were sleeping. Nothing showing yet. We'll check again after we're done with the hay.

—The hay?

The old man pointed toward the pickup by the shed, the bed loaded with the green rectangles of hay bales.

—We've got to unload that in the corral for the ewes to eat on the next few days.

—Looks like a lot of hay.

—It'll last us a while, anyway. Then we'll do it again.

—Why don't we just feed it from the back of the truck, Justin said, pointing. You know, over the side of the corral there.

Mr. Bouchard turned to the boy. He opened his mouth like he was about to say something. Then flapped his lips shut and tamped his cowboy hat that much farther down on his head. Justin rounded his shoulders beneath that gaze. He wasn't sure what had him talking so much. Most of the time he was quieter, more careful. But it had him off balance—warm water and meals and sleep and most of all the wonder of lambs, the feel yet in his hands of their birth-wet skins, their slender bones. And the whole time this old man treating him like, well—what had Mrs. Gribskov always called him? A fine boy?—like a fine boy and not some stray dog. People were always either too tender with him, as if he were about to break into fucking pieces, or, like his uncle, too hard, pushing him even that much farther down, his belly dragging on the ground. Mr. Bouchard pulled his gloves from his back pocket and started across the dirt road, that one leg of his hitching as he went. Justin followed close behind.

It didn't take the two of them long to unload the hay, though after a time the old man leaned against the side of the pickup and mopped at his forehead with a handkerchief. The scratches on Justin's stomach pulled and burned when he twisted, but he kept at it. He was still as skinny as ever but had built strong, ropy muscles across the winter hauling slash and loading wood in the mountains. He liked the pendulous weight of the bales, the way he could swing a bale by the twine from up in the pickup bed and toss it just so onto the stack below. He lifted and swung, lifted and swung, and sweat stung his eyes, salted his lips. Little bits of hay dusted his mouth, his face and neck.

Once they were unloaded, Mr. Bouchard showed him how to cut the twine — the tight strings giving way with a thwack, the dry must of alfalfa rising — and flake the hay around the perimeter of the feeder. Three more bales like that, the old man said, so Justin unsheathed his own knife and went to work. The sheep crowded in and tore at the hay. Mr. Bouchard gathered the lengths of cut twine and looped them around a corral post already draped in faded, weathered twine.

— You never know when you might need some twine, the old man said, as if etching one of the commandments.

Mr. Bouchard pulled Old Blue out of the corral, and Justin closed the gate behind him. From his station just outside the corrals, O'Malley hopped up onto the tailgate. Justin joined him, his sneakered feet swinging above the dry ground. The old man drove the pickup around the corrals and backed up to a green haystack maybe two stories tall, the face of it stepped like a pyramid. Justin had the urge to climb and even started up the first few stairs of hay but thought better of it as he heard the pickup door slam.

Mr. Bouchard came around and explained how to load the pickup: a line of horizontal bales down the middle, then two layers winged over the sides, then another single horizontal line across the top, and a bale or two on the tailgate for good measure. The old man pulled off his gloves and stuffed them into his back pocket.

— You know how to drive stick?

Mr. Bouchard wasn't that much taller than him, and they stood side by side, staring into the empty pickup bed, imagining it filled with neat rows of bales.

— My uncle taught me.

— Uncle?

Justin hadn't even thought. He'd been focused on the work, had told the truth before he meant to, and suddenly felt Heck's hands grip the backs of his arms, saw Heck shudder and fall in the camper doorway. Justin's heart scrabbled in his chest, his leg bones itching to move, to go, to get the hell away from there, from here, from his own stupid fucking sorrowful self.

Mr. Bouchard touched his shoulder. That hand steady, sure, then gone.

—You likely got a reason you're out here. You don't have to tell me nothing you don't want to. I just need to know you won't strip the gears in my pickup.

He fished the keys from his front pocket and held them out.

—Once you're finished loading, drive it on over to where I had it parked this morning. Old Blue's a bit cantankerous—watch the clutch between low and first—but she'll get you there.

—Where are you going?

—I'll take another pass through the sheep. Then I've got to see to the horses.

—You've got horses?

—Two of them. Come on out back of the shed when you're done. I'll introduce you.

The old man's eyes were the blue-gray of sage, and when he looked at you, he really looked at you. He was paying attention, was here and nowhere else. Jesus. Jesus fucking Christ.

Justin slowly reached out and took the keys. The old man told the dog to stay and started back toward the shed, one hand on the corral boards as he went.

—We were logging, Justin called after him. Sometimes we'd need two trucks, one to haul the saws and tools and one to load with camp wood. My uncle would drive the Silverado. I'd follow in the Datsun.

Mr. Bouchard nodded and looked toward the hills for a moment, as if measuring the distance between here and there. Then back at Justin.

—Logging's hard work. And those Datsuns are sons of bitches. You ought to be able to handle a Ford just fine.

The old man limped away. They watched him go, the boy and the dog. Now O'Malley turned his attention fully to Justin, cocked his head one way, then the other, and trotted over and sat down nearly on Justin's feet, leaning into Justin's legs. Justin pocketed the keys and scratched around the dog's ears. He wasn't sure at all what was happening here, in this clear light, in this raw wind, but at least he knew and welcomed what he was supposed to do. He stepped to the haystack, wrapped his fingers around the twine of a bale, and heaved it into the pickup. Turned, reached for another.

# 31

LIANNE LET HERSELF INTO the school before sunrise. No lights on in the foyer or the office. The soda machine by the glassed-in trophy case hummed. The janitor angled a push broom around the corner. She'd always relished early mornings, and after the boys showed up, those predawn hours were often the only ones she could make wholly her own. The quiet and near-dark a treasure, the stillness a vast space she could fill with her own plans and imaginings.

In the library, she opened the blinds as the sky off to the east began to glow, then unpacked her thermos and water bottle. She poured herself a tumbler of coffee and sipped. She'd given herself over to school yesterday, her second day here — morning classes, then reshelving a couple of weeks' worth of books and catching up on the previous teacher's grading — but now an image of Ves at dinner Monday night came to mind. Ves leaning back in his chair and laughing; Ves running a hand through his shaggy hair. It wasn't that any single sadness or doubt from the past weeks and months was diminished but that she could now place them next to something new: these last two days in the classroom, the evening with Ves. She could line these feelings all up like intricate figurines on a shelf arranged to catch just the right slant of light. Lianne took a swallow of coffee and turned back to her desk.

—Knock-knock. Hello?

A woman stood in the library doorway, presumably another teacher based on the fact that she'd paired a sweater and knee-length skirt with very comfortable-looking white sneakers. Her skirt set off her waist; her long wavy black hair was pulled back at the nape of her neck. It was clear as could be the woman wasn't from Delphia. She just didn't have the look of a local.

Lianne came around the front of her desk.

—Hi. Lianne Bouchard. They've roped me into doing a little teaching while I'm back.

—I heard. Gillian Kincheloe. Earth science and biology. I hope the kids have been okay for you?

—Oh, they've been great. There were a couple of eighth-grade boys who would've liked to put on a show the first day, but I think I have them corralled now.

—I bet I know just the boys, Gillian said, smiling. I was going to ask if you needed any help, but it sounds like you know what you're doing.

Gillian was strikingly pretty. She must have married that Kincheloe boy. What was his name? He was younger than Lianne, but like few Delphia kids did, he, too, had gone off to college, to the University of Montana even. She remembered a phone call with her father, Rene telling her to look for the Kincheloe boy on campus, Rene not understanding how many thousands of young men and women traipsed across the quads every day. Lianne didn't tell Rene—likely she said sure, you bet, she'd look for him—but her first thought was she'd never see him. She never had.

But now he was married and back in Delphia. What had brought him back, brought this woman back with him—what force pulled or pushed, what wind shut the other doors?

Gillian mentioned that some of the teachers were getting together for drinks down at the bar Saturday evening if Lianne wanted to join them.

The light was sharp now, flaring at the windows, and Gillian went on.

—And I'm sorry about your mom. I didn't know her. But my husband did, Kevin. He thought a lot of her, thinks a lot of your dad too. I guess Kevin was friends with your brother back in high school.

Lianne was pummeled by them again, as she hadn't been over the past two days, the heart-crushing quakes and tremors of grief, but she managed a nod and a quick thank-you.

Gillian took her leave. And it wasn't until later, the end of second period, the students gathering their things, that the stories and years finally aligned, that Lianne realized Gillian hadn't meant Keith or Dennis when she'd said *brother.* She'd meant Franklin.

# 32

RENE JUGGED UP ANOTHER set of twins and a ewe with a single. He made his notes in the lambing book, then paint-branded the ewes and lambs with dark green wool paint. He held off on the runt, though, who shivered at the back of the jug. That runt might end up a bum lamb, one they'd have to take away from his mother and bottle-feed. Had to wait and see.

He filled a bucket with oats, hiked out into the west pasture, and called for the horses. After a time, they high-stepped and shied over the hill. He talked to them, ran his hands along their jaws and necks. They rippled and tensed. The boy was pulling Old Blue around now. The horses bumped at him, wanting the oats.

—Easy, now. Don't get greedy.

Justin came up the hill, that hair of his blown every which way in the wind, the flaps of his shirttail, too, and stopped well short of the horses. Rene lifted the bucket.

—They aren't going to keep out of these oats for long. Come on and take this pail.

The boy did as he was told and held the wide-mouthed bucket in his two hands. Big Red and Nine Spot lipped at the oats in turn, and the boy looked somewhere between tickled and terrified. Rene nearly chuckled but caught himself. He knew that wasn't the kind of thing you did with a boy this age. No, they took things seriously. Themselves most of all.

—Go on, he said as Nine Spot finished. You can stroke her nose if you want. She likes that.

Justin did, just barely grazing his fingers along the horse's great long snout, and now it was the boy who was laughing, a sound like creek water running clear at the edges.

They passed through the sheep once more and headed into the camp-house for lunch. If it was just him, Rene wouldn't have thought on it, but the fact that he couldn't scrounge up much more than cold coffee, a quick tuna salad, and saltines had Rene wondering when he could get into town. There was Lianne to think of, though as it was, he expected her out here in the next couple of days, wagging her finger and trying to drag him back. No, the most of it was Justin. Rene didn't know if he could just leave him off in Delphia like he'd said he would. Didn't want to think of him, those earrings in his ears, that long straw-colored hair, standing off the highway at the edge of town, there in the verge weeds, deer bones, and beer cans. He could just about imagine who might stop. What might happen.

Twice he'd had to go after Franklin. The first time, Franklin had gotten halfway to Harlowton, had holed up in the old gym in Shawmut. He reeked of booze and stumbled as Rene led him out to the truck, was stomach-sick on the drive home. But afterward, Franklin talked with Viv and Rene, told them the story. He'd stayed a night in Roundup with that girl he knew from the FFA, and she'd driven him to Ryegate, where her older cousin had a place of her own—that much Rene had already figured—then he'd planned to hitchhike west. That night, though, the cousin threw a party. Things went off the rails almost immediately, joints and pills and some girl screaming in the kitchen, a boy methodically putting his fist through every window. Unsure what to do, Franklin walked down the night highway on his own. Made it to Shawmut, where he passed out on a wrestling mat in the gym in the abandoned schoolhouse, which was where Rene had found him. They knew it could have been worse. A boy like Franklin out there all alone. They thought that they'd gotten lucky, that the worst was behind them.

Six months later, the hard winter not yet giving way, Franklin ran again. Rene wouldn't have found him the second time except for a call from a work friend of Dennis's who'd heard that the Yellowstone County Sheriff's Office had picked up a kid on the south side of Billings without ID, a kid in bad shape. Franklin's ears and fingers were frostbit, and he'd been worked over, lots of bruises, two cracked ribs, a tooth through his lower lip. And everything stolen—pack, wallet, shoes. He wouldn't say what else. Wouldn't talk at all on the trip home. Rene mixed the pineapple into the tuna and tried to think how many more words he'd ever exchanged with his youngest son. Just a handful. Goddamn.

Rene plopped a spoonful of tuna on top of O'Malley's bowl of kibble and set it on the ground, then ferried the rest to the table.

—You don't have to drink that coffee if you don't want to, he said, watching the boy sip and grimace. Probably best you don't. I've done made a habit of it.

Rene spooned tuna onto his own plate and slid the bowl toward Justin. He rustled some crackers from the plastic sleeve and slid those toward the boy as well.

—Here you are. Eat it up if you can.

—Thanks, Justin said, and shoveled a tuna-topped cracker into his mouth. I like pineapple.

—I didn't used to have a taste for it. But my kids liked it, so I always made sure I had plenty out here.

—How many kids you got?

—We had four, me and Viv. Oldest was a girl, then three boys.

—That's why you got all those bunkbeds. Did they help you out here? Like I am?

—They did.

—That must have been nice. Four kids would be a lot of help, huh?

—Well, they were all different ages, so they helped with different things, but yes, it was nice. It was some of my favorite times, summers all of us were out here working together.

Justin smiled as if he, too, remembered those very times, then stuffed a cracker into his mouth and spoke through the crumbs.

—We lived in a trailer park once, and there was a creek there. I liked that creek. Rainier Beach was good. It wasn't an actual beach, just a neighborhood, but I liked my middle school, and our duplex was real nice. I had my own room. So did my mom.

Justin wiped at the corners of his lips, looked out the big window a moment.

—I guess those are my favorite times.

Rene thought of all the hard, sad, bad-wrong stories Justin likely had to tell. He was skinny enough to be on the wrong side of starving. He had scabbed cuts on his belly, a wash of long-ago cigarette burns on the inside of his left arm. And he slept with that knife of his under his pillow. You don't do a thing like that unless you need to. No, there's a whole world of folks who don't know about knives under pillows. Even saying the word *uncle* earlier had sent him into the shadows for a time. And still, the boy hadn't told those stories. He'd followed suit and started with his favorite times. It was enough to make Rene feel ashamed. Here was this kid at the end of any kind of rope—and still holding on. He had a thin, sharp face, but his grin was a boy's lopsided grin. And the way it lit his eyes. The cracker crumbs on his lips and chin.

—What say we save the dishes for later? Rene said, setting his plate in the sink. It's about time we check on those sheep.

# 33

THEY FOUND THE EWE in the corral, a yearling, up on her feet and chewing stems at the feeder. She worked at the old hay with quick, hard grinds of her jaw and blatted and knocked the top of her head against the feeder. Most of the other sheep had shifted away from her.

In the corral shadows, the old man and the boy came around slow and wide.

Two tiny hooves poked out of the yearling's backside, and a long glistening membrane hung from her, the end of it dragging in the dirt, a calligraphy of blood in the corral dust.

— Hell, Mr. Bouchard said under his breath. Hell and goddamn.

— What's wrong?

— She's not doing what she ought to be doing. Ought to be pushing.

— What do we do?

— That is a good goddamn question.

Of a sudden, the ewe hunched and made a long ragged sound, eyes going wide and wild, the depth of the pain clear, though after it passed, she went right back to chewing stems. The old man had slipped away and came back now with his sleeves rolled up, again that white splash of skin, and carrying a long-handled tool of some sort, a tight metal hook on one end.

— What's that?

— Even if we come up gentle-like, she's going to run. And if she gets to running, we'll lose that lamb. This here's a shepherd's crook. I'm going to catch her back leg with this to hold her, and quick as you can, you grab her and bring her down on her side. Then keep her down. Like you did the other night. You ready?

A low wind raked across the ground, skirling dust. Warm afternoon light hummed on the corral boards, on Justin's jaw and shoulders. He'd do just like Mr. Bouchard said — and then there'd be lambs. All these lambs, he thought. Wow. Holy shit. Lambs.

— Ready.

The old man took a couple of slow steps toward the feeder, then slashed out with the crook and hooked the ewe high on the leg. She reared back and smacked her head against the feeder and kept on bucking, but the old man had her. He lifted the crook so that her back legs were nearly off the ground, and Justin charged over. He wrapped his arms around the ewe's neck, slid a hand over and around, grabbing at the nubbly wool, and flipped the ewe off her feet. She fell hard, harder than he'd hoped, but Mr. Bouchard was at the sheep's backside, reaching in.

The ewe writhed and kicked. Justin fell across her to pin her down. He grabbed one back leg, then the other, so the old man wouldn't catch a hoof. He felt his heart beating against the hot heave of sheep, the sheep's heart beating back. The old man swore as he worked, the shadow of his cowboy hat falling across the three of them. Justin couldn't make out much of what was happening, had to crane his neck to watch, but it didn't look like it was going nearly so easily as it had the times before. Little bits of hay and dust whirled. Justin spit the grit from his tongue.

Now the old man was up. He had something in his hands.

— Hang on, kid. Don't let her up. We're going to have to wrestle this one into the jug.

Mr. Bouchard shuffled off, and the ewe bucked hard beneath Justin. He held her there, a dark, wild line of eye visible when she lifted her head. She nosed the air. Her lips peeled back from her square teeth. Justin began to talk to her. He told her he knew she was scared, that it must be scary, but it'd be fine, that there'd be food and water, and the old man would take care of her and the lamb, and that's what was in the old man's hands, her lamb.

Mr. Bouchard put a hand to the boy's shoulder, and Justin slowly let the ewe up but kept ahold of her middle. The old man looped a lariat rope around her neck, and together they steered her — rearing and bucking the whole way — toward the shed and into the jug, her ribbed, yellow lamb curled in the corner.

Mr. Bouchard latched the jug door and leaned against it.

— Goddamn, he breathed.

Justin slicked the mess of his hair back with his own sweat. Dust and hay and what-all covered his hands. Streaks of dirt and maybe shit and blood on his face, which he wiped now with the tail of his shirt. He couldn't help but smile. That little sheep was in there with its mama.

— That was fucking crazy, he said, grinning at the old man, but we did it. We fucking did it, huh?

Mr. Bouchard wiped his own face with a red handkerchief. Beneath his cowboy hat, those blue-silver eyes of his were shadowed, tired.

— You did good work, kid. That's sure. But we'll have to see about this one.

As if on cue, the ewe butted the jug door and made a dry, strangled sound in the back of her throat.

— She's got to clean that lamb, got to feed it. We'll give her some time, but if she hasn't mothered it in a couple of hours, we'll have to bum it.

— What does that mean?

— Means we'll jug the lamb up on its own and put a heat lamp over it and feed it formula ourselves off a pop bottle with a rubber nipple. It'd be a bum lamb, then. One without a mother.

— But it's got a mother.

— It don't if its mother won't mother it.

The old man lowered a pail of water into the jug. The ewe plunged her nose in and drank. She lifted her head and blatted once more, water running from her haired jaws. Justin was suddenly all kinds of pissed off.

After all that, she wasn't even going to mother her own lamb?

In the other jugs, new lambs were prancing and kicking, nursing furiously, their long tails shaking and dancing. Justin gripped the wood rail.

—That fucking sucks.

—Doesn't happen often. And most of the bum lambs make it, even if they tend toward scrawny.

—Still sucks.

—I know.

They washed up and fed and watered the other ewes and lambs. To his chest, Justin held the lambs from this morning—the loose, delicate warmth of them, that rich, fleshy smell. Mr. Bouchard paint-branded each one, and the ewes as well.

Once they were done, Justin checked the far jug once more. He silently willed the young ewe to do what she ought. Go on, he told her, it's what you're supposed to do, it's not even that hard. The old man came up beside him. He was rolling his shirtsleeves back down and buttoning the cuffs. He put a hand to the boy's shoulder, and beneath Justin's anger at the ewe, his wish that she'd mother that lamb, with the other part of him, the part that worked always underneath, reckoning and readying, he was tallying every touch. The first when Mr. Bouchard handed him the penlight in the shed. A few accidental brushings at the table, doing dishes, unloading hay. Then this morning, the old man had squeezed his shoulder before he handed him the truck keys. And now here in the shadow, straw, and banded light of the shed, he'd done the same.

That wide hand. The strength of it. The coolness.

Justin moved back through the moments, slowly, carefully, and yes, it was true—not a one of them had made him uneasy. As so many others had. As his uncle's touch always had.

The ewe turned once more, banging against the boards, but then dropped her head and nosed the lamb.

—That ain't a bad sign, the old man said, lifting his hand from Justin's shoulder and turning to leave the shed. Ain't a bad sign at all.

They strode the length of the empty shed, the yearling blatting once, twice. Justin looked back each time, hoping.

Mr. Bouchard kicked at the sparse straw on the shed floor.

—We'll need to spread new straw soon.

Justin swallowed. Despite how much he'd slept the past two nights, he was suddenly exhausted.

—Do we do that now? he asked.

The old man pulled his hat from his head and rubbed at his eyes, scratched at the stubble on his cheeks and jaw.

—No, we'll likely be up tonight with more lambs. We got to reserve our strength. I believe it's about nap time now.

—Serious?

—Yep.

Justin couldn't help but grin. As tired as he'd been a moment ago, the news that he could do what he wanted to do—lie down on that bed and close his eyes—had him wide awake again. He hoped he could even fall asleep.

—Shit, wow. How long does lambing last? I didn't know this was a thing people did. Did your kids like lambing? Lambing. It's something, huh? Wow.

# 34

LIANNE FINISHED WITH THE bed on the left side of the walk and started on
the right, working her way down, digging out thistle and lamb's-quarter,
turning the soil. The sky brimmed with soft afternoon light, and she
stabbed the spade into the dirt to crack the crust, picked at threads of crabgrass running this way and that. She worked for a time without thought,
falling into a rhythm. The warmth of the afternoon carried whispers of an
early summer. Lianne wiped at the sweat on her forehead.

Her third day of teaching had gone mostly well. After talking with
Gillian Kincheloe, she'd unearthed some grade-level lesson plans, so
Lianne collected the students' essays — nearly all the kids turned them
in; Amy Munroe had titled hers "All Apologies" and included an epi-
graph from the Nirvana song — then got the seventh-graders started on
common Latin roots, the eighth-graders on choosing a research topic,
and the ninth-graders on poetry. She'd been both relieved and a little sad
that she'd found the plans, as she felt obligated to stick to them, but seeing that the ninth-graders were set to begin a unit on reading and writing
poetry had more than made up for it. She had them do word associa-
tion first — what do you think of when you hear the word *poetry*? — and
then they read Robert Frost's "Nothing Gold Can Stay" together and
talked about how the poem matched or shifted their notions. Then, for

homework, they were to read the poem aloud to a parent or grandparent, have a conversation about it, and report back. The lesson plans called for the poems in the textbook — Poe, Robinson, Frost — but Lianne had other ideas. Levine, for sure. And she had James Wright's *Collected Poems* and some Mary Oliver in her suitcase as well. She dug at round-leaf weeds and stickers and wished she'd brought even more books with her. For a moment she thought she might have Marty mail her some, but that would mean she'd have to tell Marty she'd taken this sub job. The past few nights she'd been avoiding Marty altogether, calling right when she knew he'd be getting dinner ready and talking only with the boys. And just the thought of Marty squatted down in front of her shelves, thumbing through all the thin volumes — Laux, Soto, Wrigley — made her laugh out loud.

—What's so funny?

Lianne started. Mariah White Bear was crouched at the other end of the flower bed, a broad spoon in her hand, her long hair falling across her face as she scratched at the earth.

—Oh, I was just, well...

Mariah pointed her spoon at Lianne.

—My grandmother used to say a woman laughing by herself is laughing at a man.

—Your grandmother was a wise woman.

Mariah grinned. Went back to digging at a dandelion.

—They got you teaching up at the school now.

—They needed someone for a couple of English classes. That's what I teach in Spokane.

—You got my Randy. He's a seventh-grader.

Lianne mentally scanned the faces in her first period. None quite matched.

—He looks like his dad, has got his dad's last name. Randy Lang.

—Oh, right. Randy. And now Lianne saw him, close-cropped hair, slim-shouldered but thick in the chest and through the hips. He hadn't said a thing in class. She hadn't read any of the students' essays yet either. Lianne took a chance.

—He seems like a sweet boy.

Mariah, a hard hunk of dirt in her spoon, looked up. From the way her brow tightened and her lips thinned, Lianne thought the woman might very well catapult the clod at her.

—Don't let him fool you.

Lianne started to say something about how kids are always toughest on their parents, but Mariah cut her off.

—I'm serious. Keep on him. Don't let him start making trouble.

Mariah turned the spoon over and crushed the clod with the heel of her hand, went back to digging. Lianne felt like she'd done something wrong. She tried once more.

—Thanks for the help. I'm glad you knew my mother.

Mariah sat back in the grass, crossed her arms over her knees. When they first moved to Delphia, she explained, they hadn't known anybody. Dan worked road construction and was gone weeks on end. It was lonely. Viv had brought over cookies and muffins and things. Had been about the only person Mariah talked to for a time. Spoon chipping again at the earth, her face hidden by that curtain of black hair, Mariah hauled in a breath and finished in a rush.

—And after Moses…after my Moses killed himself, it was even worse.

The weight of the entire sky settled then, all those tons of blue. Lianne felt pushed to the ground, pinned, suffocated. Shit. She hadn't signed up for this. What was this?

—Oh God. I am so, so sorry.

Mariah hauled in a trembling breath and tucked a length of hair behind her ear.

—Moses could be sweet but was always in trouble. Seventh grade, he stole a car. Everyone leaves their keys in their cars around here. Down at the café, he just got in one and drove away. Got in a wreck out of Laurel, on the interstate. A bad wreck. They sent him to Landers, that juvenile center in Miles City. There was a whole bunch of months we couldn't see him. Then no phone calls for some kind of punishment. That's when he did it. We didn't even know until a couple of days after.

A wind turned in the trees; the cottonwood leaves winked silver-green, silver-green. Mariah lifted her hands to her lips, her eyes.

—After it got around—a town like this, things get around—the only people I ever heard kind words from were a couple of the teachers up at school and your mom.

Mariah's confession swirled and eddied, the smells of dirt and green weeds between them, and Lianne heard *Moses* but kept seeing in her mind's eye her brother Franklin. Lianne had tried to talk about it with Viv once. She'd been pregnant with Trent then, had come home alone for a long weekend. She and Viv were driving out to the ranch to see Rene—an early lambing season—and Lianne asked her mother about those last years, both Keith and Dennis out of the house by then and only Franklin at home. Then Franklin running once, twice, and all of it leading—inexorably, without nuance, grace, or mercy, every single one of their lives bending toward that one moment—to Franklin propping a rifle beneath his chin.

That day, Viv drove the Oldsmobile slow down the known dirt roads, dust lifting in great billowing clouds behind them, and Lianne turned to her mother and asked—and Viv shook her head. She looked at her pregnant daughter, mouth a thin line, and shook her head.

Had Viv spoken about Franklin, about what happened, with this woman?

Against the ache in her chest, Lianne sucked in a breath and willed herself not to be angry, jealous. We need to speak. To someone. Anyone. She was a teacher; she knew this. Silence might feel easier, but it wasn't. Not in the long run.

—Tell me, Lianne said, about Moses. What was he like?

—Loud, Mariah said, and laughed. You could hear him a mile away. One summer, your mom hired him to mow the grass. She'd sit on the porch and drink iced tea and watch him work. She told me later she could hear him even over the lawn mower, that he talked the whole time.

Lianne thought to ask another question, but Mariah beat her to it.

—I got cousins over on the Coeur d'Alene Reservation. One of them works in Spokane. You like Spokane?

The question felt somehow out of bounds. Lianne wasn't in Spokane. She was right here, in Delphia, six hundred miles away.

—My husband's there, with the boys, she said. We've got two boys.

Lianne dropped her spade and ran her shirtsleeve over her face.

—I'm sorry, she said. I don't know why I'm the one crying.

Mariah started to say something, but Lianne cut her off.

—God, I'm sorry. I think I need to go in.

Lianne stumbled up the walk and slammed the door behind her. One of the framed photos crashed to the floor. She breathed and wiped at her eyes and picked it up. It was the one of her curled on the chair. The glass had cracked in one corner, but the frame, cedarwood held together with staples, seemed fine.

Rene must have built the frame, all these frames. But when? Before, after? Why hadn't they ever talked with one another? Any of them? All of them. All this distance, this damnable silence.

# BEFORE

# 35

DURING THE WINTER OF her second year at the university, Lianne took the train home once more. The tracks sliced the white glaze of ice and snow, and she emptied her thermos of coffee as the hours unfolded and evening darkened into night.

The train station in Delphia had closed that fall, so she had to get off at the next closest stop, up the valley in Roundup. A single streetlight sizzled and snapped above the platform. Lianne was the only disembarking passenger.

— Pockets, Rene said, stepping from the shadows.

— Dad, she said, smiling, putting her arms around him.

The train moved down the track, revealing the valley on the other side of the berm. The river was scalloped with ice and somehow brighter for it, fuller than it ever was.

— We keep talking out here, Rene said, we'll freeze. Let's get loaded up.

Rene lifted her suitcase into the bed of Old Blue and cranked the heater. They shivered and held their hands over the vents.

— Just you? Lianne asked.

— Yeah, Keith and Dennis got a ball game tomorrow. Need their sleep. And your mother had a date with some ladies this evening. Wasn't back by the time I left.

— What about Franklin?

Growing up, Franklin was always too little to be a conspirator or adversary, like Keith, or even a hanger-on, like Dennis, but after working together out at the ranch the summer before, Lianne and Franklin had started trading letters. She often inquired, like she thought she was supposed to, about his classes and friends and girls and basketball — all the usual concerns of a boy growing up in Delphia — but Franklin never much mentioned any of that. Mostly, he asked about her or wrote about books and music and his newest passion, photography.

— Had a hard day at school, Rene said, grinding the cold gears. Said he wanted some time alone.

— He's like you that way, Lianne offered.

Rene cocked his head at her but said nothing. He pulled out of the lot and turned onto the dark highway. Another forty minutes — they'd likely catch the train headed the same way, though it didn't stop in Delphia anymore and wouldn't ever again — and they'd be home.

That holiday, the Bouchard family did all the things you were supposed to do. They cheered and stomped on the bleachers when Keith made the winning bucket. They swept a bend of frozen river clean, strapped on skates, and slipped and slid and sometimes even glided across the bumpy blue ice. On Christmas Eve day, they slept late, even Rene, and ate fried eggs and waffles at noon. Viv baked trout, a rare treat, for supper. That evening, they strung the tree — an airy, long-needled pine Rene had cut down in the Bull Mountains — with garlands and paper chains and lights. They lit candles and sat in the front room and told stories. Keith stretched out on the floor. Lianne made Dennis rub her feet on the couch. Viv delivered bowls of buttered popcorn and mugs of hot chocolate, and she didn't even cluck at Rene when he topped his up with a bite of brandy.

There in the candlelight, it seemed to Lianne like they'd come through something, like they were once again as they had been when she was a girl and they'd spent their summers together out at the ranch — like they were well and whole. Viv had taken Dennis to a specialist in Billings, and he'd been diagnosed with dyslexia, which he could get help for now. Even if they weren't close, Rene and Keith weren't so stiff around each other. And Lianne felt as if she'd finally been freed of her parents' undue expectations—she was her own woman now, a university student charting her own course.

Rene slapped his knee in punctuation to whatever story he was telling, and Lianne smiled and sipped her cocoa—and in that moment noticed Franklin in the shadows. Franklin circling the perimeter of them.

Skinny and unassuming, his wavy hair nearly the black shade of shadow, he held his camera this way and now this way, the shutter clicking, the film whirring, always his camera between him and his family—Lianne couldn't even see his face. The flash popped, and in the quick burst of light, the sudden reclamation of shadow, Franklin disappeared into the kitchen.

Lianne sat up. She'd started to think of herself as close to Franklin, as maybe the person in the family closest to him. Franklin had gone skating with them, right? Was he at Keith and Dennis's game the other night? Had he driven out into the Bulls with Rene to get the tree? On her way home, the train cutting through the mountains, Lianne had it in mind that after trading letters, she and her littlest brother would surely spend time together, surely listen to records or talk books. But they hadn't yet. Not once.

Dennis had finished his popcorn and reached now for Franklin's. Franklin's mug of hot chocolate sat on the end table, the dollop of whipped cream melting away. Lianne slid the blanket off and started to go after her youngest brother, but Keith grabbed her ankle, told her she'd want to hear this story about last Halloween, about how old man Franzel moved his outhouse forward a few feet and when the Benson boys went to tip it over, they fell right into the old hole.

# 36

SOMEHOW, JUSTIN'S MOTHER FOUND him.

It was early October, a couple of weeks since his key had quit working at the duplex. He'd been going to school off and on, hooking hot lunch when he could, but mostly living in the park, busking for meals, cigarettes. But then a few hard days of rain dried up the foot traffic. Hungry, Justin followed what passed for a friend to where a trail led into the jungle camp beneath I-5.

Traffic shook the concrete pilings. The wind tore at their hair, the holes in their jeans and flannels. The night slid down like ink and stained their faces.

They descended.

Tents, tarps, flattened boxes. Rope strung here and there. Fires, drifts of trash. Men, women, even people so old it was hard to tell if they were men or women. His friend pulled him along a trail that cut through blackberry and vine maple, through a brittle hedge of salal — and now someone played a guitar, a song Justin recognized. They settled themselves down in a rough circle of boys their age. A broken, smoking lightbulb went around. As if it were a talisman, a chalice, each person held the lightbulb with great care and concentration. A girl even skinnier than Justin kept asking for a hit, beat on one boy's back, then another's, the next. Finally, one turned and held the white glass to her lips. She leaned in and breathed deep and lay back after, off in the shadows, the smoke slipping from her in a tremendous disembodied cloud.

Like his friend, Justin put his lips to the thin, grooved metal of the lightbulb pipe.

It was true, he wasn't so hungry anymore. He was instead filled with moth wings and electricity. He couldn't make sense of what he was seeing, what he was hearing — the boys one by one rising and moving in the direction of the writhing girl, traffic drumming ceaselessly above.

His head hissed like a balloon.

His friend had fallen over. Justin took him by the shoulders, shook him until his teeth clacked. The friend focused a moment, the whites of his eyes somehow the biggest thing about him. Then went slack.

Justin staggered away.

He wandered from camp to camp. He picked up half-full bottles of whatever and sniffed and drank. Licked the last of a greasy scatter of hash-browns from a Styrofoam takeout container. He talked for a long time with a boy who had a cleft palate, his upper lip a hard, scarred V. At some point, he stepped in shit. He soaked his sneaker in a puddle and dragged it through weeds to clean it. He broke, finally, from the jungle camp — as if surfacing from the deepest part of the lake — and reeled down the white line of the highway.

In the wet, hazed light of morning, Justin prowled the empty park. He thrashed through scrub trees and, in the bowl of rock and cedar where he'd stashed his guitar and pack, crumpled into sleep.

Woke some span of hours later hollowed out. As if with a knife.

At the lake's edge, Justin stripped and dunked his head. Worked the knots from his hair, scrubbed his pits and cock and ass and feet with sand. He soaked one set of clothes — T-shirt, flannel, socks, and underwear — and beat them against a rock, then hung them on a branch. He'd have cleaned his jeans, but he had only the one pair and didn't want to be without as long as it would take for them to dry. He watched the sun shift and break on lake waves. He stood there cold and naked and itching, the whole of him an itch he couldn't scratch hard enough. The sun not even down, he slept deep and still in the trees at the water's edge, the duff beneath him soft, offering back some portion of his heat.

The next day, he woke early and felt better and hustled to claim a good spot along the walking trail, near where there was a view of Mount Rainier. He played the better part of the day, slipping away only once for something to eat at the 7-Eleven when there wasn't much foot traffic so as not to lose his busking spot. Near dark, he packed up and headed toward the Subway.

Waiting to cross Rainier Avenue, he saw her — his mother. She was on the other side of the street. She gave a small wave.

The light changed. Leaves and shadows swirled in the gutter.

Justin's first thought was to run. He didn't. He crossed Rainier. He stepped from that life into another, into this one, and embraced her. She was still a few inches taller than he was, though just as skinny. He didn't know which one of them smelled better, worse. Maybe about the same.

They ordered three foot-long subs — meatball, tuna, and ham and turkey — along with chips and cookies and large drinks. They both ate and ate. When Justin asked, she said she'd been looking for him for a while, said she knew he hung out at the park. She was staying at Rick's place. Rick was away. Justin asked, with Rick gone, if he could stay with her. She pushed the last big cookie across the table to him — a snickerdoodle — and shook her head.

— He'll be back, J. No telling when.

They walked up Rainier to the Fred Meyer, where his mother bought him two pairs of jeans, a pack of T-shirts, some underwear and socks. A new pair of Chucks. He picked out a couple of flannels as well, and she loaded the cart with food that wouldn't spoil — granola bars and beef jerky, Pop-Tarts, crackers. The checkbook she was using didn't have her name on it.

In the parking lot, she showed him where he could catch just one city bus all the way to the Greyhound station downtown. She'd talked to her brother, she said, his uncle Heck, who was back from the Gulf War and living up in the mountains in Montana. If Justin would help out around the place — her brother was a logger, had his own equipment — Heck and his wife would give him a camper to live in and make sure he was fed. He could even go to school in one of the nearby towns.

What did he think? Small towns were safer. People were nicer. He'd grow big and strong working in the mountains. Wouldn't be so skinny anymore. *Right?* she asked, and kept asking. *Right? Right?*

She had a picture of Heck — stocky, short-legged, just another man in dark glasses leaning against a pickup — and wrote his number on the back, then pulled five twenties and a wad of smaller bills from her pocket, closed his hand around the cash. Touched his hair, his cheek.

He didn't understand. If it was so good in the mountains, in a small town, why couldn't they both go? Together? Right now? With all this stuff they'd bought? All this food? He had some money, too, he said, and dug furiously in his jeans, showed her what he'd made busking, all the crumpled singles and heavy quarters. It was enough, probably, for two tickets.

— Let's go, he said, and took his mother's hand. Please?

But she straightened up and looked out over the parking lot and down the road. She was already a long ways away.

# APRIL 1994

# 37

SLATS OF LIGHT FELL from chinkholes in the weathered boards. A yellow-ish gap shone between the overhanging roof and the side walls. And on the door, a glassed cut-out moon revealed a crescent of sky. Even if the outhouse didn't exactly smell nice, Justin had smelled far worse where folks squatted in the park. Three long curlicue strips of flypaper hung from the ceiling—and a hairy-legged spider in the upper left corner was easily the size of his thumb. He glanced up now and again, thankful each time to find the spider as still as ever, right in the center of its web. He finished up and, like Mr. Bouchard showed him, shook a tin cup of white lime and ash down the hole against the worst of the smell. He made sure to latch the door when he left. It might have two holes, the old man said, but you don't want to share with a badger or a coyote.

These past days on the old man's ranch had been as enormous as the every-which-way blue of these prairie skies, almost blue and big enough for Justin to forget what he'd been running from. Almost. He came up the trail now as the sky deepened in color and edged toward evening. A wall of stony clouds assembled in the west.

Justin opened the camphouse door to the sizzle of grease and meat, the tang of pepper.

—Get washed up, Mr. Bouchard said without turning around. We're about ready.

They sat up to a platter of potatoes fried in rounds and some kind of meat on the bone.

—Antelope chops, the old man said, forking a couple up, then tilting a tumble of spuds onto his plate. I don't got much in the way of lunches, but there's enough meat in the freezer for us to eat decent at dinner for a time yet.

Justin sawed at the meat and chewed a hunk. Peppery and earthy, it tasted sort of like sagebrush smelled. He finished off one chop and, like Mr. Bouchard was doing, picked up the bone and bit at the last of the meat. Then served himself another. More potatoes too.

—What's antelope?

The old man chewed and wiped his fingers with a cloth napkin.

—You've seen them, likely. Look a bit like deer but white across their bellies and rumps. And horns instead of antlers, forked horns. The fastest thing out there on the prairie. Move like the wind.

Justin had seen them streaming up the hills east of the camphouse, though he hadn't known what they were. Now he studied the bones on his plate, the shine of grease on his fingers.

—Did you, like, shoot this antelope? Are we eating something you shot?

Mr. Bouchard shook his head.

—Used to have to hunt just to keep food on the table, but I don't so much anymore. My boy Dennis and a couple of his friends each got an antelope out here last fall. They gave us some of the meat. I've always liked it.

Justin stared at the slender bones on his plate, the puddle of clear grease and pinkish blood.

—I've never thought about it like that, Justin said, like you could see an actual alive animal and then kill it and eat it.

—Done it many times, the old man said, forking a potato. Better that way. Then you know it's done right, done clean. Then you've earned it. Antelope, beef cow, lamb. Why—

—You kill lambs? You eat lambs?

Justin felt something hot and hard begin to build behind his heart.

—*Lamb* means any sheep under two years old. We slaughter most of them when they're a year, year and a half. I don't mean lambs like you're thinking.

Justin hadn't realized he'd stood up. He sat back down. For the first time in he didn't know how long, he wasn't hungry.

—I think, he said, standing up again, lifting his plate, I'm about done. I'm gonna go have a cigarette.

—Suit yourself, the old man said, sawing at a chop.

Justin stepped out onto the porch, the clouds in the west dark and low and shouldering closer. The look of them full of storm.

Last fall, living out on the mountain had felt so strange at first, the drizzle of rain on the camper roof, the tight pines and winding switchback miles into town. But out here, here on the Bouchard Ranch—this was even farther. Its own world entire. The elemental laws and directives that governed weather and gravity and birth and death all encompassing.

Justin drew smoke into his lungs, blew the white billow of it—which was nothing, which was gone—out into the night.

# 38

Off to the west, a black snarl of cloud had built above the Bulls. Lianne hoped the storm brought rain, though clouds as dark and low as those were just as likely full of lightning or hail.

She came away from the window and settled on the sofa with a cup of coffee. When she'd had the students in her composition sections at the community college turn in papers, it often meant over a hundred essays to grade at once. It'd be different in Idaho next year; it'd be poems and stories, though likely still plenty of them. For all three classes she was teaching here in Delphia, Lianne lifted a stack of just over twenty essays and set them on her lap. She almost laughed. She thought of her first years in college, how delighted and truly terrified she was each day to see so many people on the quad, in her classrooms, on the streets of Missoula. It had taken such pure force of will to minute-by-minute negotiate those strange new spaces that when she'd met Marty, as steady as he was, she'd hung on to him as ballast. It didn't matter if you wanted to leave or where you went — there was a vast, difficult sea of difference between Delphia, Montana, and anywhere else.

Lianne clicked her pen and tilted the pages to the lamplight. All the students had begun with the same sentence starters — *If you really knew me, then you'd know...*; *My best days are when...*; *Sometimes I dream...* — and the first couple were predictable, the dreams detailing rodeo fame, basketball stardom, or new pickups. Lianne shuffled through and found Randy's paper, the handwriting faint, the smeared pewter of a dull pencil. Randy's dream was that his dad had never moved their family to Delphia, because maybe then his brother wouldn't have started getting into so much trouble, and maybe he wouldn't have stolen that car and gotten sent to Landers — and maybe he'd still be alive. The next student wrote that her best days were when she and her little sister, who'd gone deaf years ago when a fever burned away her hearing, rode their old palomino horse up into the hills all by themselves, away from their parents. One boy wanted to make his dead father proud; one girl dreamed her older brother would quit drinking. Another said his only good days were days he got to shoot something.

Lianne sat back and breathed. It was like this in her writing classes at the community college too. You were never prepared for all the many hurts young people carried, never ready for how hungry they were for the chance to tell somebody. Lianne thought again of Viv looking her way and shaking her head, of Rene saying nothing and running off to the ranch. Of how coming home from school today, she'd walked right past Mariah. Lianne couldn't help, it seemed, but continue the silence.

She'd saved Amy's essay for last, the notebook sheets only slightly wrinkled, the girl's handwriting even and precise. Lianne took a drink of coffee, cool now, and started in.

Amy wrote about feeling like she was always having to apologize for things — for not being like her sisters, for listening to music that shredded her mother's nerves, for wanting to look different and do different things and, sometimes, even live a whole different life. Though in the very next paragraph, as Amy outlined her best days — hunting agates and mussel shells along the river, driving with her dad because he always let her pick the music, watching the sun drift behind the Bull Mountains — an honest joy shone through. Amy reminded her of herself at that age, both wanting to be elsewhere and loving the place she was. Lianne wrote a quick note in the margin — *Good examples here, and clear, effective sentences!* — then finished the essay.

She sat back on the sofa and clicked her pen closed.

It was true that most every farm or ranch needed someone earning a bit of extra money to make ends meet. Usually the wife subbed at the school or cut hair in her kitchen. Viv had picked up sewing, mending winter jackets and letting out hand-me-down prom dresses. Some women even traveled to Roundup to work at one of the bars downtown, but very few went as far as Billings, like Connie Munroe had, and Amy's dream was that her mother would come home for good and her parents wouldn't fight and it would all be like it used to be.

Evening brushed against the windows. Everything blue, burnished, still. And Lianne was three states away from her own family. Over the Christmas break, on a trip downtown to see *The Lion King*, Frank had asked why it was always either Mommy *or* Daddy and never Mommy *and* Daddy. She handed him his popcorn, butter translucing the red-and-white-striped paper, and said they'd talk later, they'd better get their seats now. The theater, as they stepped in, was empty.

It wasn't quite eight, but Lianne felt wrung out. She clicked off the lights downstairs. The darkness of the house rose like water around her. Out the front window the first strikes of lightning sliced the sky. Thunder rumbled.

Viv, who hadn't been afraid of much of anything, was terrified of lightning. No matter the time of night, she wouldn't dream of being upstairs during a storm, that much closer to it, and so would hide in the kitchen or the bathroom. Franklin usually joined her, the two of them reading or playing cards. Lianne, Keith, and Dennis always lined themselves up on the couch by the window, knees on the cushions, elbows on the back, and thrilled to the jigsaw strikes, the cracks and echoes of thunder. The best, of course, was being out at the ranch, where the window in the camphouse offered long views to the south and west. Sometimes, too, they hustled out into the wind before the true storm hit and cheek by jowl squeezed into the cab of Old Blue, even Franklin—but not Viv—and Rene would drive them up some nameless knob of hill where they'd watch the storm come toward them and over them, slashing and cracking and battering, and for the thrill of it they'd shriek and hold one another as they never did when the sky was clear.

Now lightning streaked down, strike after strike. Thunder cracked and rang. And the storm faded into a steady rain, the front passing over town. Just as Lianne put her foot to the first dark stair, three knocks sounded at the front door.

She clicked on the porch light and cracked the door—and there was Ves Munroe, blinking in the sudden brightness. His cowboy hat in one hand, he motioned with the other.

—I would've been by earlier, but with supper and homework and what-all, I didn't get away until just now. We might be able to catch it yet, if we hurry.

—What are you talking about? Catch what?

—The front of the storm.

Lianne struggled to make sense of the man. His eyes shone bright as a boy's, and his grin hung lopsided in the wind. Ves had always been sort of loose-jointed, big and quick and wild in the way he moved his hands, the way he walked. Beyond him, pulled to the side of the gravel street, a two-tone Ford F-350 chugged and rumbled. Rain slashed the headlights.

—Have you been drinking?

—Not a drop, Miss Bouchard, I assure you. I just thought, considering how long you've been gone and all, you might like to see a good old-fashioned Montana thunderstorm come across the prairie.

Lianne had nearly forgotten a night ride like this was the kind of thing you did when you lived close to the land, that this was something you could choose. The wind touched her neck, the inside of her arm. It carried the clean, mineral scent of rain.

—Let me grab a jacket.

Ves drove south out of town, dog-legging down the old Delphia–Colter Road and across the Musselshell River and up into the Bulls. The rain slacked and fell away as they wound their way deeper into the mountains. At the first high pass, Ves turned onto a nameless ranch road that cut through pines and junipers, wound around wildly shaped sandrock scarps and ridges.

The truck crested the south side of a bald, and Ves cut the engine.

There it was, the front of the storm—a wall of massive, anvil-shaped clouds scudding in from the west, lightning dancing brightly beneath. The far, tinny rumbles of thunder.

—Jesus, she said.

—I know, he said.

The storm ran a curving line from well south of them, over the river valley and into the north country as far as a body could see. Surely over the ranch, Lianne thought, maybe even all the way to the Missouri Breaks. They watched in silence. The black clouds from west to east slowly ate the stars; lightning flashed close and closer. The first fat drops of rain, the very rain they'd driven out from under, again rang on the windshield.

Lianne pushed open her door and stepped into the night.

The heady smells of sage, pine, and dry grass, coppery waft of petrichor—she took in a great lungful of air and circled the nose of the truck and leaned back and lifted her face to the rain, which fell harder by the second.

Lianne sneezed, laughed, ran her hand down her face, through her suddenly soaked hair. She couldn't see him in the dark but knew he was there beside her.

—Ves, she called over the clattering rain, the gusting wind.

—Yeah?

—I'm sorry about Connie.

His rancher's hand, wide and calloused, slid into hers, and she could feel the line of his shoulder and hip against her own. She leaned that much closer to him, under the brim of his hat, and the rain against her face lessened.

—You're still married, she yelled over the wind.

—Last I knew, he shouted back, you were too.

—Hell with it, Lianne said, I'm going to kiss you anyway.

—Okay, then.

And in the rainy dark they turned to each other and touched, tenderly, as they had when they were young and new to touch and didn't yet know that in this world, tenderness was not a given but a gift. Thus, knowing grief, knowing sadness, this tenderness mattered all the more, and so they held each other, and the rain came down, and the rain diminished, and the wide, black night—which held all dreams, fears, and possibilities—plunged toward the sharpening stars.

# 39

Rene held the penlight steady on the lamb. The marker ewe, one of the few he kept with dark wool — one per fifty was the usual, for a quick count at distance — licked at her just-born lamb and lifted her head, blatted as if to no one, and nosed the lamb again.

— Why isn't it moving? Justin asked. Why isn't it getting up?

— It's dead.

— Did she not clean it up right? Did we wait too long to check?

— No, it don't look like it ever had any kick in it. Looks born dead.

— That happens?

— Yes.

— What do we do now?

— We make a jacket.

Rene explained that this ewe clearly wanted to mother a lamb. And she had the milk for it. But you couldn't just stick her with any old lamb. She wouldn't take it. She'd want her lamb. So they'd skin this dead one, wrap that jacket of skin around the runt from the other day, and tie the skin off with fishing line, then rub the jacketed lamb in this puddle of afterbirth, blood, and shit, and hopefully, jugged up, the ewe wouldn't notice, would smell her lamb on that lamb, and in time, even after the jacket dried up and crackled off, they'd become one and the same.

The boy's mouth hung half-open. He stared at Rene. He looked angry. Scared. Both.

—Are you serious? You're going to skin that lamb? Like, with a knife?

Rene clicked the penlight off and dropped it into his shirt pocket. He slid his hat from his head, worked a hand over the wiry scratch of his old man's hair. The first time Lianne had brought Marty home with her from college, for a week after their spring term, Marty had happily eaten his lamb chops with mint jam and horseradish at dinner but the next day was nothing short of horrified at the work of docking—catching lambs and giving vaccinations, clipping tails, wethering the little bucks with hard green rubber bands. On that long-ago May morning, Marty had begged off after less than an hour in the corrals, and Rene had felt at first disappointed, then annoyed, and, finally, ashamed, as if he should apologize or somehow atone for this dusty, bloody work he loved. Ranching was life distilled: birth and death, the hard winter giving way to spring, and spring to the heat and fast black storms of summer. There was a violence in it, a violence you tried in all ways to diminish but a violence you nonetheless had to know and hold. In this tilting world, when so many had gotten away from anything resembling the actual, were living what Rene thought of as supermarket lives, ranching at least kept you close to what mattered, to what was real.

That day Rene hadn't said a thing. He let Marty go. He let all his boys go. In the end it was only Lianne—he would have bet the ranch that it would be so—who'd stuck with him through Viv's last hours. Then, after the funeral and the burial service on Cemetery Hill, once they'd all traipsed back into the house and loosened their collars, grandkids parked in front of their Game Boy video game machines or taken away to naps, Keith had sat down next to Rene at the kitchen table and put his big, soft hand on Rene's shoulder and asked, as if it were already decided, as if it were the only reasonable thing to do, when he planned to sell the ranch to Orly Pinkerton and what he, Keith, could do to help. He wanted, he said, to help.

Goddamn.

It wasn't anger that he'd felt but sorrow. Keith and his money. Keith and his plans. At his golf club in Denver, Keith would never let on he knew someone like Orly Pinkerton, but they were cut from the same cloth — men with dollars and schemes in their eyes. Rene almost grieved for them.

Here, though, was this boy, this runaway, Justin — he'd helped birth a handful of lambs, and now Rene had asked this next, hardest part of him. Would the boy stay through the dying? Rene patted his shirt pocket, the slim cylinder of the penlight a promise, touched his hat back onto his head, and slid his good Buck knife from his pocket. Thumbed open the short, sharp blade.

— That mother's a good one, but it'll be hard for her to take care of three. This way that runt has got a better chance.

Rene set his knife on the table and lit the Coleman lantern. Justin didn't move.

— Go ahead and lead the ewe over to the jug with the lamb, like before. Once you got the ewe jugged up, bring the lamb over to the table.

— That dead lamb? Lead her in there with her dead lamb? Like it's alive or something? Then bring it to you so you can skin it?

The boy stepped from lantern light into wavering shadow.

— No way. No fucking way.

Rene winced at the glass and scatter in Justin's voice. Goddamn if he'd ever figure when to keep pushing, when to hold back. He started to explain that if they worked quickly and well, they might end up down only one lamb instead of two. That runt needed the good milk a mother could give or it might not make it — but Justin interrupted.

— That's fucked up. I show up out here, and you're talking about eating lambs and skinning lambs? You've gone crazy out here. You're just a crazy fucking old man. No way I'm going to trick the mother, make her think this other lamb is hers. No fucking way.

Justin was breathing hard, crying. Rene braced himself against the table. He thought the boy might charge him, knock him to the ground. Justin wiped at his face and swore again and pushed his way through the sheep and was out the shed door into the evening.

Then the only sounds were the milling sheep, the black and building wind of the storm.

Rene damn near felt like crying himself.

He took up the dead lamb and led the ewe to the jug, closed the wooden gate behind her. Not finding her lamb in there with her, the ewe circled and blatted, headbutted the wooden jug.

Against the grind in his hip, Rene ferried the dead lamb to the table and hung the lantern from a nail above. To make sure he could see each cut, he held the penlight in his mouth as he worked. He sliced a circle a few inches above each tiny hoof and cut through the hide up the inside of each of the legs, then carefully down the neck and chest and over the belly. He cut wide around the little cock and anus—it didn't need to be perfect—and finally an inch below the lamb's head circled the thin neck. Then he peeled, slowly, gently, so as not to tear. The fascia gave way with a sigh.

The runt was asleep. Rene lifted the little thing onto the table and worked the jacket over its back and tied the legs and neck and belly off with fishing line. His knees and hip cracking, Rene knelt where the ewe had given birth and rubbed the jacketed runt in the mess of afterbirth and blood, made sure to get it all over the runt's nose and back end, parts the jacket didn't cover. The runt, finally coming all the way awake, kicked and blatted. Rene told it, as he'd tried to tell the boy, that this was the best thing for it. In the long run, it was. He hoped it was.

Without her lamb, the ewe had begun to beller and stomp. Rene dropped a pail of water in the jug and waited until she'd dipped her nose to drink, then set the jacketed runt in with her. The ewe turned and knocked the runt over. Stood there with her head lowered, looking at it. The runt got to its feet once more and, after a time, tottered over to nurse. The ewe's eyes went wide. She sniffed at the lamb. Sidestepped once, twice. Then sniffed again. And stilled. She turned back to the pail. The runt kept searching. Finally found a teat. His little tail wiggled and danced as he sucked at the thick colostrum, the first milk. He likely hadn't gotten any of that the other day, not with those two big lambs around.

The ewe closed her eyes. The jacketed runt kept nursing. Well, hell. Sometimes it was like that. Hard, then easy. Not always. Just sometimes.

Rene washed his knife, hands, and arms, the red water pinking down the drain. With a pitchfork, he piled the skinned lamb and afterbirth where the other sheep couldn't get at it and covered the mess with a layer of straw. He didn't quite have it in him tonight; he'd bury it all out back of the shed tomorrow.

The wind whipped and turned. Thunder cracked and rumbled, the first hard spats of rain. Rene held his hat to his head and followed O'Malley across the road. He slowed as he came near the camphouse.

The door hung wide. Swung on its hinges and banged in the wind.

# 40

THE RAIN CAUGHT HIM halfway up the steep cutaway face of the hill above the creek. Runnels of dirty water slicked the loose dirt to mud in seconds. Justin slipped and fell to the ground.

Thick, sticky mud coated his knees, his right hand and elbow. He tried to keep his guitar case out of the mess but slipped again and slid maybe six feet down the hillside, mud gumming up everything. Fuck. He'd tried to find an extra set of keys for the pickup but came up empty. Had to run again on his own stupid feet. He didn't want to go down the road in case the old man came after him. He made it over the hill's shoulder and in a bowl of grass and shattered bits of stone attempted to scrape off what mud he could. The rain fell hard and half rinsed his hands and face. The rest of him was still a mess. His pack had long ago been oiled and that might keep out some of the rain. He hoped the paperboard guitar case wouldn't fall apart. Justin huddled himself over his guitar and sat there in the grass and mud and gravel and couldn't help it — he was crying.

He was thinking about that little lamb skinned down to meat, about those salmon on the creek firecrackered into silver shining bits, about Kurt Cobain lying dead in his house for days.

Fuck, fuck, fuck.

That old man was out here all alone. Where were his kids now? That had gone to shit too. Everything did.

Below, a light in the camphouse flared.

Through the slant of rain Justin could see the smear of it at the windows, yet he couldn't make out any movement or shadows and so had to imagine the old man taking it all in, then bending in his stiff, aching way to stow the magazines back in their rack, the utensils in their drawer.

For a long time now, Justin had needed to take what he could when he could, and so after he'd gathered his things, after he'd come up empty with the truck keys, he found himself without even really meaning to rifling through cupboards, dumping dresser drawers.

Turning the better part of the camphouse inside out.

In the end he hadn't taken all that much. Not really. He'd stashed the rest of the tuna and pineapple in his pack, along with a can opener and a fork. He already had a knife and didn't need those stupid boots the old man had offered him, but he'd rolled a blanket and strapped it to his pack — fucking soaked and covered in mud now, what good would it do him? — and grabbed a fistful of wooden matches, two long candles, some socks and handkerchiefs. In the bottom dresser drawer in the room he'd slept in, he found a camera and a stack of photos. He took the camera, thinking if he ever made it back to civilization he'd pawn it for maybe a couple of bucks. Though he wasn't sure why, he pawed through the photos and kept some of those too: One of the old man, years younger, sitting in his easy chair and laughing, really laughing. One of the shed and the hills beyond at sunset, the colors thick and swirled. He took a photo of an older woman walking along the creek with a red-and-white-furred dog that wasn't O'Malley. One of a young woman on horseback. And one, finally, of a thin, dark-haired boy holding the camera at his chest and taking a picture of himself in the cracked mirror over the dresser, the reflection of the bunkbeds and the window behind him. Justin had looked at the boy a long time, had wanted to look longer, but the storm was coming. He had to get the hell out of there.

The wind flung curtains of rain across him. The lightning and thunder far off now, over and gone. It'd be something to do later, he thought, study those photos. It'd be almost like company, though as soon as he thought the word *company*, he remembered this evening, how after dinner Mr. Bouchard had joined him on the porch. *There's a lot of company in a cigarette*, the old man had said, smoke obscuring for a moment the first stars.

Justin hugged his knees all the more tightly. He was soaked, just totally fucking soaked. His hair, his flannel and jeans. His stupid shoes. He couldn't be sure it was the last day, but he thought it was—yes, it seemed to him now that the last day his key had worked at the duplex in Rainier Beach was the very day he'd found those other photos. He'd been dumping drawers again, looking for whatever might mean a meal, a modicum of safety, warmth, or oblivion—and the thick, square photos curlicued and drifted in the still air, spilled everywhere.

Why hadn't he kept any of those?

He tried to call to mind the one of his mother on the coast, and he could get most of it—her long curly hair taken in the wind, the wet black rocks, the waves—but he couldn't put together the pieces of her face. Couldn't make her out for anything. There were photos of his father, who was no better than a ghost to him now—see-through, insubstantial. And one of Justin at a long-ago birthday party, yellow streamers on the walls and everyone wearing pointy hats, stretchy cords under their chins. Lots of little kids he didn't recognize in the background, and him in the center standing in front of a chocolate sheet cake, five candles in a row. It was his own dumb kid face he remembered, how scared he'd looked, how he was just a little kid and shouldn't have been scared. How there were about a thousand fucking reasons he might have been in that moment terrified.

Justin had been scared for so long, almost as far back as he could remember, and here in the rainy dark on this muddy knob of hill, he was again—and that was the difference; that was what had marked the immensity of these last days.

He hadn't been scared. Not out here. Not here at the ranch.

Silent tracers of lightning flashed off to the east, the rain above slowing to an irregular patter. He wiped his face with his shirtsleeve as best he could. The wind cut at his wet clothes and skin. He balled himself up and closed his eyes and drifted for a time.

Sleep spit him back up on the shore. The stars like mouths opening and opening, a bright scream across the black sky.

The light in the camphouse was off.

Justin slid down the hill, muddying himself up again — fuck it — and crossed the creek and came around well south of the camphouse, hoping O'Malley wouldn't smell him or hear him and start barking. He rolled the shed door open and squeezed in and rolled the door closed, starlight winking out.

The belly of the shed was stone dark but dry and out of the wind. He leaned his guitar and pack up against the wall and rummaged in the side pocket for matches and one of the candles. He attempted to light a match on the zipper of his jeans like he'd seen the old man do to start the fire in the stove. It took him half a dozen tries, and he broke the first three, but the fourth match flared. He touched it to the wick.

The dark rolled back. The sheep grunted and turned their drowsy heads. Straw scuffed and crunched beneath his soaked Chucks. In the flickering candlelight, shadows shifted and swung. Dust and shadow, straw and light — he was trying to reckon what it was that stilled him here, that slowed his heart as his breaths began to harmonize with the slow nighttime breaths of sheep.

At the lambing station, Justin took stock. That pile of straw by the wall was likely covering the skinned lamb. He'd look, he told himself, he would. But not yet.

Instead, he lifted the candle and peered into each of the jugs, the mothers down on their sides, the lambs curled up against them, their little heads nodding against one another, against the great warmth of their mothers' bellies. He found the newest mother in the last jug. Her wool was the same plum and umber shade as the bark of the cedars that sheltered his long-ago creek.

Her back was to him, head leaned in sleep against the boards of the jug. And the runt lay curled below her heart. The tiniest thing. The other lamb's skin, thin and blood-stained, hung on the runt crudely. The jacket didn't fit. But it did.

# BEFORE

# 41

Now that tilt leaned the world all the more precipitously — the years of work and family, everything Rene thought he understood, was somehow just beyond reach. The world not what he'd believed it was, what he'd taught his children it was.

After Lianne graduated from college — in just three years — she announced that she and Marty were going to be married that August, and in September, she'd start in the graduate program in literature at the University of Montana. Rene didn't exactly understand what graduate programs were, but he'd always been proud of how well Lianne did in school. Keith, too, had already gotten married, by a justice of the peace after his first year at the community college in Glendive. He was the star of the basketball team there, had led them to some kind of championship, and his new wife was the head cheerleader — and four months pregnant by the time of the wedding. When Keith told him over the phone, Rene knew better than to say what was on his mind, that Keith ought to have given a thought to this girl and what she wanted, that he ought to have given a thought to how he planned to support a family. But more and more, what Rene thought he knew, it turned out he didn't, and so he handed to phone to Viv, which was how he always dealt with his oldest son — let Viv take the lead. Keith had an offer to play at Montana State next year,

Viv reported, a hand on Rene's shoulder. He and his family would live in married-student housing, and Keith would finish his degree, then get a job teaching and coaching. They'd have some debt, but they'd be fine, Viv assured Rene. He shook his head, said nothing. The spring of his senior year in high school, Dennis watched the fall of Saigon play out on the television and, along with one of the Benson boys, promptly enlisted in the U.S. Army. He shipped out for Oklahoma and basic training not long after he graduated.

With everyone but Franklin out of the house, life in Delphia felt to Rene somehow airy, unfastened. It used to be not everyone left the place they were born. It used to be there was some continuity, some community. Wasn't that the way it used to be? Rene was relieved when Lianne decided to spend the week before her wedding at home. What's more, she announced that she wanted them all out at the ranch and insisted that, as a gift to her, they had to take a few days to just enjoy their time on the land—like the Bouchard Ranch was some fancy dude ranch, Lianne said with a laugh. Rene didn't pretend to understand such a request, but he went along with it, and those few days were indeed full of summer light and the soap smell of sage, the calls of meadowlarks and red-winged blackbirds in the mornings, swallows and nighthawks carving the evening air. They rode the ridges, walked the creek, and took in the sunset from Viv's bench—and the whole time, Franklin's camera clicked and whirred, whirred and clicked.

That fall, after Franklin had sent the film away and finally got the pictures back in the mail, the thick, wide paper sleeves, Rene and Viv sat down with him at the kitchen table. It was a cool late-October day, the sky a fragile blue, and they went through the pictures together. Rene had mostly thought of cameras and picture-taking—the posing and smiling, the pretending—as frivolous, more or less a waste of time, like basketball and television, but these pictures were different. Franklin never told anyone to say cheese or look here. Rather, he took pictures of what was already happening, of their days going along. Rene held the photos up one after the other.

Here was Viv walking along Willow Creek, one strand of silver hair falling across her face, their little red border collie, Henri, at her heel.

Here Lianne reined her horse hard, as if about to cut a figure eight.

And here was Rene, leaning back in his easy chair in the camphouse, the oil lamp shining over his shoulder, the laughter in his eyes something he could feel just by looking, by holding the photo in his hand.

Rene turned the picture over as if on the back he might discover the source of the magic. He took another look at the front, picked up the next. He was as thankful for these photos as he'd been for anything in a long, long time. He put a hand on Franklin's shoulder, squeezed.

— These are real nice, son. Just awful good.

Franklin blushed at the praise, finger-combed his hair out of his eyes, then scooted his chair that much closer to his father and continued telling Rene about aperture, shutter speed, and focal length, about shadow and gradations of light, about the way looking through a camera lens helped him pull the world into focus, helped him find what was true and beautiful.

Months later, in the dead of a late-winter night, Rene woke to someone banging on the front door, and those photos rose once again in his mind.

It was Franklin's one friend from school, Kevin Kincheloe. Kevin was a year older than Franklin and had initially been more of a friend of Keith's and Dennis's, but he'd been by the house so much that with the older boys gone, he'd sort of taken Franklin under his wing, encouraging him to join the pep band and the FFA. Kevin Kincheloe stood in the doorway now with tears streaking his face, one eye bruised and likely to swell shut. Rene asked and asked again where, to make sure, then told Kevin to go on home. That his mother was likely worried, late as it was. Rene told Viv to ready a bath, and he pulled on jeans, boots, and a jacket, made sure he had his knife, and grabbed an extra box of shells for his .243.

Better than a month ago, Rene had convinced Franklin to drive over to Lavina with him to look at a new little sheepdog. Sitting in the cab of the truck, the wind on their faces, Rene told Franklin he thought Kevin had been a good influence on him, that maybe he ought to do more of the things the other kids did — go to the basketball games, hang out over Cokes down at the Lazy JC. Might help him fit in.

Franklin chewed his lip a moment, looked at his father.

— Would you do that, Dad? Do things just to fit in?

The question didn't make sense to Rene. He took to this country like an antelope or a coyote, like he was born to it and nothing else. And others, men especially, valued what he did and did well — sheep ranching, cowboying. Rene kept his eyes on the road, but his heart was traveling way out in front of him.

—I guess I was talking about you, son. Some things you could do.

Now stars blued the dirty snow in the ditches, the freeze scalloping the prairie, and Rene drove through town and down the highway with his lights off. He crossed the bridge and turned onto the rutted dirt road that led to a stand of willow and cottonwood above a deep bend in the river, a place people sometimes swam or fished for bullhead. Rene killed the engine. He could see the glow of a bonfire and went wide around and came up through the grass and scattered willows, close enough to make out the flames at play on the boys' faces. Rene took a knee and fired a volley of rifle shots over their heads.

Curses and screams, and they all drunkenly piled into pickups and tore out of there. Rene stepped into the light. He found Franklin tied with a lariat rope by the ankles, hands, and throat to the biggest cottonwood on the bank, close enough those bastards could laugh at him as they passed the bottle.

Franklin was naked save for his socks, was shivering, was so cold he was barely making sense. Rene cut through the ropes with his knife and caught his son as he fell away from the tree. He wrapped his coat around Franklin's naked shoulders. The boy's hair was all wet. They'd probably stripped him down and tossed him in the river before they tied him up.

Franklin slipped, stumbled. He couldn't get his feet under him. Rene cradled Franklin in his arms and carried him down the dark wing of gravel road. The stars looked on with cold, hard eyes.

Rene got him situated in the cab of the pickup and was trying to get around to the driver's side to start the engine, get the heater going, but Franklin grabbed hold of his father, hugged his father's neck, and wouldn't let go. The boy was saying something and at first Rene couldn't make it out for his hiccups and sobs. Then he could.

—I was only trying to do what you said. They invited me last week, and I thought since Kevin was going it'd be okay. I thought I'd try to do things the other boys did, to fit in.

That's when Rene saw those pictures again, saw them with such force and clarity it staggered him. Here was this boy looking for beautiful things. And such ugliness had found him.

# 42

THE WORKSITE WAS HALFWAY up Iron Mountain, an inholding in the national forest that butted up against the Absaroka-Beartooth Wilderness, a steep quarter section thick with fir, whitebark pine, and old, gnarled spruce that hung above a massive granite outcropping, the view from the rocky ledge simply astonishing, a hundred miles or more.

The first time the new owner—Heck said he was from Connecticut or some-fucking-where—had them up, he wore chocolate-colored boots, shiny pants with lots of pockets, and wraparound sunglasses. A gold watch winked on his wrist. He hiked at double time up and down the mountain and pointed here, here, there. Heck shuffled obediently behind, marking tree after tree with pink ribbon—like a beat dog, Justin thought, astonished at how much physically smaller Heck looked, slouching that way and never meeting the owner's gaze.

Justin stood at the edge of the outcropping and couldn't get over how far you could see. Hills and ridges and steep, shadowed folds, the braided course of a river, and flat fields beyond. If he looked hard enough, he thought, he might be able to catch a glimpse of downtown Seattle, the blue waters of the sound. From way up here, he might be able to see clean to wherever his mother had gone off to.

—Imagine it, the owner said, without all these fucking trees in the way! He slapped Justin on the back, that fat watch striking the boy's shoulder bone. It's a good thing your uncle still has a pair, the owner went on. I certainly don't have time for all these pissant environmental laws.

Now, the morning sky lacquered with dark clouds, a scrim of hard freeze in the dead leaves and old needles, Heck pulled to a stop in a cold swirl of dust—he always drove mountain roads like they might get away from him—and Justin, new to driving, eased the Datsun up the road and in behind the Chevy. Even though the winter had been mild, the work was a risk. The freeze would be slippery underfoot. Trees could shatter and sheer, fall where you didn't want them to fall. And it was illegal as all get-out, in breach of the scenic easement with the forest service and who knew how many other environmental regulations. But the pay was in cash, and this far from the park, Heck said, spreading his arms wide, as if out here he could make himself as big as he pleased, who would ever even fucking notice? What's more, Heck liked the idea of messing with the government, of putting one over on them. If the VA wouldn't take his headaches seriously—he could still smell all that crap they'd burned in Iraq, that stink forever up his fucking nose—why should he pay any attention to their pinko Commie laws about trees and fish and shit?

The saw roared. Heck felled and limbed, Justin drug slash. He lost count of how many trees Heck laid down, the chainsaw in Heck's hands quick, shining, and sure, a supremely loud and graceful instrument. Sharp, cold air bit at his lungs and eyes. Pitch and sawdust filled his hair and ears, the skirts of his gloves. After a time, the sun warmed him, then it was too warm, fucking hot, and everything stank of gasoline, chain oil, and green wood. The day became a buzzing, biting thing.

The sun slid behind the ridge. Heck killed the saw, looked around.

—What the fuck? You already cleared all the slash?

Justin stood there dazed, a shiver sizzling up through him. He'd worked nearly ten hours on a few slugs of water and had indeed cleared most of the slash. He wrapped his aching hands around the last few pine limbs and pulled them toward a pile. Justin had been doing chores since he got off the Greyhound two months ago, and he'd done some work for Heck on the weekends, loading and bundling camp wood, hauling fir and pine rounds and stacking them to dry, but this was the first time he'd been out on an active logging site. Heck had said he couldn't trust anyone but family on a job like this, and considering the circumstances, he needed to finish up as soon as possible. Justin horsed the last limbs up onto the pile and turned to face his uncle and thought for a moment that things might move a different way, that Heck might nod and offer a compliment. Justin began to imagine he might even end up with a wage, some pocket money. Get himself a can of pop, like all the other kids did, from the Pepsi machine after lunch. Or see if he and the few friends he'd made at school in Absarokee couldn't pass for eighteen and buy a pack of smokes at the gas station.

— You been holding out on me, Heck said, and sniffed. You never told me you knew how to work like this.

Justin didn't know what to say. He looked around again, as if among the logs and sawdust and churned earth he'd missed something. Heck strapped the saw into the back of the Chevy with bungees and slapped his work gloves against his thigh.

— That's the last of school for you, bucko. Holding the fuck out on me like that. I don't care if it's Monday tomorrow. You're coming right back up here with me. Boss has got a skidder for the big ones, but we get anything we can haul for camp wood. It'll take us most of the rest of the week. I'll cut, you load.

Heck spit and wiped at his mouth with the back of his hand. Eyed Justin up and down.

— I should've had you doing a man's work sooner. You're just so god-damn faggoty-looking, I didn't think you'd be worth much. Well, kid, welcome to the logging business.

APRIL 1994

# 43

Rene dreamed again of water, an ocean of it he was under. He swam hard but his bum leg held him back. He drifted sideways, drifted down. Light glinted above, and he kicked and kicked but couldn't reach it, the dream waters thick, dark, impossible — he woke gasping, his heart a flapping fish.

Not yet daybreak, and the damp chill of last night's storm filled the room. The wood walls tightening, the window glazed with rain.

The whole of him hurt. A catch in his chest. His hip and back cried at him. The very knuckles of his fingers throbbed. He tried to shift up onto an elbow, swing his legs out from beneath the scratch of the flannel sheets, but his muscles strained and failed, and he collapsed back into the depths of the feather bed, where he breathed, waited. Remembered.

Last night he'd been too tired to be angry, the mess in the camphouse more than he could get his heart around. Last night, he'd simply set about putting things to rights. Now, though, the anger flooded him as the waters had flooded his dreams, the blackness of it, the force.

Yet he couldn't focus it, couldn't see the one boy without all the other boys — Keith, Dennis, Franklin, Kevin, Marty, Justin, those two Lang boys next door.

He remembered now that a while back, the older Lang boy had stolen a car and wrecked it on the interstate — nearly killed somebody, the paper said. Then, after he landed in juvie, that boy hanged himself. Viv had been broken up over it, but Rene couldn't bring himself to feel one way or another. He hated to think it, wouldn't have admitted it to Viv or anyone, but what had happened to the Lang boy hadn't surprised him in the least. More and more, it was the way of things. *Goners,* the principal had said those years before.

Rene rolled onto his side to grab at the windowsill. He saw behind his eyes Keith and Dennis naked and scowling in the stock tank — a different kind of gone, but goners again. And now this other boy was gone as well, this Justin. Well, good goddamn riddance. It'd be a clean break now. He'd lamb out the herd, take in one last sunset. Then be done with it. All of it.

Rene gripped the worn wood of the sill and pulled himself to the edge of the bed. Slowly, rust grinding in all the gears, he sat up.

Goddamn.

He hobbled out of his long johns and into his jeans, a red-checked work shirt, two black socks. His boots snugged up onto his feet, and a cup of coffee loosened him some. He and O'Malley shared a can of fried Spam for breakfast. At the feeder, a flock of chickadees whirled, and one dark, round nuthatch clung upside down before winging off — devil down-heads, his grandmother had always called them. Rene took a last bite and sipped at his coffee. Better this way. Better those who can't handle it leave off and let the work be done by those who can. He was trying to be angry at Justin. He kept seeing Keith. He kept seeing his own young face, the wild cowboy he was.

The braided rug squelched beneath his boots from the door being left wide open in the rain, and Rene bent down and with some difficulty lifted it and hung it over the bench to dry, then mopped at the floor with a rag. He put a hand to the table to steady himself, the pain in his knees and back trembling him. But that was the last of it — the cleaning up, the wreckage Justin had left. Rene put it from his mind. He clapped his hat onto his head and set himself to the day's work.

No sooner had he cracked the front door than O'Malley gave a short, sharp bark and tensed on the porch. Rene scanned the road, the shed — and, hell, the sheep were already out in the corral.

He'd closed that side door, hadn't he? It had been a long day, and he'd had to jacket that lamb on his own in the dark, the storm coming in. Still, he wasn't getting so senile as all that, was he? If he'd forgotten to close the shed door, he might well be looking at half a dozen coyote kills. He didn't know if he could stomach something like that. Not now.

The sun rimmed over the eastern hills, the high, splashing sound of Willow Creek tumbling with rain, and quick as he could, which wasn't all that quick, Rene shuffled across the dirt road and let himself into the shed.

He hadn't forgotten.

No, the side door was rolled open and the sheep were already crowding the feeders, fresh hay thrown down. And at the lambing station, the jugged ewes were watered and fed, the skinned lamb gone. Rene kicked through the straw to make sure. Nothing but a black stain of blood on the hard ground.

Out back of the shed, as he'd thought he might, Rene found Justin digging a grave.

Though for a beat or two he slowed in his work, the boy kept at it. Rene let him. He stood there in the shadow of the shed he'd built with his own hands, on his land, his ranch, the ranch he'd saved for and bought and raised his family on. Rene Bouchard stood there thinking that what he ought to do was knock the shovel from the boy's thieving hands and send him on his way. In the rain-wet bunchgrass and sage, Rene Bouchard stood there trying to puzzle why above all things he felt again ashamed, as if he'd failed to live up to his part of this bargain, this contract of dust and blood.

The grass shifted in the wind, beads of held rain raining down.

Justin hollowed a hole in the prairie earth a bit better than two feet deep and a foot and a half across. Rene watched as he slid the blade of the shovel under the skinned lamb and — careful of the loll of the head, the splay of the legs — lifted the tiny red thing into the grave. Settled it down.

Justin studied the lamb a last moment. The sadness of it, the intricacy. Then buried it and tamped the dirt down and, for the first time, looked Rene full in the eyes.

— You fed the horses too? Rene asked.

— Yeah.

—They give you any trouble?

—Not really. That bigger one knocked the pail out of my hands once. Rene took a step closer. Justin swallowed but kept his head up.

—I can't have that again. You're as free as any man to go your own way, and if you'd've asked, I'd have given you all the tuna fish and pineapple you could handle. But the way you did it was mean. Cruel. I can't have that again. You hear me?

The boy dropped his eyes, that yellow hair of his hanging. Then lifted his chin, nodded. His eyes were slicked. A tremble at his jaw.

—I hear you. I'm sorry.

Justin wiped his face in the crook of his elbow. He was filthy, his clothes wet and muddied. Like a worried bird, his one hand lifted and fluttered through the air as he spoke.

—That lamb, the one you put the skin on—I mean the jacket. Did the new mother take it?

—She did, Rene said. I believe you know she did.

—Yeah, the boy said, wiping at his eyes. I just wanted to make sure.

# 44

Shouts and whistles, shoulder slaps and the clang of lockers. Lianne stood in the library doorway as the hall chaos slowly cleared. The second bell sounded, the last few lollygaggers scurried for their classrooms, and she closed her door, breathed.

Teachers are always supposed to be ready for the exigencies, to not take things personally, but she couldn't help it. She'd been so disappointed with the ninth-graders. After she handed back their essays, which were, she told them, amazing, and after yesterday's strong discussion of Frost, she'd hoped for a good discussion of the packet of Wright, Oliver, and Levine poems she'd assigned—and yet no one said much. Amy Munroe slouched down in her seat and stared out the window. The boy she'd been paired with earlier in the week, perhaps taking his cue from Amy, was just about as sullen. Lianne couldn't get anything of substance out of them and so had them turn to one of the poems in the packet, Levine's "You Can Have It," and read the poem aloud, twice, and just as she was going to have them write about a favorite line, the word they found most interesting, and their biggest question about the poem, the fire alarm rang—a drill she hadn't known about—and there went the class period.

Now Lianne took a quick slug of coffee and pulled a tall stool around in front of her desk. She set out construction paper circles, each with one of the kids' names, at staggered intervals on the bright green oval rug. Harney had assured her that this part of the job would be easy, but beyond her own boys, Lianne had never spent much time with young children, not even babysitting in high school, as she'd usually been busy at the ranch. On Thursday, with the third- and fourth-graders, Lianne had simply let them paw through the stacks. Today, though, perhaps feeling a little guilty, in addition to checking out books for them, she planned to read *Where the Wild Things Are* and talk about any wild animals the kids had seen and if they ever felt like being wild themselves.

Last night, as the wildness of the storm pressed on and the rain slacked, the stars drying, sharpening, Ves drove them back into town. They were both soaked, and at the house, Lianne changed into sweatpants and a T-shirt. She rustled up a pair of old long johns and a flannel for Ves. As his clothes turned in the dryer, they sipped hot tea in the kitchen. They stood near to each other and said very little. It wasn't that they'd talked themselves out. It was that they were filled and overflowing with how good and needful it felt to be close, for hips to brush and shoulders to nudge, for her hand to rest against his chest, for his hand to hold a moment the curve of her ribs.

Lianne cried for a time, quietly, as if she, too, had need of rain, and Ves held her all the closer. The dryer dinged. She handed him his warm clothes, and he took them, and before Lianne could ask him to stay, Ves said he ought to get home, ought to be there for the girls in the morning.

For a long time after, Lianne lay awake in bed.

Now a fidgeting line of tiny first- and second-graders filed into the library. They lolled and wiggled, and Lianne helped them find their spots on the rug, then introduced the book and read it aloud; half of them covered their eyes and only peeked between their fingers as the wild rumpus began. She got an earful of wild stories afterward, and though she knew these kids were likely better acquainted than most with animals of all kinds, their stories were wilder even than that — whales and lions on the loose in eastern Montana! After the kids checked out books, Lianne walked them back down the hall. They made a game of doing so silently, like sneaky wild animals.

As she was packing up her things, the lines of the poem she'd read with the ninth-graders yet running through her head—*Give me back the moon / with its frail light falling across a face. // Give me back my young brother*—Lianne heard her classroom door sigh open. And there was Mariah's boy Randy. He scuffed his black sneaker against the hard carpet.

—That was a good assignment, he said, different. I never got an A on something I wrote before.

—I find that hard to believe. Your writing was honest and wise, Randy. You went right to what mattered most. That's what real writers do.

Though he tried to hide it behind his hand, Randy broke into a grin. Even if he didn't much look like his mother, Lianne thought, he moved like her. Slow, then quick.

—I was gonna tell you about your car, Randy said, drifting a step or two into the hall.

—My car? Lianne had just capped her thermos and slung her backpack over her shoulder.

—Someone soaped it.

—What? Lianne started toward the boy, but he turned and ran down the hall, disappeared into the jostling scrum headed for the lunchroom.

A hard noon sun shone on the dirty water in the ruts, the damp gravel, every car in the lot pocked with runnels and dots of dry rain. Lianne touched her finger to the soaped letters on her windshield. SLUT!!! in all caps, from top to bottom and corner to corner. Principal Harney came huffing out—she'd forgotten how fast news moves in a small town—and he was keen to get Randy Lang into his office for questioning. Might have even been him that did it, Harney said, smacking one meaty hand into the other. Or maybe the boy had been put up to it by some of the more popular kids. Maybe—

Lianne shook her head. It wasn't Randy. She was sure of that. She fished a handkerchief from her purse and dipped it in a mudpuddle and scrubbed at the soap, the letters sudsing away, leaving the windshield streaked and swirled with dirt. Could have been wax, she thought, which would have been nearly impossible to get off. Lianne saw the girl—she was sure it was Amy Munroe—deciding that morning against slipping a candle into her backpack, reaching for a bar of soap instead. The damage, though, was done. Half the town, Lianne suspected, knew she and Ves

Munroe had taken a ride last night. Now half the town would be thinking this same thing. More than embarrassed—and this was what confused her—Lianne was furious. Not so much at Amy as at Rene, at herself.

Harney was saying something about consequences and life lessons. Lianne threw her things in the back seat and left him there in the lot.

At the Mosby cutoff she squealed the brakes and cranked the wheel. Then hit the gas again. She'd sit her father down and make him talk. She'd ask why he'd run away, why he'd left his dying wife in those last moments, why he always expected so much of her, why he let go of his sons so easily. Why they'd all collapsed into such deafening silence. The Corolla clattered over a cattle guard and fishtailed a moment in the gravel. Lianne realized that to ask would necessitate that she, too, confess. All right, then. She would. She whipped the Toyota onto the ranch road. All the joints and bearings screeched and wheezed. Despite last night's rain, a great cloud of dust billowed up behind her.

At the bottom of the Seventy-Nine Hill, Lianne hit the brakes and bumped off the road and cut the engine. She stepped into the dust, sun, and stone-and-water song of the south fork of Willow Creek. Took her first breath of pure prairie air in years.

The creek ran quick and muddy with rain. There was no way she'd get her Toyota through. Lianne pulled off her shoes and socks, shimmied out of her jeans.

From a cloudless sky, the midday light fell golden and warm, though in an instant, the cold creek tightened her skin. Stones beneath her feet, and the milky brown water rushed and pulled at her. Lianne couldn't help but shout at the bright shock of it. She toed her way across, quickstepped up the opposite bank, and hopped about to warm herself, brushing at the bits of grass and dirt on her wet legs.

The susurrus of grass in the wind, the metallic, two-note calls of red-winged blackbirds. Despite herself, Lianne couldn't help but lean into the landscape, into being once again back at the Bouchard Ranch. She strode on down the dirt road, carrying her shoes and jeans. Marty had been out to the ranch only once, early on when they were courting, and since the boys showed up, they'd kept their visits to Montana short, a couple nights at most. But Trent and Frank would love it out here, she thought. Why hadn't she ever brought them? They could feed horses and nurse bum lambs and eat those hard camp biscuits Rene fried for every meal. Balancing on one foot, then the other, Lianne pulled on her jeans. She didn't worry about her shoes, as dirty as her feet were.

The corrals, shed, and camphouse came slowly into view, reifying before her, and for a moment, Lianne didn't register or quite believe what she saw. Like one of the first-graders' lions or whales, it didn't seem possible — a boy with long hair, baggy jeans, and a flannel shirt, a boy looking like so many she saw slouching along a downtown Spokane sidewalk, but this one was here at the ranch, was sliding the shed door closed and walking across the road toward the camphouse. No, toward Old Blue. The boy opened the pickup door and, like he knew what he was doing, like he belonged right where he was, hauled himself up behind the wheel.

— Hey! Lianne called.

She was yet some ways off. She shouted again. Then ran, a thin layer of soft, rain-damp earth giving way to dry dirt beneath her footfalls.

Seconds later, as she came even with the corrals, as the driver-side door of Old Blue swung open once again and the boy slid down from the bench seat, something bit at the ball of her left foot, the hot shock of it sending tracers up her leg. A rock, Lianne thought, just a sharp rock. But another running step, and pain bloomed through her. She buckled, fell. Her knees skidded in the hard dirt. Then her palms and elbows. Her shoulder smacked down, her head.

She found herself on her back. The warm prairie sun above. Smell of churned dust, crinkle of grass — and her foot on fire. Lianne gripped her knee to her chest.

The long-haired boy crouched down beside her.

— Holy fuck, lady, you really bit it. Are you okay? You cut your foot or something. There's blood.

Lianne swallowed, focused on him.

— Who are you?

The boy's face was thin, sharp. Eyes a startling blue, messy blond hair. He looked somehow familiar. Or was this just how they all looked?

—I'm Justin, he said, as if a name would solve any of this.

—No, Lianne said, what are you doing out here?

The boy pointed at the corrals.

—I just checked for lambs and was gonna go get a load of straw bales. We need more straw in the shed. For the sheep.

Lianne tried to sit up. The boy held out a hand. She hesitated, but took it. Pulled herself up to a sitting position. Her shoulder sparked, her head throbbed.

—Where's my dad?

—Mr. Bouchard?

The way the boy said the name, some mix of reverence and hope, the thinnest edge of sorrow. Lianne slashed out and grabbed the kid by both wrists.

—Even if he didn't ask, I am. Who are you? And what are you doing out here?

# 45

Hell and goddamn.

Rene told O'Malley to stay and was out the camphouse door hitching his way across the road. Lianne was on her backside in the dirt. Had ahold of the kid by the wrists like she was planning to wrestle him.

Rene had heard her shout and about knew what was going on — the creek was running too deep for her car to cross, which was why they hadn't heard her coming, and now she'd seen this kid and was wondering what in the hell. Well, okay. He'd been expecting her one of these days. Still, this was more of an entrance than he'd anticipated.

— Pockets, Rene said, catching his breath, leaning down to her as best he could, his weight on his good leg, hands on his knees. You okay?

— Dad, she said, letting go of one of Justin's wrists and reaching for Rene.

— Let's get you up. Rene braced himself and took Lianne's hand and elbow. Justin did the same. Together, they hauled her up.

Her good foot under her, Lianne put an arm around Rene and leaned into him.

— I cut it on something, she said, pointing at the foot she held just off the ground. Took my shoes off to get across the creek.

— I figured. Your car back there at the crossing?

Lianne nodded and with her free hand smoothed her hair.

— Here's your shoes. Justin handed Lianne her flats, then lifted something up between the three of them. Think this was it? What you cut your foot on?

The boy held a curved four-inch triangle of faded purple glass, one edge shattered into a glassy dagger, a smear of blood and dirt at the tip. The other side looked to be part of the neck of a wide-mouthed jug or jar, a scribble of writing just below the threads.

The boy turned the shard and thumbed the glassy letters, squinted.

— Says, uh, *Milwaukee.*

The glass caught the light, a dusty lavender in the light.

— Homesteader's glass, Rene said. Used to be things came in glass, whatever it was you needed. Wasn't any plastic. And this whole country was homesteaded, if you can believe it. Most didn't make it. People didn't have enough land, didn't know how to work what they did have. Tried to plow it. Planted wheat, turnips, apples — all kinds of things that wouldn't ever grow. Not in this dry country. So they pulled up stakes for Yakima or turned back to Iowa and left their shacks and clapboard houses and beds and stoves and plows. Left crates of empty glass too. And the glass froze and cracked and washed out in the spring and weathered and was buried and unburied by wind and rain and what-all. Used to be you couldn't drag your toe through the dirt without finding homesteader's glass. Or arrowheads.

— You found arrowheads out here? the boy asked, eyes going wide. Like, real arrowheads?

Rene started to answer, but Lianne cut him off.

— I see you're still in prime storytelling shape. Mind helping me inside before you really get going?

Rene tried a grin.

— I'm old and set in my ways, Pockets. Justin, give us a hand here.

The boy was shorter than both of them, but Rene could feel him take the better part of Lianne's weight. Together, they hobble-walked to the camphouse. Justin fumbled open the door, and Lianne lifted her arms from their shoulders and palmed both sides of the frame.

Rene stepped back and breathed. Here we are, he thought. The three of us. Well, we'll see. He motioned to Old Blue.

—Justin, how about you take O'Malley and load up that straw?

O'Malley, sitting obediently just inside the doorway, shook with expectation and delight at whatever it was that was about to happen.

—Go on, Rene said, and the dog bolted after the boy.

The engine rumbled to life. Dust lifted in the truck's passing and drained down through the warmth and sudden stillness of the day.

Rene shut the camphouse door. Lianne hopped over to an easy chair and settled herself down.

—Dad, who is he? The kid? What's going on?

Rene shook his head and said they ought to get that foot cleaned up first. He filled a bucket with warm water and ferried it over to Lianne. She stared at him, clearly frustrated, but finally lowered her foot into the water, wincing as she did. She let her foot soak, then scrubbed the cut carefully, and rinsed again. Rene handed her a towel. She patted her foot dry. Rene had hauled the old metal box of first-aid supplies from beneath the sink, and now, as he'd done when the kids were little and needed doctoring, he eased himself down onto his knees in front of her. From a cracking metal tube, he squeezed a greasy dollop of ointment and carefully worked it over the cut, then crosshatched Band-Aids on top and wrapped Lianne's foot in gauze. He held her foot in his two hands for a moment, as if his father's touch might be enough.

Rene tried to lift himself off the floor and faltered. He got a hand and an elbow on the bench behind him and slowly hauled himself up onto it that way.

—Dad?

—I'm all right. Just sometimes the old knee gives out on me.

Rene could tell she didn't quite believe him. But she had other things on her mind just now.

—Okay, Lianne said, leaning forward in the easy chair. Tell me.

—I don't know much to tell. Rene pulled his cowboy hat from his head, set it brim up on the table. I seen the kid one day down near the creek.

—And you just invited him to stay?

—Wasn't quite so clean and easy as that. But yes, I told him he could stay. Asked him to help out around the place. I know he doesn't look it, that hair and all, but he's not a bad hand.

Lianne pursed her lips. For all the world, she looked like Viv, ready to give one of their own a good talking-to.

—Dad, she said, you don't have any idea who this kid is. And you don't know kids these days. It's a different world out there. He could take your truck, your rifle. Do something terrible to you. Maybe he's already done something terrible, maybe that's why he's on the run. Why—

The wooden bench legs screeched against the floor. As sharp and sure as he could, a hand on the table behind him, Rene stood and reached for his hat.

—I may be old, Pockets, but I ain't senile. I know how it goes as well as you do.

Rene started for the door, turned back.

—Tell you the truth, I might know it better. You didn't have it so bad growing up. But I been that boy before. And I had one of those boys myself. And one day I found that boy of mine dead not a hundred yards from here.

—Dad.

Rene rubbed at his eyes; his breath ran from him like water.

—I'm sorry. That wasn't called for. He was my boy. He was your brother. I know that. And this Justin, well, he ain't either one. He's just a kid at the end of his rope, a kid who needs a place to stay. And this is as good a place as any.

—Dad.

Rene pulled open the camphouse door, and a sideways river of light spilled in, motes of dust lifting and spinning. Years ago, when Viv would drive back on Sundays to drop the kids off for the school week or when everyone was readying to leave the ranch at the end of summer, Rene carried a sense of violation, even desecration, as if what was run through with rightness, what was spare and weathered and useful and true, was being set upon by the unnecessary, the frivolous and fabricated. He'd felt it again today, Lianne showing up at the ranch and upending the routines he and the boy had built. But standing there in the doorway, in such light, he forced himself to call up and, for the first time, name that feeling of trespass. The root of it was pride. His expectations hadn't always been fair, especially those he levied on Lianne. The boys, each in his own way, had at least been able to tell him no. He hadn't given Lianne enough daylight to tell him much of anything. Goddamn.

Rene Bouchard turned back to his daughter, his hat in his hands.

—You headed out to the lambing shed? Lianne asked before Rene could offer anything. I'll go with you. Give me a minute.

Rene started to protest, but Lianne hushed him.

—My foot's feeling better. Probably be good to get the blood flowing. She was already putting her socks on. She lifted her flats. But these shoes won't do. I'll need a pair of boots.

Rene plunked the old pair from the kids' room down in front of her.

—Justin turned his nose up at these, he said. Likes those sneakers of his.

—Good, Lianne said, pulling on one boot, then the other. Dad?

—Yeah?

Lianne stood, tested her weight.

—Why'd you leave without telling me? You had Bassett out here watching the sheep, right? He could've taken care of the lambing. You and I could have come out for a while before I went back to Spokane. Just to check on things. Wouldn't that have made more sense?

Rene shaded his eyes against the slant of light. Turned to find Lianne standing there favoring that one foot, waiting for him to explain.

What could he ever on earth hope to explain?

It seemed to him now he'd never known his own self, let alone his family. Or he had, for a time, but those known to him had deepened in intricacy and become fathomless, the way you might ride a certain ridgeline trail in all weather for years and still be surprised at what the April rains uncovered, what came blooming up from the dry and ancient earth.

Vanity again, thinking he could end any of this by putting an end to himself.

It would all go on — the hurt he'd borne, the hurt he'd caused, and, most of all, the land itself. What right did he have to saddle Willow Creek with another sad, dead-wrong story? Saddle his daughter with the same?

— Dad, she said, shatteringly, I love you.

Rene put an arm around her shoulders. Lianne hugged him tight.

The tang of old rain and bunchgrass, the inerrant prairie dust, this April light, warm and improvident. Together, they stepped into it.

# 46

THE BALES SWUNG EASILY up into the truck. Justin loaded it deep and high, as he'd done with the hay, even if these straw bales felt airy, as if they might bounce out of the pickup bed on the way back to the shed if they weren't tied down, the whole load jump and lift at a rut in the road and drift right up, up into the jailbreak sky.

O'Malley stood guard, and when Justin dropped the last bale into place, the dog came over and sat on the boy's shoes. Leaned into him. Justin shook a Winston from the pack — he was down to three — and lit it with a wooden match. Mr. Bouchard had told him he damn well better be careful with fire out here, and after a first deep drag, Justin plucked the Winston from his lips and spit on the tip of the burned match, then dropped the match into his shirt pocket. He took another drag. O'Malley gave the faintest whine, and Justin parked the Winston in the corner of his mouth and reached down to give the dog a scratching behind the ears. It was late afternoon, and down the hills, the wind came just this side of warm, pulled and rattled in the grass and sage, then swept off for the green curves and crescents of the creek, the cottonwoods, some thick with furrowed bark and greening buds, others slick, bone-white.

The moment she'd grabbed him like that, by the wrists, Justin thought of what that one fly fisherman had said in the dark parking lot along the interstate—he'd said his girlfriend, the teacher, knew kids like him. Mr. Bouchard's daughter did too. He saw again the broken loll of his uncle in the camper doorway and dragged hard on his cigarette, hard enough to hurt. The billowing cloud of smoke slipping from his lips seemed by far too big for him to breathe.

He'd known this time here at the ranch wouldn't last—what did?—and now Mr. Bouchard's daughter was out here reminding them both of that fact. This work the old man had him doing hauled the world into depth and perspective, trued the day, and all he wanted was to stay and help finish the lambing. That right there would be enough, that right there was all he'd hope for.

If by some thieving luck it might come to pass.

Justin took a last drag of his cigarette, spit on his thumb and fore-finger, pinched the burn of it to ash, and dropped the cold butt into his shirt pocket alongside the matchstick.

—Load up, he said, and slapped the sidewall of the pickup.

Like he'd been listening to the boy all his life, O'Malley leaped up onto the tailgate and was ready for the drive back to the shed.

Old Blue rode a good couple of feet off the ground, and Justin creaked the heavy door open and put a foot on the runner and grabbed the wheel. He hauled himself up onto the bench seat, dust and straw wheezing from the springs. The clutch stuck some, but he ground it down to the floor and mashed the brake with his other foot. Then fired the engine. Justin drove back around the corrals and up the dirt road carrying a load of straw for the shed, for the new mothers and lambs.

# 47

At first, the work felt awkward. Soon, her muscles and bones began to remember.

Lianne and Rene jugged up two new pairs of twins and paint-branded the ewes and lambs from the evening before, including one little lamb in a jacket. Rene took his time at the logbook, and for her foot, Lianne moved slowly, dropping flakes of hay into the jugs and refilling water buckets and sometimes just looking at the lambs and ewes, patting their withers. With only a few jugs empty, and the lambs growing fast, they'd have to let the first sets of mothers and lambs out into a corral of their own soon. So Rene and Lianne measured off a square on the west side of the shed and an adjoining square in the horses' pasture to form a small rectangle pen with cover and grass. They pounded steel posts into the ground at the corners of the pen, tied wooden panels to the posts with twine, and set a small, round stock tank inside. Then they ran a hose from a spigot, hooked on a float, and filled the tank. Tomorrow, the oldest lambs would be ready to get out and run. Lianne put her hands to the top of a panel and gave it a shake. Makeshift, but it'd hold.

Rene predicted hurt feelings on the horses' part, and Lianne, not even sure the last time she'd ridden, about fell over herself offering to saddle

them up and give each plenty of attention. But just then, Justin showed up
with the straw.

The boy tossed the bales down and, as Rene instructed, dropped them at
regular intervals around the interior of the shed. Lianne took the first bale,
Rene the second, and thus they kept up with Justin, cutting twine and shaking straw flake by flake onto the shed floor. Angled shafts of light fell from
the high, south-facing windows, the light twice golden for being run through
with bits of straw. The yellow, grainy smell of it hung heavy in the still air.

Lianne pinched at her nose, sneezed. Unlike Keith, she'd never had
hay fever or allergies, but just now, the dust in the shed was thick enough
to cut and carve. Lianne and Rene shook out the last flakes, then made for
the main corral, where they blinked and breathed the clear air, the rich
smell of sheep manure a balm after the dry scratch of straw.

They were into the thick of lambing now. On the far side of the corral,
Justin was hauling a single by the back leg toward the jugs, the mother
bleating after it.

— You make sure it's just a single? Rene called.

— I saw the stuff, the boy said, and paused a moment, the wet lamb
kicking weakly in his fist, the mother hurrying up to lick it even as it dan-
gled upside down. The afterbirth. That's what that means, right? She
doesn't have any more lambs?

— That's what that means.

Justin continued on into the shed, the new mother nosing the lamb,
and Lianne studied her father, noted the way he'd talked to the boy, the
way he didn't follow to check on his work but turned back to the herd,
then shucked his cowboy hat a moment and scratched his steely hair.

— How long has he been out here? Lianne asked.

— Three nights now.

— So, Tuesday?

— Monday.

— That doesn't quite add up.

— He took a little time off. Showed up again this morning.

— And you let him?

Rene sucked his teeth, slapped his hat back onto his head.

— Guess I'm getting soft.

The shadows stretched and thinned, the sun bleeding out behind the hills. Lianne and Rene slowly herded the sheep into the shed for the night, clapping, talking, the sheep grunting and murmuring. Justin was at the lambing station, recording the birth in the notebook. He asked Rene to check that he did it right, and Rene ran a thick finger across the page and peered down and nodded. Then the three of them made for the camphouse.

Rene filled the washtub on the porch, and they all scrubbed their hands and faces and blew and blinked as cold well water dripped from their fingers and noses. The boy draped his flannel over the back of a chair, and through the thin, tatty T-shirt he wore beneath, Lianne saw that he was skinnier than she'd first noticed. And dirtier. Dried mud was smeared on the insides of his arms, on his neck, and in his hair. She asked if he had any clean clothes she could get for him, and he looked from Rene to her nervously and said yeah, in his pack. She found socks, underwear, a flannel, and a pair of jeans that were damp here and there but mostly clean. It must have been last night he'd spent out, his pack muddy, which was just about like Rene, Lianne thought, putting the boy to work just as soon as he showed back up. She brought the clothes out to Justin and found Rene had brought out a bucket of warm water as well. They left the boy alone to finish washing.

Rene set to making dinner. Lianne lit the kerosene lamps and stoked a fire in the stove, then turned to find Justin in the doorway. She took the empty wash bucket and told him he ought to take everything out of his pack and hang the wet things up to dry. If anything was muddy, she'd get another bucket of warm water ready and set it on the front porch. There was an old washboard out there he could use.

Rene side-eyed her for a moment, knife and half an onion in hand.

— You give camphouse orders just about like Viv.

— Well, Lianne said, draping a rag over the lip of the bucket. Good.

Lianne's foot had begun to throb, and she sat now in an easy chair and carefully peeled off her sock, unwrapped the gauze dressing. The cut was maybe two inches long, but it didn't seem deep. It had bled some. She rebandaged it and leaned back in the chair, into the watery shadows of the oil lamps, the pop of grease in the cast-iron, the smell of frying onions.

O'Malley's tail thumped the floor beside her. She closed her eyes.

She slept until dinner. Would have slept right through it, but Rene had the boy wake her.

— Hey, lady, he said, and lightly shook the back of the easy chair. Mr. Bouchard says it's time for dinner.

Rene's idea of a meal was usually some kind of meat and either potatoes or biscuits, so Lianne was pleasantly surprised to find he'd made a passable spaghetti and meat sauce, had even fried slices of store bread in the cast-iron, beef grease and onion flavoring it as good as garlic.

— Lianne's mother, Rene told the boy as they all tucked into their plates, she was always making this here foreign food. I ate it so much, I got to liking it.

Lianne elbowed him.

— This is just about as foreign anymore as your mutton stew, Dad.

The boy sat at the end of the table on a ladder-back chair hauled in from the porch. He was looking at the two of them, smiling, forking up another tremendous bite.

— It's Justin, right? Lianne asked.

The boy, his mouth full of noodles and sauce, nodded. Lianne went on.

— I'm Lianne, Rene's daughter. I don't know that we'd gotten to that yet. I live in Spokane, Washington, but I've been back helping since...since my mother got sick. She died two weeks ago.

The boy dropped his fork.

— So Viv died? Mr. Bouchard, your wife?

For a man who'd lived his whole life close to the fact that life means death, that on a ranch you say goodbye and goodbye to sheep and good dogs and even the best horses, Rene had never worn grief well. Though perhaps that's not quite right, Lianne thought. It was that he'd never worn his grief at all but hung it like a dark suit in the back of the closet. They'd lose a lamb, and he'd go quiet for an afternoon. The death of a good dog might mean a week of silence. And after Franklin's funeral, Rene more or less shut himself away from everyone — the few friends he had in town, his children, even Viv — for years.

Justin was looking at Rene and asking how, saying he was sorry, and

Lianne thought maybe she'd gone too far. Maybe she shouldn't have said anything.

Rash, like Marty always said. Honest but rash. She tried to turn Justin's questions in another direction—but Rene cut her off.

—Cancer, Rene said and took a slow drink of coffee. So we knew it was coming. But still. It's a hell of a thing. You spend forty-five years with somebody. Then they're gone.

—You were married forty-five years?

—Almost forty-six. Would've been forty-six in May.

—Oh, man. Wow. Is that some kind of record?

Justin still hadn't picked his fork back up. He was looking right at Rene, those blue eyes of his wide as could be.

—No, Rene said, and chuckled. It's no kind of record, but it sure meant something to me.

Lianne couldn't quite believe this was the direction the conversation had gone, couldn't quite believe the way the boy called her father out of his silences and into the texture of the moment. She rubbed Rene's back and leaned into him, rested her head a moment on his shoulder.

—Me, too, Dad. It meant something to me too. Meant everything.

Justin shook his head.

—I don't know. I don't know anyone who was ever married that long. I mean, my parents were married, like, I don't know—five years? I think forty-five might be a record. You should check.

The boy bent again to his plate, and Lianne wanted to ask about his parents but held off. She'd made dinner awkward enough. She sopped her toast with sauce and took a bite. Dropped the last corner of crust on the floor for O'Malley.

Again, Rene surprised her.

—You in touch with your parents?

Justin twirled noodles.

—Haven't heard from my dad in about forever. I guess my mom is still in Seattle.

—I imagine she misses you.

Justin laughed. A hard laugh.

— My family's not like yours. No way.

— You might be surprised, Rene said.

The boy looked at Rene and opened his mouth as if to say something, but stopped. His hair fell into his eyes.

— That's who you remind me of! Lianne broke in. That singer from Seattle. Kurt Cobain.

Justin looked pleased but pained, too, and Lianne understood that the connection mattered to him, that the death must have mattered to him as well.

— I'm sorry to hear he's gone, she said. A lot of my students really liked him.

— Who's this, now? Rene asked, turning from one to the other.

Justin's eyes went wide again.

— You never heard of Nirvana? Kurt Cobain?

— You wouldn't believe all the things I haven't heard of, Rene said.

The boy wiped his mouth on his shirtsleeve and shot up. Before Lianne and Rene could get properly turned around on the bench, he was perched on the kitchen stool and tuning an acoustic guitar. Lianne took the boy in, that long hair, his slenderness, and thought, suddenly, about what Ves had said the other evening at the café—Orly Pinkerton had seen a girl with a guitar case. No, he hadn't. Orly had seen Justin. And now here was this Justin with his guitar, ready to play for them. Where had he come from? What had he run from? And what happens—Lianne leaned forward—when Orly finds out he's here, at the ranch?

The boy's bright voice cut across her fear.

— Oh, man. I can't believe you've never heard Nirvana. This one's probably my favorite. It's called "Come as You Are."

Justin began to play, hard-strumming the guitar, each chord change slipping on the strings, bending and shifting, and now his voice ached into the spaces between them, a low and sonorous moan, a gravelly shout. The boy played and sang, the fire popped in the stove, and Rene took her hand. She let go her worry and leaned into him, listened to the music.

# 48

THERE WAS NO ELECTRICITY out at the ranch, which meant you couldn't just pack a night-light, so Rene had long ago nailed a glow-in-the-dark star to the ceiling in the kids' room. When Franklin was little, after he'd brushed his teeth but before he had to get into bed, he would sit on his bunk and shine a flashlight up at the star. He was storing up the light, he'd say, saving it for when he needed it in the night.

Roughly the size of a child's open hand, the star shone a weak green now, the light of the moon ghosting the window as well.

—What's that sound? Justin asked. I've heard it the past couple of nights.

—Coyotes, Rene said, shifting in his bunk. The mattress was thin, slim, and broken-backed, but for propriety's sake, he'd given his room over to Lianne.

The howls and chuckles of coyotes rang close and closer.

—If we didn't have the sheep penned up, those old dogs would take them apart.

—That happens? They eat sheep?

—Happens all the time.

—Oh, man, the boy said. I don't want them to get any of the lambs.

—Me neither.

The calls crescendoed, quieted, and then started up again, though fainter, drifting farther and farther away.

— Must be on the move, Rene said. Must be after something.

— What?

— Antelope, maybe. Someone else's sheep. Hard to tell. Coyotes keep their own counsel.

The boy said nothing, and Rene laced his hands across his chest, closed his eyes. He could feel sleep waiting just beyond the edges of him.

After dinner, Lianne had rustled up a can of fruit cocktail and portioned it into bowls and rimmed the bowls with vanilla wafers. She begged off checking for lambs, said her foot hurt. She'd take care of the dishes instead. Rene and Justin made a final pass through the sheep and jugged up another set of twins, then went back to the camphouse. The oil lamps snapped and whistled, thin trickles of smoke rising from the wicks. Rene tightened the flames. They stayed up for a time, Lianne and Rene listening to the boy strum his guitar. At first, he kept trying to growl the lyrics like that Cobain must have done, but as the evening wore on, his voice had lifted and sweetened, the chords softening as well. Lianne kept at Rene until he finally pulled out his harmonica and played a few old songs. Justin attempted to follow on his guitar, laughing as he tried to keep up.

They washed, and Rene lifted the mug of toothbrushes and a box of tooth powder from beneath the sink, the box almost falling to pieces as Rene thumbed open the worn flaps. Lianne handed an old toothbrush to Justin, and they all stood around looking silly, brushing their teeth. When the boy slipped off to the outhouse, Lianne took Rene's hand. She told him Orly Pinkerton had seen the boy on the run, had seen that guitar — was talking about it down at the café.

At the mention of the man's name, a spring tightened in Rene's chest. He had thought this was theirs and theirs alone. What right did Orly have to be wrapped up in any of it?

— The man tires me out, he said.

Lianne, he could see, wanted to say more, but just then the boy stomped back into the camphouse.

The night swirled and deepened, poured itself into every coulee, wallow, and camphouse corner. Rene Bouchard breathed and closed his eyes and wondered what dreams might meet him after an unexpected run of hours such as this.

The boy's voice pulled him back from the threshold.

— That star for your kids? For Lianne?

— Not so much Lianne. She wasn't ever scared of much.

— I bet, Justin said, and thought a moment. Your boys?

— Mostly the youngest, Franklin.

— Did he sleep in this bunk?

Rene cocked his head so that he could see the boy. His yellow hair was almost white in the moonlight, his sharp face in shadow.

— He did.

— I figured, Justin said. See, Lianne and the older boys, I bet they took the top bunks. And this is the best of the bottom bunks, because you have the window. That's why I like it.

Justin rolled over, the old springs squeaking, quieting. His breaths quickened a moment, then just as quickly slowed into sleep. A steady, feathery song. That music of his, Rene thought, it was from someplace else but from deep down in him too. Franklin's pictures were like that. Franklin had subscribed to a photography magazine for a while and studied on it, practiced. But his photos shone with something all their own.

Say a boy up and offers the inside of himself, and no one, not even his family, knows how to make sense of what they see.

Say a boy holds it all in.

Jesus, what chance did some boys have?

The moonlight drained away. The green star dimmed. Sleep got up on its haunches and shook and padded down the creek and over the hills, went the way of the coyotes. Rene thought to get up and have a whiskey but didn't want to wake anyone. So, as best he could, he lay back into the sure, still hand of the ranch at night, the wooden frame of the camphouse, the plank walls and sixpenny nails, the cedar shakes, the road and the grassy drift down the middle of the road, the empty corrals, the fetid warmth of sheep filling the shed, the creek dropping hour by hour into its channel, the flats and hills and bits of homesteader's glass and arrowheads and old bones and all of them held and holding one another.

# BEFORE

# 49

THE DARK TORQUED DOWN. Each day a quick, cold blaze of mountain light flanked by shadow. In the woods with Heck, Justin worked the fingertips and palms from his gloves, his hands worn raw, his arms nicked and bruised, back a bundle of nerves. The brief, bright day swallowed by night, they drove home. Justin laid himself down in the slim camper bed and slept as deep and still as a downed tree.

It was late January, and he woke past midnight to the sweat of his work frosted in his hair, the chatter of his teeth, the muscles of his jaw and neck firing of their own cold, furious accord. Only a couple of weeks had passed since they'd filled the propane tank, and Justin hoped maybe the wind had knocked the pilot light out. He crawled out of bed and clicked and clicked the sparker. No flame leaped to life. He bundled up, tromped outside into the black trees, and checked the tank. Empty. Fuck. Heck would be all kinds of pissed, would say Justin was using too much fuel, was a goddamn candy-ass from the city who needed to get used to a little Montana winter.

Justin thought on it for a time, but the chatter of his teeth eventually knocked all thought from his head. He ran for the house.

The moon—oblong, distended—leered over the ridge.

Heck always locked and bolted the door, but Justin knew where he could lift the screen from the living-room window, which wouldn't latch, and crawl in. Justin let the blinds back down behind him — no light at all now — and moved by feel along the wall, around the back of the Naugahyde couch. He stoked the woodstove to pulsing and sat so near he could see the cast-iron stretch with heat, his jaw anyway clicking for another fifteen minutes. Finally warmed through, he fell asleep right there on the floor.

Which was where Heck found him. And so was where Heck beat him. Justin had been hit before, knocked around. But never beaten.

Later, he would liken it to drowning, to knowing you'd never make the surface, never taste the good air again, so you curl up and sink into the black depths, let some nonsense dream play across your mind's eye even as your blood screams and screams.

Justin's every muscle was pulverized. He couldn't open his right eye, couldn't walk without help, could barely chew. His aunt and cousins nursed him, little Gracie sitting by his bedside and pretending to read him books in her best teacher voice. She was in the second grade and still couldn't read.

A few days on, his aunt brought him a ham and butter sandwich and whispered to him that she'd scavenged an extra propane tank, so every other time he emptied a tank, he should tell her. She had squirreled away a little money, she said, and could get the tank filled in town. Justin could make it longer this way, make it seem like he wasn't using so much fuel.

— Because no matter what, you can't do that again, she said, and helped him to his feet. You can't break into the house. Not ever.

Justin slowly made his way toward the bathroom, his every step stiff, uncertain. His aunt held the door for him.

— Heck's sensitive about that kind of thing. He probably thought you were Saddam himself. Here, go ahead. I'll look away.

From the moment he'd arrived in Montana, Justin had been doing the addition and subtraction of survival. Here in the mountains, he was fed. He'd been, in the beginning, warm. He had his privacy in the camper, but he could use the bathroom in the house to clean up. School hadn't been too bad. The teachers were a wash, and all the boys in boots and Wranglers sneered at his hair and earrings, but there were a few who thought him cool, who wanted to hear about Seattle, who were always begging him to bring his guitar and play at lunch hour. And, too, he loved the mountain, the pines, the white, roiling run of Burnt Creek. It was different from the overgrown ravine back of the trailer park — not so many shades of green, more buckskin, umber, and dun — but wild and redolent and big enough to let him be as wild and messy as he often felt. It had all added up, was better than scavenging, busking in the park, and being inexorably pulled toward the jungle camps beneath I-5 — in the beginning, anyway.

Heck felt bad about the beating. Not that he would ever say anything, but he piled three more wool blankets in the camper, bought Justin a new set of work gloves and a good Carhartt flannel. Justin slid his arms through the sleeves of the flannel, felt the thick, soft give of the gloves, and was even more terrified. It was something in the wide way Heck moved his elbows, the sizzle and shift of him come five o'clock. Were men always like this? Would he end up like them? He didn't know.

Justin knew here in Montana the subtractions were coming quick and quicker. He began to consider when and how to run.

Heck must have seen it in Justin's eyes.

Heck screwed a latch and staple hasp onto the outside of the camper. Once Justin was fully healed, Heck woke him early each morning and padlocked him in at night. The logging work tapered off to nothing, and most days Heck started drinking after breakfast, can after can of Keystone Light. He made Justin ride with him as he drove winding mountain roads and told long, meandering stories about convoys and camels and sand in all the moving parts, oil smoke staining your eyes. After he finished up with Iraq, Heck gave his heart and soul over to cursing that rich fucker from Connecticut who'd shorted him nearly five hundred on the job they'd done, who suddenly wouldn't take his calls. Then he started in on what a complete and total asshole his old man was.

— This one time, Heck said, tossing a can out the window, your mother'd been out too late with some guy or another, and she said something smart. Well, the old man decked her. Right in the mouth. That's how she lost those teeth, why she had to get that bridge.

Heck reached for another beer.

— I think I was twelve, thirteen. I saw her there, on the floor. She was holding her mouth, all this blood dripping from between her fingers, and I grabbed a lamp and swung it at the back of his fucking head. Which was dumb. I should have grabbed something that could do some damage. The bulb popped, the fucking lamp shorted out, and the old man turned around and slapped me so hard, my head rang for days.

Now Heck drank deep.

— He slapped me. Slapped me like you would a woman. He must have left then, because it was just the two of us lying there on the floor, all fucked up and bleeding.

Heck sniffed again, wiped at his nose with his can.

— Anyways, that's the kind of man you come from, kid. That's your fucking inheritance.

Justin listened. He cataloged, waited.

Over dishes one evening, his aunt whispered to him that winters often went like this. She scrubbed at the char on a thin pan and said that once the logging work picked back up, Heck would lay off the drinking, might even, if he got on with a crew, let Justin go back to school.

Justin rolled the word around in his mind — *school* — and it sounded now like another language altogether.

Each day, more light leaked down. Some nights, Heck forgot to lock him in. It was yet too cold to make a run for it, but Justin woke early those mornings and tromped up and down the creek. Snowmelt quickened the waters.

Then, in March, two federal investigators showed up. They asked Heck about his work, asked if he knew anything about a logging job up on Iron Mountain. Heck shook his big head, played dumb, would barely meet their eyes. A damn mess, they said. No environmental review, missing permits, and on top of that a good number of the trees that had been dropped were actually inside the border of the wilderness area. Would he know anything about that? Could he help them out?

Heck stared at his shoes.

The investigators buttoned their jackets and pitched the little cream-colored rectangles of their cards onto the kitchen table, told Heck that if he remembered anything — anything at all — to call right away.

Heck was on the phone now morning, noon, and night, calling that rich fucker from Connecticut again and again. No answer, no answer, no answer. Heck cursed and raged.

A week later the feds drove out once more, this time with the county sheriff. The landowner was cooperating in the case, was claiming he'd been lied to and taken advantage of by an unscrupulous local logger. They confiscated Heck's chainsaw, his Silverado and Datsun. The investigators said Heck shouldn't leave the county. Said it might be a while, but they'd be back.

Heck didn't say a word.

Everyone cleared out of his way as he stomped into the house, sat on the couch, and commenced to drinking and watching TV. He'd set his beer on top of the television to go take a leak when Gracie, forgetting, came skipping through and spilled it. Smoke boiled out of the back of the set. Heck, his pants not even buckled, grabbed Gracie by the arm and swung her at the wall.

Early April, and the days had begun to shift. The buttery cups of glacier lilies shone along the creek. His aunt's van kicked up dust for a long time as she drove away, the dust hanging over the road, snagging in the pines.

Justin looked around then and found himself out on the mountain alone with Heck.

# 50

When she thinks of those years, which she doesn't often, not if she can help it, she sees a river braiding into course and riffle, threaded with islands and gravel bars, willow, milkweed, and wild hollyhock, the sharp, metallic calls of a thousand, thousand blackbirds, and the sudden rock gap rising, narrowing into a tight chute—the river constricted now, running deep and hard, digging at the channel and scouring the banks. Everything gone, as the walls fall, to lifeless flood and wrack.

That August, after those long lovely days at the ranch, the wedding in Missoula was over in a matter of minutes—Rene walking her down the short aisle of folding chairs in his suit and bolo tie, the impossibly young campus chaplain officiating, the potluck reception on the same quad—and the next Monday, after two nights at the lodge in Lolo, Marty started work at a patent firm in Spokane. As he'd always planned.

Still in Missoula, Lianne moved out of the dorms and into graduate-student housing, a second-floor studio with a shower down the hall, a two-burner stove, and a set of French doors that led to the tiniest landing, barely enough room for one. She had her graduate courses in literature and taught one section of freshman composition each semester. She sometimes wished she had applied to the MFA program, though Marty was likely right that the MA would give her a better leg up when it came to landing a spot in a PhD program. Still, her favorite evening of the week was Thursday, when she and a dozen other grad students met for a women-only poetry workshop at the Missoula Club. And, too, all through the riotous fall colors, the winter half-light, the cool, muddy spring, Lianne took long walks on her own, crisscrossing Rattlesnake Creek or switch-backing up the mountain trails east of town — that's where she wrote the best, out on the trails, in the wind and weather.

That next summer, the summer of the bicentennial, she packed her suitcases and took the Greyhound to Spokane. Marty met her at the station and drove her to the bungalow on Perry he'd put a down payment on. It had two bedrooms, a dishwasher, the first Lianne had ever seen, and one enormous ponderosa rising from the corner of the backyard. Marty was putting in sixty-hour workweeks, so, alone and without a car, Lianne walked the hills of the neighborhood. She took the city bus to the riverfront, the remnants of the '74 World's Fair in various states of dismantling or repurposing. And the Spokane River — uncaring, unchastened — crashed down through the middle of it all.

For the fireworks show on the Fourth, they carried a picnic to Grant Park: a basket of ham sandwiches, potato chips, and cold beer. Lianne lay back on the blanket they'd spread out and laced her hands behind her head as flowers of color exploded across the night sky. Maybe it was one beer too many or too many days spent wandering anywhere instead of getting somewhere, but she felt something lurch within her, like when the bus came to a quick stop after barreling down the South Hill. She wanted to go home.

Though even as she thought the word — *home* — her heart shuddered and ran. Where, now, was home?

Missoula? Though she loved her studies, teaching, and the Thursday workshop, she'd always understood that college and graduate school would be temporary, just a place on the way to some other, more permanent place. But was that place here? Spokane? The little house on Perry and the many hours she'd struggled this summer to fill? All the neighbors she didn't know? The city unrolling in every direction? She'd been married a year, and this was the first time she and her husband had lived under the same roof for more than a few days, and it had been, well, fine — even fun at times. But all this, too, felt like a lark. A stopping-by.

Against the color and spin, the shriek and crackle of rockets, Lianne closed her eyes and saw — as she always did when she daydreamed — the slope of the prairie as it dipped down to cottonwood, willow, and choke-cherry, the gravel bar where the two forks of Willow Creek came together, the sage-studded hills rising abruptly beyond. She heard from Viv now and again, bits of news about Keith and Dennis, the latest from the ranch. Rene only ever got on the phone to make a joke, to tell her, *Take care of yourself there in the city, Pockets.*

The last letter she'd received from Franklin had arrived the very day she was packing up her apartment in Missoula. She'd sliced open the top of the envelope with her pocketknife and shook the letter out. Took the pages to the landing to read.

Franklin wrote in an old-fashioned hand that reminded her of Viv's slanted, precise lettering, the way she labeled mason jars of canned toma-toes and frozen packages of lamb chops. It always took Lianne a moment to get used to it, to be able to see and read it again — and this time, it took a moment longer. There was no preamble, no discussion of the weather or whatever oddity was going on about town, no disquisition on photogra-phy or questions about what new music he should be listening to — *Dear Big Sister*, Franklin wrote at the top, and then asked if she knew about the man who'd saved the president's life last fall, Oliver Sipple, the former marine, the one who wrestled the gun away from the woman who was trying to kill the president.

He asked if she knew that Sipple was a homosexual, was gay.

Even just reading those words, Lianne had gripped the landing's rail-ing, the white paint cracking and chipping beneath her hand. She'd read and loved the poems of Allen Ginsberg and Adrienne Rich, but rather than printed on the thin, nearly transparent pages of some broken-spined anthology, here were these words written on the cream stationery Viv kept in a wicker bin in the hallway closet. Here were these words — *homosex-ual, gay* — in her little brother's hand.

Her kind, quiet sixteen-year-old brother.

The one always taking pictures. The one who tried so hard out at the ranch. The one who didn't play basketball, who didn't listen to the right music, who didn't slap and laugh and joke like the other boys. The one who used to set up an easel in the backyard with Ethel Kanta and paint pictures of white sheep and green meadows, of blue skies and sunshine. Viv had hinted at some trouble at school, had mentioned the names of a couple of boys who were especially mean to Franklin. Once, the winter past, Rene had stayed on the phone with her a few minutes longer than usual. He said he'd gotten hold of some nice lengths of cedar and was going to frame some of Franklin's pictures. Some of the ones Franklin took out at the ranch before her wedding were awful nice. He said it again that way: *Awful nice.* He mentioned Franklin's friend Kevin Kincheloe and started to say something else, too, the register of his voice shifting, like the wind dying down come evening, the dwindling of the stars as dawn undoes the dark, but he stopped. In the silence, over the hum of the line, Lianne could hear the scratch of his thick hand over his whiskers.

— Pockets, he said finally, with a cough, you'll have to excuse me. I get to rambling. I'll let you go now.

Come mid-May, the air over Missoula had cleared some, the winter inversion of woodsmoke lifting and swirling away. The flattened grasses on the hills winter-dead and dull. The river ran to froth and slate. Lianne folded the letter in half once, twice, then held it nearly hidden in the palm of her hand as she climbed onto the kitchen stool, reached up, and slid the folded square of paper into the highest, tiniest cupboard. She closed the small door and stepped off the stool, wondering who else Franklin might have told — her parents? Kevin? — and then, like a cold drink of well water hitting your belly, she understood that he hadn't told anyone, because he hadn't even quite told her. Franklin was waiting for her. To be able to truly say it, he needed her help. He needed her to step toward him, to be brave enough to ask.

But she was headed west for the summer. The wrong way altogether.

That day, she'd tucked the letter away and finished packing. She hauled her two blue vinyl suitcases down the steps and used the phone by the front door to call for a car. She smoothed her blouse, her skirt. Soon, the car that would take her to the bus that would take her to her husband would arrive. Only the faintest smell of smoke stained the air that day. The mountain sky was a heartbreak blue.

And here, in Spokane, where that car and then bus had indeed taken her, Lianne felt the press of the earth up through her bones, the night vaulting faultlessly above. She opened her eyes to cascades of purple and green sparks blooming and sifting down.

She hadn't yet written Franklin back.

# APRIL 1994

# 51

THE LIGHT AT THE window shone a pale blue, the far hills and low clouds fringed with gold and rose. The blankets were warm and heavy. The press of his body over the past days had hollowed the feather mattress such that it felt nearly impossible to extricate himself. Justin rubbed his eyes and forced himself to sit up. Framed just so out the glass panes, the prairie held still as a painting, save for the arcs of what he knew now were swallows and the faint, fading calls of killdeer.

He'd slept in his flannel and socks and so only had to pull on his jeans. He belted them and jammed his feet into his Chucks. Mr. Bouchard's bed was already empty, the blanket pulled up and folded down beneath the pillow. He could smell coffee and hear the two of them talking. Justin studied himself a moment in the cracked mirror. His hair hung messy and yellow and longer than he'd ever worn it. His face hadn't exactly filled out, but it wasn't quite so knifelike. He looked fine, he thought. Like a boy his age ought to look. Rested, ready for the day.

He pushed the heavy curtain aside. Mr. Bouchard and Lianne quieted and leaned away from each other. Mr. Bouchard slid a plate of biscuits and a bowl of stewed plums toward him. There was coffee, too, as always, and Mr. Bouchard drained his cup before excusing himself to the outhouse.

Justin said he'd check on the sheep before he sat down to eat, but

Lianne stopped him. Said Rene had been up to check in the night, that she'd turned them out of the shed this morning and fed and watered the ewes in the jugs. And no, she went on before he could say anything, he shouldn't feel bad. A growing boy needed sleep.

— How old are you anyway, Justin?

He poured a spoonful of thick, fleshy plum sauce onto a biscuit.

— Sixteen.

— So that'd make you a sophomore?

— Yeah, he said, holding a fist to his mouth so he didn't spray biscuit crumbs. He was trying, as best he could, to be polite. Also, he wanted every last crumb of biscuit he could get.

— Where were you last in school? Seattle?

He'd just spooned up a soppy plum half and so shook his head, was about to say something about going to school for a few months in Absarokee but caught himself. He hadn't even told Mr. Bouchard that much.

Lianne sipped at her coffee. Glanced out the big window, then back at him.

— I don't mean to pry, but when you're ready, I think you owe my dad some answers. You don't need to tell us — sorry, *him* — everything. But — and here Lianne looked right at Justin — he needs to know it's safe to let you stay, that you're safe. Does that make sense?

Justin wasn't sure if it did or not. Some mothers hugged their sons goodbye forever on street corners. Some boys curled themselves up to sleep in the straw. Justin felt Heck's hands on him, the splitting maul's coarse wooden handle.

He shook his head, his hair in his eyes.

— You don't have to worry about me, he said. Once I'm done out here — helping with lambing, I mean — I'll go.

Lianne set down her coffee cup, the ting of it against the wooden table. She was young-looking and had a lightness to her, the way she moved her hands, turned her head, her thick, dark brown hair shining as his mother's never had, at least as far back as he could remember.

— That's what I'm trying to get at. I don't think you should go. A kid your age shouldn't be on his own. But we need to find a way for you to stay.

Justin's heart scrambled about in his chest.

— What if there isn't a way?

Lianne reached out and put a hand on his arm, just below his elbow.

First Mr. Bouchard, now his daughter. And before that, who had known him and touched him with kindness? Gracie, maybe. Or one of the boys in Seward Park. Mrs. Turnbull. Mrs. Gribskov as she handed over his check.

— There's a way, Lianne said. I promise.

Mr. Bouchard's boots hit the porch, the door swung open, and the cool morning air swirled through the stove-warm camphouse. Mr. Bouchard was saying something about Lianne's car, about the horses, telling O'Malley to stay.

— Eat up, Mr. Bouchard said. It's time to ride.

The horses broke the horizon line and came on hard-trotting, slowing and sidestepping, tossing their heads. Lianne moved immediately toward them. The horses snorted and breathed her in as she worked her hands over the long, dark flowers of their noses, their necks and shoulders and bellies. Justin hung back behind Mr. Bouchard, though as Nine Spot chewed oats, he reached up and stroked — lightly, quickly — the planes of her underjaw.

Mr. Bouchard haltered both horses and led them down the hill to the tack room, a small lean-to built onto the back of the sheep shed, right near where Justin had buried the skinned lamb. Mr. Bouchard and Lianne brushed Big Red and Nine Spot down, checked the horses' feet, and set about saddling and bridling. As they worked, Mr. Bouchard told Justin to open the gate in the barbwire fence. Justin jogged over, wrapped his arm around the gatepost, and put his shoulder to it. He lifted the wire, then pulled the gate all the way open and leaned it up against the fence just like Mr. Bouchard had taught him.

Behind him, he heard the syncopated clomp of hooves.

Lianne rode at a gallop through the gate, turned Nine Spot sharply, and stopped dead in the road, puffs of dust drifting from beneath Nine Spot's hooves. Mr. Bouchard reined Big Red around in a wide arc. He rode up and clucked and lifted the reins. The horse stilled, trembled. Mr. Bouchard reached his hand down to Justin.

— Put your foot in the stirrup there — no, the other foot — and, yep, give me your hand. There we go!

Justin could feel the heat of the horse beneath him, the astonishing breadth and power of the animal, its muscles and blood and big, shifting bones. He wrapped his arms around Mr. Bouchard's middle and with a shake of the reins, they were riding.

They rode fast and faster, and even so, Mr. Bouchard wasn't keeping up with Lianne, who flattened herself against Nine Spot's mane and galloped past the camphouse and down the straightaway. Far ahead, Lianne reined Nine Spot to a walk and turned a circle. She rubbed the horse's neck, her hair gone wild with wind and sunlight.

She was laughing, her smile as wide as the sky. They rode up beside her.

Lianne asked Justin what he thought. Though he kept his arms tight around the old man, he said it was all right. He smiled because she was smiling, because the wind was in his hair as well, quick at the corners of his eyes.

# 52

FOR BETTER THAN A mile, the road fell in with the serpentine wanderings of the creek's south fork, and where the creek doglegged west-southwest, the road bent down into and through a riffle, Lianne's car on the other side. Rene didn't slow but reined Big Red across. A quick splash of water, and they were through. Lianne had crossed ahead of them and already dismounted. She worked a hand down Nine Spot's neck.

Shading her eyes, she handed the reins up to Rene.

—Dad.

—Pockets.

Early this morning, while the boy still slept, Lianne had poured them each a cup of coffee and asked Rene to sit and let her talk and not say anything until she was done. He'd joked that this sounded like more of a second-cup-of-coffee conversation—but the look on her face quieted him. She had some things, she said, to sort out with Ves Munroe. She had some things to sort out for herself too. She didn't know how long ago she'd begun feeling like home—Spokane—wasn't home, but she had. And Marty was part of that. The better part of it, maybe. She wasn't sure.

To keep himself from saying something easy and dumb, Rene took a big slug of coffee. Once, when he was young, couldn't have been more than six or seven, he'd overheard his grandmother talking to his mother. The two women were boiling rags in a smoke-black pot on a coal fire in the yard. They weren't even blood relations, but his grandmother was telling his mother she might want to think about cutting her losses, that it didn't look to get any better with Floyd. Rene, the boy he was, was stunned, furious. That evening, he waited at the end of the road for his father to come home, waited past dark and wouldn't even come in for dinner. He couldn't remember anymore whether he'd told him, as he'd planned to do, or whether his reaction alone was enough to shame his mother. Floyd died in his early fifties. Though Rene had never been close to her, he was glad now that his mother had had a few years to herself there at the end.

Rene Bouchard held his tongue. The underwater light that presages dawn hung at the windows. Lianne went on.

It wasn't that this—and by *this* she meant the prairie and stars and storms and teaching at the school and Ves Munroe and all of it—was home. It wasn't that she knew but that she'd like to know. That's what she was trying to figure. As much as wanting to help out, that's why she was still here. And even before she'd come back to Delphia, she said, all in a rush, she'd had an offer to teach writing at a university in Idaho for the next year, and though she hadn't told Marty, hadn't even really admitted it to herself, she'd been, until now, planning to take it. One way or another, she said, she wasn't going back to the way things were. She was choosing something different.

Lianne sat up straight and smiled, a sad smile, and Rene couldn't hold back any longer. He asked after Ves's wife and daughters, if she'd thought on them, if they'd factored into her starting whatever it was she'd gone and started. Lianne winced and breathed and told him what she knew and even about Ves's youngest girl soaping her windshield.

Goddamn but things were always a notch or two more complicated than they seemed. Every family was a mystery; every four walls enclosed a world.

Rene asked about Trent and Frank then, and it was suddenly as if Lianne had swum up from the very bottom and surfaced for air.

—I'll see if Marty will meet me in Missoula tomorrow, she said, standing up from the table. He flies out for work Monday, and the boys have spring break. I'll bring them back here.

—Will you tell him?

—Maybe, she said, sitting back down. What do you think?

Rene blew a shot of air out his nose.

—Hell, Pockets, I'd like to say you can't go wrong with the truth, but I don't even know anymore. I'm not much good to you here. I wish I was. I'm not.

He hadn't thought it much of an answer, but Lianne wrapped him in a hug, held him close.


The day grew into warmth and brightness. Lianne worked a hand through her wind-tangled hair, told Rene she'd be back out Monday after school, with groceries, and she'd bring Trent and Frank for a quick visit. Maybe they could stay a night or two on their own later in the week?

She turned and reached a hand out to Justin.

—Come on, she said. I'll help you get situated.

—Get what?

—Situated. On Nine Spot. So you can ride her back.

—Shit, the boy said, tensing. Do I have to?

—Ain't no one else for it, Rene broke in.

Justin swore again but took Lianne's hand and slid off Big Red, stood there stiff and awkward as Lianne went over the basics. The kid put a foot in the stirrup, took a couple of hops, and swung himself up into the saddle. Nine Spot shifted and stilled. Justin's eyes were the biggest thing about him.

—You look good up there, Lianne said.

—Jesus, the boy said, gripping the pommel. Oh, fuck.

Lianne started her car, then waved out the window, bumped back onto the dirt road, and drove away, dust rising in the blue-white sky.

Rene had ahold of Nine Spot's reins.

—You ready?

—I don't know.

—If things go sideways, she'll likely listen to me, but that ain't exactly ideal. What you want is for her to listen to you. Do like Lianne said.

Justin looked truly terrified. Rene resisted the chuckle welling up in his belly.

—It's okay to be afraid, he told the boy, handing the reins over. But it'd be a shame to let that keep you from trying.

Justin swallowed, clutched the leather straps tight.

Rene touched his heels to Big Red's belly and started forward. A quick splash through the creek and a scramble up the other side, and he could hear Nine Spot behind him. She was about as good a horse to learn on as you could hope for. He could likely even get Trent and Frank up on her later in the week. They rode slow and easy, Rene trying not to look back too much but doing so now and again. The fear hadn't left Justin's face but had shifted some, begun to transform into something kin to fear but not fear, the way that what is best in us shares the same bloodroot as what might bring us to our knees.

The road widened out of its ruts, the lift of grass down the middle thinning, and Justin rode up alongside Rene. They went on like that together, the boy ramrod straight, reins clenched tight in his fist, and Rene never more at home than when in the saddle. There was yet more to sort out, but they'd get it sorted. He hoped they would.

—Nighthawks, Rene said, pointing at the quick, dark birds skimming over the creek. They're done feeding. That's how they drink.

—Nighthawks, the boy said, trying out the word, shaping this place that much more into being with his breath.

—Yes, Rene said, and meant the word, the ride, the day at its height and measure.

# 53

Lianne came up the walk to the house and lifted the grease-spotted paper bag, warm to the touch, that had been left by the front door. There were a half dozen rounds of fresh fry bread inside. In the kitchen, Lianne set the grocery bag on the counter and unfolded the white note taped to the side: *Randy told me about what went on at school yesterday. Said he wanted to do something nice for you. We made fry bread. My grandmother's recipe. If you'd like more help with your gardens, let me know. Mariah.*

Lianne leaned into the counter. She saw Randy hiding his grin behind his hand as she told him he'd done what real writers do. She saw the welcome grief on Mariah's face as she talked about Moses. Lianne opened the bag once more and breathed the good, warm grease, then crossed the kitchen and lifted the phone.

The buzz worked its way down through her as she dialed Marty.

He answered, as ever, on the second ring, his hello bright and chipper, but his next questions strained—where was she? Was she on the road? Why wasn't she home yet? As calm and clear as she could, Lianne explained that she was in Delphia, that they needed to make a plan for the boys for this next week. Marty cut her off.

—Listen, Lianne, I know you've been through a lot. But you're not thinking straight. You're not Pockets anymore. You don't have to do everything your dad tells you to do. You've got your own life to live. He's never treated you fairly. He—

Marty wasn't wrong, but he wasn't right either. She stopped him.

—I don't want to do this over the phone, Marty. I know it's a drive, but will you meet me in Missoula tomorrow with the boys? I'll bring them here for spring break. Then you can fly out to your meeting.

She could hear them in the background, Trent and Frank, what sounded like the beginnings of a squabble. Marty was quiet a long time. This, he wouldn't have planned for.

—What happens, Marty finally said, when I get back?

—I don't know. I don't know how this works any more than you do.

Marty almost never cursed. He cursed now. Then told her where he'd be and what time and hung up.

The bevel and grain of the wooden doorframe was hard against Lianne's back. The wind worried the window glass. The kitchen clock ached along. The tears came quickly, silently. Lianne felt shame and sadness but relief as well, as if she'd surfaced for air. She wiped her face with a kitchen towel and slathered a piece of fry bread with butter and honey. Ate greedily, licking each finger.

She showered and rebandaged her foot. She made grocery lists, one for her and the boys, one for Rene and Justin. Then stopped short, pen in hand. He hadn't said where, but Justin had been in school since leaving Seattle. Maybe he'd been living with a relative or a family friend, then that household disintegrated. Or maybe he'd broken a rule and gotten kicked out. Or, Lianne thought, seeing again the glint of those earrings, his long hair, maybe he hadn't broken any rules and had still been kicked out. She was trying to consider Justin's situation but kept seeing Franklin's face. *Sixty Minutes* had run a story about it a couple of months ago, the flood of young men kicked out of their homes and streaming into San Francisco, LA, Seattle. All these runaways.

Lianne had never answered Franklin's last letter. She'd left it there in that little all-but-unusable cupboard. It might yet be there. Yellowing, gathering dust. In the months after, she'd made excuse after excuse for herself—she was busy with her studies, Franklin was too old to be pen pals with his big sister anyway — but even then, she could feel her silence growing by the day bigger, darker, more monstrous.

My God, she thought now, and the tears rivered up and out of her, an animal sound uncoiling from her throat. She touched again the note Mariah had written her. She took the stairs two at a time. Even through her tears she could see her journal waiting for her on the corner of the dresser, a fine-tip pen beside it.

With salt on her lips and the sweet of honey, she drove east out of town, up Cemetery Hill, and around the gentle loop to the far corner, where the wind stacked tumbleweeds in the fences. Her mother's rose-colored stone shone bright, the many bouquets beginning now to fade. Her brother's stone was smaller, grayer. One crown of plastic roses leaned against it. She sat on the hard prairie earth and touched, lightly, the etched letters.

From up here, you could see for miles in all directions — the Bull Mountains, the river oxbowing and curving, the hills and plains, and, above it all, intricate feathers and notions and stacks of bright, white cloud cut with blue filigree, the vault of sky, the entire sky. It felt possible now to say what needed to be said, to choose the new and necessary.

Lianne Bouchard began to write a long-overdue letter.

# 54

JUSTIN SWUNG HIMSELF DOWN, and his feet felt different on the earth, his every step novel, consequential. They unsaddled the horses, brushed them, slid the bridles from their noses and turned them out, Big Red and Nine Spot tossing their manes and cropping each a mouthful of grass before galloping up the hill. Justin felt both himself and not himself. He shook his head and could feel, in aching detail, the slick, complex assemblages of shoulder and neck, muscle and bone, the wind in the cups of his ears. The whole of him trembled.

Without a word, he and Rene made for the shed — This is what we do, Justin thought as he bent to the work, what we always do — where they turned the first sets of mothers and lambs out into the makeshift pen, the little lambs bucking and running circles and, after a time, closing their eyes in the sunlight or flopping down in the grass. Justin was about to let the coffee-colored marker ewe and her jacketed runt out, but Mr. Bouchard told him to hold up. Even though the lamb was old enough, he wanted to give it another day, just to make sure. Justin let the jug's wooden gate fall back into place.

Mr. Bouchard showed him how to clean out a jug with a pitchfork, getting the tines underneath the matted shit and piss and straw, then how to disinfect the earth beneath with three good shakes of a coffee can filled with chalky slaked lime. A few flakes of new straw on top, and the jugs were ready again. A set of twins had dropped in the corral, and another young ewe was beginning to show. Mr. Bouchard caught up with the logbook. Justin jugged up the twins and fed and watered all the ewes in the jugs. The older lambs in the pen pranced and kicked and of a sudden ran over and dropped to their foreknees and nursed furiously at their mothers. Justin watched and marveled and trembled.

The day blurred into the good work, and some hours later, while Mr. Bouchard made coffee and set about thawing a pound of frozen stew meat for dinner, Justin checked once more on the sheep. He circled the corral and understood that he once knew but had forgotten this trembling. It carried him back to those first months in Rainier Beach, his mother readying for work at Boeing in the mornings, their Sunday shopping cart full of stuffed tortellini and Gatorade, his teachers at the middle school nodding as he spoke, as if what he was saying might even matter. Justin trembled because he had reason and grounds to hope, because he had begun to imagine the world Lianne had spoken into being just before she left—he had begun to imagine that this place, the Bouchard Ranch, wasn't just somewhere to rest with a roof over his head, to sock away a few good meals and carry when he left the memory of lambs in his hands. No, he had begun to imagine that he might stay.

The Bouchards, he thought, were the kind of people who could make things happen. Lianne especially. Unlike him, unlike his mother, they could turn the world another way. Lianne had said the word *stay*, and Mr. Bouchard had said Justin rode a sight better than some on their first go-round, and here he was, hauling another set of triplets to the shed. He noted these lambs in the logbook and fed and watered the new mother and rolled the door open and squeezed through—and someone was at the camphouse.

He melted like that back into the shadowed gap of the shed door.

They'd shown up unannounced like this the first time they came to question Heck about that logging job up on Iron Mountain. The men had worn thin jackets, though it was winter, and their trucks were dark and buffed, with clean white government plates.

Justin collected himself and peeked through the gap again.

The pickup out front of the camphouse was a boxy cream and brown Ford, the windows down, the sidewalls speckled with gouts of mud, the back plate nearly mudded over as well. This was no government truck. Whoever it was, Justin thought, stepping out of the shed, rolling the door closed, the old man wouldn't want him to hide. It'd be a shame, Mr. Bouchard had said, to let fear keep you from trying.

Justin tucked in his shirt and finger-combed his hair and strode across the dirt road to the camphouse. He didn't know if he should knock or not and stood there for a time with the sun at his back, the smells of sage and green grass and creek bottom wafting in the late-afternoon air. Finally, he knocked but didn't wait for an answer before he went in.

Mr. Bouchard and another man stood in the kitchen, both holding coffee cups. The man was younger than Mr. Bouchard, though outfitted the same in boots, jeans, and a snap shirt. He looked somehow familiar to the boy, hair shaggy and dark and poking out in tufts from underneath his cowboy hat, his face clearly built for a smile.

— This is Ves Munroe, Mr. Bouchard said. And this here is Justin, my latest hire. He's new to sheep ranching, but he's proved a pretty fair hand.

— Justin, the man said, and reached out to shake.

— Mr. Munroe, Justin said, gripping the man's hand.

The old man went on.

— Ves and his girl came out to pay us a visit. They're what passes for neighbors out here. How long is the drive over to your place, Ves? Half an hour?

— About that, Ves said. A real nice drive. You see my Amy out there?

Justin stood there a moment before realizing the man was talking to him.

— I, uh, just came from the shed. I didn't see anyone.

— Well, she likely isn't in the mood for shed chores. I hear you got lambs dropping?

— Yes, Justin said, then corrected himself: Yes, sir.

— No need to *sir* me. Ves'll do just fine. Maybe check down by the creek. Amy might've wandered that way. Tell her, if you would, that it's time to go. I got just a few more things for Rene here.

The sun a coin in the sky, meadowlarks calling in the cottonwoods,

Justin made his way past the outhouse and down the creek path. He found the girl sitting on the gravel bar where the two forks of Willow Creek came together.

She was maybe his age, wearing a blue flannel shirt. Her curly hair fell long and loose. She was hugging her knees to her chest, winging rocks now and again, the rocks blinking into the deep, slow water. O'Malley sat on his haunches beside her, leaning into her, the way he liked to do.

Justin pushed through the willows that choked the trail's mouth, and the dog's ears perked. The girl, Amy, scrambled to her feet.

—Who're you?

—I'm Justin.

The girl seemed to relax a moment, as if just his name made sense to her. She brushed at the back of her jeans and patted O'Malley on the head. Turned to the creek.

—I'm sorry about Viv, she said, then turned back to him. You're not from Roundup, right? Are you one of the ones from Colorado? One of Rene's grandkids?

That he might be Mr. Bouchard's grandson, that this girl looked at him and thought it so.

—No, he said, smiling, I'm not related or anything. I just work for Mr. Bouchard.

Amy crossed her arms over her chest and stared at him with renewed suspicion. Justin tried again, gesturing toward the camphouse.

—Your dad said I'd find you down here. He said it's time for you to go.

—Why are you dressed like that?

—Like what?

—You know, not like any ranch hand I've ever seen.

Amy came toward him, her shoes crunching in the gravel.

—Are those earrings? Are your ears pierced? You've got two earrings!

She was inches away from him now. He thought she might grab him by the ears. O'Malley gave a quick little woof and wagged his tail in the gravel.

—You gotta tell me where you're from. You're not from around here, right? I mean, around here there's only cowboys, jocks, and burnouts.

Some of the burnout guys wear earrings, but usually just one long dangly one and always, always, always in the left ear. Not in both ears. And burn-outs are kind of over anyway. It was more of an eighties thing. Now —

— What are you? Justin interrupted.

She was maybe an inch taller than he was, gangly and bright-faced. She grinned.

— I'm not any of those.

— Yeah, he said, I'm not any of those either.

She laughed. He did too. It had been a long time since he'd laughed with someone his age.

— Duh, she said, I could see that, like, a million miles away. Just tell me where you're from.

— Seattle.

— I fucking knew it! You look just like him!

Pleased but wary, knowing he was on the outside of everything here, Justin shook his head, bent down, and palmed a creek stone.

— It's just a coincidence. It's not like everyone in Seattle looks like Kurt Cobain.

— Okay, sorry. That was maybe kind of dumb. I hate it when people do that too. About here, I mean. Assume everyone dresses like a cowboy and rides a horse and chews tobacco.

Justin nodded and lobbed the rock into the water.

— But you probably ride a horse, right?

— Yeah, she said, of course.

They both laughed again.

— Well, it's, uh, nice to meet you — Amy, right? Anyway, your dad sent me down here to tell you it's time to go.

A quick frown washed across the girl's face.

— Walk back up with me?

— Sure, yeah.

O'Malley led the way, disappearing into the willows. Justin and the girl walked side by side.

— What grade are you in? she asked.

— Sophomore. You?

— Freshman.

The grass shushed about their knees and legs; a magpie flapped and croaked and veered away. Amy looked over at him, frowned.

— Where do you go to school?

— Nowhere.

— Really? You should go here.

— Yeah?

— Yeah, for sure. There's some cool people. I'll introduce you.

— That'd be awesome, Justin said, and slowed as the camphouse came into view. The two men stood there waiting, as just up the trail Amy was waiting now for him.

Justin caught up to her, and together they walked out from under the trees and into the cloud-shadowed prairie light.

# 55

LIANNE LIFTED HER EYES from the page to find the day cooling into evening, the shadows of cactus, sage, and the cemetery stones stretching east. Better than sixteen years gone, and she'd finally written her brother back. She was tired and cold and sad, but something like gladness blew through her as well, a good wind—in emptying herself, she'd spoken Franklin into being again for a moment. She'd missed him. She told her little brother how sorry she was, just what she should have done. Lianne wiped at her wet eyes and brushed the dust from her jeans. She drove down the hill and into town.

It was Saturday evening, and the gravel parking lot out front of the Snakepit was packed. She'd planned to call, but maybe Ves was here. How good it would be to drink a beer with him, let him know what she planned. She couldn't quite remember what his pickup looked like but nosed her Corolla into a slot between a flatbed and a big Dodge Ram and got out.

The ding of poker machines, clink of beer bottles, laughs and shouts—after the windy, wide-sky silence of the afternoon and early evening, Lianne was staggered by the dissonant noise of the bar. A hard light shone on the pool table, and colored Christmas lights ringed the mirror reflecting all the clear and amber bottles, but the rest of the room was bathed in shadow. She slid behind a couple dropping quarters into the jukebox and cut between two tables, a cowboy-hatted man scooting his chair out of the way for her. She turned a slow circle and was about to leave — when she felt the press of a hand at her back.

— Not often we get such high-class visitors. I'd bet dollars to cow-pies we ain't never had a college professor take in a Saturday night at the Snakepit!

Orly's hand was thick and wide. The blunt insistence of his fingers pushed Lianne toward the bar.

— Let's get you a drink, Miss Bouchard. Or is it still Mrs. Something or Other? I don't mean to be rude, but sounds like there's some question about that these days.

Orly winked, his closed eye disappearing in the flesh of his face. He'd hooked his whole arm around her waist now. She pulled away, but he was stronger. His fingers gripped her hip. Lianne was about to say something when she felt someone take her other arm.

— Orly, it's good of you to find Lianne for me.

That young science teacher, Gillian Kincheloe, pulled Lianne to her side and stabbed a pool stick straight up and down between Orly and the two of them.

— But we've got teacher business to discuss. Kind of stuff that would go right over your head. Lianne, I'll follow you.

Orly started to say something, maybe make a joke, but Lianne was gone, was out the door kicking gravel in the lot. She set the flat of her hand against her stomach, breathed. Blue and red neon snapped and hissed. Gillian had two bottles of Bud Light. She offered one to Lianne. Lianne took a big swallow.

— What a fucking asshole, she said, and wiped at the beer on her lips.

— That about sums it up. You okay?

— Yeah, thanks. I wasn't expecting that. Just looking for someone.

Gillian crossed her arms and leaned against the corrugated tin wall.

— When we first moved here, I worried that everybody would be like him. I was always on guard. And he definitely has money to throw around, and plenty of dumbasses laugh at his every joke, but it's mostly Orly that's like Orly. And like you say, he's a fucking asshole.

Lianne laughed. Mariah, Gillian. She could have friends here. Maybe she did already. She took another swallow. Risked the question.

— Was Ves at the bar this evening?

— No, but I thought you might be looking for him. Sorry. Small town and all. You know, though, they're branding out at his place tomorrow?

— He mentioned that. I'm not sure I'll make it. I've got to pick up my kids.

— Right, kids. Gillian lifted her bottle to her lips. My husband and I are switching off. I get to play a couple rounds of pool with the other teachers tonight, and he gets to go to the branding tomorrow. Speaking of, I should make the most of it.

Gillian started back into the bar. Lianne called another thanks.

— Don't worry about it, Gillian said. Maybe sometime we can all get together? Me and Kevin, you and Ves?

Lianne hadn't been on a proper date since she was twenty years old. She was thankful the neon hid the color in her neck and cheeks.

— Sure, she said. Yeah. That'd be fun.

# 56

RENE CARRIED THE NEWS, as he did most heavy things, in silence.

After Ves and Amy left, he and the boy walked the herd. Justin didn't ask, but Rene offered that Ves had been out here hoping to talk to Lianne, that he must have missed her on the road. The boy nodded as if this made good and reasonable sense, and they went on circling the sheep. One was down on her side near the feeder. She strained, kicked at the dirt. Blood and membrane pooled at her backside. Justin held her, as before, and Rene delivered triplets, the runt the first one this time. While the boy jugged the ewe and her lambs, Rene tried to get up off the ground, but his knee and hip failed him. Goddamn. He crawled through the dirt to the feeder, where he could get a hand on the lowest board, then the corner post, and slowly haul himself up. He slapped at the dust and sheep shit on his jeans and felt unaccountably thinned, as if he weren't much more than dry cottonwood limbs snapped in any old wind.

Rene did the logbook, his hand shaky and weak, the blue ink wicking into nonsense whenever he paused, then he begged off and let Justin take the better part of the work: unloading the hay from Old Blue, checking again for lambs, and herding the sheep into the shed for the evening.

Rene sat on the porch with a glass of whiskey. The rich onion smell of the stew he'd had on the stove all afternoon drifted out the open front door. The light as ever in his eyes until the dark hills and far buttes lanced and drained the sun.

Shadows reeled up and over him.

Justin washed, and when he'd finished, Rene bummed a cigarette — the ask and glance down as easy as it was all those years ago when he was working as a cowboy for Schuster — and Justin rooted for the pack in his shirt pocket, handed one to Rene, shook one out for himself, and crumpled the empty pack. Rene thought he'd be able then to bring it up, while they smoked, but before he could, Justin mentioned that Ves's girl Amy seemed nice, that she'd said something about going to school in town, in Delphia, how she'd show him around. And Rene couldn't do it after that. Not with a spark like that in the boy's eyes.

Three bowls of stew later, Justin looked fit to fall asleep at the table. Rene told him he ought to wash up and get to bed. By the time Rene was done with the dishes, the boy was indeed asleep, the green star on the ceiling still shining.

Rene dropped the curtain over the bedroom doorway. The night wasn't so cold that they'd need to bank a fire. He blew out all the lamps but one and poured another glass of whiskey — leaving maybe two fingers in the bottle — and sat once more on the porch as night settled over him and everything.

He wished maybe that Justin had stayed in the shed. Then no one would know. Then they could have gone on for a little while yet. Sometimes even a day matters, Rene thought. A day, an hour. Another handful of words. If you were wise and brave enough to say them.

Rene strained whiskey through his teeth. At his feet, O'Malley twitched in a dream.

Ves had held his hat in his hands and been right up front about Lianne even before Rene had poured him any coffee. Ves had made Amy come with him to the house in town, and no one was home, so he figured Lianne was out here. Rene hadn't been so sure about Ves Munroe, as full of silliness and trouble as he'd been in high school, but he'd indeed found his way up to being a good man. They sipped coffee and turned to the weather, the early spring and what it might portend. His hat back on his head, Ves invited Rene to their branding tomorrow if he could take time away from the sheep. Ves had turned and been about to leave—when Justin came in.

Bats and nighthawks scissored the sky's dark cloth. The dim stars.

After the boy left for the creek, Ves scuffed at the camphouse floor with the toe of his boot. Ves apologized but said he wouldn't feel right if he didn't mention that Orly Pinkerton had seen someone on his place the other day, a drifter, someone young, carrying a guitar case about like that one right there leaning against the wall, and so he, Ves, had been keeping an eye on the Billings paper, just in case there was—and Ves had looked right at Rene when he said it—just in case there was a kid in trouble. A kid who needed help.

—Well? Rene asked, not wanting to ask.

—I saw it yesterday, Ves said, and toyed with his empty coffee cup, which he'd set on the counter. Didn't think much of it. Seemed so far away. But there's a man dead out of Nye, dead maybe a week now.

—And he didn't get that way himself.

—No.

—Goddamn.

—The paper mentioned a relation of some sort, a boy, high-school-age. No name, though. And they can't find the dead guy's wife and kids either. They likely wouldn't have found him at all except that they were coming out there to arrest him. Some kind of illegal logging operation.

Ves paused, looked up.

—How long has the kid been out here?

Rene worked a hand down over his face and looked away. His silence said enough. Ves cursed under his breath.

—How's he been? I mean, should I be headed down to the creek to make sure Amy's all right?

Rene took a step forward, his heat up before he could help it.

—Hell no. He's just a kid. Kind of goofy sometimes, but he listens. I meant it when I said he's a good hand, I wouldn't lie about something like that. And that story in the paper, it doesn't have to be Justin.

—No, it doesn't, Ves agreed. There's likely a heap of kids on the run out there. All kinds of things we don't know about. I just didn't want you to be surprised. Wanted you to know the shape of things.

Rene could feel even then that thinness in him, the whole of him emptying. Before he could offer anything more, some context or reasoning that might sort this out, they heard Amy and Justin coming up from the creek—laughter and the loose, easy voices of young people.

Ves pushed the camphouse door open, then held back a moment, his face set.

—I might listen in, but I don't do much gossiping downtown. And you know as well as I do that Orly Pinkerton isn't one to read any newspapers. We don't know each other all that well, Rene—just neighbors, I suppose—but there's not many I trust more. Whatever you decide, is what I'm saying.

Now the lamp in the camphouse dimmed and shook and after a moment stilled. Likely the wick needed turning up. Rene sat where he was. He held the whiskey glass in his two hands, lifted it to his lips. Not a drop left. Empty of everything but the night.

# BEFORE

# 57

AGAIN, JUSTIN SLEPT. AGAIN, though this night, warm and full and unafraid to let himself all the way down into the depths of sleep, he dreamed of the many hours beyond repair, the cloth of things ripped.

Tatters, tatters.

Hungover, or still teeteringly drunk, Heck sometimes forgot to let him out of the locked camper until late in the morning, even past noon. Justin rinsed out an old milk jug and kept it full of water, squirreled away some chips and packaged cookies and things like that. When he had to, he pissed in the sink. It drained directly under the camper and stank. What could you do?

One long, locked-in morning, after working out the chords to "Heart-Shaped Box," which was new to him, a song he'd heard for the first time just days before he left Seattle, before he got on a Greyhound headed for Montana — playing quietly, so quietly, in case Heck was near — Justin set his guitar down, lay back on the thin camper bed, and studied the sky-light, the sun-bleached patterns whirling through the half-opaque yellow plastic.

With one foot on the bench along the small table, a knee on the tiny counter by the sink, Justin balanced himself and reached up to feel around the edges of the skylight. It wasn't screwed in or riveted, not that he could tell. He rubbed the dry grit of old adhesive between his fingers. The plastic, too, was beginning to vein and flake, crack at the corners. A way out, he thought, and just as the thought firmed in his mind, he heard Heck clomping down the dirt walk. He threw himself back onto the bed.

With his aunt and cousins gone, he didn't have as many chores — just hauling firewood, chopping kindling — and with Heck's trucks and saws confiscated, there wasn't any logging work or any long, rambling drives through the mountains. So Justin had time. About the only thing he could do on his own, though, was play guitar. For everything else — walk the creek, get something to eat, shower — he had to ask permission. He wished he had a notebook and pen. He wanted to make a list like he used to do for all the music, listening to the radio and carefully charting each song in the Top 40. He needed to start planning, to note what he had, what he might need. When the time came, he wanted to be ready.

Heck drove his four-wheeler, the only vehicle left on the place, into Nye for beer and what passed for groceries — frozen meals, canned stews and baked beans, white bread, bologna. He always left Justin locked in the camper when he was gone.

Justin used those afternoons to work at the skylight.

He couldn't just punch through it. Heck would notice and board it up. No, he had to be able to set it back in after he lifted it out, which one April afternoon he finally did, a corner sliding out cleanly from between the layers of plywood and metal, the other cracking, though Justin thought he could prop it up in such a way Heck wouldn't notice.

Justin hauled himself up onto the camper's white roof, dry needles and hard glops of birdshit, and slid down the bulbous end of the trailer and went to work. He used the one window to let himself into the house, which smelled of beer and cooking grease and piss, the ammonia reek so strong that when he went by the bathroom he nearly gagged.

A backpack, a knife, a map — what else?

He wished he'd been able to make that list, was sure he was forgetting something. No food, not yet — there was so little food in the house that Heck would note anything missing. But he lifted Heck's old army surplus backpack off the shelf in the unfinished basement. He scrounged a paring knife with a good wooden handle in the kitchen, a rain poncho in the mudroom, a flashlight in the junk drawer.

Justin risked two pieces of bread and a spoonful of peanut butter and ate the quick sandwich standing up, then hurried back through the house and crawled out. He made sure the curtains hung the way they had, pulled the window closed, and fitted the screen back in the frame. After the dark of the house, the stink, he blinked in the light, pulled the piney air deep into his lungs.

He didn't know how much time he had.

He scrambled up the sloping camper roof and dropped the pack in with a clunk. Then he lowered himself down through the skylight and onto the counter. He stuffed the backpack with what clothes he could spare—four pairs of socks and underwear, a handful of T-shirts, three flannels, a pair of jeans. In case he had to run at night in the rain, he stowed the flashlight and poncho beneath his mattress. The knife under his pillow.

Then poked his head up out of the skylight once more.

He looked down the road as far as he could. No one. And he didn't hear the growl of the four-wheeler. He hauled himself up and slid down the top of the camper with the backpack and his guitar in tow and ran to the old barn. Took the stairs two at a time, hid both in there, beneath rotting handfuls of straw. Then sat back and breathed.

A good day's work, he thought. Another afternoon like this—find a map, snag some food—and he'd be ready. He'd go, he thought, early in the morning, before dawn, the likeliest time for Heck to be passed out or otherwise incapacitated.

Outside the barn, the sun shone high and white-yellow, the sky feathered at the edges with cloud. It was hard to tell when Heck might be back—sometimes he didn't come home until dark—and Justin would have liked to walk the creek, study the greening leaves of snowberry, tug at last year's pearly fruit still hanging on the stalks. He settled for crouching on a wide, flat rock and pulling off his T-shirt and rinsing his pits and neck and face. He washed and shook dry and wished he could scrub his greasy hair with soap. Heck hadn't let him use the shower for days. Burnt

Creek glugged and crashed down the mountain. Wind licked at his wet skin.

Justin dressed and loped back to the camper. He was perched on the roof, legs dangling in the empty skylight hole, about to let himself down — when he heard the crack of a beer can.

# 58

Up north, in that high, wild country where the Musselshell charges hard for the Missouri, seams begin to appear on the prairie. The thinnest hairline cracks. Keep following, and the fissures widen into gullies, into breaks that shift and drop, plummet suddenly into chasm, scarp, and canyon—and what seemed a solid and forever range of plains falls from beneath you.

Rene and Viv talked with the parents of the boys who'd tied Franklin up, and for a time things were better. Slowly, though, the bullying and meanness came bubbling back up. Knowing the ways of boys, or thinking he knew, Rene hesitated to step in much more. He was just damned glad Franklin had a friend—and a good one at that. It would have been easy for Kevin to drop Franklin after what had happened. But he hadn't. Rene thought a lot of old Elner Kincheloe too, Kevin's mother, who, after her husband died young, had been running the Kincheloe spread for years. Rene himself first hired help in '77. The summers before, he'd tried to do it alone, but without Lianne around and with Viv spending more of her time in town, the work of the ranch simply got away from him. Rather than readying for the season ahead, he was always fixing the next busted thing, patching over what he could just to keep things going. Franklin helped some, and Kevin tagged along and helped out as well. They were good boys, kind and easy to get along with, always willing to try, though with all the exploring, storytelling, and general daydreaming they did when they stayed out at the ranch, Rene sometimes wondered if it wasn't mostly for the company that he brought them along. Rene fixed up one of the old sheep wagons that summer. The construction was yet true — the wheels and axle and wooden frame, even the tiny stove and chimney pipe in good condition — but the wagon hadn't been used in years. He set Franklin and Kevin to pulling mice nests from the cupboards and drawers, chipping the hard mud cups left by barn swallows from beneath the eaves. They tightened and glued every corner and joist, nailed down a bright tin roof, put new hinges on the Dutch door, replaced the window above the bed, horsed in a new mattress, and finally painted most everything that could be painted a shamrock green, Viv's favorite color.

Once the wagon was ready, Rene let word filter through town that he was looking for ranch help. Delphia, and eastern Montana in general, was the kind of place you could find a man, or sometimes a woman, willing to live out on the prairie for months at a time in a six-by-twelve sheep wagon that lacked electricity and running water. Some simply couldn't get along with people and even in this far place needed a place that much farther away. Others were running from the bottle, or to the bottle, or from or to similar devilments. Most did decent work, although decent work was barely good enough for Rene, and a few were true geniuses with their hands and backs. A very few were miserably lazy. Regardless, they seldom lasted long, taking their pay and disappearing down the road, stepping into another story altogether.

That August, after they'd gotten their first hired hand settled in — a man named Leforge from out of Hardin, his long black hair in two thin braids, the ends tied off with chewed hide — Rene, Franklin, and Kevin stayed on an extra night at the camphouse. Rene peppered beefsteaks and cooked them on the cast-iron. He slathered potato and onion slices with butter, wrapped them in foil, and nestled the hobo packs in the red-orange coals in the woodstove. He had bottles of root beer and strawberry pop in the fridge for the boys, an extravagance he never would have allowed Keith or Dennis, and he'd stowed a bottle of whiskey beneath the sink for himself.

After dinner, they scrubbed the dishes, and even though the long summer twilight blued the window, they lit the lamps, settled into playing poker for pennies. Rene eventually cleared both boys out—two jacks in a game of stud settled things—and they leaned into the lamplight and told stories. Or, rather, Rene told stories, and Franklin and Kevin breathed life into their many wishes and imaginings. Unlike Franklin, Kevin had played on the basketball team and, as far as Rene understood, was popular at school. He was quick to joke and laugh and was nice-looking in the way boys were supposed to be nice-looking, wide-shouldered and square-jawed. Yet Rene could see why the boys were friends. Kevin, too, was serious, was someone who paid attention. He held Franklin's photos close to his nose and commented on the framing or the focus. He was always going on about what he called *the science of ecology*. A year ahead of Franklin in school, Kevin was going to the university in a month to study forestry, not just to play on the basketball team for a season or two, like most boys around here who tried college did. Kevin and Franklin dreamed and schemed about the wider world, and even if this world right here was the one that mattered to Rene, he smiled to see the boys happy in each other's company.

Stars sparking the window, that last glass of whiskey swirling behind his eyes, Rene excused himself to bed. He stripped down to his long johns and, given the warmth of day, pulled just the cotton sheet up and over himself. Even as he slid into sleep, he could yet hear the boys talking, talking.

Rene woke early, as he always did, the sun not yet risen but the world anyway beginning to shine with a dull, pewter-colored light. A dream teased the edges of his vision as he heated water for coffee. An argument, a sundering. He sometimes dreamed Viv had left him, but those dreams were vivid and terrifying, and he usually woke remembering every painful detail, every little thing he'd done wrong. Standing now at the window, he sipped coffee, waited for the chickadees and larks to take up their daily work, and he couldn't put together whatever the broken dream was. The glinting bits of it.

The boys slept late—must have stayed up for a good long time—and Rene set himself to the chores of closing up the camphouse. He trimmed the wicks in the lamps and wiped down the counters. He heated a pot for wash water, then shoveled the last of the ashes into an old coffee can and dumped the can down the outhouse hole. Once the fridge was emptied and wiped out, he propped the door open with a hunk of driftwood against mildew, packed the few things that would spoil into a cardboard box, and loaded the box into the bed of Old Blue. When he came back in, Kevin was up. He'd already dressed and packed his duffel bag, and he stood there rubbing at his eyes, waiting. He washed and took his coffee and plate of biscuits and bowl of canned peaches. Rene finally had to go in and get Franklin up. He found him awake, just lying there in his bunk by the window.

— You boys must have stayed up late, Rene said, leaning over Franklin and shutting the window. Well, you gotta pay the piper. Let's get moving.

— Okay, Franklin said, though he didn't. He didn't move at all.

Rene cocked his head, lowered his voice.

— You all right there?

— No, Franklin said, and squeezed his eyes shut. Then opened them. Yes.

Rene felt wooden in his movements after that but didn't know what else to do besides clean up the last of the dishes, sweep the floor, and drive the boys home, the sun boiling up in the east, the day already a light-rinsed, blistering thing. As the roadwind spilled in, they didn't talk much. Kevin stared out the window. Franklin, sitting in the middle of the bench seat, sagged into his father and didn't say a word, even when Rene tried to get a little conversation going, even when Kevin, always polite, obliged. After they dropped Kevin off at his place, the Kincheloe ranch right at the north bend of the Musselshell River, just south of the highway, Franklin buried his face in his father's shoulder and shuddered, began to cry. Rene knew he ought to do or say something.

He didn't know what to say, didn't know what to do but drive.

Something had happened. He didn't understand a goddamn thing that had just happened.

# 59

THE BONFIRE SUCKED AND shuddered, great gouts of flame leaping into the mountain night. Heck's face reflected that fire.

Empty gas can toppled on the grass behind him, Heck tipped his beer back and back. He tossed the empty onto the flames, pulled another from the rack. When something big caught — oily black smoke funneling up from the old recliner, the pop and sigh of half a dozen capped milk jugs — Heck grunted in satisfaction.

Justin stood deeper in the shadows.

He swayed, closed his eyes, and held his hands out for balance, as if he might grab hold of the night. Each time he blinked and glanced up, the fire grew that much bigger, roared that much louder. A pile of keyholed beer cans lay in the dust and pine duff at his feet. He'd gulped down three quick, before he felt anything, so Heck made him do two more. Heck had already drunk the shoulders and belly out of a fifth of Rich & Rare. He laughed at what a lightweight Justin was, slapped him on the back.

Justin staggered. Swallowed against the hot metallic gorge rising in the back of his throat.

Earlier, Heck had hauled him out of the trailer by his ankles, dragging him, his head hitting the camper floor, his back ripping over the aluminum sill and onto the dirt. Heck stood over Justin then, the toes of his boots pinning the boy's upper arms to the ground, and squatted down and slapped his face and head, poked at his throat, his eyes. Finally, after Justin quit trying to twist free, Heck grinned. His face was so close, his patchy beard and wide nose, breath soured by beer and Copenhagen and canned stew.

Heck chuckled, said he'd thought he'd just check how things were going when he wasn't around, a little test, so on his way back from town he'd parked the four-wheeler a mile down the road and, like the old bear, walked up the mountain just to see what he could see. Heck chuckled again, pleased with his own craftiness and guile, then lightly patted Justin on the cheek. Said they were gonna have a fire, said they were gonna drink.

The fire twisted and shook. Heck cracked open a beer and wrapped both of Justin's hands around it.

—Don't say I never gave you nothing! Heck laughed at his own joke, laughed until he coughed. He popped open another for himself and drank long and deep, then sighed, seemed to deflate.

—Shit, we've been out here on this mountain way too fucking long.

Justin swayed in the dark.

—You ever twiddle some little city gal? Heck asked, his voice dropping in volume and register. One of those ones with an earring in her nose? I think maybe I wouldn't mind some skinny little thing with a ring in her nose. Just to try it out.

Heck squatted down and picked up a handful of pine needles and tossed them on the flames. The needles sizzled, smoked, and were gone.

—When I was your age, he said, I was seeing this gal who didn't have a left hand. Just the arm, you know, and the skin over the end of the bone. Some kind of birth defect. She was eight, ten years older than me, and we had to sneak around. I'd show up at her trailer when I was supposed to be at football practice. She'd fuck the daylights out of me, I tell you what.

Heck sniffed and drank, and his face was doing strange things, the muscles twitching, his lips curling into a smile, a sneer. His eyes mean one moment, then stricken.

—She was in a car wreck. Winter, black ice. She went sailing straight off the edge of a bridge. I hadn't seen her in years. I only heard about it later, after I was back from Iraq. I guess she wasn't much. Just some big-titted piece of tail who didn't have but the one hand.

Heck was a hulking darkness now, the shape of him eclipsed by flames. He threw his great, huge head back and let beer roll down the hole of his throat. He came close and closer.

— Maybe you ain't into girls? How about a little boy or two? Is that the kind of tail you're chasing?

Justin didn't understand a thing Heck was talking about, was trying only to keep himself from falling over. His stomach heaved and sloshed. He thought he might be sick. He was sick.

Heck cursed and stepped back, tossed his empty at the flames.

— You're gonna have to learn to hold your beer, bucko. He paused and shook his head. Go wash your stupid fucking self off in the creek. Can't have you a mess like that.

Justin stumbled toward the clatter and purl of the creek. He half fell, half sat on the bank. Took off his shoes and scrubbed the sick from them in the grass. He didn't want to get them wet. Drunk as he was, the night spinning like a top, he knew it'd be hard to run in wet shoes. Better they stank, better they were stained. He lay down on his belly, lowered his lips to the cold surface of the water, sucked in a mouthful. Rinsed and spit, rinsed and spit. Then drank deep. He splashed his face, and his head cleared some. If he weren't so drunk, if the night wasn't so cold, he'd run right now. Even without his pack, his guitar. He didn't fucking trust the way things were unfolding — the lack of a beating, just the slaps, the forced drinking, the glug and stink of gas, a single match tossed onto the burn pile. And, too, before the fire, Heck had fitted a square of plywood over the skylight and tightened it down with four-inch screws, the sharp, threaded tips daggering down from the camper ceiling. Once Justin was locked inside, there'd be no way out. Not ever again.

He tried to hold it all, tried to parse and reckon it. He glanced back at the fire. There was the gas can, the case of Keystone. Where was Heck?

A stick snapped. Heck grabbed him by the hair on the back of his head and drug him, shoeless and wet-faced and writhing, deeper into the night.

# APRIL 1994

# 60

Though soon it would and the day begin, that glow at the horizon line, that blue-gold penumbra, the sun hadn't yet broken over the hills east of Willow Creek. Justin, already back after a walk through the herd, perched himself on the edge of the bench and strummed his guitar and sang low, just under his breath, that same song he'd played for them the other night. *Come as you are, as you were, as I want you to be...*

Rene turned back to the stove, where a pot of mush bubbled and shook. He cut the heat and spooned on sugar, dropped in the butt end of a stick of butter. Let it melt a moment.

—Grub's on.

Justin snapped his guitar back into the case and was up and ready before Rene could even lift a bowl and spoon for himself. The boy ladled his bowl full and asked what it was and dipped a finger in the hot mush and shouted and sucked his finger and smiled and sort of danced over to the table. Lifted a spoonful to his mouth—but caught himself.

He plopped the spoon down in the bowl and turned and waited for Rene, his knees bouncing to a rhythm all their own beneath the table.

—Go on, Rene said. You get to be my age, you don't move so quick in the mornings. You eat.

Justin started in, and Rene ferried the pot of mush over to the table and set it down on a woven hot pad, green and deeper green, one Viv had made long ago.

—I got what I need as it is, Rene said, gesturing at the pot. You eat up the rest.

Rene sat and ate, sipped at his coffee. He was feeling more stove up than usual, his chest and arms tight, the ache of two deep glasses of whiskey behind his eyes. Justin kept up a more or less steady stream of chatter, and Rene nodded and ate and answered as needed.

He was looking at the boy and trying not to see a boy but someone who'd killed a man, killed his own uncle—he couldn't do it.

All he could see was this loose, happy, long-haired kid—Justin. The boy he was now, right here.

And didn't it used to be this way? You could leave a place and show up in another and no one much cared who you had been or where you came from, only that you could do the work you were asked to do, only that you could stand up when you needed to on your own two feet. Thad Bassett—not a soul knew where he'd come from—had had the good luck to wash up on Pete Schuster's spread, and now, years later, was a known hand and sheepherder in this part of the country. Or, hell, Rene's own story was one—the son of a no-account Missouri Breaks bootlegger who'd turned himself into a rancher, who owned one of the biggest spreads in the Musselshell Valley. Was it that the world then wasn't yet stitched together? More gaps where a body might slip through? Something felt like it was hemming them in. Maybe that story in the newspaper. Maybe school records or some such. Goddamn but why couldn't this Justin, no matter what happened with that uncle of his over in Nye, just begin again out here? Become the boy he'd never had a chance to be?

First light brought the goldfinches quick to the feeder and quick on the wing away.

Justin was asking him something, and Rene had missed what it was, but looking from the birds to the boy, Rene had the thought that, hell, it was already happening. Here was a boy eating three bowls of sugared mush and just about bouncing out of his seat with excitement for the new day. Maybe there wasn't a damn thing but his own troublesome heart in the way, the cruelties of this place his own heart's failings, his own vanity and fear. Though even as Rene touched the flat of his hand to his chest, an image of Franklin tied to a cottonwood along the midnight river rose behind his eyes, then one of Orly hulking in the dark in front of the camphouse, that big red pickup blowing exhaust up into the evening sky. He hated it, but it was true—there was some thread of kinship between himself and Orly, even between himself and those boys who'd bullied Franklin. At least there had been. Up until now.

—You never did let on to me, Rene said, setting his spoon down and lacing his hands above his bowl, about a last name.

Justin blinked and shied, whatever it was he was about to say dying like that away.

—I'm asking because it'd be good to know if it's the same last name as that uncle of yours.

The boy shook his head. Rene swallowed, went on.

—Well, good. But you might want to pick a different one anyway. Rene leaned back in his chair. I been thinking on it, and it might make some things a little easier. Things like school, which you mentioned yesterday. And I'd support.

It was as if the boy stepped back into himself, his eyes somehow brightening in their blue, his shoulders going still and sturdy, the whole of him growing into the moment—the wild possibility Rene had just breathed into spark and flame.

—How about *Cobain?* the boy asked, his voice even, quiet.

Rene said it in his mind and knew he'd heard that name before and after a moment or two connected it with the singer, that one the boy liked. He nodded. Well, it'd be easy to remember.

—All right, Justin Cobain, it's time to feed sheep.

# 61

A SQUEAK OF SWINGS and merry-go-rounds, shouts of children, a dipping melody spilling from someone's boombox — Lianne skirted the edge of the park's busy green space. The sky above was a soft blue, circumscribed, the same mountain sky she'd known so many years ago. On this Sunday morning in Missoula, the lilacs were in full bloom, and dozens of families were out. Joggers and walkers crisscrossed the trails that wound along either side of the river. A troupe of teenage girls practiced a dance routine by the basketball courts. A bearded man with a tarp over his shoulders shuffled along the runoff creek. And three boys in black jeans and ratty sweatshirts shared a cigarette by the restrooms.

Lianne stopped and stretched — six hours in the car already this morning — and surveyed the park from her new vantage. She spied Marty near a budding Norway maple, the boys on the jungle gym nearby.

— Hey, she said, coming up behind Marty, touching his arm. You must have gotten here early.

Marty bent to the small red cooler at his feet, popped the top.

— You've had a long drive. I've got snacks. A soda?

— No. I'm okay.

Marty straightened up, adjusted his glasses. He'd never looked more like himself. Hair thinning up top, shoulders beginning to slope. Not heavy but soft in the middle. He was the type of man who was meant to be in his mid-forties — destined to hold a decent job, be a good dad, a faithful husband. This was going to be so damned hard.

— Marty, I just…well, for a long time now, I don't even know how long, I haven't been honest with myself. Or with you.

Marty looked one way, then the other. Anywhere but at her.

— You're staying in Delphia? You're going to live there?

— For now.

Marty started in lecturing. He spread his arms wide, his voice strained and loud. A couple walking nearby turned their way — and Marty stopped. He held his hands up in front of himself, as if pushing all this away.

— I'm sorry. Wow, I'm just really angry. I didn't know I could get so angry. But this is such a dumb decision, Lianne. You can't let your father run your life forever. You can't —

Lianne hadn't expected anger. Not from Marty. And his fury, his voice like she'd never heard it — loud, serrated — brought out her own. He didn't have any idea, she told him, what he was talking about.

— It's not Dad. It's not even because — and here she paused, met his eyes as she said it — I'm seeing somebody else. It's way before all that, Marty. Way before.

Like that, Marty's anger fell in on him, the flames collapsing into ash. He closed the cooler and zipped up his jacket. He was already, she could see, planning his next steps, her confession finally making this real for him.

— I'll call when I'm back, he said. I fly home Thursday.

Marty went over to the boys — Trent getting in on a game of basketball now, Frank playing on the monkey bars — and Lianne gathered their things. Marty patted each boy on the back, hugged them both, and told them to be good. He straightened up and, for the first time, looked right at Lianne. She cursed herself for it but couldn't help it — she started apologizing. She had plenty to atone for, but not this. This, she told herself, was just the truth.

The first miles on the road, the boys were full of stories and jokes — Trent was on a joke kick, and his best audience by far was his brother — but the boys had been up early too. An hour out of Missoula, as she slowed off the interstate and turned onto Highway 12, which paralleled the Little Blackfoot River before rising to the Continental Divide, Lianne glanced in the rearview and found Frank asleep, his head resting against the door, Trent with his nose buried in a book.

On both sides now, the mountains rose and buckled and rose up once again. In her mind Lianne repeated the words she'd written yesterday, the letter she'd finally answered — *I'm sorry, Franklin, for not asking. I'm so sorry for seeing you and not seeing you.* You had to see things as they were, and you had to tell yourself in words what you'd seen. We lie to ourselves if we don't look and shape the true words in our own mouths, if we hold them unsaid in our hearts.

The engine strained against the grade. Lianne gripped the wheel and turned her Corolla into switchback after tight switchback. At MacDonald Pass, the spine of the continent, the engine notched down its whine, and the mountains themselves resolved for a time before descending into canyon, ridge, and aridity.

From here, all water ran the other way, toward the Missouri, and Lianne felt the whole of her rushing that way as well.

# 62

THEY'D SEEN TO THE sheep and the horses, and with nothing showing in the corral, Mr. Bouchard said they might as well stop by the Munroes' branding. He put a hand on Justin's shoulder and said a branding was work, don't get him wrong, but it was a chance, too, to catch up with folks, to drink some soda pop and eat some hamburgers. If we're thinking you might start school and whatnot, he said, well, maybe we ought to make an appearance.

Justin slid the flannel he'd scrubbed on the washboard over his shoulders — the cloth stiff and smelling of soap — buttoned it up, tucked it in, and cinched his belt tight. He shifted the sheath of his knife over so that it hung almost behind his hip. In front of the mirror above the dresser, he brushed his hair, feathered it back behind his ears as best he could, his part falling just a bit to the left. He took out one earring, started to take out the other, but stopped. Looking at himself in the mirror, he thought of the girl, Amy, and put the earring he'd taken out back in.

O'Malley had already loaded himself up into the back of Old Blue, and Mr. Bouchard was waiting for Justin out front of the camphouse. The old man had traded his usual straw hat for a wide-brimmed hat of gray felt, an iridescent black feather stuck in the band. The snaps of his checked shirt shone a creamy pearl. He jangled his keys at Justin.

—I was thinking I'd have you drive, the old man said. That way I can do a little sightseeing.

With both hands on the black wheel, Justin brought the truck around and started down the dirt road. The tires shushed in the ruts. Midday sun streamed down. Willow Creek laughed alongside them. And Justin knew this for what it was. He was driving Mr. Bouchard to this get-together, this branding, and people would see him driving Old Blue, the man's keys in his pocket, and that would mean something — he wasn't sure what, exactly, but it was no small thing. That he knew. And so he drove, slowly, carefully, and Mr. Bouchard hooked his elbow out the open window, watched the prairie roll by like he hadn't had a good look at it in years.

They splashed through the creek and came up the Seventy-Nine Hill, and Mr. Bouchard pointed off to the southwest as they gained the crest.

—Antelope. Fifty head or more.

On willow-thin limbs, the antelope streamed across the flats, the duns and whites of their backs and rumps and bellies liquid in the sun.

The ranch road dead-ended at an oiled gravel road, the berm slightly higher, the ditches along either side deeper, and Mr. Bouchard pointed south once more. The back end of Old Blue fishtailed a moment, then trued as they picked up speed. At the county line they hit pavement, such as it was, potholed and cracked and not a painted line to be found. Fifteen minutes on, they rumbled over a cattle guard and turned east onto the highway proper, crossed a bridge, the river below bending north, and Mr. Bouchard pointed up the highway at the mouth of another gravel road. Less than a mile on the gravel, and they turned onto a dirt road that led, Justin realized, his gut hollowing, to the very same farmstead he'd found himself contemplating not so long ago from the back of a stock trailer. He looked at Mr. Bouchard as if they were both in on the secret, but of course they weren't, Mr. Bouchard not paying any attention to him, only smoothing back his gray hair, touching his hat to his head.

Nobody needed to know, Justin guessed. Another something he'd carry on his own.

He slowed and nosed Old Blue into a gap in the long column of pickups that stretched down the road maybe a hundred yards from the house.

He cut the engine and offered the keys to Mr. Bouchard. The old man shook his head, told Justin to hold on to them.

With O'Malley at heel, they came clean of the pickups and walked toward the noise and commotion.

The screen door to the house slapped open and closed as women ferried bowls of potato salad and pasta salad and jugs of iced tea and lemonade to lines of folding tables. Nearby, two grills smoked and spit. A small, aproned man with an enormous mustache wielded a pair of tongs and a long metal spatula. At the end of one of the tables, Justin noted, a plate of hamburgers and one of hotdogs were already there for the taking, along with a tray of ribs glistening in sauce. He wondered if maybe they might not stop and get a little something to eat first, before they went to work. The women called hello to Mr. Bouchard, and he touched the brim of his hat and kept on. Justin glanced once more at the tray of burgers, then hurried to keep up. Off to the side of the house, an old metal swing set screeched and rocked. Little kids, too young to help, ran about clutching lassos and sticks and toy six-guns. O'Malley woofed in frustration at the shame of all these little critters running here and there without any proper herding.

Nearer the corrals, they came on the cattle work, men and women and boys and girls busy with one thing or another, though some leaned in twos and threes up against the corral boards and talked and laughed. They all wore boots and fitted blue jeans, and while most of the men wore snap shirts like Mr. Bouchard, a few of the boys had on T-shirts or tank tops, ball caps instead of cowboy hats. They circled to one side of the corrals, and Justin wondered which group they'd join, where they'd go — more than a few were staring at him, sizing him up, wondering why this long-haired kid was following Rene Bouchard around — and as if in answer, the man who'd been out at the ranch the other day, Ves Munroe, came striding toward them.

— Rene. Justin. Good to see you.

Ves pumped their hands in turn and asked how they were, then guided them over to a low wooden stand built so you could see above the highest corral boards, see the action. The bellows of calves, calls of cowboys, drifts of dust and shit and sunlight, metal slam of gates — the whole of it was like nothing Justin had ever witnessed. Ves knew it and had a hand on Justin's shoulder, explaining that there were different operations going on in each of the main corrals. In the far one, they were running an old-fashioned branding, with cowboys on horses heading and heeling the calves, and wranglers laying them out—and they were even using a fire of juniper and coal to heat the irons. Ves grinned, said a couple of the fancy restaurants he sold to liked to advertise that the beef was ranched using traditional practices. In the other corral, where they had the bulk of the herd, they were running the calves into a squeeze chute, an iron contraption that held the calf while it was doctored and branded. The chutes and squeeze made the work faster, more efficient.

—Amy's over there, Ves said, pointing toward the squeeze chute. All right if she gets you lined out? I'm gonna take Rene over this way. See if he can't teach these knuckleheads how to properly heel a calf.

Mr. Bouchard nodded and so Justin nodded as if to say, yes, that was okay, as if he knew what he was doing. He watched the two men walk away, O'Malley as ever at Mr. Bouchard's heel, and Justin wondered what it would be like to know a place and to know the people in that place and to be known in turn. Whether it would be welcome or a weight.

He stepped off the riser and came around the corral, one hand on the worn wood, the grain of it slipping beneath his fingers, and watched as a man set a hot branding iron—its red-orange glow almost liquid—against a calf's haunch. The calf squealed and tensed, but the man held the iron steady as the smell of burning hair and hide bloomed in the air, then pulled the iron away. Working beside the man, Amy Munroe flipped open the two metal levers that opened the squeeze bars and the gate, and the calf bucked out of the chute, ran headlong into the pen, skidded to a stop in the dust, and gave one long, sad bawl—then seemed to forget its troubles and ambled toward the feeder, where the other branded calves and mother cows milled about.

Justin screwed up his courage and walked over.

—Let me know what I can help with, he said.

Amy turned from the squeeze and beamed, then punched his shoulder.

—Hey! Cool! You're here!

Amy was done up like the rest in boots, jeans, and a wide-brimmed hat, her curly hair in a thick braid. There were streaks of dust on her face, her hands work-dirty.

—Here, she said, positioning Justin, you work this lever. That's the squeeze. The calf'll come running in, and I'll catch it in the head gate, and then you set the squeeze. Got it?

Justin nodded. The man who'd done the branding stepped over. Glanced at Justin, then Amy.

—Ready? he asked.

Amy nodded for the both of them, and the man pursed his lips and whistled.

At the whistle, a boy—a bit older, maybe just out of high school, the sleeves of his T-shirt cut off to show his ropy muscles—jumped down from where he'd been perched atop the corral boards and swung open a wooden gate and slammed it shut just as quick, letting a single calf go. The calf broke for the daylight at the end of the chute, but Amy slammed her lever down, catching its head, and Justin swung his lever down, tightening the squeeze.

—There we are, the man said, and set about checking the calf.

Justin stepped back, his heart charging in him. It was different, this work with cows, everything that much bigger, the bang of the calf against the gate like a gunshot.

He thought maybe he liked the sheep better, but he'd see.

—What all do you have to do to them? Justin had leaned toward Amy to ask her, but the man answered.

—Well, we gotta make sure their feet are good, their joints. Then give them their vaccinations. If they're boy cows, we band them. Slip this little green rubber band around their nuts to cut off the blood flow and eventually turn them into steers. Then we brand them.

—So it's kind of like docking, Justin said. A little bit, anyway. What you do with sheep.

A high wooden table stood behind them, and before he answered, the man took another green band from a plastic sack of them, worked it onto the bander, then refilled the vaccine syringe. He was a big man, tall and wide-shouldered, but like Mr. Bouchard, he moved in a gentle, sure way. And he was one of the only men wearing a baseball cap and a T-shirt.

—I'm Kevin Kincheloe, the man said, sticking out his hand. You must be one of Rene's grandsons. I saw you walk in with him. I knew your uncle Franklin. He was a friend of mine.

Justin shook the man's hand and started to explain, but Amy, who'd wandered off to talk with the boy perched on the top corral board, was back.

—He's not a relation, she said. Just works for Mr. Bouchard.

Kevin eyed Justin again, then squatted down to the metal cylinder — a silver barrel laid on its side — that contained the propane fire, the long handle of the branding iron sticking out the end of it. He turned the iron once, twice. The fire roared steadily, invisibly.

—Except for that yellow hair, I thought there was a resemblance.

Kevin pulled the branding iron from the barrel and, in a clean, practiced motion, set it against the calf's haunch, held it steady even as the calf bellowed and tried to buck. Seconds later, he pulled the iron away. Justin undid the squeeze, and Amy loosed the head gate. The calf bucked and tried to run — but it had kicked its back leg over the edge of the squeeze plate. Scared, it continued to buck and kick, wedging its leg all the more tightly.

The calf slobbered and screamed, its hard head banging and clattering against the iron.

—Shit. Kevin scrambled to get the still-hot iron back in the barrel.

Amy whirled around the side of the squeeze chute and tried to lift the calf from there.

Justin considered a moment, then climbed right into the squeeze itself, spidered up and over the bucking calf, reached down, and hefted its whole backside so Amy could unhook the calf's hoof — and just like that, the calf was out, running and bucking with the others.

Justin dropped to his feet and stepped out of the squeeze. Pushed his hair behind his ears.

—You sure you're not related? Kevin asked. That's just about the kind of performance I'd expect of Rene Bouchard's grandson.

Amy laughed. Justin grinned.

—No, he's just a good teacher. I'm learning out at his ranch.

—I imagine, Kevin said, and turned and whistled for another calf.

# 63

LIANNE SPUN THROUGH THE radio dial looking for something that wasn't ag reports or Paul Harvey. The NPR station out of Billings cracked and chirruped, the pure, high sounds of violins shot through with what sounded like the grab of tires and gravel. Another spin down the frequencies, and she punched the radio off. She'd try again once they were past the Crazy Mountains.

Frank began to stir, and in the rearview Lianne caught Trent readying to poke his brother in the ribs. She thinned her mouth and shook her head. Trent, catching sight of her in the mirror, shrank back in his seat.

—Mom, Frank said, rubbing at his eyes, gulping. Mom, I had big dreams!

Frank sat ramrod straight, seat belt straining against his small shoulder.

—Hey, Frankie. You had quite the nap. I bet you feel good.

—Yes, I do, but I also have to tell you about my dreams. They were very big dreams!

Frank lifted his hands into the air, arms and fingers splayed wide, as if this might illustrate to his mother the true immensity of what he was about to relate. Lianne grinned at him in the rearview and held up a finger.

—I am super-excited to hear about your dreams, Frankie-Doodle, but let's do a quick check-in. Do you need a drink, a snack? Do you need to pee?

Frank was stone still a moment, then grabbed at the crotch of his jeans and nodded his head vigorously. Lianne slowed and pulled to a stop on a gravel forest service road.

— Everyone out. Last stop until Delphia!

Lianne stood and stretched. Both boys hustled off into the grass and sagebrush. Trent finished and hopped back in; Frank stood there staring up into the bare, wind-rattled branches of the cottonwoods, the bluebird sky beyond, his pants not quite below his bottom.

— Frankie-Doodle, let's move!

When they were back on the highway, Frank pulled a rock from his pocket — he must have picked it up after he finished peeing — and worked at it with his thumb.

— Mom, I think it's an agate. Is it an agate? Like the ones you and Uncle Keith and Uncle Dennis and Uncle Franklin used to find?

Lianne reached back for the rock, held it up, and looked at it as best she could.

— I think it's just a rock. It's pretty, though. Those white squiggles in it are probably quartz.

Frank sighed and took his rock and sort of melted into the seat, his disappointment always so palpable.

— How about your dreams, buddy? Want to tell me now?

Frank screwed up his face but said nothing. Lianne drove on for a time. The highway skirted a reservoir, a few big white RVs docked at the treeless campground, and joined the course of the north fork of the Musselshell.

— Earth to Frankie-Doodle — the dreams? The very big dreams?

Frank shook his head.

— They're gone, Mom. They were very big and bright and right there. And now they're gone. I don't know where they went.

He shook his head and threw up his hands, this going-away another mystery to add to the great heap of mysteries.

— That can happen with dreams.

— Yeah. Mom?

—What's up?

—Can you tell me about Uncle Franklin again?

Lianne had told the boys they'd had an uncle—like Uncle Keith and Uncle Dennis—who'd died before they were born, and Frank was even named after him. Usually, that was enough. Usually, that was as far down that road as Lianne had to go.

—Sure, Lianne said. What do you want to know?

Frank rolled his head around on the back of his seat. Trent stuck a finger in his book and lowered it to his lap.

—I was wondering what kind of agates Uncle Franklin used to find.

—Oh, we all found agates. When we were in town, in Delphia, we'd go agate hunting down by the railroad tracks, and when we were out at the ranch, we'd go agate hunting along the creek.

—Mom, I mean a specific time. You know, it's like this: One time Uncle Franklin found an agate, and that agate…and, you know, then you keep going.

—Oh, is that how it goes?

—Yes, Frank said, and crossed his arms dramatically. That's how it goes.

—Okay, Lianne said. She put on her best storyteller voice: One time Uncle Franklin found an agate, and that agate was as yellow as a lemon.

—Really? Frank sat forward, the seat belt catching his shoulder again.

—Yes. A bright, shining yellow, and when he brought it home and washed it up in the sink, it was even brighter. He sat it on the windowsill, in the light, and sometimes it was so bright it looked like the sun wasn't shining on the rock but from inside the rock.

—Wow. Where'd he find an agate like that? Do you think I could find one?

—He found it out at the ranch, on Willow Creek, and yes, I was thinking we should go out there this week. Maybe you could even stay with Grandpa Rene one night. Have a sleepover.

Trent gave an immediate thumbs-up and said they needed to bring the rope to practice roping, then went back to his book.

Frank was still thinking, his face tight again.

—But isn't the ranch where Uncle Franklin died?

Even as the car hurtled down the highway, Lianne felt the inside of her slam up against her son's words—that wrenching, that here then gone. She swallowed. She hadn't eaten much today. One hand on the wheel, she fumbled in the snack bag beside her.

—Yes, it is. Where did you hear that?

—I don't know. I just know. How did he die again?

This, Lianne hadn't shared with the boys. Not yet.

—It was a kind of sickness. He was sick and sad in his heart. And then he, well, he hurt himself and died.

—But Uncle Franklin wasn't very old and usually people who aren't very old, like kids, usually they don't get so sick, right? Right, Mom?

—Right, young people don't usually get so sick.

—But why did he get sick, then? Why did Uncle Franklin get sick and hurt himself and die?

—It was a certain kind of sickness, one that's hard to know or see. This was more than she'd said about her brother to anyone in years. Maybe ever. Lianne swallowed, went on.

—He needed help. We should have paid more attention. We should have helped.

Frank scooted as far forward as he could. He reached up and touched her hair, twirled a length of it around his finger like he used to do when he was little. Lianne could feel the motion of his hand, his breaths close to her ear.

—If we know anyone, Frank said, who needs help, like Uncle Franklin, we should help them. We should help them so they don't die.

The ridge slid away, and the great, high peaks and scarps of the Crazies reared up again, the mountain shadows beginning to stretch east across the prairie.

—Yes, Lianne said, gripping the wheel, we should.

# 64

Amy told him to, so he did; he filled a plate about as high as it could go—a hamburger, a hotdog, big wet spoonfuls of potato salad and taco salad and a red Jell-O salad with hunks of strawberries and whipped cream, and a fistful of potato chips on top of everything—and then they snuck around the side of house to the back door and went up the narrow stairs to her room.

— You sure you don't want some?

With one hand, Justin hefted his burger, and with the other he pushed the heaping plate toward Amy. They were sitting crisscross applesauce on the floor of her room, the soft shag of a pastel blue throw rug beneath them.

— Totally sure, she said, and held up her hands. I already had lunch. Besides, she added, eyeing him, looks like you're hungry.

Justin pulled his plate back and took another enormous bite.

Amy cracked open a CD jewel case and popped the silver disk out, lifted it carefully between her thumb and middle finger.

— You really haven't heard it?

— Not the whole thing, Justin said, swallowing. I heard "Heart-Shaped Box" on the radio, and a kid at my last school let me see the CD case during algebra. I just looked at it. Couldn't play it or anything.

Amy's bedroom was tucked into the corner of the house that faced the river, with just enough room for a bed, dresser, and bookshelf, the bottom two shelves filled with books, the top with tapes and CDs. The very top of the bookshelf served as a bedstand—a small reading lamp, three lustrous purple river shells, and a black Sony stereo with a tape and CD player, the radio antenna, like his used to be, flagged with tinfoil. She had posters and cutout magazine pages of Nirvana, Pearl Jam, and Soundgarden plastered all over her powder-blue walls, her bed heaped with pillows and stuffed animals, the one window propped open with a stout length of driftwood. Afternoon light filtered through gauzy green curtains, which lifted now and again in the breeze.

Amy shone in that light, her eyes wide, a few curls of hair escaping her braid and framing her face.

—It's so good, she said. I can't wait for you to hear it.

Justin popped the last of the burger into his mouth, spoke as he chewed.

—You sure it's okay we snuck away? We're not going to get in trouble or anything?

Amy rolled her eyes and shook her head, opened the top of the CD player.

—I've been working since breakfast, and so many people showed up that you have to take turns. See, even the big talkers want to do at least a little work before dinner. Makes them feel better about eating two plates of ribs and drinking all my dad's beer. So, really, sneaking away like this, we're doing them a favor.

Justin laughed. She was putting on a show. He liked being her audience.

—If you say so.

He scooped up the last of the taco salad with a potato chip and chewed and swallowed, wiped his hands on his jeans. Then he feathered back his hair, slouched against the wall.

—Okay, he said, I'm ready.

Amy grinned and crawled over to him. She smelled of dry grass and sunlight. Freckles across her nose and cheeks, the dark copper of her hair, green of her eyes. She kissed him on the mouth, a slow, easy kiss.

314

—Is that okay?

—Yeah, Justin said. That's way better than okay.

He moved toward her, and she kissed him once more, a longer kiss this time. She pulled away and sat next to him, the lengths of their legs touching, their hips and shoulders brushing. She laughed. He did too. At the lovely strangeness of the day, at the sudden, wonderful closeness of this unexpected other.

—Hold on to your shit, Amy said, and pressed Play on the stereo. With a little electronic ping, the disk started spinning.

A click of drumsticks, a whisper of reverb, and the first clanging, playful, discordant sounds of "Serve the Servants" filled the room and spilled out the window, that music mingling with the light, the dust, the calls of wranglers and calves, the river, and the insistent prairie wind.

# 65

THE HOUSE SMELLED AS it always did, of the old rug in the front room, of dust, hard water, and so many pots of coffee. Lianne had half hoped it would feel like her own when she stepped inside. It didn't. It felt like her parents' house, like its own inscrutable, atavistic space. Outside, the boys bargained and argued. Trent had the lasso, and Frank had found a cottonwood branch he could imagine into something. Still, this wouldn't last. They'd need dinner soon. The pound of ground chuck she'd put in the fridge last night was mostly thawed. She poured off the blood and set the meat to frying in the cast-iron with a chopped onion, dusted on garlic salt, paprika, cumin, and chili powder, then went for the groceries yet in the car.

By the time Frank stomped in — not crying, but sniffling, frowning — Lianne had lettuce, tomatoes, and black olives chopped, cheese grated, a pot of refried beans warming on the stove, and the taco meat ready to go. Frank had never seen fry bread before and just about instantly forgot his complaints and troubles.

— Trent, Trent! he called out the front door. We've got a new kind of tacos! Indian tacos!

The boys held their rounds of fry bread with both hands and took awkward bites. They laughed at the beans and sour cream smearing their faces, at Lianne sweating out all the hot sauce she'd put on her own. Fingering up the last crumbs of cheese and lettuce, they talked about the upcoming days, about Mariah, the neighbor woman who'd watch them while Lianne was teaching, just like Ethel Kanta used to watch Lianne and her brothers when Grandpa Rene and Grandma Viv were at the ranch. They talked about going out to the ranch to stay for a night later in the week, and Lianne thought to mention Justin but Frank announced he had to go to the bathroom and left the kitchen.

Lianne set Trent to clearing the table. Then stepped into the mudroom and closed the door, picked up the phone.

Shadows gathered, the slice of sky out the back window shot through with buff, tangerine, and vermilion. It had been three long days. She spun Ves's number into the rotary.

One of his daughters answered. Lianne asked for Ves. He was busy, at the branding. Shoot. Lianne had forgotten. Well, she'd try tomorrow. Lianne started to pull the phone from her ear, but the girl's voice sounded down the line.

—No, wait.

A moment of movement, muffled voices, and Amy—Lianne was almost positive it was Amy now—was back.

—Miss Bouchard?

—Hi, Amy.

—I just, uh, want to say I'm sorry.

A pause, and Lianne waited for the girl to go on. Music and an occasional call or shout reverberated in the background.

—I wish my dad would have told me things were, well, like they are—over, I guess—but that doesn't have anything to do with you. I shouldn't have soaped your windshield. I don't even believe what I wrote. I was just mad, I just did it. I liked your class last week. You're a good teacher.

Lianne shifted the phone to her other ear.

—It's really mature of you to say all this, Amy. I appreciate it. I want you to know, though, it hurt. What you wrote.

—I know. It was awful. I'm really sorry. Also, you should probably just drive out here.

—What?

—It's branding. There's lots of food and drinks and stuff. Your dad's out here. And Justin. And I know my dad would like to see you. This morning he called you, like, ten times. My sisters about lost it, they needed to use the phone so bad.

With one hand on the doorframe, Lianne steadied herself.

Her dad had brought Justin to the branding, which meant he must want people to see the boy, must have decided, despite all they didn't know, to see if it might work. And just as quickly, those thoughts fled. Ves had been calling her. She felt like a girl—the delightful sense of being chosen—and very much not like a girl but a woman understanding what mattered to her, what kind of happiness she might work toward.

This wasn't an obligation. This was her choice to make.

—Okay, Lianne said. We'll be out in twenty.

# 66

THE DAY FILLED AND gathered, a bright, dusty thing, loud in the ears and hard on the hands, burn of rope and hide, the clatter of hoof and tack, the bite of the sun through the long afternoon — and at the day's almost imperceptible turning, there came a cool lick of wind. A slowing, a softening of sound. Rene shook out a handkerchief and wiped at his eyes, the back of his neck.

The last of the calves were branded, the ropes coiled and put away, and most everyone had already called it quits. Only a few yet closed up gates, stowed ropes and irons and banders and the like. Rene whistled once for O'Malley, who perked his ears and ran wide around from where he'd been stationed at the gate the wranglers used to get in and out of the corral. Rene patted the dog's head. O'Malley loved with all his heart any work he could get, and Rene had enjoyed a day of cattle work as well, work he'd done as a young man, and he'd enjoyed the company, though he'd lost track of how many times folks had hung their heads and said how sorry they were about Viv. Each time, he'd waited for that grief to come hard for him, and it did, though he didn't let the silence and distance close over him. No, he tried to face it — said thanks, nodded at the offered stories.

Rene gave a stretch, and the silver of his watchband caught the light.

It wasn't quite suppertime. But close. He and Justin had been gone since noon. Maybe two or three ewes, he guessed, had lambed out back at the ranch. He hoped there hadn't been any complications. Likely there hadn't. Likely the ewes were just mothering up in whatever corner of the corral they'd dropped their lambs. Still, he and Justin needed to get back soon, to make sure. And with the work done here, O'Malley would be getting nervous. The poor dog wouldn't feel right until they were loaded up and headed north. Rene wasn't much for this kind of commotion himself, had really only thought to come for the boy, so Justin might see Ves's Amy again, so he might be seen and maybe then it wouldn't be such a big surprise if he showed up one day at the school there in Delphia.

And where was the boy now? Rene scanned the buffet lines, the makeshift tables, circles of folks standing around drinking, letting down the tailgates of pickups to sit on and swing their legs.

—Rene, can I get you a cold one? Ves came barreling out of a group of men, gesturing toward an ice-bathed keg of beer sunk in a silver stock trough.

—I don't drink nothing, Rene said, thinking he likely had time for one, if it ain't eighty proof.

Ves laughed, said they were prepared for just such a thirst, and disappeared again into the throng. Rene took the chance to walk O'Malley down the road a ways. Once they put eyes on Old Blue, Rene told the dog he wouldn't be long. O'Malley bolted down the road and leaped into the pickup bed. He lifted his black-and-white head over the sidewall and blinked at Rene, then flopped down.

You don't ever deserve a dog as good as that, Rene thought, and lifted his hat, smoothed it back down onto his head. No one does. Not ever.

People milled about, gossiping as they filled their plates, kids darting between gaps in the line to grab rolls and cookies and wedges of melon. Rene wasn't sure if you just picked a line or if you were supposed to go from table to table in some kind of order. Well, hell, he'd do his best. He stepped up to the nearest line and took his turn, loaded fruit salad, some kind of pasta salad, and a few potato chips onto his plate. He'd grab a burger later with Justin. Rene looked about again for the boy.

—Mr. Bouchard.

He turned at the sound of his name and found a man holding a tumbler of whiskey out to him, better than three fingers—more than he'd ever pour himself—ambering the bottom.

Rene took the glass and sipped, lifted the tumbler toward the man in thanks. Then he turned back to the buffet table, where he gathered a fork and napkin and, after hesitating a moment, slid a hotdog onto his plate, squeezed a couple of splats of mustard on it. Even though the kids had whined about it, he and Viv had never gone in for hotdogs or lunch meats. There was always lamb in the deep freeze, and antelope or deer, and they often traded for beef. Viv didn't like that store-bought stuff anyway, because of the cholesterol. But as he did for most things that weren't good for you, Rene had a taste for hotdogs.

He got his plate balanced on one hand and lifted his glass with the other and looked around for a place to sit—and the man was still there, as if waiting on him. A big man, sandy-haired, a ball cap high on his head, the shadow of a beard beginning to show at his jaw. Had they worked together today? Had someone already introduced them? Likely.

—Hell, Rene said, gesturing at his plate and glass with his chin, you get to be an old man, you can't remember much but what's right in front of you. Let me have your name again.

—Kevin, the man said. It's Kevin Kincheloe, Mr. Bouchard.

And it was. Rene had somehow framed Kevin in his mind with Franklin, framed him as a boy. But that was all wrong because Franklin was the one who would always and ever be a boy. Not Kevin. Rene had heard he was back in town, that even after being gone a good dozen years and living who knows how many different places, he was back working as a game warden out of Roundup, his wife, the one folks always said was so pretty, teaching up at the school. Lianne was at the school now too. Maybe they'd met? And had Rene seen Kevin since he'd moved back? Had he only now forgotten the man? Rene felt himself swirl and list, the years unthreading, crossing and tangling, knots everywhere.

—Let me help you find a seat, Mr. Bouchard.

Kevin took his elbow and guided him to a big wooden spool that had once held fence wire but was turned on its side now for a makeshift table, a couple of straight-backed wooden chairs pulled up to it. The sky had reddened in the west.

They both sat, and Rene took a quick swallow of whiskey.

— Thank you, Kevin. It's been a while. I didn't recognize you.

Kevin had a red plastic cup of keg beer. He lifted it halfway to his lips, set it back down.

— That's my fault. I should have stopped by and said hello some time ago now.

— How long have you been back in town?

— About three years, since just before our little girl was born.

— A little girl. That's good news. Congratulations.

Kevin grinned and took a slug of beer. He was clearly smitten with the whole situation.

— Yeah, Maddy. She can make some noise, but we're awful happy with her.

— Changes about everything, that first one, but I'm like you. I don't remember being happier.

The booming bass notes of a country song Rene had heard but didn't really know sounded from close by, and both men turned to see some high-school kid throw the doors open on a pickup. Old Blue had an FM/AM dial and five plastic buttons you punched for preset stations, but anymore people drove around with the fanciest kinds of stereos. You could hear the music even with the doors closed, the whoomp and jangle of it. Rene thought again of Justin, the way he hard-strummed that guitar. The boy wasn't with the other teenagers there.

Rene turned back to the conversation, was about to ask after Kevin's work, when Kevin started talking all in a rush.

— I should have been by to say more than hello, Mr. Bouchard. I should've been by to say how goddamn sorry I was, am, about Franklin.

Kevin drained his beer and dropped his elbows on the splintery wooden face of the spool.

— I don't know if you remember, but I, well — I didn't come back for the funeral. It was my first year at the university, and for some reason I just couldn't do it. No, shit, that's not true. It wasn't that I couldn't. I didn't. And there's not a day goes by I don't regret it. Even before, hell,

I could have sent him a letter, given him a call. I went off to college and pretty much dropped him. I wish I hadn't. Franklin was a good friend. I miss him.

Kevin worked a hand down over his eyes and mouth.

—God, he said, I'm just so sorry.

The years more than tilting—slipping, spilling, piles of thread and you don't know which end to pull, what might unravel any of this or what might tighten the knot down hard, hard as bone.

The music crested and broke, the light leaning over the hills and river trees, the sky bleeding out, and Rene lifted his whiskey. Set it back down without taking a drink.

Something was wrong with the sound of the evening, with the voices and the lack of voices. A bark of laughter, a stilling.

Kevin heard it too. Was up and moving before Rene could even haul himself out of his chair.

# 67

JUSTIN STEPPED OUT THE back door and stood in the dirt yard, still as a post. In front of him, above him, everywhere, the wide sky was studded with high, white popcorn clouds, the sun just now setting over the river valley, that low, shallow bowl of horizon not even enough to hold the red-gold-orange-pink spill of light, light leaking out all over the place.

He'd seen a few good sunsets — over the city proper when he was camping in Seward Park, up in the mountains of Nye — but those displays paled in comparison to these prairie sunsets. Almost didn't seem to be the same phenomenon, just like there was Nirvana and every other band.

They'd spent the afternoon in Amy's bedroom listening to *In Utero*. Justin couldn't even understand how "All Apologies" was so good. Amy said it was her favorite too. They put it on repeat. She touched her fingertips to the cigarette burns on his arm. He set his hand on her hip. "All Apologies" played half a dozen times, and the smell of the song was her smell, the touch of it her touch. Justin thought he'd be able to pick out the chords on his guitar when he got back to the ranch. He hoped he would. After a time, he asked for a piece of notebook paper and started transcribing the lyrics. Amy snuck out and grabbed a couple of Mountain Dews, filched a whole bag of Doritos. They listened and ate chips and licked the powdered cheese from their fingers and washed the salt down with sugar.

Amy asked him about school. He told her he figured he needed to finish lambing, but then he thought Mr. Bouchard and Lianne were going to,
well, do something. They'd both mentioned school. Amy went quiet for a
moment. She reached for another chip, held it as she talked.

—Do you like her? Lianne?

—Oh, yeah, Justin said, wiping Dorito dust on his jeans. She came
out and stayed the night at the ranch and was really nice. Mr. Bouchard
says she's super-smart. She even knows about Nirvana. And you should
see her ride a horse!

Amy began to gesture with her chip—and the phone rang.

Amy bounded down the stairs, and Justin followed. She picked up
the phone, and after a moment held the receiver to her chest and told
him—her voice suddenly not so loud, not so full of mischief—to go on,
she'd catch up.

Now Justin took a last look at the sunset, or not really a last look but
a new look, as the colors and gradations and intensities streamed and
shifted, the undersides of the clouds painted like certain bright rocks he'd
pulled wet from Willow Creek. Then he came around the house.

The yard and gravel lot out front were packed with more people than
Justin had seen in a long time. Men held red plastic cups and threw their
heads back and laughed. Women leaned into the sides of pickups, one boot
held up against the sidewall of a tire. The older boy who'd been working
the gate stood in a circle of teenagers just down the road, near the mouth
of the shed. The boys were still in their work clothes, sleeveless shirts and
dirty jeans, and the girls—had they changed?—wore clean pastel boots
and the tightest, bluest jeans you could imagine, their makeup peach and
rose and violet and flawless.

A few nights ago, Justin had lifted himself from the straw and slipped
out of the back of a trailer right there, near the shed—how many nights
ago now? He wasn't sure. He attempted a tally, but the last days at the
Bouchard Ranch had grown so immense in his mind that they didn't seem
like days at all but each an epoch, a reordering of time such that all that
had come before balanced equally on the scale with what had come since
he'd crossed Willow Creek and followed the trail up to the camphouse.

An older woman elbowed open the screen door, a platter of deviled eggs in her hands, and sidestepped down the concrete stairs with some kind of hitch or limp in her movements. Like Mr. Bouchard, Justin thought. The woman hustled off toward the nearest folding table, pushing her way through the talkers and plate-fillers.

Justin tucked his shirt in and belted his pants a bit tighter, finger-combed his hair. He'd get another plate and wait for Amy, keep his eyes open for Mr. Bouchard. He stepped into line behind a woman and her two little kids, a girl in a jean skirt and a boy in blue overalls, the boy's hair buzzed short enough, you could see the white of his scalp. Justin put three deviled eggs on his plate and tried the baked beans this time, plus a scoop of pasta salad sheened with oil and vinegar. The mother attempted to get her daughter situated with a hamburger, and the little boy, waiting his turn, stared up at Justin.

— Are you a boy or girl?

The boy was barefoot, the cuffs of his overalls dragging in the dirt. Justin reached for a handful of potato chips. Pretended he didn't hear.

— Hey, the boy said, louder, pointing a stubby finger up at Justin. I asked if you were a boy or —

The boy's mother, who wasn't the only one who heard him raise his voice, shushed him and started fixing his burger, but the boy didn't want ketchup or mayonnaise, he wanted barbecue sauce, and Justin stood there waiting, a hollow opening inside him. Mr. Bouchard and Lianne. Ves and Amy. That guy branding calves today, Kevin. All these people had been so nice to him he'd almost forgotten. But in school at Absarokee, going to the post office in Nye or on beer runs to the Trading Post, he'd caught the stares, heard the whispers. And, often, it wasn't whispered but said plainly, as loud as could be: *You ought to get yourself a haircut. I got a knife right here. You want me to give you a haircut? Carve those earrings out for you?*

The little boy mashed his bun down onto his burger and turned back for another look — and Justin slipped out of line. He held his plate with both hands against the worry and shudder working up through his bones and veered off toward where he knew Old Blue was parked. He'd eat there, come back for a burger later if he was still hungry. Though of course he'd still be hungry. He was hungry right now for a hamburger, a cigarette, something, everything.

The gold-red light came like a wind almost perpendicular to him, spilled across his shoulders, and threw long shadows down the road, the dirt and gravel packed hard and cut with old tire ruts. That circle of teenagers just off to his left. Justin lifted his plate and hopped over a rut, and a man — a big man, enormous, the wide shine of his belt buckle not so far below Justin's nose — slid from between the line of pickups and stepped directly in front of him.

— You ever hear the one about the cowboy and the cocksucker? the man said, moving with the ease of someone used to taking up space, moving close and closer.

Justin swallowed. The man smelled of beer, cowshit, and smoke. His snap shirt was stretched tight over his chest and gut, a scatter of long curly hairs at the V below his throat.

Against the angle of the sun, the man tilted his hat. The teenagers had quieted, were looking at them. The man rubbed his nose with a knuckle.

— Shit, now that I think about it, I can't remember the goddamn punch line. Can you believe that? It's a good one, though. I wish I could remember. Anyway, it don't end good for the cocksucker. I know that much.

The man let out a bark of laughter and quieted. He steadied his gaze on Justin.

— I heard about you. You can't hide nothing around here — you know that, right? Even if you got something to hide, you can't. Anyways, I heard some long-haired kid was staying out on Willow Creek with old Rene Bouchard. Didn't sound right to me. Sounded fishy. Don't it seem a little fishy to you? I mean, shit, old Bouchard might not be as sharp as he used to be, but the rest of us want to know why a boy would go and pierce his goddamn ears, wear his hair like that. Like he was a cocksucker or something.

The man leaned toward Justin now, the thick, warm bulk of him shifting the light, the air. His voice was even louder, loose and rattling, unwound.

— Cowboys and Indians. Cowboys and cocksuckers. You'd think the fuckers would learn. It's fucking historical. Rule number one, you don't mess with cowboys.

The man poked a thick finger into Justin's chest, and Justin slapped his plate of food into the man's face. Baked beans on his cheek and chin, the yellow of deviled egg in his eye.

A great collective in-suck of breath, someone saying, *Oh, shit,* and even as Justin leaped away, the man had him by the wrist, his shirt front.

His feet left the earth, the man simply lifting him into the air like he was skin and sticks, like he was nothing, and Justin felt a sad, sickening rightness rain down through him.

This was what happened to boys like him, all the lost boys.

# 68

THE CROWD SHOVED FORWARD, drawn to the fight, and Rene couldn't see for a moment. He tried to push through. Stumbled, felt himself begin to fall—and someone had him. A shoulder under his own, two arms around his middle. It was Ves's daughter, that Amy. He hadn't realized she was almost as tall as him, and strong. She held him until he had his balance. Rene nodded, and together they shouldered through the crowd.

Orly flung Justin like a sack of meal; the boy's head and back crashed against the tailgate of the nearest pickup. The bone-and-metal sound rang across the evening, and Justin crumpled in the dry grass below. Orly gripped the top of the tailgate for leverage and kicked at the boy. Someone yelled for Orly to lay off, someone else said let the little shit have it. A child's cry, a gasp, more than a few laughs. Rene didn't know much of what he'd do but get between that bastard's boot and Justin. He was just about there when Kevin Kincheloe burst through the crowd and football-tackled Orly.

The two men smacked the hard-packed dirt of the road, and Kevin cried out, cursed, his left arm bent awkwardly under the heavy bulk of Orly's middle.

Kevin stumbled to his feet, his left arm held to his chest. Orly rolled and without really getting all the way back up lunged at Kevin. The two men went down again, a mess of arms and legs in the dirt and grass and gravel.

Orly was up first. He wiped at the blood dribbling down his lips, sluicing from between his teeth. He'd lost his hat. Most of the buttons on his shirt had popped. His heavy gut swayed above his silver buckle.

Kevin Kincheloe was tall and fit, but Orly had most of sixty pounds on him. He stalked toward Kevin, who was scrambling up, one-armed.

—Once a faggot lover, Orly growled, always a faggot lover. You should have stayed gone, Kincheloe. This is cowboy country.

Rene stepped between Kevin and Orly. He was smaller than either man but didn't hold himself like it.

—Orly, Rene said, if there's a dumber son of a bitch up and down the valley, I don't know him. Just because you got oil under your acres and buy yourself a new rig every year, you think you're a cowboy? There's not a cowboy I used to ride the Comanche with who would've put up with the likes of you. Beating on a boy like that, you're a coward. A goddamned embarrassment.

Orly sniffed and blood burbled from one nostril. He wiped at the baked beans on his chin, his mouth turned down in a child's frown.

—You're always talking Comanche, Bouchard, always talking forty, fifty fucking years ago. How about now? What are you doing for this town now? Where are your boys, Bouchard? You're such a cowboy, how come they're not here, not cowboying with you? At least your last had the balls—

—You shut your mouth. You shut your filthy mouth right now.

—to shoot himself and rid the world of one more—

Kevin stepped around Rene and swung; his good fist sank into Orly's gut. Amy wrapped her arms around Rene's middle to pull him back to safety. And Ves pushed through the crowd, a shotgun held above his head. He fired a single, crowd-quieting blast into the sky—all this just as Justin, belly-crawling from the grass and weeds, slammed his knife hilt-deep into Orly's right ass cheek.

The blast rang and echoed. Orly screamed, hopped once, twice, and fell to the ground, writhing.

# 69

Darkness gathered along the course of the river, in the deeper folds of the Bulls, and Lianne leaned toward the steering wheel. The whole of her trembled with exhaustion and expectation. She'd skipped a shower and hustled the boys into the car again, promising lots of treats when they got there, then driven too fast down the highway, the county road, the ranch road — and now here she was, pulling into a grassy field at Ves Munroe's place, a line of pickups and even a few sedans leading maybe a hundred yards on toward the house.

She killed the engine and stepped out of the car into the cool of the evening, the crinkle of dry grass — and heard a shotgun blast, a scream. Those twin echoes sounding the hills, the river bottom.

— Boys, she said, stay in the car. Keep the doors locked.

Trent was wide-eyed, Frank ready to cry. Nothing to be done for it. She had to go. Her first thought was of Franklin — no, not Franklin. Justin. Justin would need her help; Rene might need her help.

She took off running, keeping close to the long line of pickups, and slowed as she came near the crowd, found herself crouching down.

Orly Pinkerton was on his belly in the gravel, writhing and swearing, blubbering. Ves faced the crowd, away from her. She could see the butt and barrel of the shotgun in his hands. Another man stood by him. And

331

there, finally, was her father—his hand at his chest, something about to break in his eyes.

Where was Justin?

Above her own sizzling blood, and in the silence that followed the blast, she heard quick shouts, scattered bursts of laughter, voices rising above the others: *That long-haired kid just stabbed Orly! Get that kid!*

Lianne stood straight up and finally spied Justin off in the tall grass and shadow, hugging his knees. He was bleeding from the back of his head, hair clumped in wet hanks. The meat of his cheek was zippered open below his right eye. His jeans were wet. He shivered, shook. Franklin, too, had been beaten up. Is this what he'd looked like? This bad? Oh God. Why did this happen to these boys?

Orly was still screaming and swearing. A few people were trying to see to him.

Lianne moved toward Justin. So did Rene. Rene said the boy's name, said it quiet and slow—*Justin*—and reached out his hand.

—This here ain't your fault, Rene went on. You did as good as you could. I'm sorry. I'm just awful goddamn sorry.

—Justin, Lianne said. We're right here. Here with you.

—That goddamn faggot kid! Orly yelled, and pounded the earth.

At Orly's voice, Justin scrambled to his feet; his back knocked against the side of the pickup. He looked past Rene, past Lianne, his eyes wild. Lianne took another step, reached out, and touched his arm. Said his name once more.

Justin turned and ran, the tail of his shirt flapping.

Lianne started to follow but saw her father take a single step—and fall. She caught him. He was pale and trembling, a sheen of sweat on his cheeks and neck. Now Amy Munroe was there as well, was helping her lay Rene down in the gravel.

—Leave me be, Rene was saying. Help the boy. Get my boy.

An engine turned over. Old Blue whipped around in the field and raised a roostertail of dust the other way down the ranch road.

—Hell, Rene said, his eyes fluttering closed. Hell and goddamn.

Lianne screamed for help.

# BEFORE

# 70

THE BIRD—ASHY UNDERSIDE, black and white feathers across its back and tail—hopped once, twice across the forest floor. It cocked its head one way, then the other. Dug at the ground with a stout black beak. Justin watched. His cheek was pressed against the earth, the dry needles and mossy duff.

That was as much as he knew.

The bird dug and ruffled its feathers and winged away, and in the bird's absence, Justin began to understand his vantage, that he was laid out on his belly, head to the side, arms and legs splayed. The forest rose above him at a perpendicular, the scaled, reddish bark of pines, here and there knots of sagebrush, the sound of the creek. He shivered.

He was alive. With that realization came all the rest.

The pounding across the back of his skull. The burn in his belly, throatful of stale beer and sickness. His lower back throbbed; a knee had been pressed there. His wrists felt stretched to sinew, all the bones jangling and loose. He'd been gripped hard, could feel the deep blue-black bruises rising, though all he could see were the foot of the forest and a soft blue light feathering the edges of things.

He tried to push himself up. His pants were undone, halfway down his legs.

Justin's breath scattered. Shards of night, of memory, crashed across him. Cut him to the quick once more.

Heck with a fistful of his hair, dragging him across the forest floor.

Heck dropping onto his back — a knee here, a knee there.

Heck yelling at him, *Say it! I know you are, so go ahead and say it. Say I'm a faggot, I'm a faggot, I'm a faggot. Say it!*

The piney air filled him, and he was up on his elbows, sick again. Nothing came up but hot strings of bile.

He crawled for the creek. The sound of it a bell, the one good thing.

Burnt Creek ran fast and milky green with snowmelt. On the bank, Justin stripped off his clothes, stripped down to blood and bruise, to smoke and sick and filth, and stepped and slid and nearly fell headlong into the water. It was shatteringly cold. He sat down, water up to his chest, and like a trout fell forward into the current, the flow of it over his nose and mouth. He opened his eyes under there. If he could but breathe water, if he could fin and swim away.

He sat up gasping, his every bone and joint clacking with cold. As best he could, he bent and scrubbed with sand and fern fronds, his backside yet bleeding some. He dunked himself once more, felt lines of blood unthreading and slowing, and he rose and came up the bank. The light touched him now, and though cold, it was warmer than the creek. He didn't dress but left his stained clothes there on the rocks, covered in filth. Carried his shoes.

He ran wet and naked through the forest. He crouched down at the edge of the trees. Watched for a time the camper and the house. Nothing moved. The sun at its zenith, the shadows shrinking back into themselves. The burn pile smoldering.

Justin made for the trailer, pulled at the door — but the padlock was closed tight in the hasp. He worked at the knob for a time thinking he was somehow both inside the trailer, locked in, and outside the trailer trying to get in.

Then he stilled, understood.

After Heck stumbled away he must have forgotten where Justin was, must have been so blind drunk he'd forgotten he'd only just left Justin behind, brutalized on the forest floor. Like he did every night, Heck had locked Justin in the trailer — only he wasn't in the trailer — then Heck had gone into the house to pass out.

In the barn, Justin dug his pack and guitar out from under the straw. He dressed in the clothes he'd stowed, laced his Chucks up tight. He clattered down the barnstairs with his guitar and got his pack situated on his shoulders, was just about to go, to run, when in the straw-and-rot-scented dark of the barn, he heard the screen door slap open.

A moment later Heck coughing, pissing in the weeds.

Heck's heavy step in the direction of the trailer.

If he ran now, Heck would follow, and he wouldn't even make it off the mountain. But if he didn't run, Heck would soon enough realize he wasn't in the trailer and come looking for him. Somehow blame the fact that he'd blacked out last night on Justin. Which meant Justin could expect even worse. Was there worse?

Oh, fuck.

Fuck, fuck, fuck.

Justin looked around wildly. Saw hanging from two thick nails on the barn wall the splitting maul. The wide, promising face of the blade.

# 71

April, and the long winter had only days ago given way to the tough green shoots of bunchgrass, the blue-gray burgeoning of sage. Rene had been reluctantly planning for lambing in the snow, keeping the sheep in the shed all day for warmth, chopping the thick skeins of ice on the water troughs come morning, feeding out extra hay — but now that the season had turned, he didn't have to worry. He drove Old Blue down the familiar roads with his arm hooked out the open window, prairie wind and sunlight touching every part of him.

He rode thankful, too, that his boy Franklin was beside him.

Franklin slouched against the passenger-side door, head against the window glass. He hadn't said a word all morning. But he was here. Rene held on to that.

As he drove, he stole glances at his son. Franklin had grown in the last year, was taller now than Rene, though not quite as tall as Keith. His shoulders had broadened as well. With his dark hair and serious dark eyes, he was turning into a good-looking kid, Rene thought. The wound on his lip wasn't quite so angry anymore, though he'd have a scar. The bruises already fading. You couldn't see his cracked ribs, but those ribs, Rene knew, were what hurt the most. They'd take months to heal. Though it meant he'd now be sending all his boys away — Franklin had gotten into

Missoula, like Lianne, like that friend of his Kevin Kincheloe — Rene hoped Franklin might find a place for himself off at college. Because there wasn't a place for him here. Rene wasn't sure why or how, but it was so. He loved his boy. He didn't understand his boy.

They unloaded their bags, the boxes of groceries. The camphouse was cold and stuffy, the smell of mice and dust, the slow, steady drip of the sink. Rene got a fire going in the stove and lit the fridge, opened the windows to air the place out, the wind quickly gusting, circling. He asked Franklin to let the sheep out of the shed and check if any lambs had dropped, if any ewes were showing. The boy did as he was told, though he did so silently, with his head down, as if moving through deep water.

He and Viv had picked Franklin up from the hospital in Billings two weeks ago, had talked with the police and the doctors, signed the papers, and helped Franklin into the clothes they'd brought for him, an old pair of jeans and a sweater. Once they got Franklin home, they had cared for him like he was little again, blankets and library books and all his favorite meals. Rene still had to drive out to the ranch daily to see to the chores and ready the place for lambing, but he hadn't stayed, had instead driven back to Delphia every evening, even in the dark on icy roads. And each night after Franklin went to bed — he was sleeping fourteen and fifteen hours at a stretch — Rene and Viv sat up in the front room, the lamps whining, their cups of coffee and tea cooling; they didn't know if they were doing this right, didn't know at all what this was. Sometimes, careful not to wake their sad, sleeping boy, they argued. You pushed him too hard; you didn't push hard enough. We should have moved to Billings, where they have photography classes at the high school; we should have homeschooled him early on and kept him from all that would hurt him. We should have treated him like the other boys; we should have recognized he was different. And why, why, why was he so different? Who was he? What the hell was going on with him?

Viv had talked with his teachers and gotten all his assignments. At least he'd be able to finish his senior year at home, which they thought was good, though, again, they weren't sure. With Kevin gone off to college, Franklin didn't have any friends up at school, and many of the teachers were happy to be rid of him as well. Even if he didn't disrupt class, he was a target. The other boys, and even some girls, wouldn't let him alone.

Rene always got the report from Viv when he got back from the ranch. Franklin slept late, ate toast or half a grapefruit for breakfast, and was done with his schoolwork in an hour. Then he wrote letters most of the afternoon, to Lianne, to Kevin, to that girl in Roundup who'd helped him run the first time. Franklin hadn't sent any of the letters yet — they just piled up on his desk — and more than once Rene thought about sneaking in there and opening them. What would he find? Would his son suddenly make sense to him? Or would whatever he read confuse him all the more? If it had been Keith or Dennis, he would have opened the letters without a thought. That didn't make it right, but it made Rene wonder. From boy to boy, how had the world shifted so? How had he gotten it — them — so wrong?

The camphouse warmed, the air freshened. Rene put the percolator on for coffee. Earlier, he'd heard Franklin getting something in Old Blue, maybe the grocery sack of toilet paper they'd brought for the outhouse, and now he could hear Franklin cleaning his shoes on the boot scraper on the porch. The door swung open. Until Franklin looked right at him, Rene hadn't realized he'd been standing stock-still, waiting.

— No lambs, Franklin said. And nothing showing. He paused there, at the threshold. I think I might go for a walk along the creek. Take some photos.

Rene nodded. It had been Franklin's idea to come out to the ranch. He'd said he could get his schoolwork done out there just as well as he could in town. And he could help with lambing too. Viv resisted. She knew Rene would be busy all hours of the day and not able to keep an eye on the boy. And it was just so far away — what if Franklin tried to run again?

Rene had shaken his head. He said it might be the best thing, to get some distance from town, from all the high-school kids driving their pick-ups up and down Main Street, to have a chance to take his photographs in peace, hear himself think.

— Sounds good, Rene said now. We'll have hamburger steaks for dinner.

Franklin lifted his camera and aimed it out the window, getting it ready somehow. Rene watched him crouch and fiddle with the knobs and lenses, saw how he made himself even smaller than he was, almost disappearing behind the black eye of the camera — click.

— Look all right? Rene asked.

— Yeah, Franklin said, and almost smiled. The light's nice.

— Well, good.

Franklin turned and stepped into that light. Rene rushed to the door and called after him, called into the gusting wind:

— I'll see you later, son.

It was hard to tell, the way the light and shadows fell from the choke-cherries and cottonwoods, tall dry tufts of last season's bunchgrass, but Rene thought Franklin looked back once before he disappeared down the creek trail.

# 72

THE ONLY THING THAT damps the fear is doing something. He learned this long ago. If you're scared—and he has been so often in his life terrified—you steal something, you put the cigarette out on your own skin. You play hard and loud the loudest fucking song you know. You sling a Pepsi at his face, you roll a bum, you run.

Inaction was not a luxury granted to people like him. He knew this.

Justin hefted the maul.

Through a knothole, that slant of light meeting his eye, he watched Heck lumber toward the camper, cursing and grumbling the whole way. Heck hammered on the camper wall and called out, fumbled with his keys—and dropped them in the weeds.

In barn shadow, Justin willed his heart to unthump, his breath to still.

Heck cursed, kicked at the cracked camper tire. He bent over and grabbed for the keys and banged his head on the wheel well. Cursed again and stood there rubbing at the knot. Then closed his eyes and breathed through the tremors of his hangover.

Sunlight washed across Heck's stubbled face, his hair sticking out in tufts from sleep. However old Heck was, he looked younger in this light, like the few framed pictures of him in his uniform on the mantel by the woodstove—Heck standing slim and tall and straight. His aunt once told

Justin that Heck came back from Iraq different and the same. All of one or the other would have been better, she'd said as she dried the dishes. Now he's split down the middle.

Of a sudden Heck hollered and keyed the padlock open and swung the camper door wide, stuck his head inside.

That's when Justin rose up and ran.

He held the maul close to his chest. He closed the light-shot distance between the barn and the camper in a matter of seconds. He slowed and choked down on the thick, hand-greased haft. Raised up the maul.

Heck turned and blinked. His face flashed with confusion. Then filled with fear. He screamed once, a quick, high sound without direction or constraint—and Justin swung.

There was the sound of the maul meeting neckflesh, and Heck looked for a moment like he was about to say something. He didn't say anything.

Lines of blood ran from the wound, and as if his strings were cut, Heck fell. The great bulk of him rattled the camper.

# 73

ANOTHER NOTE ON HER apartment door in her landlady's blocky handwriting:

*Your husband says you have to call your mother. Call her as soon as you see this.*

She tugged at the slip of paper, a small white square tearing away beneath the tape, and unlocked the bolt and turned the knob.

Inside, Lianne kicked off her shoes, rolled her bag off her shoulder and onto the small round kitchen table. Carefully, reverently, she extracted a cardboard box and lifted the top—and there it was, a thick ream of typed pages. Her thesis. The final draft. Edited, typed, and formatted exactly the way the library demanded: "Necessary Beauty: Working-Class Poetics." The first in her cohort to have a finished product, she planned to deliver it to her adviser's office on Monday. Lianne pulled a bottle of Rainier from the fridge, popped it open, took a big swig, the beer buzzy in her mouth and throat.

The bottle foamed over. Lianne squealed and made for the sink, where the beer bubbled and spilled, the cold stickiness of it on her hand. Smiling, she took another drink.

Her mother had called three times yesterday. Lianne had gotten the notes—taped to her door, a row of them—when she came home from the library after midnight. She woke early this morning and was back at the library again before sunrise, typing all day.

Most likely it was just about Keith. He and his cheerleader wife seemed to be on the one-a-year plan when it came to having babies. She took a swallow of Rainier, set the bottle on the counter, and rinsed her hands. Still in her socks, she padded downstairs to the phone. It wasn't too late, not yet, and she was thinking she'd make the call quick, thinking she'd say what she needed to say and then go see if anyone wanted to do a little celebrating. She turned the numbers into the rotary and leaned against the wall. The hard rings jangled down the line.

Viv picked up—that soft, distant click—and even before Lianne comprehended the words, she understood the hollow, undone quality of her mother's voice. Understood that this person who had always been to her a giant, a mountain, was suddenly wrecked, was staggering through ruins.

Lianne's vision thinned. She slid to the floor.

On the other end of the line, Viv regained herself. She said Keith and Dennis were already back, said Marty was on his way to Missoula right now to pick her up, said—but it was Lianne's turn to thrash and roar, the sounds coming out of her urgent, loud, and animal.

—I want to hear what happened, she finally got out. I want to hear it from Dad.

A pause.

—He hasn't said a thing since they took Franklin away.

—I don't care, Lianne said. He'll talk to me.

A longer pause. And she heard her mother's muffled voice: It's Pockets.

And then her father, Rene Bouchard, breathed down on the line. Whiskey sawed at the edges of his voice as he told her Franklin had gone for a walk, told her Franklin wanted to take some pictures.

He must have lifted the .243 from Old Blue earlier in the day, must have stowed the rifle somewhere near the creek.

Rene had been frying hamburger steaks. He'd sliced onions to cook alongside; the onions had watered his eyes. He heard the gunshot and thought maybe Franklin had seen a coyote, thought maybe a neighbor was hunting coyotes up the creek. Maybe.

He dropped the spatula and busted out of the camphouse door and ran as best as his bad leg would let him.

He didn't know where the sound had come from and ran a long way through the trees down the creek yelling for Franklin.

When he finally stopped to reconnoiter, he heard only his own sick heart.

And the wind, the goddamn wind.

On his way back to the camphouse, the sound of the gunshot fading, the urgency along with it—had he really heard what he thought he heard?—he saw across the creek in the slant of late-afternoon light the sunset bench. One thread of smoke unwinding from below. And the crumple of his boy in the grass.

Franklin had made a little fire, burned all the letters he'd written over the last weeks.

He must have pulled the trigger with his toe. Blood and other things all over.

Franklin had taken some pictures—that wasn't a lie; his boy hadn't lied about going for a walk to take pictures—that camera of his still strung around his neck. Rene tried to wipe off all the blood, tried to save the boy's last pictures, but he must have been holding the camera wrong because the back clicked open.

—I ruined the goddamn film, he said to Lianne, and took one great breath, then fell into many small pieces. Hiccups, sobs, and curses, the keen of grief traveling like light itself the hundreds of miles between them.

Slumped to the floor, Lianne almost felt sorry for her father. Almost felt sorry for herself, the last to know. Sorry for her mother, for Keith and Dennis—she was feeling sorry for everyone, she realized with a start, but Franklin.

—Dad, she said, her vision narrowing once again, thinning down to the summer the three of them stayed together at the ranch, to the tight folded square of Franklin's letter in that half-size cupboard two stories above her.

—Dad, Lianne said again, it was me and you. We were the ones.

—I know it, Rene said, those loose pieces of him whirling in the wind. And that's what hurts the most, that I know and don't even know.

MAY 1994

# 74

THE DINNER DISHES DRYING in the rack, she tears off a piece of warm fry bread and lets the butter melt before drizzling it with honey. She eats quickly over the sink, the slow roll of honey oozing onto her fingers, grazing the heel of her hand.

Late May, school out for the summer, and the sky fades now from light to light, the evenings golden and Arctic in length. Cottonwood fuzz drifts softly against the window. A breeze bobs the lilac's heavy heads of blossom. Next door, the lawn has greened, gone thick and shaggy. Trent, Frank, and Randy take turns with the lariat. The other day Mariah's husband, Dan Lang, stacked two straw bales and stuck a black plastic longhorn's head anchored by two long metal rods in the top bale. Ever since, the lariat has been in heavy rotation. None of the boys are very good. Most of their throws land short or well off to the side. But Randy, being the oldest, lands the loop over the horns now and again. Then he pulls the rope tight, and Trent and Frank pretend to wrangle the big calf as if they're at a branding, leaping on the straw bales, toppling them over. Lianne rinses the butter and honey from her fingers and looks up just as Frank catches a horn and jumps up and down, forgetting he's supposed to hold on to the rope. It doesn't matter. He gets high fives from his brother and Randy, then the boys all dive at the bales together.

Lianne readies a plate of fry bread with peanut butter and choke-cherry jam for them. They'll eat outside and get blue-black jam every-where, dust and straw sticking to their mouths and fingers. After, it'll be time for Trent and Frank to head in for showers and then bed. The past two days, Frank handled it reasonably well. She hopes he does again, these summer days so epic to Frank that they're hard to say goodbye to. Every sunset, every story and its inevitable end a cause for grief.

From the front room, Lianne hears her father rise from the easy chair, the slow, focused process of it.

—Dad, she calls, can I get you anything?

—Hell, Pockets, ain't no end to the things an old man needs. Right now I just want to get out there and catch the sunset. I'd take a piece of that fry bread, too, before the boys eat it all up.

—You know you're not supposed to have fry bread. How about I put a little honey in your tea?

—Tea? Rene calls back as if offended, as if he hasn't been having herbal tea—his doctor's prescribed substitute for black coffee, dessert, and whiskey—all hours of the day.

Lianne hears him muttering as he fumbles with the door.

—Hell, he says, the screen door squealing. Hell and goddamn.

He's as predictable as the quick, cracking storms that begin to boil up each afternoon as the summer comes on, fast black clouds and rumbles of thunder—the relief, then, of a few minutes of rain.

About as predictable as she is, she guesses, and grips the edge of the sink, crying silently.

In the beginning Lianne thought something was wrong. She thought these sudden sunset tears bespoke fear or miscalculation, that she'd once again failed to choose or had chosen poorly, that home would ever remain away from her. Many things do remain away, but she knows now these tears, which come each evening, are thunder and rain, grief and grief's slow release, the silences of the past years slipping away. The heart ready-ing, making room for something new.

She rinses her face and pats it dry. Sets the kettle to perking on the stove.

# 75

RENE WRESTLES THE SCREEN door open with one hand, leans on his cane with the other. The step down to the porch is a little tricky, but he negotiates it. The screen door clatters shut behind him.

The boys look up. Trent and Frank call, Grandpa! Grandpa! The Lang boy holds back.

Rene gets himself settled on one of the ladder-back chairs, the light's golden angle cutting across him, and tells the boys he'd very much like to see a roping demonstration right about now, it is in fact the very reason he came out, so they better step to it.

Serious as can be, the boys oblige.

Without his hat — his straw is still out at the ranch, and he doesn't feel right wearing his good felt hat here at home — Rene shades his eyes and notes that Randy lets Trent and Frank go first, lets each have more than their fair share of turns. Notes, too, that Randy doesn't hold back once he does get the lariat. He catches a horn on his first throw and both horns on his last, the boys all scuffling with the straw-bale calf.

Weeks ago, Lianne had told him about Mariah White Bear, that she'd be watching Trent and Frank while Lianne was teaching, and Rene counts it now a failure of his own imagination and character that he never once thought about Mariah's boy Randy — that his grandsons would surely play with the neighbor boy, that he, Rene, would have to question things he'd long ago decided to leave alone. He's been doing that a lot lately, reckoning and re-reckoning, watching boys play. Afternoon storms rage, and week by week, the prairie flowers lift themselves up on the thinnest, toughest stalks—Rene seeing it all once again.

And for the first time.

Lianne carries out a platter of fry bread for the boys, a cup of peppermint tea swirled with honey for him. Ah, well. Whiskey or no, he'd sit here forever with the light like this.

The tea is hot and just sweet, and Rene holds the cup beneath his nose, breathes it in. Now he lifts his hand to Mariah White Bear, who's stepped out to talk with Lianne. She nods back. She had Trent and Frank three nights while Lianne stayed with him at the hospital. The fourth day, Mariah drove Viv's Oldsmobile—which is more or less hers now, as he and Lianne don't need it—down to Billings so the boys could see him and their mom. Rene was getting discharged and was able to dress in his own clothes. With Trent and Frank staring wide-eyed, their grandfather in a wheelchair and strangely at their height, Rene unsnapped his shirt and showed the boys the long scar, ridged and stapled, running down the middle of his chest.

—They opened me up with a chainsaw and a crowbar, Rene said, then that doctor reached right in and set my ticker ticking again.

Trent grinned, Frank burst into tears. Lianne wheeled Rene out to the parking lot.

Mariah was leaned up against the Oldsmobile, smoking. She stubbed out her cigarette, and the boys ran to her, wanting to introduce everybody.

—Mom, this is Mariah, the boys said. She looked after us, she told the best stories!

—Don't be silly, Mariah said. I know your mom.

Rene started to introduce himself—it felt shameful, to have lived next door to somebody for years and not properly met them until you ended up in the hospital with a heart attack—but Mariah shook her head as if he needn't bother and handed him a paper sandwich sack. Rene could smell it even before he opened it.

—Hetanévánó'ėstse, she said, white sage. My grandmother called it *man sage*. It's good for healing.

The light leans ever down, gilding the front porch, and Rene sips at his tea. The women talk. The boys sit on the toppled straw bales, lean greedily to their rounds of fry bread.

Ves Munroe had called earlier in the day, said he'd be by tomorrow. It'll be Rene's first trip out to the ranch since the branding, since he watched Old Blue raise the dust of the road, the dirt settling back down as the full pain of the heart attack galloped through him.

He has never once in his life had to set an alarm. He simply wakes when he needs to wake, as he does now, just after five a.m., the house still, twilight at the windows, the birds trying on their first, soft morning songs.

He's downstairs not long after, rooting around in the front closet for a hat. He finds an old Delphia Broncs booster cap, blue corduroy with a rearing bronc stitched across the front in gold thread. Maybe it was Keith's or Dennis's. Or even his when he used to go to the boys' games. Anyway, he pulls it down over his head. It'll work.

Rene cooks himself an egg in that nonstick pan Lianne got him so he doesn't have to use any grease on the cast-iron. No butter on his toast either. He shovels the egg onto the dry wheat toast and ferries the plate to the table. Sits himself up to it alone. A blue and trembling light fills the windows.

—Viv, he says, folding his hands, steam rising from the peppered egg. Viv, I'm sorry. Sorry I left you there at the end, sorry about our boy.

After, he doesn't have to wait long on the front porch before a flatbed farm truck pulls up. Just minutes after sunrise, the world laved with light, Rene starts down the walk, expecting to shake hands with Ves. But it's Ves's girl Amy who comes around the nose of the pickup.

—Mr. Bouchard, she says.

—I was expecting your old man.

Amy cocks her head and hooks her thumbs in her back pockets. She's doing a hell of a job, Rene thinks, navigating all this. Whatever this is.

—After he called, he got it in his head that he was going to bring Lianne and the boys out to the ranch too. He figured you'd still want to go early. So he asked if I'd give you a ride.

Amy picks at the dry bones of a tumbleweed stuck in the truck's grille, goes on.

— During school I was out there on the weekends, helping with the lambing. And last week I spent three nights at the camphouse with my dad and Kevin Kincheloe. We finished docking and trailed the herd into the southeast pastures, across the creek.

— I heard. Thank you. And your dad's right, Rene says, hauling open the passenger door of the farm truck, the gears creaking with years of dust and straw. Early's the best time for it.

This hour of the day in eastern Montana may as well be magic.

First light — a pale, watery light — fills the world, softens the sky, and long shadows delineate and define, call into relief and attention butte and coulee, cottonwood and juniper, barb of wire and lean of fencepost, the red and black dots of cows in the fields. Nighthawks dive, meadowlarks key up their six-note songs, and the only wind is the wind of the road, the clear, green, bitter smell of late spring on the prairie.

Rene rides with his arm hooked out the open window, the wind on his face. Dennis nearly blew a blood vessel arguing with him, but Rene shook his head. No, he said, he wouldn't do it, wouldn't report Old Blue stolen. It would have been a gift anyway, if Justin would have asked. Anything the boy might have asked. Even O'Malley.

— Say, he says, what was the name of that fellow again? That singer you two liked?

Still new to highway driving — though, like most ranch kids, she's likely been driving dirt roads since she was eight or nine — Amy leans forward and peers out the windshield, both hands tight on the wheel. She's dressed for work: boots and jeans and, against the morning chill, a faded yellow sweatshirt with a hood, her bushy hair pulled back in a low ponytail. Her cowboy hat sits on the bench seat between them. She glances at Rene, back to the road.

— Kurt Cobain?

— That's him. Read about him while I was in the hospital. Was sorry to learn he killed himself. Sounds like it was those drugs.

The pavement quits, and Amy slows as the truck's tires catch gravel, dust billowing up.

—I guess, she says, but he, well, he had this awful stepdad, and he ran away a couple of times when he was a kid. In high school he was teased and beat up. You know—Amy pauses, glances at Rene—how boys make fun of other boys. They did that to him. Called him gay and things.

The roadwind, the gravel, the words—all of it so suddenly loud, Rene can barely hear himself think. When he speaks, his voice even in his own ears is quiet, strained, faraway, as if he's asking from years and years back.

—Was he, then? Was he gay?

Rene asks and realizes it's the first time he's ever said the word aloud.

—No, I guess not. I don't know. But he talked about being proud to have gay friends, and he said people should, you know, be nice to gay people. I read that in something he wrote, in one of his albums. Living around here, that was the first time I'd ever heard anything like that.

Amy knows the turn before Rene has to say a word. The ranch road quieter, the shush of dirt and grass, long plume of dust.

—He sounds like someone worth listening to, Rene says as Amy gears down and the world plunges toward Willow Creek. A shame we lost him.

# 76

AT THE CREEK, LIANNE and the boys toss rocks into the deepest pool and strip half the fuzzy seeds from a cattail. They watch water striders skitter and count red-winged blackbirds until they lose count. Just as Lianne spies an agate and is about to show the boys, put them on the hunt, they hear Rene holler — he must have gotten back from checking the sheep with Amy — and Trent and Frank hightail it right back up the trail after Grandpa, the spring leaves of sandbar willows and chokecherries winking silver in their wake.

Lianne bends down for the agate now. A small one, but a beauty. Clear to pale gold and run through with dark, mossy inclusions. She slips the agate in her pocket and hikes down the creek. The sage is in bloom, and the prickly pear cactus, those astonishing pops of yellow fringed with rose. Though she knows across the long, hot summer these plains and hills will dry down to so many shades of dun, dust, and burlap, today the prairie fairly shines, greening and burgeoning before her eyes. On days like this, it's about the easiest thing to do, to imagine her young parents first walking Willow Creek — Viv's thick hair piled on her head, Rene's brown jacket draped over his arm — and deciding then and there to put everything they had into it, to tie themselves to this place and name it home for them, for their children.

And maybe her boys too, Lianne thinks. Maybe.

After the initial shock — the heart attack, the boys suddenly thrust into Mariah's care, Justin gone with O'Malley and Old Blue, Orly Pinkerton threatening lawsuits against her father, Ves, Kevin Kincheloe — everything seemed to slow. And the days became days, each hour the hour only for what needed to be done that particular hour — cooking oatmeal for breakfast, helping her father to the bathroom, telling the boys a story before bed. Evenings, she stayed up in the front room or on the porch beneath the stars, grading papers, planning, and even at times working on her own poems. Just after Rene got back from the hospital, Dennis came over from Roundup for a few days, and his wife stayed for a week to help. Keith sent flowers, chocolates, boxes of fruit — likely there was another package at the house even now. Marty called, ready to fight, to win — and got Mariah on the phone. Lianne can't help but smile thinking about it. She would have loved to hear that conversation. After spring break, she enrolled the boys in school here in Delphia. Last they'd talked, Marty let her know she needed a lawyer.

— Mind if I walk with you?

Ves had come up beside her. Over the clatter of the creek, the wind sawing at the cottonwoods, she hadn't heard him.

— Please do, Lianne says, sidling closer. If you like, I'd even let you hold my hand.

— All right, then, I believe I will.

They walk that way for a time in their own sweet silence.

— I talked with your dad before he called for the boys.

— Did you?

Lianne waits a moment, then winds up and socks him in the shoulder.

— Okay! Okay! I'll spill, Ves says. He's decided he wants to sell me the ranch.

— And this was really his idea? He was the one who brought this up last week?

Ves gives her a nod, goes on to tell her Rene set a per-acre price well under what he could charge. Part of that is Rene wants to run a small sheep herd and his horses out here as well as use the corrals and shed and camphouse after the sale goes through.

—I'll get a hell of a deal on good land, Ves finishes, though it'll be plenty tight the next few years, and Rene gets a no-cost lease.

—It's just like him not to consult any of us about this. Lianne laughs. Keith will probably be pissed and not want him to sell now.

From atop an old cedar fencepost, a meadowlark lets loose, the bird's song sounding above the rhythm of the creek.

—I love the idea of you buying the place, Ves. Still, you should think about it. It's so much money. And this is all new enough — here she takes his other hand as well — you ought to be hedging your bets, at least a little. I guess what I'm saying is, don't do this for me.

Now it's Ves's turn to laugh.

—Oh, he says, chuckling, I'm mostly thinking about that meadowlark right there.

Lianne swats at him again, but he insists.

—I'm serious. I gotta make a living, but there's a reason I'm doing it the way I am. I could have left, like Kevin, like you — and if you gotta leave, that's fine — but me, I want to live right here. I want to take care of cows, I want to take care of this land. Hell, I'm even thinking we'll put a good number of sections into the conservation reserve program, just let the grass rest. Folks like your dad, the ones who did it right, who knew what it took, are leaving the work. And I'd hate to see Orly Pinkerton get any more acres than he's got. It'd be a goddamned travesty if he ended up owning Willow Creek, grazing it all down to dust the way he does. Hell, he'd probably put in another one of those big center pivots and raise corn or do some other dumbass thing. I think we can do all right both ways, make a living and keep the land healthy.

Ves looks down the creek, back at Lianne. Tries a grin.

He's embarrassed, she thinks, being so unguarded and honest about what he loves, what matters to him. And she suddenly sees herself, her own sputtering attempts to explain what it means to her to write poems. How just the act of putting words onto paper rearranges the world. How that work binds the pieces she is together.

—That, Lianne says, pulling him into a kiss, is a speech I think I'll keep all to myself.

— Well, good, Ves says, acting relieved. I'd hate for it to get out and ruin my decidedly mixed reputation.


Lianne and Ves wander up from Willow Creek to find Rene, Amy, and the boys feeding oats to the horses. Trent reaches out and strokes Nine Spot's rippling shoulder. Frank hangs back until Amy picks him up — he's still so little — then runs his quick fingers through the horse's wind-tousled mane.

Ves wants to see how the artesian well is running and hops in his truck. As if blown the other way in the wind, Amy and the boys charge off toward the creek.

The horses lift their great heads, they shy and drift. Father and daughter stand there for a time watching them, their soft eyes, the strong and graceful movements of their muscled necks. Weeks ago, after she'd brought her father home from the hospital, they'd all sat up that first evening at the dinner table to beef-and-noodle soup — one of Viv's classic quick dinners: leftover roast, macaroni noodles, grilled onions, and a can of stewed tomatoes — she and her father and her sons, the four of them sitting around the oak table in the small dining room off the kitchen in the old house in Delphia, and she was as glad and sorrowful as she'd ever been. She'd cried silently all through supper, little Frank reaching out again and again to rub her back.

Later, after she put the boys to bed, she came downstairs to find Rene waiting for her in his wheelchair. He told her about the man dead out of Nye. Rene coughed then and had a hard time stopping, and Lianne drew him a glass of water. I'd bet the ranch there's more to the story, Rene finally said, his breath evening out. A whole hell of a lot more. Though Lianne agreed, though she could begin to imagine all kinds of justifications and exigencies, there rose in her, unbidden, a weed of relief that Justin was gone, that they didn't have to deal with whatever might come of this news. Like folding away a letter, like not answering a brother's letter, it was a meanness in her, one Lianne has wanted to dig up by the roots.

She's kept up with the Billings paper ever since — there hasn't been anything for the past weeks — and once school let out, she drove to Roundup to go over Orly's filings at the courthouse. His lawyers had the name Justin Cobain, which must have been as much as Rene had given them when they called. There weren't any criminal charges at all, which didn't surprise her — you don't start and lose a fistfight in Montana and file criminal charges. The civil claims mostly had to do with Ves, since it was his property Orly'd been injured on. From the basement pay phone, Lianne called the Stillwater County Sheriff's Office and asked about the man who'd been killed up Burnt Creek. Who? the deputy asked. Lianne explained, and the man set the phone down for a time and came back. She could hear papers shuffling, the screech of a chair on wheels. The investigation was, the deputy said, yawning, ongoing. Did she have something for them? Did she know where the man's wife was? Lianne hung up.

Lianne takes up the empty grain bucket, puts her other hand to her father's elbow. Lambing season over and done, the shed is still, sepulchral, leaning shafts of light swimming with motes of dust and straw. Lianne tosses the bucket into the oat bin, and the shift of grain, the ting of metal, are sounds she's heard and loved a thousand times before. The day has warmed, is nearly hot, and the wind when it gusts lifts the dust of the road. Halfway to the camphouse, Rene slows and stops, pulls his elbow away from Lianne's grip.

— I was thinking, he says, how the first time I ever saw a motorcar was when my daddy drove a Ford Runabout up Canyon Creek. My own grandfather thought it a silly thing, loud and impractical. I was scared to death of it. But my daddy made me ride with him into Billings, and I saw some dozen other cars putting around downtown. I even got to liking it, the zip of it when my daddy turned a corner, the sound of the horn, the wind.

Rene had left his cane back in Delphia. Lianne had thought to bring it for him when Ves picked her and the boys up, but then thought better of it. He shifts his weight now — his bad hip, the unsteadiness of his weak legs, his healing heart — and goes on.

— I'm old, but there's older. And that was in my own lifetime. I guess what I'm trying to say is I used to think you could do a thing the right way, and the rest would take care of itself. I used to think the world would go its own way, and I'd go mine. Hell, Pockets. I've been a fool.

Lianne reaches for her father's hand.

—I've been talking to Franklin, she says. I've been telling him all kinds of things. And then I feel bad about that, ashamed, and I try to listen instead.

—What does he say? Rene asks. He looks for a moment like he did before the heart attack, like he did that day the two of them and Franklin drove out for their last summer at the ranch—undefended, blown wide open.

—Oh, Dad, she says, we should have listened when we had the chance.

—Yes, Rene says. Christ Jesus. Goddamn.

With a quick, sure hand Lianne blots the tears tracking her father's cheek.

—But we can listen to each other, Dad. We can at least do that.

# 77

As if from above, as if he could saddle and ride the light, Rene sees far below him the yellow-haired boy and the good dog, floodwater lapping at their ankles, water rising as together they run. Waves of water now, and Rene spurs hard his rearing horse of light. Mountains ahead, and for their great height the water sloshes back. *Run for the mountains!* he calls. *Run for whatever safety you can find! Goddamn you, stay alive!*

Rene wakes to the sound of wind, the dry whinge of blown dust. He flaps his lips and blinks and tries as best he can to gather himself, to remember. He's in his easy chair, the one at the camphouse, and the other chair, Viv's chair, is empty. Yes, he thinks. And there are others who have gone away as well.

It comes to him. He'd tired, so Lianne had followed Amy and the boys down to the creek. He'd thought he'd just sit for a moment.

How long has he been asleep? Fifteen minutes? An hour? He tries to gauge the sunlight at the window, but these late-spring days are long and lavish with light, and his mind is yet sleep-addled. Rene pushes himself up and fills the percolator with water and spoons in coffee grounds. Sets it to heating on the stove.

The first bubbles of boiling water break against the jeweled knob atop the percolator — and he remembers he's not supposed to be drinking coffee. Well, hell. He'll let it brew. Maybe someone else will want it.

He heats a separate pan of water on the stove in case anyone needs to wash and ties back the cloth hangings to air the bedrooms out. Stands there for a time staring into the bunkbed room, and something isn't right. The star on the ceiling, wool blankets on each of the beds, the light at the uncurtained window. The boy's green backpack right where he'd left it, leaned up against the bottom bunk.

But that guitar of his is gone.

That's what's wrong. That guitar had been leaning against the wall, the scuffed case. Rene can see the boy's thin back and shoulders, see him running as the dream waters rise. He can see, too, Justin's astonished face as he strokes Nine Spot's neck. Justin beyond delighted with a new lamb in his hands.

And now Rene is shuffling out the camphouse door, looking for Old Blue, for O'Malley at the boy's heel, for Justin himself brushing that long hair of his out of his eyes—but there's only the road, the corrals, the hills beyond, the sky above so big and blue and straight-up knee-buckling.

The wind loud in his ears, Rene Bouchard touches his bare head. He's forgotten that stupid ball cap inside. Or in Amy's truck. Somewhere. And his straw hat, too, which he knows is sitting on the camphouse table.

Of course the boy hasn't come back. Goddamn.

Rene Bouchard squeezes his eyes tight shut against the wave of sorrow rising in him—but then hears on the wind plucked strings, a high, sweet voice. He comes around the camphouse and down the trail a ways. Sees the shadows they are—there, across the creek at the sunset bench.

With the flat of his hand he shades his eyes.

Lianne and the good neighbor, Ves Munroe, sit close together. The girl, Amy, perches on the back of the bench, her feet on the seat, Justin's guitar nestled on her knee. She must have been so quiet, he thinks. Must have slipped in and out while he slept. She's trying to play, and even this far away, Rene can hear that she doesn't know what she's doing. She's just strumming, singing lines now and again. His grandboys are there. Frank trying to sing as well, Trent digging in the dirt. For fossils? Agates? Bones? It'll be good, Rene thinks, whatever he finds.

Lianne waves to him. Rene waves back.

Soon, he'll go to them, and likely someone will meet him to help him across the creek — maybe the boys with their jeans all wet; maybe Lianne with her jeans smartly rolled to her knees — and they'll sit together and watch the sun go down, and the glory of it will be as true a thing as there is in the world. Rene Bouchard will go to them, and he'll be a broken old man among those who love him, which might well be the best good luck.

Just now, though, he's got coffee on the stove, a few chores in the camp-house to finish up. And, too, he'd like a little more time with the wind and the dust. He'd like to believe for just a little longer that Justin might be on his way.

That his boy might be headed back to the ranch.

# 78

WE ALL KNOW WHICH way this likely goes.

We've seen these boys, seen them hitching up their pants, heard the chuckle and shake of their last-ditch laughs, the way they're always walking away. Long before the boundaries began to soften and the breaches sprout flowers and beguiling weeds, these boys dressed themselves up with polish and rings, let their best girl friends draw pictures on their wrists and ribs. They have sad, hard, wild eyes, eyes dull as roaddust or bright as stove coils. They come in various shapes, colors, and styles, these boys, though whatever size they are, they are good at being small. They're the kind who ask why, what's in it for me, can I have a little more, please? They pick and pick at the scars on their arms. They live with Mom and Dad, but Dad doesn't really count. They live with Mom but don't see her four nights a week. They live with aunts, older sisters, cousins, teachers, kids they met last week in art class. For all kinds of reasons, they sleep some nights in the back seat, curled beneath the drapery of ferns along the irrigation canal, or locked in the bathroom and not coming out no matter how hard anyone pounds. Then maybe for a run of ten thank-God days on the couch in a friend of a friend's dank basement, the coal furnace coughing all night long. Their numbers are legion in trailer parks edging forgettable cities, in stucco apartment complexes squatting near warehouses and distribution centers, four-lane highways roiling all night with cars. Like thin stalks, they rise up in small towns, where they bend in the wind, where they break.

We tell ourselves all kinds of things, but mostly we tell ourselves these boys don't mean anything, that they are not somehow an indictment, a prophecy, a metaphor among so many for the failure of the republic. Still, despite our dissembling, our looking away — yours and mine — there are possibilities.

There's the river, for one, which the boy follows west.

Some hours on, he coasts off the highway — out of gas — and drifts down a short dirt road that dead-ends above the river. His heart a sad hammer in him, he strips down and in the slow, brown shallows washes the blood from his face and neck and hair. He sits a long time on the tailgate, lets his body ache and dry.

The sky gone to crimson and fishbelly, he wanders the highway west. Unhinges himself from shadow and hooks a gas can from the back of a truck at a roadside saloon. Then the long walk back through ditchweeds and trash — he's always, it seems, walking ditches and highways, washing the blood and grime from himself in creeks and rivers — and the good dog is waiting, as he's been told to wait, in the truck bed.

Later, the stars hard and sharp, there's the boy and the dog curled together on the bench seat, neither sleeping unless the other's sleeping.

Two evenings on, he's sitting on a picnic table at a roadside pullout in Ryegate when a carload of boys his age drives up. Like him, they're lost. Some further gone than others. They ask if he goes to school in Harlowton, if that's where he got beat up. And where'd you get your ears pierced? You want a cigarette? Hey, climb in, we're going to a party.

A double-wide out in the greasewood and trees. Keystone Light, vodka mixed with Mountain Dew. The whole place saws and throbs with heavy-metal music. It's so dark you can't tell who's who — cowboy? long-hair? good girl, burnout, jock? — but then a shout, a broken window, a rifle shot. And the boys are out of there fast, are driving around the hills and pine ridges for hours, talking nonsense until their teeth hurt.

Later, one of the boys — lost, but not so lost as the others — sneaks our boy into his basement, which means three a.m. plates of leftover spaghetti and a plastic jug of SunnyD, a Van Damme movie on the VCR, a couch and nest of blankets. It means these two let their guard down and sleep snuggled up like little kids, like brothers.

But our boy, always hedging, always skirting the edges, wakes early and extricates himself from the blankets and slips quietly up the dark basement steps. Stands there for a time in the carpeted front room. A big white refrigerator hums. In a bowl on the counter, bright rinds slant around oranges and grapefruit. The heater clicks on, blows its good, warm breath all over him. Against his better judgment, he leaves without stealing anything.

The next handful of days, he travels west twenty or thirty miles at a clip until the next crossroads town, where he parks behind some abandoned building and locks the dog in the cab. He hooks cans of gas from open garages, cases the TownMart or three-aisle IGA, slipping slick packages of lunch meat, hotdogs, and jerky sticks into his pockets. It's barely enough for him, not nearly enough for the dog, who whines all night to work and run, who begins to bald across the belly.

In Townsend, the boy pulls over by a park—always a good place to cadge something from a picnic, to find a faucet and wash up and suck a cold drink right from the spigot—and hears clear voices, melodic music. He wanders into a church across the street, the sanctuary doors wide open. It's youth night, so there's pizza and Pepsi and *Everyone, let's circle up.* Later, as all the scrubbed teenagers mill about and hug goodbye, as the young, fresh-faced pastor angles to get this new boy on his own, to get his story, he hides in the bathroom, stands on top of the toilet—he knows the youth pastor won't dare open a single stall door. After everyone has left, he sneaks out with the rest of the pizza and a beautiful twelve-string in a hardshell case.

The light shifts and lengthens.

He takes to busking in downtown Bozeman. College girls are pushovers, especially if he brings the dog, and when he sets up by the co-op, there's almost always a couple of sandwiches in his case by day's end, sometimes two big chocolate cookies or a paper box with a piece of carrot cake inside, the frosting so thick and sweet, the first bite swims his vision. He makes most days around twenty bucks. Half of that keeps him and the dog fed. He saves the rest. He figures he needs close to two hundred to drive straight through, to cache enough groceries and kibble — even with the right food, the dog keeps losing hair, little scabs ringing his muzzle — and stop only for gas on the way back to Seattle.

Up Hyalite Canyon, the boy sleeps each week in a different campground, his arms curled around the dog. He dreams of fishermen and jerky sticks, of horses and straw, cold well water and hard biscuits, lambs and the death of lambs.

He jerks awake in the cab one morning. The dog whines and licks at his face. Thick pines and firs hem the sunrise view, the creek rising day by day into froth and snowmelt roar — and a ranger raps again on the pickup window.

— It's nearly the summer season, the ranger says, peering in. We let you have a few weeks, but now all these sites will be reserved. You're going to have to start to pay if you want to stay up here. Say, that a sheepdog?

As fast as he can, the boy is the hell out of there.

He tumbles down the canyon, and with Bozeman in his rearview, he's on the interstate driving west. He reads the green signs — BUTTE, DEER LODGE 71, MISSOULA 151 — and doesn't know any of these towns, if they'll be good for busking or if he can even make it that far with what money he has, less than a quarter tank of gas.

Later that morning, he sips coffee at a diner in Whitehall. He hopes coffee will curb his hunger. After a time, the waitress wanders by with a plate of toast. The boy says he didn't order any toast. She ashes her cigarette on a saucer.

— Eat, she says, your goddamn toast.

The boy slathers all the butter in the packet on one triangle and takes the littlest bites, to make it last, the rich, dripping crunch of it. Another triangle, and he's eating too fast. He goes out, the little tinkle of the bell above the door, and pours a small pile of kibble in the truck bed for the dog. Comes back in and butters the next piece.

Let's imagine now beyond the pure powerful kindness of those who've known some reasonable amount of struggle, shit luck, lucky breaks, and maybe even love, another kind of thing happens.

Let's get specific. Let's say, having seen Old Blue nosed into the lot, having seen the good dog O'Malley and patted him on the head, the old rheumy-eyed sheepherder Thad Bassett walks in and sits two stools down from Justin. Let's say these two runaways get to talking. The talk turns to work, and Justin says, proudly, that he's done some lambing. Bassett mentions he's a herder, been herding sheep all across the state. Says he's in the market for a dog.

— That dog out there for sale?

Justin is down to his last bite of butter-soaked toast. He looks up at the man, the gaps where his teeth once fit, the salt-and-pepper whiskers spiking his wrinkled cheeks and swept-back chin.

— I'm headed east, Bassett says, to a spread I've worked before. I bet that dog would be just what I need out there.

The waitress leans over the till, looks from one of them to the other.

— For a work dog like that, Bassett finishes, I'd pay good money.

The sun bores a white hole in the sky. Big rigs whistle down the interstate. Justin opens the tailgate and calls to O'Malley. The dog leaps lightly down and sits nearly on the boy's foot, leans into his leg. Bassett counts out twenties all the way to two hundred.

Justin can almost taste the bills, can smell gasoline as it falls into the pickup's tank, the exact heft of a cold-cut sandwich in his hands. He pats O'Malley's head and blinks back tears. He can't help himself. He falls to his knees and hugs the dog's neck, squeezes his eyes shut and almost believes when he opens them, he'll see hills and grass, the prairie sloping down toward Willow Creek.

There's only the blacktop streets of Whitehall, the gas and rubber smell of interstate.

— I'm sorry, Justin says, standing, wiping at his eyes. I guess he's not for sale.

Bassett shoves the wad of bills back into his front pocket as if it's nothing to him at all and slaps his sweat-stained slouch hat against his thigh.

— Well, if you won't take my money, kid, at least let me give you some advice.

Justin nods, as if he has any say in the matter, as if he isn't a tumbleweed blown in whatever wind.

— I know a dog about like that one, Bassett goes on, then cocks a thumb at Old Blue. A pickup too.

Now Justin can't believe he let that two hundred pass, can't believe this toothless old fuck is about to call the cops or pull a gun or do whatever he's going to do.

— The man who owns them, Bassett goes on, well, he's a hard-to-please son of a bitch is what he is. I believe over the years he's fired me near on a dozen times.

Justin's heart seizes and stumbles. The old sheepherder smooths his greasy hat onto his head.

— Thing is, he's taken me back a dozen and one.

Now the waitress steps out of the café and toward these two as if their business is hers and always has been. Bassett beats her to the punch.

— Son, I don't know the story, but if you need a place to go, I know one. I believe you know it too.

As if to anchor himself against the world's sudden lurch, Justin takes hold of the thick, dirty fur at the nape of O'Malley's neck. Puts his other hand to Old Blue's cool metal hide.

— I went and made, he says, too much trouble.

Justin looks down, looks away. Swallows at the pure, bone-shattering sadness welling up in him, sadness overflowing like a mad, muddy river.

— I did, he goes on, something you can't take back.

— Well, Bassett says, and sucks at his lips, that wide gap where his teeth should be, I guess you'll have to live with that. But don't flatter yourself, kid. Don't go thinking you're the only one who's ever made a bit of trouble.

At this the waitress can't help but give a loud *Mm-hmm*.

— Boys, she says, let's see what extra we got on the grill. You got miles in front of you. You need a proper meal.

She disappears into the café, the ting of the bell, the glass door sighing shut, and Bassett asks Justin to thank her for him, but he's got to be on the road. Bassett crawls into the cab of his yellow pickup and gets situated, as if the one thing he's got in all the world is time.

Finally, he fires the engine and bumps onto the highway, turns up the on-ramp and disappears down the interstate. The light edges past noon.

The waitress is at the door again.

— Get in here and eat an omelet. I got two cooking. Goddamn

sheepherders take off at the drop of a hat. Can't trust 'em much farther than you can throw 'em.

Justin does what he's told, and the waitress plops a big steaming omelet in front of him, along with another coffee.

— You remind me of my own boy, she says. He wore his hair long too. Just about couldn't wait to leave Whitehall.

— Did he find someplace to go? Justin asks between big, cheesy bites.

— He did. Minneapolis. He liked it there. The waitress pulls her cigarettes from her blouse pocket. A couple years ago now, he got awful sick. He'd always been such a big kid, but he was just skin and bones at the end.

— I'm sorry.

— Don't be. I take any chance I can get to remember him. I see you, and I remember him. Does me good.

She props a cigarette in her lips and lights it, slides the other omelet into a Styrofoam container.

— Feed this to that dog of yours, she says. That's a good-looking dog. You take care of him, you hear?

Justin ferries the omelet out to O'Malley, who eats it in a single wolfing bite. Then for a long time, still as a post, he stands there in the lot. The wind flips his hair across his face, licks at the corners of his eyes, the soft places back of his ears.

The concrete wings of the interstate spread west and east, the sigh and thrum of traffic, of people going wherever it is their fears or shames or loves are carrying them.

Those things we're always carrying. That carry us.

Justin hopes the old sheepherder and everyone else are headed somewhere good, somewhere they'll matter, somewhere that feels even a little bit like home. He climbs into the cab of Old Blue, jams the clutch to the floor. He turns the key and maneuvers the gearshift into reverse. The mountains wheel in his mirrors; the golden mountain light shines straight down.

He's got a good number of miles on the interstate. Then Highway 287, Highway 12, the Mosby Road, and the Seventy-Nine Hill — and by then he's almost there. Almost home.

# ACKNOWLEDGMENTS

Thanks to Lex Runciman, Alexis Bonogofsky, Taylor Brorby, and, especially and always, Liz Wilkins, who read early chapters and drafts and offered encouragement and wise guidance. Sally Wofford-Girand has long been an advocate for good writing from the American West; I'm honored to be working with her. Ben George sees inside a story and sees what it needs to be; his expertise and insight have been essential. Thanks as well to all the good folks at Little, Brown — Maya Guthrie, Betsy Uhrig, Tracy Roe, and so many others — working to bring books into the world. A final thanks to Linfield University, St. Lawrence University, the Pine Meadow Ranch Residency, and the Spring Creek Project's Residency at the Cabin at Shotpouch Creek for the time and space necessary to write.

# ABOUT THE AUTHOR

**Joe Wilkins** is the author of the novel *Fall Back Down When I Die*, which was short-listed for the First Novel Prize from the Center for Fiction, and the award-winning memoir *The Mountain and the Fathers*. He has published four books of poetry, including *Thieve* and *When We Were Birds*, winner of the Oregon Book Award, and his stories, essays, and poems have appeared in the *Georgia Review*, *Harvard Review*, *Orion*, and elsewhere. He is a Pushcart Prize winner, a three-time High Plains Book Award winner, and a finalist for the Pacific Northwest Book Award, the National Magazine Award, and the PEN America literary award. He lives with his wife and two children in western Oregon, where he teaches writing at Linfield University.